Sol Gate

The Disclosure Files - Book Three

Nancy J. Nelson

Brown Leaf Press

Published by Brown Leaf Press. Los Angeles, CA.

Copyright © 2025 by Nancy J. Nelson

ISBN: 979-8-9919647-6-0 (Paperback)

ISBN: 979-8-9919647-7-7 (eBook)

Cover Art by David Leahey

Interior Formatting by Atticus.io

First Printing edition 2025

Contents

Chapter One

J erry sat across from Vicki, eyes flicking to the stack of papers between them. Mary sat at Vicki's side with a tablet, logging meeting requests and speaking invitations as they came in. The strain of the last few months pressed down on all of them.

Disclosure was now official. Governments around the world had admitted what had long been denied: extraterrestrials were real, and they were here on Earth. For most people, it might have felt like triumph. For those sitting in this room, it felt more like responsibility piling higher.

For Vicki, it seemed to have drained the last bit of enthusiasm she had for this role.

Jerry watched her, studying the way she glanced at the papers before her without much interest. Her eyes, normally sharp, were unfocused, and she flipped through the meeting requests without really reading them. It wasn't that she was slacking—Jerry knew her too well for that—but there was something missing. He couldn't quite place it.

"Vicki, you've got a lot of meetings lined up for the next few weeks. You sure you're up for all this?" Jerry was trying to gauge her mood.

She sighed, leaning back slightly in her chair. "I don't know. I mean, sure, I *can* handle it. But should I?"

Mary, now widely accepted as the most efficient office administrator in the entire Department, didn't look up from her tablet. "These are meetings with foreign dignitaries, industry leaders, and environmental organizations. Your role is to be a key part of all of it. Of course, you should—"

"I'm not talking about that," Vicki interrupted. "What I mean is, why am I still doing this? Disclosure is out there now. What am I really contributing to at this point? We've created this system—and it's a good one—but now our job is just to keep it running. It's turning into a bureaucracy. Other people are rushing to meet with us because they're want their piece of the pie."

Jerry blinked, surprised. He had seen Vicki struggle with certain aspects of her role—yes—but this was different. She sounded tired.

"You're asking yourself why you're doing this," Jerry said slowly, repeating her words back to her. He had always thought of Vicki as someone in a position of real importance. She was one of the most visible figures in government, leading the work on interspecies relations and holding the attention of political leaders, industry heads, and senior military officials.

"Yes," Vicki said, looking up and meeting his eyes. "Jerry, it's not about the power. It's about purpose. And I'm not sure that I'm fulfilling it here. This," she gestured to the piles of papers around her, "is all a lot of political theater. We've gotten to the point where the truth is acknowledged. Good for us. But what happens *next* is what really matters, and I'm not sure I'm the best person to be stuck in this bureaucratic mess. Or—just as important—if I even want to."

Jerry's mind raced. "But... this—what you're doing—is *huge*, Vicki. You're one of the most powerful people in the country... in the world. You can do so much. You've *been* doing so much."

She rubbed her temples in frustration. "I get it. But the real work that's left—it's not about public speeches anymore. It's not about handling diplomacy or cleaning up press coverage, or any of the things I've been doing these past few months. It's about shifting consciousness. If humanity is going to move forward, it won't happen through this office or another round of meetings. It has to happen on a deeper level—helping people raise their vibration and reach a higher state of being. The Hum—the vibrational shift—is where we should be focused. Not this."

Jerry felt a pang in his chest. He hadn't anticipated this—this feeling of resignation from her. For months, he had watched her throw herself into this work and seen how much it meant to her. She had fought, uncovered secrets, and put herself at risk—all for Disclosure. To hear her say that she might walk away from all of it now that Disclosure was "done" was hard to process.

"You don't think this work is important?" he asked carefully.

Vicki exhaled slowly. "I think this work is *vitally* important, but I'm not sure this is the right way to do it anymore. At least not for me. Disclosure was just the first step. What comes next is about consciousness—and I can't do that if I stay in a world of infighting and backroom deals. I don't want to stay locked in the lower vibrations of this reality. Everyone will have to choose. My decision is whether to keep my focus here, on *this,* or to learn to vibrate at a higher frequency and help others do the same."

Mary paused, her eyes glancing briefly from her tablet to Vicki. "You mean you'd leave your position? All of it?"

"I'm not just going to drop everything," Vicki replied quickly. "But I admit I'm feeling a pull toward something different. Something bigger than politics or power. Not just for myself—I think I could be doing more for humanity by helping people understand their own potential, rather than by managing their perception of what's already happened."

Jerry opened his mouth to say something but stopped. Vicki was a visionary. He knew that better than anyone. The work she had done—the work she continued to do—had changed the world in ways no one could have predicted. But now... now she was questioning her place in it all.

"I get it," Jerry said after a moment. "The world's changed. I know you're thinking bigger than this. But this position... You have the power to change more from here than anywhere else. You can reach so many so many people."

"I'm not saying I'm walking away from it completely," Vicki said. "But there's a part of me that thinks there's another way to contribute. Another path that might be even more valuable."

Jerry didn't know what to say. He had never seen Vicki like this before. She had always been the one pushing ahead, seemingly fearless. But now she seemed unsure—even detached from the mission that had once driven her. Something inside her had changed.

"You're saying you want to help people learn to vibrate at a higher level," Jerry said, trying to find his footing. "But isn't that sort of what you've been doing already? Teaching people how to see things differently—how to think differently about their place in the world?"

Vicki nodded slowly. "Yes. But it's one thing to be the voice of something that's already happening. It's another thing entirely to be the catalyst for it. I'm starting to wonder if I should put my energy somewhere else. Maybe I could help people find that higher level of awareness—that shift in perception. Right now, this job ties me to politics and paperwork. I think I might need to move on to something different."

Jerry watched her carefully, and for the first time in a long while, he saw that familiar spark—the one that had been missing earlier. She wasn't giving up. She was trying to find a new way to contribute.

"Okay," Jerry said finally, nodding. "I get it. You're ready for something new. Something bigger. And you're right—the world's ready for that, too."

Vicki gave him a tired smile. "I don't want to get stuck in a bureaucracy, Jerry. I'm ready to help others reach the next level."

Mary stood up, finally putting the tablet down. "So what's next for you then?"

Vicki paused for a moment. "I honestly don't know. But I have a feeling it's time for the real work to begin."

* * *

The community hall chairs were arranged in two sections with an open space down the middle. On one side sat the Suede Nation elders, reserved and watchful. On the other side were a small group of young people—mostly Suede, along with a few humans, and two whose elongated heads marked them as Alpha Centaurians.

Junia was nervous—too nervous to sit. Some of the elders already looked upset, even though no one had spoken. She took a breath to calm herself. She had practiced what to say, but now her words felt unready. The other young people were standing behind her. They were here because they wanted change. No more hiding all the time. No more waiting for bad things to happen.

Junia wanted the elders to say *yes*. She wanted them to say it was okay to try something new. She wanted them to help the young people, not try to stop them. She didn't want to fight. She just wanted everyone to work together. The shift was already happening. Pretending it wasn't real wouldn't keep anyone safe.

Alun remained in the center, the quartz spire behind him. His eyes moved between the two sides of the room, as if waiting for someone else to begin—or for permission to speak.

Junia sighed as she looked at her uncle. Alun didn't understand—waiting for permission wouldn't change anything. Junia opened her mouth to start talking, but Elder Tarran spoke first.

"This gathering is irregular. This conversation should not be held here."

Junia fought to keep from making a face. Tarran was usually nicest one. Since he was already grumbling, the others would probably be worse.

"This is where everyone can hear each other," she said. "That's why we chose it."

"We did not agree," said Elder Morcan. "You dragged us into this."

"We asked," Junia replied, "but you ignored us. So we came anyway. Now we're here to talk."

One of the human youths shifted beside her. The boy was maybe sixteen. Behind him, a girl nodded in agreement.

"You're putting us at risk," Morcan said. As one of the matriarchs, her words had influence. "The humans can't all see us yet—but soon more will. And when they do, they'll remember their fear. And they'll act the way they always have."

Alun finally spoke up. "The young ones believe the danger lies in continuing to hide—and that the time to hide is over."

"Hiding has preserved our lives," Morcan snapped. "You've forgotten the ones they burned. The ones dragged into camps. The ones left on the ice. We haven't."

Junia kept her voice level, but now there was a bite to it. "I know those stories, and I know that reality. *My* parents were burned. *My* cousin was killed defending us. But that's not what this is about. The vibration is rising. You know it. Some humans are already beginning to see us. We can't stop that. We can't run from it."

"We don't plan to run," said Tarran. "We plan to stay quiet. To let it pass over us, just like the other times. Then we'll continue with our lives."

"But this time isn't like the others," argued Junia. "This one decides if humans can see us. And they will. There's no going back."

Junia wanted to bang her head against the wall—or maybe bang the elders' heads against the wall. How could they not get it? How could they not understand that the only way to get to a future they wanted was to help build the path there? She wanted to cry and shout and shake them all. Not because she was mad. (Okay, maybe a little, because she *was* mad.) But mostly because she was scared. Not scared of the humans. But scared of losing this chance. Scared of the elders being too afraid to try, and then of it being too late.

Another elder spoke up from the back. "You want to lead them to us."

"I want to walk *with* them," Junia said. "And I'm not the only one."

Now she motioned behind her, and the other young people sat straighter. They weren't many—maybe a dozen—but they were mixed. Some Suedes with their coppery dark locks and topaz cat's eyes. The two ACs with with their light-colored hair covering elongated heads. The rest human. Teenagers, all of them. The sort who had already stopped following the old rules.

Morcan scowled. "They will turn on you."

"Maybe," Junia said. "But maybe not. We've already started working together. Small things for now, but real things. They're not attacking us. They're helping."

Morcan looked directly at Alun. "And you? Do you approve of this?"

"I listen," Alun said. "I advise when asked."

Then he added, more pointedly, "They're not asking for permission. They're informing you. They'll keep doing it whether you agree or not."

A ripple of murmurs moved through the elders.

Junia took one step closer. "We're not saying the past doesn't matter. We remember—we know what happened. But we don't want to be scared forever. We want to make something better. We want something new."

"You will not have our support," Morcan said.

"Then we'll do it without you," Junia answered.

The tension did not break, but it shifted. No one offered blessing or farewell. But no one stood to block them either.

Alun turned his head slightly. "Then it's done."

Junia looked to the elders. "We'll keep coming back. We'll still listen. But we're already moving forward."

No one replied.

The young people turned and walked out.

CHAPTER TWO

The conversation had been simmering for a while, and Captain Samuel Burger could feel the tension growing. Rear Admiral Folsum had just made his point about the military's longstanding role in keeping information under wraps, and Colonel Mathers had countered with his usual skepticism about civilian oversight. Sam let the words drift past him, the familiarity of the arguments washing over him like faint static in the background.

The question on the table was what role the military could play in Disclosure, now that the Department of State's Office of Multispecies Relations— OMR—was clearly in charge. The group had been divided on this issue for some time. The military, especially figures like Colonel Mathers, had once argued that it should take the lead, using force if necessary. If alien technology posed a threat, it seemed logical for the military to control it.

But that position had lost support after the scandal involving Colonel Riley's hardline approach—which targeted civilians—and his subsequent court-martial. The military had lost much of its credibility.

Now Sam found himself at the table—one of the lowest-ranking officers present, and with less influence than most—trying to help decide the next steps.

"I just don't see how we *don't* continue to assert military control in some capacity," Mathers said, his voice steady but insistent. "We've handled national security for decades. Alien or not, we're the ones who should be calling the shots."

Sam took a slow breath, pausing before he spoke. Mathers had previously supported Riley's position—the one that had led to disaster. But Sam didn't want to get bogged down in old arguments.

"Colonel," Sam said, his voice calm but firm. "I'm not suggesting the military should be out of the picture. But we need to face facts—*control* isn't an option anymore. Not with what OMR has done in bringing aliens to the public's attention, and not with the other events taking place in the world."

Mathers leaned forward, his gaze sharp. "Are you saying we just sit back and let *them*—the civilians—run the show?"

Sam didn't back down. "No, Colonel. But we can't operate like we did before, either. The idea that we're the ones who should 'control' Disclosure... *That* mentality is what got us here. We need to adapt, work alongside OMR, and help shape the military's role in this new environment."

Rear Admiral Folsum raised an eyebrow. "That's quite a shift, Captain. Do you think the military can actually make that kind of adjustment?"

Sam didn't hold back. "It's not just about what we *can* do, Admiral—it's about what we *must* do. Disclosure isn't about control anymore. It's about cooperation, sharing knowledge, and seeing the bigger picture. We kept things secret for too long, and now we need take on a new role. The real question is: how can the military contribute in this new era?"

There was a brief silence. Mathers and Folsum exchanged glances, but neither one spoke. It wasn't easy to accept that things were changing—and that the country wasn't looking to the military to fix things anymore. But Sam wasn't going to back down.

"We've had our time in charge," Sam said firmly. "That's done now. Our strength isn't in holding on to power—it's in adapting and finding new ways to contribute. We still bring valuable skills. We still have a role in protection, security, and supporting our allies. But we need to let go of the idea that the military should lead Disclosure—or that we get the final word."

Colonel Mathers scoffed, shaking his head. "You're asking us to surrender authority. The military *always* should have the final word. What happens when OMR can't protect us, when they can't handle the full scope of what's out there? Do you think they'll be prepared?"

Sam didn't flinch. "I'm not suggesting we abandon our role in national security. But the days of operating like we're in control are gone. If we try to hold onto power, we'll be left behind. There's more at stake than just protecting our own interests."

Mathers shot him a pointed look. "So what, you want to just hand this over to the civilians?"

The person who responded wasn't in a uniform. No one had introduced him, so Sam assumed the man was from one of the intelligence agencies.

"Colonel, you might not have noticed, but we don't have anything *to* hand over—that ship has sailed. There are Galactic Federation representatives in the United Nations who are talking directly with foreign governments without any U.S. oversight. People everywhere are building their own free energy and healing devices from the alien tech schematics that showed up on thousands of websites. New history is coming to light that changes how we see ourselves. And it's only a matter of time before we're faced with even more alien species. *That's* where we should put our energy—not trying to put the genie back in the bottle."

Oooh, that was harsh. Sam was relieved it had been said—and even more relieved he wasn't the one who had had to say it.

Folsum's voice broke the silence. "It's not going to be easy to shift the way the military thinks about this. We're going to face resistance. But I think you're right about one thing: *control* can't be the priority anymore. Our priority now needs to be securing our place in the new paradigm."

Sam nodded. He knew tougher battles were coming, but the military would have to change if it wanted to stay part of the Disclosure process. And that was a fight Sam was ready to take on.

"As much as we might want to, we can't go back to how things were," Sam said, more quietly. "It's time to redefine our role in this process. We need to be proactive, but we need to be *partners*—not just in charge."

The room fell silent for a moment. Sam could see the others thinking it through. For the first time, he felt a spark of hope that maybe—just maybe—the military could find a way to contribute while not running the show.

* * *

Jessica was in the back room, sorting gear into the labeled crates. James had finally finished the new inventory system, and she didn't want to be the one to mess it up. One bin was full of electronic parts. One had blank DVDs. Another had tools she still didn't know how to use.

She heard the heavy footsteps before she saw him.

Lewis stood in the doorway. He didn't come in right away. His hands were still. His face didn't change.

Jessica stayed crouched by the bin. "Do you need something?"

She admitted it to herself—she was nervous. More than nervous. Lewis was a biologic construct, a super-soldier, and he had been part of the team that kidnapped her only a few months ago. Larry had often said the Partnership had chosen psychopaths for the super-soldier program because they were more willing to carry out cruel and abusive missions.

So when Lewis appeared, offering protection to the Four, the decision hadn't been simple. They had let James decide whether to accept the offer—they had let him because Larry had been his uncle.

But who was she facing now—the protector or the psychopath?

In either case, she was facing this guy alone.

He blinked. "No."

She waited. Lewis didn't move. Jessica stood up, brushing her hands off on her pants. Should she be looking for a way to escape? Not that this room had any exits besides the one Lewis was currently blocking.

"I want to say something," he said.

Jessica nodded. "Okay."

If she remembered correctly, the bin with the tools had several sharp objects. She took a position behind, keeping it between her and Lewis, and casually rummaged around in it. There! Lewis couldn't see she had a metal rod in her hand. A *sharp* metal rod.

"I was on the team that kidnapped you. I helped bring you to the place where they locked you up. But that was wrong—I'm not supposed to do that. Not to a woman. Not to someone young."

Jessica couldn't school her expression—she glared at him. "It still happened."

"I'm sorry," Lewis said.

Jessica didn't answer. The rod was still in her hand.

He stood there for a few seconds. Then he said, "I saw you leave."

She frowned. "What?"

"I saw you leaving the house. The place where they kept you. You were alone walking down the alleyway. It was dark, but I saw you. You walked fast."

Jessica's breath caught. "You saw me escape?"

"Yes."

"You didn't stop me."

"No. I was told to catch you, but I let you go. I didn't tell the others."

Jessica looked at him. "Why are you telling me this now?"

"Larry said it matters to say what you've done. Even if no one asks. Even if it's late."

Jessica swallowed hard. "Why didn't you stop me?"

Lewis's face didn't change. "I told you—it was wrong. I like fighting; I've even killed people. But women and children are supposed to be left alone. Family is supposed to be left alone. Those people who hired me would have hurt you. I didn't want you to get hurt."

Jessica felt heat rise in her chest. Not anger. Not fear. It was something strange she couldn't identify.

"You're working with us now."

"Yes." His expression didn't change.

"You're protecting us."

"Yes."

"You won't change your mind about that?"

That was the million-dollar question.

"No," he said. "Larry showed us that we could make a choice—on what to do and who to be. I choose this."

She looked down, then back at him. "Okay."

She had asked the question, but she couldn't be sure he was telling the truth. She needed Vicki—Vicki with her truth-telling gut.

He turned to go. Then paused. "Thank you for not yelling."

Jessica let out a breath. "Thank you for letting me go."

He left the room. She put the metal rod back in the tool bin and went back to sorting supplies. But now her hands were slower.

* * *

OMR OBSERVATION MEMO
Classified Briefing – Internal Use Only

Subject: Escalating Global Deviations – Environmental, Sociocultural & Cognitive Frequency Shifts

- **[BFEMU Regional Sensors: Composite Update]**
  The Hum – Discontinuity and Regional Intensification
  Signal mapping confirms significant shifts in the Hum's

amplitude and patterning. Regions including southern Chile, parts of coastal West Africa, and the interior of Mongolia now register null Hum signatures, while frequency amplification is noted in urban northern India, the U.S. Midwest, and Central Australia. Populations in these areas report intensified lucid dreaming, time distortion episodes, and electromagnetic interference.

- **[The Denver Times]**
  "High School Exodus: Classrooms Sit Empty Across State"
  Districts report widespread, coordinated absences. Students cite feeling "called elsewhere" or "needing to unplug." Some administrators note students gathering in wooded areas or near bodies of water. Reports of synchronized chanting or quiet meditative behavior have been confirmed.

- **[The Des Moines Register]**
  "Middle Schoolers Join Walkouts in Solidarity with Older Siblings"
  Younger students mimic high school exodus. Teachers describe a "weird calm," a "lack of fear," and coordinated movements during exit. Some students refuse to speak, communicating only with hand signals or by drawing geometric patterns.

- **[[The Omaha Sentinel]**
  "Veterans Rally Against AC Integration"
  A group of retired service members gathered outside a civic center hosting an alien resilience workshop. Protesters carried flags and signs reading "Service, Not Surrender" and "Never Forget Earth First." Event proceeded under local police supervision. No incidents reported.

- **[TechPulse | Trending AI Metrics Division]**
  Psychic Pet Videos Trigger Algorithmic Misfire
  Instagram reels showing animals responding to human
  thoughts, locating hidden objects, or mimicking human
  speech patterns (without vocalization) have reached over
  320M views in 72 hours. Virality traced to cross-platform
  reposting, with comments often referencing a "connection
  opening" or "the veil thinning." BFEMU notes spike in
  user-reported synchronicities and anomalous behavior in
  pets.

Action Items

- School-age behavioral monitoring to shift from passive
  logging to direct ethnographic engagement (w/ Consent
  Protocol 12-B)

- Veteran group sentiment tracking to integrate Service Co-
  hort Archives and conduct longitudinal attitude mapping
  (per Defense-Civic Interface Directive 4-D).

- Digital media analysis unit to apply psycholinguistic filters
  to viral pet content and comment threads for subliminal
  pattern markers.

END OF BRIEF

Chapter Three

K iran stood behind Brad, watching the shifting patterns on the screen. The map was dense with data points, the colored indicators representing the Hum's active and fading zones. Brad tapped on a few keys, zooming in on the United States. The frequency pulses had expanded again around the Great Lakes. But the earlier spike in northern Idaho was now gone. Not just smaller—it was totally gone.

"Another one just disappeared?" Kiran asked.

He never would have thought to map the Hum's locations—what they were now calling "quiet zones"—on his own. But Brad's mind worked differently from most, partly because of the DNA upgrade, but mostly because of who he was. He had been sending his reports to Vicki's office at the State Department, and she, in turn, was sharing them with different government agencies.

When speaking with those agencies, Vicki stayed vague about her source. She didn't want to draw attention to the Four or to their base at the former flower shop. Most likely, the agencies assumed she was getting the information from an extraterrestrial contact.

Brad nodded. "Yeah. That whole region was active for nine days. Then it just stopped. No trace."

"But during those nine days, the quiet zone had grown, right?"

Brad leaned back in his chair. "It started as a ten-mile ring. Expanded to nearly seventy. Then began shrinking, like the others. Finally flatlined about six hours ago."

Kiran kept his eyes on the map. "This has happened in how many locations now?"

"Thirty-seven," Brad said. "That's only counting the ones I've had reliable data on. Could be double that, depending on what we're missing in remote areas or places with no sensors or reporting structure."

Kiran folded his arms. He didn't bother asking what type of sensors or reports Brad had access to—his friend was a genius-level hacker. "And the Hum's intensity in these places—it starts strong, peaks, then fades?"

Brad nodded. "Every time."

"But then what happens after it fades?" Kiran asked. "What about the people there? Are you tracking that?"

Brad clicked a few times, bringing up a secondary overlay. "In the early stages, there were consistent reports of more cooperation, less conflict, fewer emergency calls, and better health markers. Those trends didn't completely disappear when the Hum did. They plateaued. Some dipped. But most of them stayed higher than before."

"So, the peace doesn't leave," Kiran said. "The Hum fades, but the higher vibration remains."

Brad looked at him. "I don't know that we can prove that."

"But we can observe it," Kiran replied. "The Hum might not be the vibration itself—it might just be the signal. Like scaffolding around a building that's under construction. Once it's no longer needed, it's taken away, but the structure remains."

Brad didn't answer right away. He zoomed out on the map again. "I don't like assuming permanence."

"You're not assuming," Kiran said. "You're observing. The theory doesn't need to be perfect for it to be useful. Harmony doesn't mean that there's no conflict ever. But isn't it significant that people start living more in sync—even without knowing why?"

Brad sighed. With a few quick clicks, a new window appeared on the screen. It looked like police report data. "Sure, but let's not romanticize it. There's still crime in those places. There are still car crashes and fights and people making bad choices."

"I'm not saying that everyone's problems disappear," Kiran said. "But think about it. People still have free will. If you're in a higher vibration zone, you feel the difference. At the same time, you can still choose to stay angry and afraid—if that's what you want. You can still choose to behave badly. But the gap between the higher vibrational environment and the way you live your life will become like an itch you can't scratch. And as time goes on, it will become harder and harder to live in those areas because it will feel too uncomfortable."

Brad turned in his chair, giving Kiran a skeptical look. "So people will just begin... what, self-selecting? They'll pack up and move to some low-vibe city because their bad attitude doesn't fit in anymore?"

"Maybe not consciously," Kiran said. "But yes. Over time, people gravitate to where they resonate. If someone doesn't want to change—if they feel more comfortable in chaos or in the lower-level patterns they're used to—they'll find somewhere that matches their frequency."

Brad tapped a pencil on the desk. "Why would anyone *want* that? Why would someone choose the lower frequency?"

"Fear of change," Kiran said. "Fear of losing who they think they are. Or maybe guilt—feeling like they don't deserve anything better. There will be some who choose to stay behind to be with people they love who aren't ready yet. Others just won't know they have a choice."

"Everyone always has a choice," Brad muttered.

"Not if they don't know one exists," Kiran said quietly. "Or if they think choosing something higher means abandoning everything familiar—their friends and family, their way of life."

The two looked back at the screen. Now that they had put it into words, Kiran understood there would be a real emotional cost to the vibrational shift. Families split between different vibrations. Friendships unraveling not from conflict, but from a growing discomfort—like wearing shoes that were too tight. Most people wouldn't easily walk away from those they loved. Even if staying meant living with pain.

He thought about Jessica. If his parents hadn't accepted her, things could have turned out very differently. He was close to them—weekly calls, shared jokes, little family rituals—and losing that bond would have left a hole. Yet he had been ready to walk away, because Jessica mattered that much to him.

Still, he was relieved it hadn't come to that. His mother asked only a few direct questions before deciding Jessica had a good heart. His father didn't ask anything—he just gave him a long look, nodded once, and left it at that. They had probably talked it over in private, but they didn't let it affect their relationship with him.

His sister, Aija, had been another story. It wasn't personal—she didn't care about Jessica or Disclosure. Aija just wanted eyes on her, and spinning a dramatic narrative about a threat from "warmongering" aliens got her plenty of attention. Kiran had tried to ignore her antics, but then Amanda Riley's report aired, with Aija front and center, making fearful, veiled accusations.

Their parents had been furious—not with Kiran, but with his sister. The very next day, Aija was packed off to an auntie's household in rural India to "learn how to behave." Kiran doubted it would last. Aija was too comfortable in her role—thriving in drama, clinging to denial, and quick to judge. If the vibrational shift forced a choice, she would almost certainly stay right where she was: vibrating low and loud.

He let out a slow breath, thinking about the awkward silence after he moved into Jessica's room. He'd expected some kind of joke or ribbing from Brad or James, but neither had said a word, and he didn't forget that. The rest of them had been through a lot together before he showed up. He was the outsider who had come in after the fact. Their acceptance wasn't something he took for granted. And so far, nothing between them had changed. They were still working together as a team.

Kiran came back to the present as Brad spoke.

"So the Hum... it's not the thing we're chasing. It's just the indicator."

Kiran nodded. "It's something that signals transformation. Not the transformation itself."

Brad sat still for a while, watching the shifting data. The map showed dozens of flickering zones. Some pulsing brighter. Others fading out completely. He tapped one, then another. "So this is it, then. A global pattern of activation."

"More like alignment," Kiran said. "The Hum initiates resonance. Once that resonance stabilizes, the scaffolding drops away. And then people either adjust or relocate."

Brad gave a short laugh. "We're watching humanity sort itself without being told what to do."

Kiran didn't smile. "We're watching individuals choose whether they have a future."

* * *

James sat across from his parents in the tai chi studio's small office. The walls muffled the distant sound of people moving in the training room, but the air inside the office was still. Mona sat with her hands folded tightly on the desk. Cal stood just behind her, arms folded, feet planted wide. His expression wasn't hard, just watchful—tense in the way James had come to recognize as fear, not control. He knew the difference by now.

"I want to move to the flower shop," James said. "I want to room with Brad."

Mona's reply came fast. "That's not going to happen."

"I'm serious."

"So are we," Cal said. "You're sixteen. You're still in school. And we're your parents."

"I know," James said. "But school isn't preparing me for anything real. Not anymore."

"You've just started junior year," Mona said. "You don't get to decide what's real."

James let out a short breath, somewhere between disbelief and frustration. "How can you even say that? We're all seen what's coming. The vibrational shift is already happening. People are waking up. The world that school's preparing me for? That doesn't exist anymore."

"You're still our son," Cal said. "And you still need structure—you still need our guidance. You can't just walk away from that because you think you know better."

"It's not just what I *think*," James said. "We have the memory crystal. We've seen the real history. We've seen how humans and extraterrestrials have been connected for thousands of years. That history changes everything about who we thing we are. And I'm the one responsible for putting that out. That's what matters now."

His parents exchanged a glance. Mona looked like she was going to say something, then closed her mouth again. They both knew that Vicki had given James the memory crystal and asked him to review and publicize the historical information. They both knew what was on it.

James kept going.

"The stuff they're teaching in school? It's wrong. The history is edited. Our science classes claim the tech we're uncovering is impossible. Free energy, biological healing platforms, non-linear communication—none of it fits their models. The Four have already uploaded some of the schematics. There's more coming.

He leaned forward. "And people are starting to listen. That's the education I want. That's what matters. That's what I want to be a part of."

"You're talking about walking away from your entire future," Mona said, her voice low and even. "From college, from a career, from stability—"

James cut in. "From a system that's already collapsing. Our entire educational system was built to teach us how to obey. To work a job for someone else. To fit into boxes. And people know that now. That's why students all over the world are walking out. You've seen the news stories."

Cal's jaw tightened. "We're not saying you can't be part of what's happening. We're saying you can do that while staying home. While finishing school. You can still graduate."

"No, I can't," James said. "Because that version of me—the version that just keeps showing up at school and pretending like the world hasn't shifted? That's not me anymore. It doesn't fit."

Mona finally looked directly at him, her eyes steady. "We're not losing our son because he thinks he's found something to replace his family."

"You're not losing me," James said. "You taught me to pay attention and act with integrity. That's what I'm doing. This isn't rebellion. It's growth. It's purpose. I love you. But I need to be where I'm meant to be."

James hadn't expected them to say yes today. But he had to start the conversation. The pull toward working with the Four, toward the shift, was too strong to ignore. And deep down, he hoped his parents would feel it too.

Before it was too late.

* * *

Mei wasn't trying to eavesdrop, but the wall between the studio's office and the storeroom where she was putting away towels was thin. The Cooper family was arguing, and as soon as she heard the raised voices, she froze. Memories slammed into her—the quarreling, the putdowns, and the insults. She thought she had left those when she walked out of her family's house, but here she was right in the middle of it again.

But I'm not there anymore; I'm safe. She mentally shook herself and started on the towels again.

No, she wasn't trying to eavesdrop, but it was hard not to hear. James wanted to move in with the Four, and his parents disagreed, saying he was too young. Mei wondered what Calvin and Mona thought of her—she was a few months younger than James, and she had already left home. Not for the same reasons that James had for leaving, but, still.

James made a good point when he said the future was dissolving—his parents had to know that. But Mei realized they were just frantic about keeping him safe, about making sure he stayed part of the family.

She wasn't part of a family anymore, not since she had packed a bag and left home. No one had tried to stop her. No one had reached out to see how she was doing since then. Mei envied James—she envied that he had parents that loved him. She had no one. She was grateful to the Coopers for offering her the spare bedroom in their home, but that could always change. She wasn't family.

Mei thought about her grandmother—the only person in her family she truly cared about. At Mei's age, her grandmother had left China and moved to the United States for an arranged marriage, starting a new life. Maybe she and her grandmother had more in common than it first seemed.

Mei waited until she was sure the office was empty before she left the storeroom.

Chapter Four

Just how many entrances to the Suede Nation were there?

Probably as many as they wanted.

Jessica stood outside a small cave entrance. This time they were in a canyon in the Santa Monica mountains, just a 20-minute drive north of Santa Monica Pier. She was always amazed that you could find true wilderness so close to California's biggest city.

And it was very, very private—which was a good thing, considering who was with her.

There were nearly two dozen of them now—more people than she was used to seeing together since everything changed. Jessica took in the familiar faces first: Brad, Kiran, and James. Mei sat on a rock near them, knees pulled up, watching everything carefully. The high school students from her breathing class were seated beside her. Junia stood tall, arms crossed, surrounded by Suede teenagers. Three Alpha Centaurian youths—they were introduced as Nevik, Astran and Calix—were spaced out along the edge of the group.

Junia was the one leading. No one had to say it. She had taken up the role naturally, and no one seemed inclined to question it. Especially since they had all seen the video of her claws.

"So," Junia said, voice clear and direct. "Now we're finally in one one place. At last."

Everyone turned to look at her.

She continued. "The Suede Nation elders don't like this. I told them what we're doing, and they said it was a bad idea. Some of them aren't even pretending to listen anymore."

One of the Suede teens beside her muttered something, and Junia nodded. "They want everything to stay the same. They say they're protecting tradition, but they're just scared. If something new happened, they'd have to change. And change means something might go wrong."

An AC youth stepped forward. His voice was even, but Jessica noticed how he didn't make direct eye contact. "It's the same with us. The adults—the ones who liaise with your people—they've been given orders by the Galactic Council. Until Vicki gives the signal and coordinates directly, we're supposed to stay out of sight."

Another AC added, "We were told it would be dangerous. That it might set back progress if we appeared too early."

That ship had already sailed.

Jessica thought back to the video the Four had made, when Junia—joined by other Suede teenagers—introduced the young ACs. It hadn't been part of the careful plan that Vicki and the Galactic Council had set up, but it turned out better than anyone expected.

Later, when Jessica spoke with Vicki, she had heard the relief in her voice. The job of introducing the Alpha Centaurians to humanity was no longer hers, and Vicki had seemed grateful for that.

Jessica glanced at the others, before speaking. "It's a little different for us. Humans have a bigger population—about 25,000 times bigger than the Suede and AC populations combined. And since the vibration on the surface is lower, the shift feels bigger. It's not just scaring people—it's dividing them. Some want to evolve. Some want to exploit it."

One of the high school students asked a question. "Exploit it how?"

Jessica looked at him. "Some are trying to make money from it. Selling fake cures. Offering 'vibrational consultations.' People want to be special without doing the work. Or they want to sell the idea of being special. The change is happening, but they're trying to put a price on it. They're not even wondering about what wealth actually means in a new higher vibration."

Junia nodded once. "That sounds like humans."

One of the Suede teens tilted their head. "We get it. Not everyone in our Nation is ready either. But at least we know what the shift *is*."

Kiran looked around the circle. "Which is why we're here. We train together, we align together. That's how we help others. It starts with us."

James stepped into the middle. "We'll start at the very beginning. Thirteen Postures. Humans need it the most. But all of us can benefit from synchronizing."

Jessica watched as the others spread out, finding space. James began calling out the postures, his body moving through the familiar patterns. One by one, the others followed. The Suede teens moved easily. The AC youths had slightly different stances but adapted quickly. Jessica felt her breathing shift, slow, deepen.

Midway through, one of the ACs—Astran—paused, looking toward James, confused. "You said Thirteen Postures. But just now you said something about 'gates'?"

When guiding the others through the movements, James had counted off the "gates." At Astran's question, James—and everyone else—came to a stop.

"Yes. The eight gates of tai chi are the eight fundamental energies. The gates open and close depending on intent and alignment. Then there are five steps—the direction or footwork. Eight plus five equals thirteen—the Thirteen Postures."

"There are gates that open and close?" One of the high school students looked puzzled.

"The gates aren't like doors you push open," explained James. "They're more like... energy circuits. If your body's aligned right, and your focus is locked in, the current flows. That's when a gate 'opens.' But if your structure's off, or your intent wavers, the flow gets scrambled. The gate closes, and you have no power. It's not magic—it's just resonance and geometry doing their thing."

Astran looked toward her fellow ACs. "Aren't there stories? Stories about Eight Gates and resonance and geometry?"

"And about space travel," agreed a male AC. Jessica thought this was Nevik. "It was one of the old stories, from the beginning times. But I don't remember the details."

He glanced at the Four. "The adults don't like talking about the beginning times because there is so much shame there."

Yes, the survivors of the Alpha Centaurian expedition felt ashamed of their ancestors for nearly causing humanity's extinction. Jessica knew Vicki saw that shame as useful for negotiations. But for Jessica and the other young people—human, AC, or Suede—the past didn't matter. Their focus had to be on the future.

"We'll ask when we get back home," Astran said. "There's something important about it. I can feel that much."

They continued with Thirteen Postures, James calling out the movements. The only other sounds were coordinated breathing, shifting stances, and the breeze through the pines.

Jessica tried to focus on James as he began calling out the movements again, but her mind held onto the phrase: *Eight Gates and space travel.* She didn't know what it meant yet. But it didn't feel random.

* * *

Lewis stood behind the old maintenance shed on the edge of the abandoned industrial lot. The metal walls were streaked with rust. He knew it well. It had been a meeting place for men like him before everything fell apart. He had come here because he was asked to, which surprised him. Usually he was ordered, not invited. The message had been short: *Come alone. Just to talk.* The message had arrived on an encrypted data pulse. Coded. One of the old frequencies.

He didn't have to wait long.

Malcolm stepped out from behind a row of storage containers. He walked with his hands in his coat pockets, posture relaxed but eyes watchful. His gaze moved over Lewis like he was scanning for faults. He stopped a few feet away.

Lewis smiled—he couldn't help it. It felt good to see someone like him. Someone with enhanced hearing and sight. Someone incredibly fast. One of the strongest men alive, with the entire internet downloaded into his brain. Someone trained to be deadly.

A super-soldier. Just like him.

"So the rumors are true," Malcolm said without smiling back. "You're with them."

"Yes." Lewis didn't move. Suddenly he was on alert.

"You're with them," Malcolm repeated, starting to pace slowly in front of him. He moved in tight, measured lines, each turn sharp, as if restraining violence. Lewis recognized the movement—he walked that way himself.

"You're with the ones who brought down the Partnership. The ones who exposed everything. The ones who destroyed it all."

Lewis said nothing.

Malcolm looked at him, eyebrows raised. "You always were quiet. Thoughtful, they used to say. But *I* always thought you were stupid. I just didn't think you'd be *this* stupid."

Lewis shifted his stance slightly. "I'm not stupid."

Malcolm smiled without warmth. "Then explain it to me. Why them? Why do you protect them? They're not like us."

Lewis looked past Malcolm for a second, then back. "They didn't run. When everything got dangerous, they stood their ground. That's honorable."

He didn't talk about how you were supposed to leave women and children alone. That wasn't something the Partnership taught him. That came from his father.

"They were the reason everything become dangerous," Malcolm said sharply. "They're the reason our lives were destroyed. We were made to protect the mission. To be better. Stronger. Not to follow civilians around like guard dogs."

Lewis felt the familiar tension in his shoulders, the kind that came from being spoken down to. "I made a choice."

Malcolm laughed once. "You think you get to *choose*? You think people like us get to rewrite what we are? You can't change what you are, Lewis. You can't change the fact that our bodies were made in a lab, trained from day one to fight, to obey, and to execute. And you shouldn't *want* to change that. We are better than regular humans. They should listen to us. Don't try to be like Larry."

"I'm not Larry," Lewis said.

"No," Malcolm agreed. "You're not. Larry broke protocol. He died for it."

"He chose it," Lewis said. "He thought for himself."

Malcolm stepped closer, voice low. "And where did it get him?"

Lewis didn't answer. He thought through what Malcolm had said.

Super-soldiers *were* made. They had been built, augmented, trained, and then reinforced with metamaterials. That was just the truth. He could still remember drills, training sequences, the sound of alarms that told him when to stop thinking and start acting. But things had changed. Larry had shown it was possible to break away. Not just to defect—but to live a different kind of life. To put someone else's life before his own and mean it. That hadn't been programming. That had been a decision.

Malcolm watched him. "You think they'll ever see you as anything but a tool?"

Lewis looked him in the eye. "They already do."

"Then you're a fool," Malcolm said, stepping back. "You should be with us. We're all that's left—just six of us, counting you. And when this new world turns against them—and it *will*—they'll throw you in front first."

Lewis considered that. Maybe it was true. Maybe he'd never really belong. But he didn't want to live in the kind of world Malcolm was trying to rebuild. One built on control, on hierarchy, and on old orders.

"We're a team," said Malcolm. "You'll feel better being a part of *our* team. A place you'll really belong. With men who are just like you.

"I'm staying," Lewis said.

Malcolm stared at him. "You're lost."

"I'm not the one hiding," Lewis replied.

Malcolm didn't argue further. He turned and walked back the way he'd come, disappearing into the maze of metal and concrete.

Lewis stood alone for a few minutes. He didn't move. He thought about loyalty—not just the word, but what it meant. Was it to those who were just like him? Or to those who accepted his choices? Larry had chosen to protect people who weren't like him. And in doing so, he had become more than what the Partnership had made him to be—more than the Partnership had *wanted* him to be..

Lewis wanted that as well. Not because he was trying to be human, or better—but because he was trying to be free.

Chapter Five

T he corridor was quiet, as it always was during the fifth rest
cycle. Astran's mother stood at the terminal, her hands moving through layers of spatial layouts. Astran paused to watch her.
People in their community often said they looked alike, and that
made Astran proud. With her elongated head, flowing blond hair,
and tall, graceful build, her mother was considered a beauty. She
was also known for her extraordinary architectural vision, and it
showed—their city was considered the most beautiful of the three
underground Alpha Centaurian cities.

Astran stepped closer, holding the glowing lichen she had
gathered before coming into the house.

"Mother," she said. "What are the Eight Gates?"

The spacial layout projection collapsed with a sharp flick of
fingers. Her mother turned to face her, eyes wide, posture suddenly
rigid.

"Where did you hear that term?"

"Earlier today on the surface. We joined the humans in their
tai chi practice—their 'moving meditation'—and they talked about
eight gates. One of them said it had to do with energy flowing,
resonance and geometry. And I told them we had a story about Eight
Gates and star travel. I heard something about it when I was little,
but I couldn't remember anything more."

Astran's mother reached forward and snatched the lichen from her hands. "You are not to speak of that again. Ever."

"Why?"

"It is forbidden knowledge. It was buried for a reason. If anyone asks, say you misremembered. Say nothing more."

"But—"

Her voice snapped, suddenly tense. "Enough, Astran! Leave it alone. If you care for this family—for our people—do not ask about this again."

Astran nodded. She would obey—at least to a point—but her mother's fear had etched the word into her mind more deeply than curiosity ever could.

* * *

Naturally, Astran, Nevik, and Calix compared their experiences afterward. That's how they discovered that each of them had hit the same invisible wall when they'd tried, at different times, to ask about the Eight Gates.

Nevik had brought it up to his father during a quiet evening, expecting an explanation or maybe a story. Instead, his father had slammed a drawer shut and snapped at him—his voice rising not just with anger, but with something that felt like fear. "Don't ever bring that up again," he'd said, pacing the room like something dangerous had been let loose just by the mention.

Calix hadn't even gotten that far. The moment he said the words, his grandmother went pale. She spoke the old code phrase—the one few people recognized anymore—and whispered, "The use of the Eight Gates is banned. We don't talk about it. We don't think about it." She refused to answer any questions and had insisted he go outside and cleanse himself with silence.

Which is why they were now all sitting at a table in one of the city's chamber rooms across from Representative Brandori. Even if their parents were afraid to talk about the Eight Gates, *he* would surely know.

"We have a question," Astran began.

Brandori's expression was noncommittal. "Proceed."

It wasn't normal for Representative Brandori—one of the most important Alpha Centauri leaders on the planet—to meet with young people. But he had been there when Junia refused to speak to Vicki on the representatives' behalf, and when the three of them walked out with her. He and the others had seen the video where Junia introduced them to humans. Astran figured he probably wanted to know what they and the other young people were up to.

But it was clear that Brandori did *not* expect to hear the question they asked next.

Nevik leaned forward slightly. "Do you remember the term... the Eight Gates?"

The AC representative blinked once. The silence was absolute.

"We don't know what it means," Calix added, his voice level. "Not really. But we remember it—at least a little bit. We heard something about it when we were children, and when we asked our parents, they all said the same thing: that it was dangerous and forbidden. Best forgotten."

Nevik added, "They wouldn't even explain why it was dangerous. They just shut down. My father left the room. Calix's grandmother made him leave the house."

"They acted like they might be hiding something violent or shameful," Astran said. "But that can't be right. This morning we practiced tai chi with the humans and the Suedes. The movements reminded us of shapes—spatial alignments, like the kind my mother thinks about when designing buildings. There's geometry in those postures. The human boy said that in their tai chi tradition, the Eight Gates are like circuits, opening or closing the flow of energy depending on resonance."

Brandori did not move. *"You are making a dangerous mistake by speaking about this."*

The fact that the representative switched to mind-speak showed how alarmed he was. Alpha Centaurians usually reserved that way of communicating for adult conversations.

"But you know something," said Calix. "Don't you? There's something about geometry, resonance, and the Gates. We remember old stories. The Eight Gates had something to do with space travel. With the beginning times. When we first arrived."

Brandori leaned back in his chair, looking at them. "*You are not wrong.*"

They said nothing. They waited.

Brandori took a deep breath, as if he'd made up his mind. "The Eight Gates," he said, once again speaking out loud, "aren't a myth. They're real. Our ancestors knew about them. They're not physical structures exactly, but nodal points—locations in space, or space-time. All stars can act as portals for space travel at higher vibrational levels, but only for a few destinations within their home galaxies. The Eight Gates, however, are hubs that allow travel to anywhere in the universe under specific conditions involving resonance and geometry. The energies and vibrations of the Eight Gates are much more powerful and complicated than other portals."

The silence that followed was unbroken for several long seconds. Then Astran said, "So why are we not taught this? Why are the adults behaving as if this is something dangerous?"

"Because," said Brandori, "using the power of any of the Eight Gates *can* be dangerous. Our ancestors—to our great shame—abused it."

Nevik tilted his head. "You mean they used it in a wrong way?"

"No," Brandori said. "They used it as intended, at least at first. You've all been told our ancestors came to Earth on a sanctioned research mission through Sol Gate. But what you weren't told is that Sol Gate is one of the Eight Gates. After passing through, our ancestors tried to make their work easier by pulling Sol Gate's vibration toward this planet. That was their mistake. At the time, Earth's vibration was not compatible with Sol Gate's resonance. Our ancestors were arrogant and thought their geometric calculations would be enough. The math was correct, but it couldn't override the natural bond between a planet and its sun. For over two centuries, the system stayed stable as they waited for rescue. But when the Galactic Federation came through Sol Gate to bring them back to Alpha Centauri, the resonance collapsed—and nearly destroyed humanity. That's why so many of us stayed underground instead of going home. We couldn't face the shame."

Astran felt... confused. "Sol Gate is one of the Eight Gates? And there are seven other gates? Where?"

Brandori looked as if he wasn't going to respond, then sighed. "Don't ask about those locations. We honestly don't know anymore."

"What happened to the information about the Eight Gates?" Nevik asked.

"At first it was just locked away," Brandori said. "Then we destroyed it. The risk was too great that one of us would decide to try and use it for their own profit."

"So we're not so different from the humans as we like to believe," murmured Astran. More to herself than to the others, but Brandori heard her.

"No, we aren't," he said. "That's why we were able to merge our cultures so easily all those millennia ago." He shook his head sadly.

"But some of the humans know something—at least part of it," Calix said. "Or maybe they're rediscovering it. In tai chi they're using movement to access resonance—they call this the eight gates. They don't have the geometric equations, but they're aligning something."

"Every species has to find its own path to the Eight Gates," Brandori said. "The humans are just beginning."

"And what are we supposed to do," Nevik asked, "when the humans discover fragments of the patterns? When they find the vibration?"

"Nothing," came the sharp reply. "Humans and Alpha Centaurians are not the same, and need to find their own way."

"Are *we* ever going to find our own way, again?" asked Astran. The thought of never flying through the stars made her feel sad. "We don't want to live this way forever. That's why we joined Junia's group."

"They're different," snapped Brandori. "You can't be like them." He stood up and went to the door, then paused.

"If you want to remain a part of our community, you will stop asking questions. Immediately."

Then he left.

* * *

Amanda Riley sat in the back booth of a nearly empty café in Arlington, browsing through websites on her laptop. The latest article she'd posted about her uncle—framing him as a loyal patriot betrayed by a corrupted chain of command—had barely registered. The views were low. The comments were worse. Most accused her of spinning lies. Some called her a relic. One particularly concise reply read, *"You lost. Get over it."*

She looked up. No one had recognized her. A year ago, that might have stung. Now, she found it useful. The Heirs had cut her off weeks ago, refusing interviews and ignoring her messages. Even Aija—once eager to vent every suspicion and frustration—was unreachable, banished by her family to some extended relatives in India. Amanda had tried contacting her, but the messages bounced back. No forwarding address. No social accounts. Just silence.

The news landscape had shifted. People wanted stories about energy shifts, vibrational changes, and establishing contact with aliens. They wanted to read about Suede music, about AC architecture, and about whoever was behind the *Truthsplosion* information portal. Amanda didn't believe in any of it. This curiosity about the aliens all felt orchestrated—manufactured, even. Was someone trying to distract them?

But her instincts told her that beneath the surface, resentment was still there. People didn't just forget their distrust. It simmered. It spread. It needed a voice.

She opened a new folder and titled it: *The Hidden Cost of Aliens.* She began listing potential angles:

- The shuttering of hospitals due to the increase of reverse-engineered medical devices.

- Preferential treatment in energy allocation.

- Alien technologies replacing human jobs.

- Schools forced to adopt "vibrational education," and students refusing to learn and study.

The narrative had to be smarter this time—less emotional and more calculated. She wouldn't defend her uncle anymore. That angle was dead. He was now a symbol of failure, not rebellion. Instead, she would make herself the authority on the costs of Disclosure—the voice of the rational opposition. Not a denier, just a skeptic. A patriot asking hard questions.

She noted names—think tank figures, economists, ex-military officers passed over for promotions post-Disclosure—the kind of people who might be willing to go on record if she framed it right. Maybe even a few younger influencers who had begun posting sarcastic takes about "raising your vibration" and "galactic mindfulness." She could get traction there.

Amanda's expression didn't change as she typed. She had learned a lot working with her uncle, but that chapter was done. She wasn't going to wait for permission anymore. She wouldn't ask gatekeepers for access. She'd build her own sources. She could dig into zoning disputes near rumored Suede Nation entrances or expose records showing human workers replaced by alien tech.

She would highlight every case of alien interference—every decision made without public consent.

The story wasn't over. It had just changed shape. And Amanda Riley knew how to survive in a changing political landscape.

She picked up her laptop, paid the bill, and left the café without looking back.

Chapter Six

M ei moved slowly across the wooden floor of the Cloud Hands Tai Chi Studio, sweeping in long, even strokes. The faint scent of sweat still lingered from the class, though the students were gone now, their chatter and laughter replaced by silence. She paused, using her forearm to brush a strand of hair off her forehead, and looked around the reception area. The space felt like hers, even though it wasn't.

She leaned the broom against the wall and sat for a moment on one of the lounge chairs. She remembered the evening she left home, her bag packed quickly, a few bills in her wallet, her parents and extended family not trying to stop her—not even bothering to look up from their phones. She hadn't known where she would sleep that night. But Calvin and Mona had taken her in without asking questions, clearing out the spare bedroom and putting fresh sheets on the bed. They hadn't asked for anything in return. They just said, *You're welcome here.*

It was nice to have some time to think without anyone yelling at her. The Four were doing something important. They were doing something real—not just demonstrations or theory, but work that was shaping the future. They were standing at the center of a shift that involved aliens, humans, and the question of what comes next for both. And somehow, *she* had been invited into that circle. Her.

The girl who once had to lie about just about everything to avoid her family's judgment.

The high school students had started coming to the studio just looking for ways to help change things. Mei had been the person who had offered to help, and suddenly she had her own class. Not a tai chi class—she wasn't good enough for that—but a breathing class. And now, some of those same high school students had been brought into Junia's group too. Mei was a part of that group. Not just standing on the edge—she was inside it. Junia had trusted her. The Four had welcomed her. The AC youths shared notes with her after meetings, and the high school students considered her to be their spokesperson. Mei felt lucky every time she showed up and they made space for her.

But under the gratitude, there was still that small, niggling doubt. Maybe they were wrong to trust her. Maybe she didn't deserve to be there. She hadn't done anything extraordinary. She had only kept going, and now she was surrounded by people who were shaping history. She hoped she wouldn't let them down.

She stood again and returned to the broom, now sweeping mindlessly. With each stroke, her thoughts loosened their grip. She wasn't trying to think or not think. She was simply *doing*. Kiran said this was something people should practice if they were trying to get better at meditation.

The door to the studio opened. Mei turned, expecting maybe Jessica or James—someone from the group. Instead, her grandmother stepped inside, pausing just beyond the doorway. Her shoulders were slightly stooped, her silver-gray hair pulled back in its normal bun, her purse hanging from one hand, the other wrapped tightly the folds of the cardigan she wore even in warm weather..

Mei blinked. "*Nǎinai?*—Grandmother?"

The elderly woman gave a small nod. She stepped forward and looked around the studio, eyes taking in the space. "I wasn't sure if I should come," she said. "But I heard you were staying here. I took the bus."

"You should have had someone drive you!" she protested. "You don't need to ride the bus."

"I didn't want anyone to know I was coming her."

Is she ashamed of me?

Mei set the broom aside and gestured to one of the chairs. "Please, sit down and rest."

Her grandmother shook her head. "No. I won't stay long."

There was a pause. Mei waited.

"I came to say I'm sorry," her grandmother said, her voice low and flat. "For not protecting you. I knew how they treated you. While I didn't agree with it, I didn't stop it either."

"You couldn't," Mei said. She understood how it was.

"I didn't try," her grandmother said. "That's the truth. In the old traditions, a wife never spoke against the family—especially not against the men. Especially not a woman from a low-status family like mine. But that didn't make it right." She looked straight at Mei. "I want you to know I'm proud of you. You left. You escaped and built something good out of nothing."

Mei felt her chest tighten, but she didn't respond.

Her grandmother reached into her purse and pulled out a small cloth bundle, wrapped and tied tightly. She held it out. "This is for you. My grandmother gave it to me when I left China. She told me to keep it safe—to keep it hidden. I never told your grandfather, or your parents, or anyone else."

Mei untied the cloth carefully. Inside lay a circular piece of dark green jade—an amulet. In its center was a small crystal, faint and almost hidden unless she tilted it just right to catch the light. On the jade surface around the crystal, there were fine etchings. She squinted, and then recognized them: the bagua trigrams.

"Is it a pendant?"

"It's not jewelry," her grandmother said. "It's not for decoration. I don't know what it does. I was just told that it was important and that I should keep it safe, and that one day—when the time was right—I should pass it on."

"Why now?" Mei asked, looking her. "Why me?"

Her grandmother looked away. "Because I see you're trying to change things. I don't know why, but I believe this belongs with you, not with someone who would keep it locked away out of fear."

Mei nodded slowly. She didn't ask more. Her grandmother was already walking toward the door.

"I'll go now," the old woman said. "I just wanted you to have it while I'm still alive to give it to you. You deserve this. Learn how to use it instead of hiding it away like I did. Don't repeat my mistakes."

Mei walked her to the door. They didn't hug. But as her grandmother stepped outside, she turned and gave Mei one last look, nodded, then left.

Mei closed the door gently behind her, sat down on the studio floor, and placed the jade amulet in front of her. She didn't know what it was meant for. But for the first time, she felt like she had been trusted with something important.

* * *

Jerry stood near the edge of the yard, arms crossed loosely over his chest. The air was cool, and the sounds of the neighborhood had quieted. The last porch light across the street had clicked off half an hour ago. Anne and a few of the other neighbors had gathered in the middle of the lawn, either sitting cross-legged or perched on folding chairs. A speaker played low-frequency tones, and someone had placed a few candles in jars at the perimeter, though they gave off little light. The CE-5 event had begun.

He looked up. The sky was clear and the stars were bright. He still hadn't gotten used to these evenings—quiet gatherings where people meditated, focused, and tried to contact extraterrestrials. It wasn't as if he doubted it—he had seen too much for that—but it didn't sit comfortably with him either. Something about intentionally opening a door without knowing what might walk through felt reckless. Or maybe that was just his fear talking.

Anne stepped up beside him and stood quietly for a moment. "You don't have to join if you don't want to," she said.

Anne had begun the CE-5 evenings without his knowledge. It wasn't that she was hiding them from him; he had simply been tied up with long days at the office and too many other things on his plate.

He nodded. "I'm not against it. I just keep thinking about the kids. About what all this means for them."

Anne glanced at him. "Then that's exactly why we should be doing this. Contact doesn't have to be something that just happens to us. We can shape it and guide it. We can help create the kind of future we want."

Jerry looked out at the small group, their quiet breathing in sync. "But what if creating it means exposing ourselves? Making ourselves vulnerable?"

"Safeguarding what we have is only part of the work. It doesn't build anything. It doesn't move us forward. The kids won't be protected by walls. They'll be protected by the example we set—and by how we live."

Her words struck him harder than he expected. For the last week, he'd been thinking about Vicki. She had been questioning her role, and she wasn't hiding it. Disclosure had happened, and now her focus was beginning to change. She was talking more about the vibrational shift, about raising awareness, and about stepping back. If she left DOS—left her role at OMR—it would create a vacuum. What would happen then? The question wasn't just hypothetical. Several colleagues had already hinted at it—if Vicki did step down, his name would be among the first considered.

He had worked hard. He believed in the mission. The title—Deputy Assistant Secretary for Intra-Species and Extraterrestrial Relations—sounded impressive. It *was* impressive., The job would give him access and influence. People would listen to whatever he had to say.

But it also came with more risk. The job would mean higher visibility, more scrutiny, and greater exposure—not just for him, but for Anne and the children.

Would accepting the role keep them safer, or put them in more danger? Would his presence help steer things in a direction that served the public good, or would he end up buried in policy fights, trying to manage chaos without truly making a difference?

He didn't have the answer.

* * *

THE DAILY SENTINEL
"Truth You Can't Afford to Ignore"
July 14, 2025 | Op-Ed | By Amanda Riley

ALIENS AND OUR CHILDREN: IS EARTH'S FUTURE BEING UNRAVELED FROM WITHIN?

By Amanda Riley, Investigative Journalist

When Disclosure happened, we were told it would be a new era of peace, science, and progress. We were told our children would inherit a brighter world—one shaped by advanced knowledge, energy breakthroughs, and contact with beings from beyond the stars.

But parents across the country are now asking: *What exactly is the next generation inheriting?*

Reports are emerging from schools in multiple states—California, Virginia, Massachusetts—where students are not just *losing interest* in traditional subjects, but are outright refusing to attend school at all. Some claim they are receiving "higher guidance." Others dismiss academic goals as "outdated" or "vibrationally misaligned." Many no longer express any interest in future careers, family plans, or stable adult lives.

"I raised my son to think for himself," said one parent from Alexandria, Virginia, "but now he just stares at the sky and talks about energy fields. He doesn't want to go to college. He doesn't want a job. He says he's waiting for 'alignment.'"

What does that even mean?

Sources close to the Department of Intra-Species and Extraterrestrial Relations (OMR) admit that there is *no formal policy* on how alien philosophies are influencing youth. Meanwhile, once-involved parents are being told to "let go" and "trust the process." Is that advice... or indoctrination?

A Breakdown of the Family Unit?

Social media is filled with glowing posts about "youth awakening" and "cosmic realignment," but beneath the hashtags, a darker trend is forming: parental authority is eroding. Children are not just disengaging from society—they're actively rejecting their families. Some teenagers have moved into communal "vibrational learning centers." Others have cut ties with parents entirely, claiming their "energy fields are too dense."

Is this personal growth? Or is it something more orchestrated?

We must ask: Is the family unit being deliberately destabilized? And if so—by whom?

No one is suggesting that all aliens mean us harm. But in the rush to embrace a new galactic era, have we allowed ourselves to ignore the social cost? Children are the foundation of our future. If that foundation is being reshaped without our consent, it's time to speak up.

What's Next?

Lawmakers are silent. School boards are overwhelmed. Parents are scared.

This is not a question of science fiction—it's a question of societal survival. We deserve answers. We deserve accountability. And above all, we deserve to protect our children.

Stay tuned. The Sentinel is watching.

CHAPTER SEVEN

V icki stepped out of the rideshare and stood in front of what used to be Beth's flower shop. The outer sign had been left untouched, its faded lettering still reading *Uptown Blooms.* She placed her palm briefly against the metal of the door before ringing the bell.

When her sister was alive, the front door had been glass. That had changed when she invited the Four to move in—security concerns made it important to block the view from passersby and to provide more protection against anyone who meant them harm. Now the entrance boasted a steel door with a solid core and 18 gauge 'skin.'

Jessica opened the door and broke into a wide smile. "Vicki! Why didn't you let us know you were coming?" Jess grabbed her into a hug, then stepped back and yelled, "Guys! *Vicki's* here!"

Footsteps thumped down the stairs, and Kiran burst into view. Brad's head poked out from one of the new offices. Both young men sported big grins.

"You should have let us know!" Kiran said. He and Brad pulled her into the shop and enthusiastically hugged her.

Vicki felt her eyes moisten. She felt *centered* again, as if she was where she was supposed to be.

The young people insisted on giving her a tour of how the flower shop had changed since they moved in. The front part of the building's first floor now held Brad's office with its computers and electronics, as well as Jessica's recording studio. In the back half, the counter where Beth once arranged bouquets was now covered in laptops, comm devices, and notebooks, as well as a top-of-the-line espresso machine. Comfortable lounge furniture dotted a common area, chalkboards with notations in four different handwritings covered the walls. Upstairs, Beth's old apartment was now given over to Jessica and Kiran. Brad had made a bedroom in what was formerly the shop's plant propagation area.

Brad saw Vicki eyeing the two beds in his sleeping area.

"That was Kiran's bed before he moved in with Jessica."

Vicki saw the couple both blush at his remark. Brad continued, "James wants to move in, but his parents are against the idea."

"I'm not surprised," replied Vicki. James was underage and their only son. After the death of Larry—Calvin's brother—James parents were probably feeling strongly about the family they had left.

"We kept it alive." Jessica said, deliberately changing the subject away from sleeping arrangements. She was pointing to a white, potted chrysanthemum. It had been the only plant that had survived in the shop after Beth's death—a message from beyond the grave about the beauty and transience of life.

And hope.

Vicki smiled.

They all went downstairs and sat in the common area while Brad made a latté for Vicki. When the back door rattled and opened with a key, she wasn't surprised to see James walk in. But the person behind him...

"Super-soldier!" she gasped, jumping to her feet. She could tell he was a biologic construct—his chi was flat and unmoving. When the Partnership created super-soldiers, they couldn't replicate the junk DNA, which seemed to play a role in how chi flowed through the body.

"This is Lewis," James said. "Remember that we told you about him? He's with us now."

James stood near the biologic construct, careful not to step farther into the room while Vicki tried to calm herself. Lewis stayed still, making sure not to appear threatening—he could tell she was panicking too.

Yes, they had told her about Lewis. But while in Washington, she hadn't really focused on it—there had been too many other things demanding her attention. Facing a super-soldier in person was different. Larry had warned her that men like Lewis were likely psychopaths, willing—and happy—to manipulate and cause harm to others. Hearing that was one thing. Standing across from one was something else entirely.

Jessica stood up and put her hand on Vicki's arm.

"Lewis was the biologic construct who kidnapped me. He told me he didn't tell my other kidnappers when he saw me escaping. He knew Larry, and he told us that he wanted to be like Larry and have a choice of who to be. I was hoping you'd be willing to talk to him and ask him a few questions."

Jessica stared at her intently as she spoke. It took Vicki a few moments, but then it clicked—of course. Since Melly had activated parts of her junk DNA, Vicki could tell when someone was telling the truth. Jessica wanted her to use that now to see if Lewis was lying.

Brad handed her the latté, and she took a sip, composing herself as she cleared her thoughts.

"Lewis," she said. "I apologize for being startled. Could I ask you a few questions."

He nodded. "Of course."

James and Lewis stepped fully into the flower shop and came over to the common area. While James sat down, Lewis remained standing. His face showed nothing, but Vicki sensed he was bracing himself in case he was turned away.

Vicki started by asking about the day he kidnapped Jessica—whose orders he was following and whether it was true he let her escape. She asked how much he had worked with Larry and what he had learned from him. Finally, she had Lewis explain why he had decided to side with the Four. Why was he doing this?

"I don't want to hurt women and children. I don't want to hurt family. It's against the code," replied Lewis stoically. "I'm also tired of people who tell me that I have to do certain things because that's what I was made for. Larry said we have a choice to decide who to be."

Vicki glanced at Jessica and nodded—her gut pinged truth. She turned back to Lewis.

"Someday you might be approached by people who supported the Partnership. Maybe by a few surviving biologic constructs or some former Partnership employees. What will you do when if they ask you to join them?"

"I'll tell them what I already told Malcolm—I'm staying with the Four."

Lewis's face stayed expressionless, but everyone else in the room looked shocked.

"What? You've already been approached?" asked Brad. "Who's Malcolm?"

"Another super-soldier. Both Larry and I worked with him before. He wanted me to join the others."

"Others?" asked Kiran, faintly.

Yeah, Vicki felt her own knees growing weak.

"There are six of us left—super-soldiers who survived after the Partnership fell. Me and five others. Malcolm told me I should join them because we're all the same. But we're not. Not anymore. I want to be something different. Malcolm said you'd turn on me eventually. But I don't care. I'm staying with you anyway."

"Maybe you should tell us when you talk to other super-soldiers," James said, just as Jessica added, "We won't turn on you."

Vicki smiled, taking another sip of her coffee. She felt better now that the Four had protection.

"Vicki," asked Brad. "Why are you here? Not that we're not glad to see you, but isn't there a world crisis or two you need to take care of back in Washington?"

All the young people turned towards her. They had been wondering the same thing.

"I'm taking a week off," said Vicki. "I'm tired."

"Tired of what?" persisted Brad. "Tired of saving the world?"

"Tired of being part of the bureaucracy," admitted Vicki.

"But... Wasn't that a bureaucracy you created? Pretty much from scratch?" James sounded skeptical. "The Department of State created an entire bureau just for you. The most important people in the world want to meet with you. And you're bored?"

"Not so much bored as wondering what really needs to be done," said Vicki. "Now that OMR is up and running, anyone could lead it—Jerry, for example. But if I stay a part of the government—no matter how important the work I've doing—I'll be staying in a lower vibrational reality. I can't be focused on government and still take part in the vibrational shift."

"Oh," said Kiran, understanding. "You'd be left behind."

"Exactly," Vicki nodded. "I'm working to change the current environment, but the Four are the ones actually creating a path forward."

"Kick-ass Quartet," murmured Brad. Everyone ignored him.

"Maybe we're more than the Four now," James said carefully.

"Oh," said Vicki. "All those young people are part of it too—the humans, the Suedes, and the ACs."

"Actually, it's Mei," said Jessica, smiling at James. "She was one of the tai chi students, and now she's living with James's family. She's a pretty good addition."

"Then it can be the Kick-ass *Quintet*," said Brad with emphasis. Everyone still ignored him.

"I look forward to meeting her," smiled Vicki.

She had not expected to feel calm. Her days in D.C. had been marked by stress and constant effort—filled with briefings, coordination meetings, public statements, and closed-door negotiations. OMR still held power, but that power was... shifting. Political structures were becoming less effective—less necessary. Vicki had always seen the government as a tool, but a tool had to match the job.

She was no longer sure if it did.

* * *

It was late, and the United Nations office was quiet for the first time that day. The last of their scheduled meetings had ended nearly an hour before, and the door to the outer corridor had been locked by the human aides under Federation security protocol. Inside the conference suite, the Pleiadians finished up their tasks. Ambassador Halbi sat at the edge of the long oval table, reviewing a report on a slim interface panel. On the other side of the room, Ambassador Charis stood at the window, observing Geneva through the window.

"They are still coming," Charis said without turning away from the view. "Today we received fifteen new requests from national ministries. Another nine from corporate consortia. One of them brought three different envoys, all arguing over who held seniority."

"And how many asked about planetary alignment, sustainability measures, or species equity?" asked Halbi.

"None," Charis replied. "Again. Did you expect anything to change?"

She finally moved from the window, crossing the room to sit opposite him. She laid her own panel on the table and activated a holographic summary display. "Corruption indicators in the United Nations have fallen seventy-one percent since our assignment began. Nepotism-based appointments have dropped significantly. The data suggests our presence has forced at least some internal restructuring."

Halbi set his own panel aside. "The internal restructuring is because we dismissed the worst among them. Would it have changed if we hadn't? The humans are performing for us. They're giving us what they think we want to see. Their core behaviors haven't changed."

"They are adjusting slowly. The systems are deeply rooted. Many of their leaders still assume that proximity to us is a way to increase their power."

Halbi nodded. "They misunderstand the function of the Galactic Federation. They think we can distribute resources, bypass restrictions, or grant them some sort of privilege. They still operate under the logic of scarcity."

"There is no scarcity," Charis said. "There is only imbalance. But that is not a message they are prepared to receive."

Halbi leaned back and let out a heavy breath. "Earth will not qualify for entry into the Galactic Federation in the next review cycle."

Charis looked over at him. "No. Not yet. But we already knew that."

There was a pause.

"Are there markers that could shift the evaluation?" Halbi asked. "Public initiatives, transnational cooperation, or post-Disclosure transparency?"

Charis collapsed the UN indicator display and pulled up a map, shaking her head. "There's very little of that, although some human groups are experimenting with new governance—decentralized, non-extractive models. But those groups appear to be more similar to cults rather than intentional communities."

Ambassador Halbi set down the latest delegation request and glanced across the table at Charis. "They keep coming as if we are gatekeepers. As if our favor will open doors."

Charis kept her focus on the holographic world map. "Because they still believe in transactional access and privilege. They believe that getting our approval will give them power over everyone else."

Halbi folded his hands."But that's not true. And no matter how much we want them to succeed, it's not our job to ensure their acceptance into the Federation. That's not how it works."

"No," Charis said. "They have to reach alignment on their own. Membership isn't given by request or appointment. It comes from internal coherence—planetary, social, and vibrational."

Halbi's voice remained even. "And if they cannot reach that coherence?"

Charis collapsed her map. "Then the vibrational shift will continue on without them. Those who rise will move forward. Those who resist will stay behind. We've seen it happen many times before."

Halbi nodded. "While we may still find alignment here, the window is limited."

Charis nodded her head in acknowledgement.

There was nothing more they could do.

Chapter Eight

The Cloud Hands Tai Chi Studio still smelled faintly of incense and wood polish. Vicki stepped inside behind the Four. James led the way, carrying a small tripod. Jessica had a camera bag slung over one shoulder, and Brad and Kiran moved slowly, checking the lighting and angles as they entered. Lewis followed, trailing them all, scanning the space in a methodical arc before settling into a still posture near the wall.

Vicki paused near the door, letting the others move around her. The last time she had been here, it was just a studio. Now it was also a production and filming space. There were mats stacked neatly in the corner, rows of chairs against the wall, and a charging station next to the sound system.

Mona Cooper emerged from the back, wiping her hands on a towel. Her hair was twisted up in the familiar little corkscrews. She stopped when she saw Vicki.

Vicki walked over, slowly. "Hi."

Mona nodded once. "It's been a while."

"I know," Vicki said. "I should have come sooner."

There was a pause.

"I made a choice," Vicki continued. "When things escalated with the Partnership, I pulled you and Calvin out. You were both targets. You know that."

"You didn't give us a choice," Mona said, folding the towel. "You just cut us off. We were part of it. And then we weren't."

"I regret how I handled it," Vicki said. "I didn't mean for it to feel like a dismissal. It was fear. I didn't want you to get hurt. But I should have said that."

Mona looked at her for a moment, then nodded again. "Thank you. I appreciate that."

The tension left Mona's shoulders. She motioned for Vicki to look into one of the classrooms where the young people had gathered. Inside, Jessica was adjusting the camera angle while Brad fussed with the audio equipment. James was getting ready to lead a class of students through a slow sequence.

"We've added two new classes," Mona said. "One in the morning, one in the evening. They keep filling up. Life is going crazy—people need to feel like they're doing something."

"We all feel like that," Vicki replied nodding.

"Jessica's been filming classes," Mona added. "They're putting them online. Some of the clips have gone viral and been shared on different forums. It's spreading."

"Did you ever imagine this would be happening? That you would be a part of all this?" Vicki asked, her eyes still on the students as they went through the form using slow, practiced movements.

Mona sighed. "No. Never. Our first wake-up call was when Larry sat us down and told us what the Partnership was really doing—what it wanted *him* to do. How it was using reverse-engineered alien technology to grow richer and more powerful than even the government. At first, I half wondered if Larry was on drugs—or maybe struggling with PTSD. But then James came to us."

Mona paused to watch her son. James was adjusting the posture of one of the youngest students. The girl looked up at him with wide eyes, then relaxed when he nodded in approval and walked away.

"If Calvin and I hadn't already spoken with Larry, I would have punished the boy for lying to us. As it was..." Mona lifted her shoulders in a shrug. "Who could have blamed me for thinking my child was inventing a story about talking to an alien during meditation? Luckily, Larry was there to suggest we keep our minds open."

Vicki swallowed. Larry had sacrificed himself to save her and the Four.

"Calvin hasn't come to terms with it yet," Mona said quietly. "Losing Larry changed him. I know it's only been a few months, and Larry always warned us how dangerous this was—but we didn't understand how serious it really was. Calvin and his brother were best friends."

Vicki didn't say anything. There was nothing she *could* say.

Mona nodded her head toward Lewis who was still standing against the wall, eyes alert.

"Then James brought that one into the studio. I thought Calvin was going to have a heart attack. And then it was James who was urging us to keep our minds open."

"If it makes any difference, I truth-checked him today," said Vicki. "He means it when he says he'll protect the Four, that he wants to live a different life than the one the Partnership planned for him."

"We're all living different lives than the ones we planned for ourselves. We thought we would be running the tai chi studio for a few more years, then retiring to the countryside when James went off to college. And then everything shifted." She glanced at Jessica, who was now repositioning the camera. "Now I manage studio schedules and monitor comments on tai chi videos that get thousands of views. Calvin rewired half the studio to handle the energy-efficient upgrades. It's not the life we expected, but it's one we said yes to."

Vicki gave a small nod. "And you're okay with that?"

"I am," Mona said. "We're helping. People are learning how to regulate their bodies and allow the chi to move. It's making a difference. It's small, but it's what we can do. And we're supporting the next generation while they figure out what comes next. That's enough for me." She turned toward Vicki. "Is what you're doing in Washington enough for you?"

Vicki didn't answer right away. She watched the rhythm of the Four's movements, the stillness of Lewis nearby, the students moving through the form. She wasn't sure what her answer was. Not yet.

Vicki looked around the studio again. "Does Junia's group ever meet here?"

Mona shook her head. "No. the kids have told me that Junia and the ACs are careful about enclosed spaces. They won't risk being boxed in—especially not after the attack on the Suede Nation. They prefer open-air spots, or places where they can move quickly if something goes wrong."

Vicki nodded. "Makes sense."

Mona glanced toward the entry where a young woman was entering quietly, carrying a water bottle and a towel. "That's Mei," Mona said. "She lives with us now."

Vicki looked over at the girl. Mei gave a polite nod and moved to one of the back mats to stretch. "I've heard about her."

"She came to us after things got difficult with her family," Mona continued. "She's reliable. She teaches breathing exercises to the high school group and helps with class sign-ups. We're glad to have her."

Vicki folded her arms and watched the Four set up the next scene. They worked well together, adjusting without needing to speak much. Lewis remained still, quietly watching the door.

"You've built something strong here," Vicki said.

"We're trying," Mona replied. "It's not the same as what you're doing, but I believe it's making a difference."

Vicki nodded. "It does."

They stood quietly together for a moment, watching as the camera light turned red and Jessica gave the signal to begin.

* * *

Jerry sat at his desk, the office quiet except for the faint hum of the ventilation system. A pile of documents sat to his right, half of which he'd already skimmed. He leaned back in the chair and looked toward the window. The sky was overcast, casting the office in a muted gray. Vicki had left for Los Angeles three days prior. She'd told him only a day in advance, saying she needed a break, and then she was gone.

He hadn't questioned it. She'd been looking worn out these past few weeks—tired eyes, and her voice lacking enthusiasm. She hadn't made any mistakes, but her focus had been scattered. She had too many decisions to make, too many competing timelines. When she told him she was taking a week off, he didn't argue. She needed the rest.

What surprised him was what came after. He had expected fallout from her sudden departure—pushback in meetings, questions about his authority, at least a little resistance. Instead, after a brief pause, everyone accepted his role as acting Deputy Assistant Secretary without question. His inbox was full, but the messages were respectful. People were copying him instead of Vicki. Everyone had adjusted faster than he would've thought possible. He wasn't sure how he felt about that.

A knock at the door broke his train of thought. Mary entered, holding a thin stack of folders.

"Morning," she said. "These need signatures."

He nodded and reached for a pen. "Anyone I need to call back personally?"

"Not urgently," she replied. "But a few people still want meetings."

"With me or with Vicki?"

Mary shrugged. "It doesn't seem to matter. I told them she was out, and they didn't react. I'm pretty sure they just want to brag that they met with OMR—to their boards, their funders, or their constituents. They're collecting proximity."

Jerry signed the top form. "Same as usual, then."

"Pretty much," Mary said. "But congratulations, you're holding your own. No one is throwing a tantrum or asking to speak to higher-ups. So you're doing something right."

He nodded slowly. Mary handed over the rest of the forms and left.

A few minutes later, there was another knock. Deputy Assistant Secretary Thomas stepped in, his jacket draped over one arm and phone in the other. "You have a minute?"

"Sure," Jerry said. He stood and offered a seat.

Thomas settled in without ceremony. "I just flew in from Geneva. I was on a late livestream with the Pleiadians."

Jerry leaned forward. "How's it going over there?"

"Productive," Thomas said. "Ambassadors Halbi and Charis have a system. They're not pressuring us, but they're making expectations clear. They've already cleaned up a lot within the UN structure—quietly. There's less bureaucracy in the way now."

"Any movement on planetary review?"

Thomas shook his head. "Not officially. But their reports are detailed. They're watching social indicators closely—education trends, economic shifts, integration efforts. They're paying attention to the younger generation and to the energy patterns coming out of community-based initiatives."

Jerry noted that. "So not the formal structures."

"I think they've given up on governments," Thomas said honestly. "Which makes my job harder, but more interesting. Before, my job was a backwater. Now? Everyone wants to talk to someone from the State Department's UN Liaison Office—government agencies, committees, and the press. Even some foreign government representatives. We're getting questions from diplomats who haven't cared about my office in years."

He stood and checked his phone. "Anyway, just wanted to keep you in the loop. Let me know if anything shifts on your end."

"I will," Jerry said. "Thanks for stopping by."

After Thomas left, Jerry sat still for a while. The office was quiet again. He looked at the signed forms, then at the calendar. His meetings were stacked, but manageable. He was doing the job.

The thought that had been circling all day returned again, clearer now that the immediate demands had slowed. If Vicki stepped away, the position would be his to take. No one had said it outright, but the signs were there—how easily people had adjusted to him being in charge, how few questioned his authority during meetings. People seemed to accept him in the role. That part surprised him more than anything.

Vicki might not return. At least not in the same role. Lately, she had been hinting more about her dissatisfaction with working in a traditional bureaucracy and her interest in focusing on the vibrational shift. She had said she didn't want to be left behind. Jerry wasn't sure if she was disillusioned with the State Department specifically or with the entire government system.

If she left, OMR would need someone to step up. He could do it. He was already doing it. The role would come with more than a title. The salary increase would be significant. The access, the influence, and the invitations to shape high-level policy—it would mark the peak of his public service career. It would also mark a shift in how he lived, and how visible he became. He'd be *important*.

But he thought about Anne. About the kids. About how much more visible he had become in just the last few days. A permanent move upward would come with trade-offs. More travel. Less privacy. More risk. And Anne had grown more involved lately, not only leading CE-5 groups in their neighborhood, but helping to start groups in other places. She didn't seem interested in turning back.

He didn't have an answer yet. But the question wasn't going away.

Chapter Nine

The common room of the flower shop was filled with quiet conversation, the occasional clink of coffee mugs, and the audio of the latest video. Vicki sat with James and Brad on one of the large cushions pulled close to the wall monitor, watching the footage from the tai chi studio. Jessica stood nearby, arms crossed, occasionally reaching over to skip forward or rewind.

Brad leaned forward, tapping the corner of the screen. "That's the part people keep commenting on—when James transitions from White Crane Spreads Its Wings to Repulsing the Monkey. It's clean. And with your narration, Jess, it actually makes sense to non-practitioners."

Jessica gave a short nod without looking away from the screen. "We recorded three versions. I used the one with the least amount of jargon. The first one sounded like I was reading from a manual."

Vicki smiled, resting her arms on her knees. "This looks good. The pace is calm but keeps your attention. It'll help more people feel like they can try it without getting overwhelmed."

Brad sat back a little, satisfied. "Traffic's been up too. Our website—truthsplosion.net—just hit over twenty thousand visits this week."

James looked impressed. "Seriously?"

"Yep. A couple of the posts about breathing techniques got shared on that vibrational health subreddit. And someone clipped a piece of our livestream for a 'Why Earth Isn't Falling Apart' compilation. We're low-key famous."

Jessica rolled her eyes, but said nothing.

Brad grinned. "You all owe me for not naming the site *The Kick-Ass Quartet.* You know I could've done it."

"No one would've taken us seriously," James said.

"Still, admit it," Brad replied. "You'd wear that on a hoodie."

"I don't know about anyone else," laughed Vicki, "but *I'd* certainly wear it on a hoodie."

Across the room, Kiran sat on a divan near the window. Mei was beside him, cross-legged. They were both drinking chai. She had been quiet since dinner, mostly listening.

Mei put down her tea, and took something out of her pocket. When she opened her palm, Kiran could see what looked like a small circular jade amulet. The center was almost smooth, but when the light from the table lamp caught it at an angle, a faint glint of something deeper became visible.

"What's that?" Kiran asked, leaning slightly closer.

Mei looked down at it for a moment. "My grandmother gave it to me me a couple of days ago. She actually came to the tai chi studio to see me." Her voice caught slightly when she said that. "She told me it had been passed down from her grandmother. She kept it hidden for years."

Kiran leaned in, curious. "Hidden? Why?"

"She didn't know. Only that it's important. Apparently we've kept this secret in our family for generations."

"Is it part of a necklace?"

Mei shook her head. "No. She told me not to treat it like jewelry. It's meant to be a tool of some sort. She was never taught how to use it and doesn't know what it's supposed to do—only that she was told to keep it safe when she left China."

He reached out carefully. "Do you mind if I take a look?"

She handed it to him.

He turned it slowly in his fingers, examining the fine engravings. "These symbols—they're the *bagua* trigrams, right?"

"Yes," Mei replied. "I've seen them in books on feng shui and the I Ching."

"But the I Ching's for fortune-telling," Kiran said.

"I thought so too," Mei said. "But this doesn't feel like something for fortune-telling."

James walked over and looked at the amulet in Kiran's hand. "In the West, people call the I Ching fortune-telling. But it's more like a decision-making system—symbolic logic, patterns of change."

"And you know this, how?" Kiran was a bit taken aback. Wasn't he supposed to be the one that told the others about eastern philosophies?

"Tai chi has the eight gates—energy points that that can open and close, shaping how chi flows. The *bagua* has the eight trigrams—they're said to represent the nature of reality. The story is that both came from the legendary Chinese hero Fu Xi thousands of years ago. I don't know if that's true, but it's striking how the number eight shows up in ancient civilizations: the eight gates of Babylon, the eight directions of Native American medicine wheels, the Buddhist Eightfold Path..."

Kiran gave up and started giving examples from their previous conversation. "...and the eight-petalled lotus in Hindu mandalas. Plus the eight limbs of yoga."

Brad came up behind James and slapped him on the back. "Nice to have an historian in the group."

But James wasn't done.

"In Platonic cosmology, the number eight represented harmonic balance. The octagon was said to bridge the square and the circle—linking earth and heaven. In alchemy, eight symbolizes balance and transformation."

By now, Jessica and Vicki had joined the conversation.

Jessica squinted at the amulet. "So... does this connect to what the ACs talked about? The Eight Gates and space travel?"

"What?" This was the first time Vicki was hearing about it.

"They're checking back and will let us know," Jessica said.

But Vicki was searching her memory.

"Sol Gate—that's what the Kewpies called the sun, right? When they took us through the portal to meet with the Galactic Council? Do the Eight Gates represent eight suns? Each one a portal to another star system?"

Everyone stared at her in shock.

"I'm probably way off base here..." she continued.

"I wouldn't assume that," Jessica replied faintly.

Brad's eyes lit up. "I bet Mei's amulet is a tool to open the portals! A way to reach the stars!"

Vicki frowned. "I'm not sure I'd agree with you there. Number one: that's a really big jump to make—like a crazy-ass-leap-off-the-side-of-a-mountain big jump. And number two: why would anyone need that? The Kewpies took us through Sol Gate. They told us that to use portals, you just need to match the vibration of the craft's navigation crystal to that of your destination. No hardware needed—except, of course, for the spaceship and the navigation crystal."

"But maybe you don't always *know* the vibration of the place where you want to travel," persisted Brad. "Maybe the amulet acts like a type of cheat code that can program the navigation crystal when the people on the ship can't."

Vicki took a sip of her coffee. *Ugh*. It was cold.

"I still think we're making a lot of assumptions. We need to check with someone."

The Four looked at each other, then looked at Vicki. They all knew who they could ask.

* * *

Lewis stood by the back door of the flower shop. His hands were clasped behind his back, and he stayed still so he wouldn't draw attention. No one had asked him to be part of the conversation, and he didn't mind. The others were gathered around the low table in the common room, talking quickly and overlapping each other as they traded theories about space travel through portals.

They were discussing the Sol Gate, sacred geometry, and vibrations. Kiran mentioned the bagua again, and Mei was passing something around to show them. Lewis couldn't see what it was from his angle, but he noticed the way they all leaned in. No one looked at him. That was fine. They didn't need to.

He listened as they talked about vibrations and sun portals—how they might possibly use them to transport to other star systems. Or at least to a meeting place with the Galactic Federation. Vicki said only people with a certain vibrational level could pass through the Sol Gate without dying.

Lewis stayed silent. He knew space travel—he'd been through it. But what they described sounded different. The Partnership hadn't used portals. He and his team had flown in ships reverse-engineered from crashed alien craft. Their movement was smooth as they passed through silent zones of black and silver. He'd been awake most of the time, though not always fully conscious. He remembered the stillness, the lack of sound, and the way the ship glided. He never got tired of it.

He had been assigned to a mining facility on Europa—the second largest of Jupiter's 95 moons. He remembered the facility clearly, with its plain metal walls and long hallways. The Partnership had sent him there to support extraction and shipment of rare metals collected from the surrounding asteroid belt. While there were plenty of humans on his team, there had also been others like him. Biologic constructs trained to endure the work and follow orders without question.

The facility had been empty and lying dormant when the Partnership was destroyed—orbital paths made space mining too expensive at certain times of the year. Moving materials from the asteroid belt required careful timing and a lot of energy. When the window of opportunity closed, operations were paused until orbits lined up again. Now the Partnership was gone, and the facility was deserted. Still, he was sure it remained operational. The systems were built to run indefinitely.

He shifted slightly and began paying attention to the conversation again. Mei was explaining something about how the amulet was a family heirloom. James was talking about about history. Vicki was asking questions about the Alpha Centaurians. None of them sounded like they were planning to turn on each other. Or on him.

Malcolm had said they would. That these people were only kind until it was inconvenient. That if things changed, they would abandon him like the Partnership had abandoned—or destroyed—the other super-soldiers who didn't meet their standards. But Lewis didn't believe that. He had been watching them. He had seen how they treated one another. He had seen how they included him, even if they didn't always talk to him. No one had asked him to leave. No one had locked him out.

He knew he couldn't follow them through Sol Gate. Biologic constructs couldn't raise their vibration high enough to pass through portals. If he tried, he'd burn to death. There were limits to being one of the strongest and most dangerous men alive, and he had accepted that.

Still, he thought working for these people had value. He carried things when they needed it. He made sure no one followed them home. He watched the perimeter. He stayed ready. This life wasn't the one the Partnership had prepared for him. It didn't follow the rules he had been taught. It was better.

Even if he was left behind. It was still worth it.

* * *

OMR OBSERVATION MEMO
Classified Briefing – Internal Use Only
Subject: Post-Contact Civilian Behavior Patterns

[Observed: Education Sector – Multiple Regions]

- Civilian use of **cranial prosthetics**—referred to online as "AC Bumps" or "Foremind Enhancers"—has increased 800% month-over-month. Marketed as fashion items, but worn with evident seriousness in Disclosure-active zones. Some wearers claim "improved thought coherence" when worn continuously.

- **Synthetic claw accessories** modeled after Suede anatomy are now being sold at open-air markets and in online stores labeled as "bioempathic extensions." Suede emissaries have issued no official statement, but several private individuals have expressed discomfort.

- **Blue-tinted facial products** are trending across streaming platforms, particularly in solidarity circles. Often paired with star-themed clothing and phrases such as "Unified Harmonic Front." Usage is voluntary and symbolic; no confirmed Pleiadian endorsement.

[Unconfirmed Reports – Youth Contact Points]

Sporadic but consistent sightings of **Suede and AC youth** in parks, libraries, and nighttime music events in North America, Scandinavia, and Southeast Asia. Descriptions match known visual markers, but all interactions are brief. Individuals appear healthy, communicative, and mobile. No photographs or verified recordings available. Statements from bystanders often include phrases like, "They didn't seem like they were hiding. Just visiting."

[Medical Notice – Device Fraud]

Unauthorized clinics and private vendors are offering "interdimensional detox units" and "scalar resonance recalibrators."

Claims include: aura realignment, pre-ascension smoothing, and vibrational leakage repair.

None have been reviewed or recognized by OMR's Technology Validation Task Group.

Several units found to contain household microwave parts and copper wiring.

Local authorities urge communities to construct verified devices using the open-source schematics widely distributed—anonymously—several months ago.

[The Hum – Status Report]

Currently not a concern. Regions formerly reporting high incidents (Utah, Lower Bavaria, Eastern Tibet) have now normalized. In locations where it persists, residents report tuning it out or incorporating it into group meditation routines. No anomalies in EM or acoustic scans. Monitoring remains in passive status.

[Digital Platforms – Engagement Trends]

The site www.truthsplosion.net has seen a significant spike in user traffic, largely driven by short-form videos of tai chi sessions, energy coherence tutorials, and citizen-recorded CE-5 attempts. Notable metrics:

- 21,000+ unique visitors this week

- 3,400 shares of "Quiet is the Signal" video segment

- Continued interest in documentary project, tentatively titled "The Kick-Ass Quartet" (internal joke, not recommended for public branding)

[Analyst Addendum]

The boundary between mimicry, transformation, and early resonance adaptation is increasingly difficult to track. Youth behavior is
leading trend shifts. Civilian adoption of extraterrestrial markers is
accelerating without formal policy direction.
No action recommended at this stage, but surveillance protocols
remain active.
Expect further shifts in expressive behavior and identity patterning
over the next lunar quarter.

End of Brief

Chapter Ten

V icki stood in the pocket out-of-time, observing the others as they stabilized. Her energetic form shimmered like theirs, outlines held by intention rather than physical mass. Jessica appeared to her left, with Brad and Kiran opposite, and James slightly behind. The space around them was neutral, without temperature, without sound, without direction. Time did not pass in the usual way here. It simply was.

Two were missing.

Mei was not here. She hadn't yet learned how to shift herself into this frequency. Truth be told, they hadn't even told her it was possible. Shifting required readiness, and Vicki wasn't sure if she was there yet. Even so, Mei appeared to be fitting into the group well: she listened without demanding attention and helped without wanting credit. She had even stepped up and to start an extra breathing class for the high school students.

But did she belong?

Vicki hardly knew Mei—the Four would be in a better position to judge. But if Mei didn't already belong, she was beginning to. Vicki had a sense that Mei was becoming a part of what they were building.

Vicki gave voice to her thoughts.

"Do you think Mei will be able to do this soon?" she asked, glancing at Jessica.

"I think she's close," Jess replied. "But I think she'll learn faster if we actually invite her—she's the type of person that needs to know she's welcome."

Brad tilted his head. "She's already leading her breathing class, doing tai chi with us, and is part of our tri-species group. There's no reason why she shouldn't."

"Has she been introduced to Melly, yet?" Kiran asked. He seemed a bit nervous.

Vicki noticed and felt a wave of empathy. Kiran was the most recent arrival to their group, and had only been around the Galactic Council representative a couple of times. Being in the presence of an eight-foot alien was enough to make anyone nervous.

"She's part of this," James said. "Whether she knows it yet or not. Whether *we* know it or not. I think that jade amulet showing up at just this exact time proves that."

No one disagreed.

Vicki let that settle and turned her thoughts to Lewis. He wasn't here either. And he would never be.

He was a biologic construct. His physiology and energetic composition had boundaries. He couldn't raise his vibration high enough to enter this space. Just like Larry, his structure was stable but limited. Vicki knew that, but it didn't make it easier.

"Lewis will never be able to come here," she said aloud, more to name the truth than to seek any reaction.

There was silence for a moment.

"He knows," James said. "I think he's made peace with it. Just like Larry did."

"He believes in what we're doing," Jessica said. "Even if he can't be part of all of it. You've already checked to make sure he was telling the truth."

"He's cut off the people he used to work with," Kiran added. "That couldn't have been easy. And he did so in person, which is even more remarkable. It's hard to reject former friends."

Vicki nodded. "He's choosing this life, but I don't know what that gives him."

"He said he didn't want to follow the old instructions anymore," James said. "Isn't that enough? At least for now?"

"We need to bring him in more," Vicki said. "Not just as staff, but as someone who has a place—someone who's part of the group."

"He's already loyal," Brad said.

"But loyalty isn't the same as belonging," argued Vicki.

Jessica nodded. "We can include him more in the planning. Let him talk. Ask for his ideas. Not just hand him tasks to do."

"He'll take it seriously," James said. "He always does."

All conversation stopped as a shift in the pocket reality signaled someone's arrival. All five turned to look at the disturbance.

Then Melly entered.

Vicki never got used to it. Melly didn't walk into the pocket reality. She didn't just appear. She *unfolded* into it—eight feet of radiant, insectoid alienness. She had the head and forelegs of a praying mantis and the body of a beetle standing upright. A long cape, four short hind legs, and bulging eyes on either side of her triangular head. But it was Melly's *eyes* that always drew Vicki's attention—their iridescent colors swirled in no fixed pattern.

To Vicki's surprise, Kiran was the first to step up and greet Melly. She could tell he was doing it on purpose—maybe as a way to face his fear.

"Melly, it's good to see you," he said, forcing a smile as he placed his hands over the first bend of Melly's forelegs in greeting. Then he quickly stepped back.

The boy gets an A for effort, Vicki thought, as she and the others followed his lead and greeted Melly in turn.

"You have accomplished much," said the alien. There was an overlay of Tibetan singing bowls. "There were many in the Galactic Council who doubted you."

"*I* doubted us," muttered James.

Brad turned to him, clearly taken aback. "But... but *of course* we were going to be able to pull it off! We had the interviews with Melly, the free energy schematics, our activated DNA abilities... We had *me!*"

Vicki hid a smile as Jessica and James both pretended to gag.

"We actually have a reason for being here," she said. "We'd like to ask you about a family heirloom that one of our friends was given."

"You are speaking about Mei?" The feeling of small bells.

Vicki and the young people all stilled. Melly knew about Mei? How? Vicki decided to ignore that question. Some things she didn't need to know.

"Exactly. It's a small jade amulet with a crystal embedded in the center, with the eight bagua trigrams engraved in a circle around it."

"We're trying to figure out what it's for," said James eagerly. "We think it's a key. Or a tool. Something linked to the Eight Gates."

"But before all that," Jessica said. "I think we need to know what the Eight Gates actually are."

Melly looked at them, and when she spoke, there was the *feeling* of gongs. "It *is* a tool. But it cannot be activated by one person alone. It requires joint activation—by humans, Alpha Centaurians, and Suedes. It's designed that way."

Kiran asked, "So it's a device? Or something symbolic?"

"It's both," Melly said. "The Eight Gates are both access points and states of alignment. The amulet can interface with those Gates, but only when the conditions are right."

Brad frowned slightly. "What kind of conditions?"

"Not technical," Melly said. "Relational, and energetic. The amulet responds when the three species are working together—when intention, focus, and action are held in balance across them."

"So Mei can't activate it alone," Vicki said.

"No," Melly said. "Nor can you. Nor could an Alpha Centaurian or a Suede by themselves. It must be done together. That's part of its design. The function depends on cross-species resonance."

James asked, "Can you tell us how to begin the process?"

Melly shook her head. "I cannot. If I explained each step, it would remove the purpose. The path of activation is also a test of readiness. The three groups must learn how to listen to one another, and how to share control without trying to dominate the others."

"So figuring it out is part of the work?" asked Jessica.

Melly looked at her. "Learning how to cooperate is the work."

"But," Kiran said hesitantly. "Why do we need this? When the Kewpies took us to meet with the Galactic Council, there were no other species working with them to access the Sol Gate portal—it was just them. Why can't we do what they did?"

Internally, Vicki facepalmed. She had worked hard to keep her nickname for the small beings who piloted that craft under wraps—but she'd forgotten to warn the Four. While the Suede Nation might have liked the nickname she gave them, she was pretty sure the Kewpies would not.

And she still hadn't know the proper name for their species.

But Melly was answering Kiran.

"The Galactic Federation does not want aggressive species to be unleashed in the galaxy. So the first time beings from a planet travel via a gate, there is a test to ensure they won't be a threat to others. In the case of Earth, it is cooperation between its three peoples."

"And since it was the Kewpies taking us through Sol Gate," said Kiran, "it didn't count—we weren't doing it ourselves."

Melly didn't answer, but there was the feeling of bells.

Then Vicki took a breath and changed the subject. "I've been thinking about stepping down—about leaving my job at the State Department."

The Four all stared at her in shock. Melly's eyes whirled.

"The Department of State is still structured for the world that existed before Disclosure. It's a bureaucracy. Yes, we keep adapting, making connections and providing new information—but the nature of it hasn't changed. Now that we have a system in place, there are others who could do what I'm doing."

Vicki paused, but no one said anything. She went on, "I mean it. We already brought down the Partnership. Disclosure has happened. Now I'm stuck holding press briefings, writing policy papers, reviewing documents, and meeting with an endless stream of people all wanting some sort of inside access. I did my part. It doesn't need to be me anymore."

"You think your role is finished," Melly said.

"No. And that's the problem—it's not finished. The position is just as important now as ever. But I can't do it anymore—not without anchoring myself to the wrong place. If I stay, I'm going to be stuck."

James looked up at that. "You've mentioned being stuck a couple of times. Stuck how?"

Vicki glanced at him. "The vibrational shift is accelerating. You know that—all of us can feel it. And I'm scared that if I stay focused on governance—on keeping the bureaucracy running—I won't shift with the rest of you. I'll be too embedded in the low vibrations of the old system."

"Then leave," James said. "We've got each other. You've told us before that the Four are supposed to lead from outside the system. Come back to us."

Come back to us. She closed her eyes for a moment. It was so tempting.

"I want to," Vicki said. "But someone will have to take my place. The post can't sit vacant. And whoever steps in will probably end up stuck in the lower vibrational state themself. I would be handing them a job that could trap them."

Jessica understood. "So you're afraid of being left behind. But you're also afraid of causing someone else to be left behind in your place."

"Yes," Vicki said. "Exactly. I'm not sure which outcome feels worse."

"You can't hold a door open forever," Kiran said. "The point is to walk through it."

"I know," Vicki said. "I'm just trying not to lock someone else out while I do."

Melly spoke—the feeling of singing bowls. "Not everything is your responsibility, Vicki."

"I'm doing it again, aren't I?" she said.

She was. Vicki had had this same exact conversation—pretty near to it anyways—with her sister Beth, who had scolded her for trying to handle everything herself when she had a team to rely on, and friends to support her.

"You do have the tendency to take the burden of everything on yourself," agreed Jessica, smiling. "I think as long as you're upfront and honest with candidates, that's enough. And we've already confirmed that, even with the vibrational shift happening soon, people will still have a few years to choose the reality they want to live in. Whoever takes your position isn't necessarily stuck there forever. Not everything has to be decided right away."

Was it really that simple? Vicki wasn't sure, but she knew what she had to do. Talk to Jerry—and Anne. Prepare her office for the transition. She had worked to define a path for humanity.

Now it was time to make her own.

Chapter Eleven

The night was warm, but dry. No wind. No moon. Perfect.

He crouched in the tall ornamental grasses just beyond the rear fence line, barely disturbing a single blade. Thirty-two minutes since the last student exited. Twenty-five since the lights inside had gone dark when the owners left. He'd counted the steps, tracked the bio-signatures. Everyone had gone.

Good.

He activated his night vision. The world sharpened into crisp monochrome: walls, windows, doors — all green-gray geometry. A possum skittered near the compost pile on the western edge of the grounds, but otherwise the place was still.

His breathing was slow—controlled. His heart rate didn't rise above 55 beats per minute even as he unclipped the flat disc from his belt. The charges were pre-programmed to collapse the roof at the lowest structural stress point, ensuring it fell without spreading debris beyond the foundation. A demolition that was clean and targeted.

It feels good to have work again.

The thought came unbidden. It felt good to have purpose, to have direction. It had taken several months, but now he had an employer—a former client of the Partnership. Someone who knew how to use people like him—biologic constructs—and who still had enough money to buy destruction like this.

And yet, no one had told him to check the building first.

Amateurs!

He did so anyway. Not out of mercy—he wasn't wired that way—but because complications meant evidence. Evidence led to discovery. Discovery led to mission failure. And he *never* failed a mission.

He lightly scaled the fence, then walked down a gravel path toward the eastern wall. A question came to him. *Why destroy a tai chi studio? What does this gain anyone?*

Fear, probably—a way to send a message. Just like in the old days—burn something beautiful and make people cower.

But the logic was flawed. Didn't his employer know? This could backfire. Disastrously.

He paused near a koi pond, one booted foot perched silently on the edge of a smooth stone. The water was black and motionless. A single frog croaked from the lily pads.

He tapped into the neural stack behind his right ear. A flicker of electric cognition opened his indexed database. The Partnership had downloaded the entire pre-Disclosure internet into his cortex during final commissioning. All of it. Even the bits the world's censors thought they had deleted.

He queried: *destruction that backfired / turned into rallying cry.* Two hits surfaced instantly.

- The Birmingham Church Bombing, 1963. Intended by white supremacists to intimidate and silence the Civil Rights Movement. Result: Outrage and mobilization. The movement swelled. International coverage. Legislative shifts. "Four little girls" became a chant for change, not a deterrent.

- The Reichstag Fire, 1933. Nazis blamed the communists and seized power. But in long-term historical framing, it became a symbol – not of fear, but of manipulation. It became a cautionary tale, not a success story. "False flag" accusations that lingered through decades, and a legacy of mistrust in centralized power.

He closed the query. What was his employer's game? Control, maybe? If so, this was a mistake. Just as easily, it could lead to more defiance.

But his employer hadn't asked for his opinion.

He reached the back door and pressed his ear against it. His enhanced hearing picked up no movement or sounds that might indicate someone inside. The building was empty. A quick biometric scan confirmed it.

Still, he paused.

This place was peaceful. Not just quiet, but *clean*. Even in grayscale, he could tell it was loved. He didn't feel love himself—he had been one of the Partnership's first psychopathic hires—but he had excellent pattern recognition. Human devotion leaves traces, even in a garden: the neat edging of the paths, the benches placed evenly around the pond, and the carefully trimmed trees.

He knelt beside the door and set the device. It took less than a minute. No one would know he had been here.

But after he climbed back over the fence, he realized he was feeling something. Deep down inside himself he sensed slight misgivings—not in carrying out the mission, since his execution was flawless, but in the strategy itself.

And he'd learned enough about history to know: when destruction starts with fear, it rarely ends in victory.

At least, not for the destroyer.

* * *

James woke to the sound of his mother's voice.

At first he wasn't even sure he was awake. The room was dark, and the frantic syllables that broke through the silence were muffled by walls and sleep. But they came again — sharp this time, unmistakably panicked.

"...how bad is it?" asked his mother's voice, cracking.

A deeper rumble followed. His father. Measured, but tense.

James sat up in bed, pushing off the sheets. The digital clock read 2:37 a.m.

He opened his door just as the hallway light flared to life.

Mei stood there, barefoot, wearing her robe with her arms wrapped around herself. She blinked at him, confused and wide-eyed, her expression mirroring his own.

Neither of them said anything. They padded down the hallway together, drawn toward the raised voices.

The living room lights were on. His father stood near the door with his mobile in his hand. His mother was gripping the back of the sofa so tightly her knuckles were white.

She turned toward them the moment they entered. Her eyes were wide, her expression shocked.

"It's gone," she said. "The studio. The Cloud Hands Tai Chi Studio. It's—" she glanced at her husband, as if saying it again might somehow make it untrue.

James' father didn't correct her.

"The fire department says they got the call at 2:09," he said. "There was no sign of anyone. The structural collapse happened just before they arrived. It was already too far gone to do anything."

James stared at him. "Gone?"

"They said it was arson," his mother whispered.

That word hung in the air like static. Mei stepped closer to James.

The studio had been their second home—their safe place. Where they'd learned tai chi, made videos, and taught students how to center themselves before attempting anything remotely vibrational.

And now it was gone.

"Who would do that?" James asked. He voice quavered.

But Mei wasn't looking at the adults anymore. She grabbed James' arm. Not hard, but firmly enough to take his attention away from his parents' shattered expressions.

"Call the flower shop," she said.

He blinked. "What?"

"If someone targeted the tai chi studio, they might go after the others next. We need to warn them."

His mother looked over, startled. "You think this is coordinated?"

"I think we're out of time to be surprised," Mei said. "James—now."

He was already heading back to his bedroom to get his phone. Would their attackers go after the flower shop too? They had tried to be careful, not filming anything from the Four's offices, varying their routes when they traveled between the two locations, but they might have slipped up.

James unlocked his phone, then pressed speed dial for Brad.

He hoped it wouldn't be too late.

* * *

The Daily Sentinel – Special Feature Op-Ed
By Amanda Riley, Investigative Journalist
Title: *The Secret Buried Beneath Our Feet: The ACs, the Cover-Up, and Humanity's Near Extinction*

"History is written by the victors. But what if the victors were from another star system?"

-Amanda Riley

They live beneath us.

Not metaphorically. Literally. Beneath our cities, our forests, and our deserts. Deep within the Earth's crust, sealed behind gates of energy and illusion. They've been watching, waiting—maybe even planning. And if you believe the sanitized press briefings or the syrupy joint-human-alien youth videos being shoved down our throats lately, you'd think the Alpha Centaurians — those crystalline-eyed humanoids from another system — are just misunderstood spiritualists.

But what if I told you this isn't the first time they've walked among us?

What if I told you that the same beings now asking for "co-creative integration" with humanity... are the very reason human civilization nearly disappeared thousands of years ago?

Sound extreme?

Then buckle up, buttercup. Because this ride is about to take you under the surface — both literally and figuratively.

Out of Place... Out of Time... or Erased?

For decades, archaeologists have stumbled across what they call "OOPs" — out-of-place artifacts. Machined metal in ancient strata. Batteries in Mesopotamia. Maps showing Antarctica without ice. We've laughed them off. Labeled the finds hoaxes or misinterpretations. Academic tenure depends on obedience, after all.

But what if these were remnants of a previous human civilization — one that had technology, culture, knowledge... and then vanished?

Dr. Halima N'Goma, a respected archaeologist from the University of Cape Town, told *The Daily Sentinel*, "We see sudden starts and stops in the archaeological record. Civilizations that should have developed never did. Whole land masses that were once above sea level are gone."

Geologists, too, are asking questions. Dr. Vijay Kapoor, a tectonics specialist, has long puzzled over anomalies in sediment layers dating back 12,000 years. "There's evidence of sudden, continent-scale shifts, but no corresponding asteroid impacts or super-volcano events. Something else happened."

They're right. And they're not alone.

The Smoking Gun: Youth Video Blows the Lid Off

Weeks ago, a "unity message" video — produced by a group of teenage Suede, Human, and yes, Alpha Centaurian youth — was quietly released by truthsplosion.net. It was meant to be a feel-good broadcast about shared evolution and interspecies collaboration. But buried in the middle of the video were a few throwaway lines by one of the Suedes:

"They hope to avoid repeating the errors of their ancestors. The scars on the planet and near destruction of humanity? That's long ago history and doesn't matter anymore."

Excuse me?

The video has since been edited. But *The Daily Sentinel* obtained a copy of the original — and you can bet I watched it frame by frame.

The implications are staggering. The crash of the ancient Alpha Centaurian craft thousands of years ago wasn't just a tragic accident. It was the beginning of a catastrophe that pushed early humanity to the brink of extinction.

Why aren't we being told about this?

Enter: The Galactic Federation, History's Greatest Censor

Sources within the Department of State's Office of Multi-species Relations (OMR) — who will remain anonymous for obvious reasons — have confirmed what many of us suspected: the Galactic Federation intervened directly in Earth's history.

"They used energy-based suppression," one source told me. "Not just of people – of memory. Of timelines. Whole civilizations erased, their ruins buried, their stories unspooled from collective memory."

Why? Because what the Alpha Centaurians were doing back then was *illegal*. Their ship crash-landed, but instead of seeking rescue, they began building – experimenting – *interfering*. Think gene-editing. Think mind control. Think planetary social engineering, done without consent.

The Federation erased it all. Covered it up.

Sound familiar?

History Repeats Itself. Or Does It?

Now, the descendants of those original AC survivors – the ones who scurried underground after the near-apocalypse they caused – are resurfacing.

They're elegant. Polished. Peaceful.

They say they're sorry.

They say they've changed.

But let me ask you this: if your great-grandparents had committed crimes so severe they were expunged from history by interstellar law, would you be *trusted* with governing the very species they harmed?

Would you be allowed *above ground*?

Because that's what's happening now.

And while some in our government – looking at you, Deputy Assistant Secretary Victoria Heywood – seem ready to open the gates and hold hands, I, for one, have questions. Questions about sovereignty. About memory. About survival.

Because no matter how many tai chi sessions they film with the Alpha Centaurians, no amount of joint youth summits will erase the fact that these beings once saw humanity as nothing more than a resource to manipulate.

They didn't ask permission.

They didn't offer restitution.

And now, they want trust?

Final Thought: Seduction Is Still Control

Beware of soft power. Beware of the spiritually enlightened sales pitch.

Because what the Alpha Centaurians are selling isn't new. It's just better wrapped.

If they've truly changed, let them open their archives. Let them show us what was erased. Let them prove they've dismantled the tools their ancestors used to warp us. Let them face consequences — not just PR campaigns.

Until then, I say this:

Let them stay underground.

Because if we forget what they did last time... we may not survive the next one.

—

Amanda Riley—Investigative Journalist. Earth Native. Uncanceled. Uncompromising.

Reach me via verified ComNet node: Sentinel.Riley/Tr uthfire

Editor's Note: *The views expressed in this article are those of the author and do not necessarily reflect the official position of The Daily Sentinel. But maybe they should.*

Chapter Twelve

Vicki, arms crossed, stood by the counter in the common area of the old flower shop. Despite the number of people in the room—the Four, Lewis, Mei, and the Coopers— there was a heavy silence as they contemplated the disaster. Mona sat on the sofa, staring into her cup, her fingers wrapped tightly around the ceramic. Calvin was beside her, his face pale, eyes hollow. Both of them were in shock. Mei, always quiet, now looked as if she was trying to become invisible. James, standing across from Vicki, was also in bad shape. Just *how* bad was the fact that he was clutching a cup of coffee, rather than his usual hot chocolate.

The Four didn't say anything. Vicki knew that everyone in the room was trying to make sense of what had happened the night before. The fire. The destruction. The uncertainty of what came next. For the Coopers, it was not just about the loss of a building, but the destruction of something much more personal. It had been their foundation, their space, and their identity.

"I don't think we can do it," Mona finally spoke, her voice tight. "I don't think we can start over from scratch. We have insurance, but it'll probably take another year before we can rebuild and start operating the business again. We can't go that long without income."

James sighed heavily. "And the tai chi studio was where we were filming all our videos; that's going to have to be put on hold until we can find another place."

Jessica, Brad and Kiran all started. They hadn't realized.

"Maybe this is an opportunity," said Vicki slowly. She wondered whether she was pushing too fast—everyone was still reeling. But events were already in motion, and the world wasn't going to wait up.

Mona shook herself out of her daze, and turned to glare at Vicki. Maybe all wasn't forgiven between the two of them after all.

"I hope you have a very good reason for saying that," she said curtly.

The others were looking at Vicki in surprise, too. Maybe this was a mistake, but it's not like they had many options.

"There's a building next door," she said. "It's for sale. It used to be a bank, then an event space, and most recently, it was retail. It's big, it's empty, and it's already set up for a lot of different things. You could buy it."

"With what money?" asked Mona, bitterly. "All our money was wrapped up in our business—which has now burnt down, if you recall."

"How much?" asked Jessica quietly.

"The mid-eight figures," said Vicki.

Jessica glanced over at her brother, who nodded. "We could buy it," she said. "Our dad made a lot of money with the Partnership—we still have all that. We also received insurance when the mansion was destroyed. And we could sell the land as a building plot—a 2-acre building plot in that neighborhood would bring a lot of money even though the buyer would need to clean out all the debris before starting to build."

The room fell into a tense silence. Mona and Calvin exchanged a look, their eyes showing both unease and hope.

"We can't accept it," Mona finally broke the silence. "It's... too much. This isn't what we need right now."

"I think it's *exactly* what we need right now, Mom," said James. "The world is running out of time. Whoever burned down the tai chi studio knew it would slow us down. Setting up next door will help us get back the time they stole from us."

"But the money..." began Mona.

"Mona, listen to me," said Vicki. "I know it's a lot, but this is an opportunity we can't ignore. The building next door is exactly what what you need—what *all* of us need—right now."

"I'm appreciative, but we can't accept it," said Mona, shaking her head. "It's too much. It's not just the money, it's the principle. It feels wrong. I don't want to rely on anyone, not like this."

Vicki saw the struggle in her eyes. It wasn't just about the money—it was about pride, about a sense of dignity. Mona and Calvin didn't want to be indebted to anyone, especially not at a time like this. She understood that, but her own thoughts were pulling her in a different direction.

"It's not about the money anymore," Vicki said, leaning forward slightly, her voice quiet but firm. "The world is changing, and we can either resist it or we can adapt. The shift—it's coming. The money, the buildings, even all of this"—she waved her hand around the room—"is all losing relevance. What matters now is what we can do with what's left. What we build with the pieces we have."

Vicki continued, "That building, the one next door—it's more than just brick and mortar. It's a space where we can continue our work, where we can focus on what really matters. Helping people raise their vibration. Teaching them how to shift and evolve. This is bigger than any of us. If we're going to be ready for what's coming, we need a place to do it."

"Mom," said James. "You're acting like it's charity. It's not—it's just shifting to a new path now that the old one's closed. I've seen the building. It's huge, and it'll let us expand the number of classes we offer. There's even living quarters upstairs. If you and Dad feel strongly about it, you could sell both the house and the tai chi property and put proceeds toward the cost of the bank building—so you'd have your own investment in it too. We could live and work there."

"I still feel like it's some sort of betrayal," said Mona, shaking her head.

"It's not about betrayal, Mona," said Vicki. "It's about survival. It's about adaptation. You've seen the way the world is shifting. We can't keep pretending that the way we've lived is going to work much longer. People are waking up to their own potential, to their ability to raise their vibration. But they'll need guidance, and they'll need a space to do it. Our *kids* need it."

Vicki noticed how Mona went still when she referred to the kids. Yeah, that was probably a low blow, but she didn't care.

But Mona was still balking. "I just don't know. It's too much. I feel like we're stepping into something we can't control."

"You're right," Vicki said. "We *can't* control it. But we can guide it. And that's the best we can do for now. Buying the bank building would help us do that."

It looked like Mona was going to say something more, but before she could, another voice spoke up.

"I have something to say," said Lewis, from the back of the room.

* * *

Everyone turned to stare at him. This was the first time the biologic construct had spoken up in a group without first being asked a question.

Lewis didn't like people staring at him. He liked to stay unnoticed while watching others, simply doing his job. But he was proud of always doing a *good* job, and in order to do that, he needed to talk now.

"I have something to say," he repeated, feeling a little nervous now.

"Go ahead, Lewis," said Vicki.

"My job is to guard—to protect the young people and the family of my fallen comrade."

Calvin blinked his eyes furiously at the mention of his brother.

"The job includes three locations—here, the tai chi studio, and the house."

When he mentioned 'the house,' he nodded towards the Coopers. "Plus seven people." His eyes glanced at Vicki. "Maybe eight."

"And you are just one person," said Jessica, suddenly understanding.

"I can *do* the job," said Lewis, "but not all at the same time. Last night, someone burned down the tai chi studio because I was not there. If I had been there, no one could have damaged the studio. But then I would have left all the people unprotected."

"You are our security expert, Lewis. What are you suggesting?" asked Vicki.

Lewis nearly lost his train of thought—he was being asked for his input, not just being told what to do. He could tell Vicki already knew what he was going to say, but she wanted him to say it himself. He paused for a moment, then continued.

"Two buildings, side-by-side. Everyone together. This is much easier to patrol. Much easier to defend. Everyone would be safer if you bought the bank building."

"The super-soldier just made a recommendation, Mom," said James. "He's our security; we should listen to him."

* * *

Mei sat quietly, her hands folded in her lap, as the conversation unfolded around her. Everyone was in shock. The others spoke with urgency about what to do next, their voices mixing with the sounds of frustration and concern. The fire at the tai chi studio had left a hole in their plans, but for Mei, the worst part was her own silent panic screaming in her mind. While everyone else debated their next move, she couldn't help but wonder what was going to happen to her.

And she felt so *guilty* about it.

Aliens. The vibrational shift. Earth's membership in the Galactic Federation. It was *all* at risk. But she could only think about herself.

Mei hated that. She felt small. Everyone else seemed focused on the greater mission while she was stuck in her own selfish worries. She knew she needed to be better—she needed to think of the greater good, not just herself. But she couldn't. Did that make her a bad person? Evil?

The Coopers were good people, but what if they told her it was time for her to leave? If the tai chi studio was gone, maybe they couldn't afford to keep her anymore. The thought made her stomach tighten. If she had to go back to her family's house... the very thought of it was suffocating. Her family never understood — and they never tried. They didn't care about the vibrational shift, the aliens, or any of it. They would tell her she was wasting her time, that she was just a young girl imagining things that had no place in the real world. They would mock her and humiliate her, telling her she could never make a difference.

Deep down, part of her feared they were right.

The voices around her seemed distant, a blur of ideas and plans, but one voice finally cut through her thoughts—Lewis, talking about the bank building next door. He was saying that buying it would make things more secure, it would make it easier for him to guard them. Mei didn't really care about the building—or the security. She just wanted to know what would happen to her. Would she be kicked out and told she was on her own?

Her fingers slipped into her pocket and touched the jade amulet with its bagua markings and the small crystal in the center. She held it for a moment, the cool stone giving her a sense of comfort she couldn't explain. She gripped it tightly—her own personal good luck charm.

And then James's was telling his mom that Lewis was a biologic construct and a security expert—and that she should listen to him when he gave advice about staying safe. That they should move the tai chi studio into the bank building. That they should sell their house and live in the bank building too—it had enough space for tai chi classes and for all four of them to live.

All *four* of them! Mei suddenly couldn't breathe. James was talking as if he assumed she would be coming along with his family. With the Coopers. That she was a part of them now.

With a surge of happiness, Mei realized she finally had a home.

Chapter Thirteen

Jessica stood near one of the walls in the small limestone cave, watching as the other humans trickled in. The air was cool and dry, and the rocky ceiling arched high above, speckled with mineral traces that reflected the artificial illumination of the portable lighting they had brought with them. They had practiced tai chi just outside this same cave when they last met, but now the group had grown.

Junia arrived with half a dozen Suede youth, coming through whatever passage connected to their community. And the three Alpha Centaurians—Nevik, Astran, and Calix—weren't alone. They were joined by several other AC youth, quiet and watchful.

Brad, James, Kiran, and Mei stood nearby. A few high school students, who had been slow to keep up, finally made their way in and gathered near the back of the group. Jessica wondered if they'd ever find a more convenient place to meet—driving out to this isolated spot in the Santa Monica mountains was awkward. Not that she'd ever risk putting the Suedes or the ACs at risk, it was just... a long way.

No one started the tai chi forms. Instead, they began to gather in a loose circle. Junia, now their accepted leader, nodded to Jessica and then looked at the ACs. "You said you wanted to share something."

Nevik looked over at Astran and Calix, and then began slowly. "We've learned something," he said. "About the Eight Gates. We believe it's important."

Jessica folded her arms and waited. The Four had something to say about that too.

"All suns," Nevik began, "are portals. But only in higher dimensions. They allow travel between places in the galaxy."

The Four exchanged glances. Larry had already told them this months ago.

Calix added, "But the Eight Gates are different. They are stronger. They allow travel not just within this galaxy, but to others. To anywhere in the Universe, if the conditions are met."

Astran continued, "But this requires specific alignments—combinations of resonance and geometry. The Eight Gates form a kind of universal access system."

"What sort of conditions?" asked Brad.

"We don't know anymore," Calix said. "That knowledge was destroyed a long time ago."

"Destroyed by who?" James asked.

Nevik answered, his voice steady. "By our ancestors. After what happened with Sol Gate."

Jessica just raised an eyebrow and waited. The explanation wasn't long in coming, although it was a little different from what the Four had learned from Melly. Nevik told them how the original ACs had extended Sol Gate's energy to Earth, triggering geological and climate disasters across the planet after the connection collapsed.

"Afterward, our people chose to erase everything they had recorded about the Gates," finished up Nevik. "They believed it was too dangerous to ever try again."

"He told us never to bring it up again," Calix said. "Representative Brandori told us we'd be expelled from the city if we kept trying to uncover more information about it."

Astran added, "We were told that the past needed to stay buried. That humanity isn't ready. But we don't agree."

Mei took a step forward. "What would happen if you got expelled?"

Nevik looked at her. "We'd be banned from our homes, our schools, our families. Everything."

The Four all went still when he said that. They all knew what it felt like to lose their home.

But then Jessica shook her head and came back to the present. "Don't worry about that—we've come across the same information from another source. And as far as I'm concerned, Federation Council Representative Melly outranks Brandori. She didn't tell us to stop looking. She said humans, Suedes, and ACs need to work together to figure it out."

This grabbed everyone's attention. The ACs brightened.

"It's all connected," said James. "The eight trigrams of the bagua, the eight gates in tai chi, the eightfold path in Buddhism..."

"And we have a cheat code to the Eight Gates of interstellar travel!" interrupted Brad, gleefully.

* * *

Junia stood quietly, listening as the Four explained the importance of Mei's jade amulet. The room was filled with the hum of eager voices, all focused on the task at hand. James, Jessica, Kiran, and Brad were speaking, each one contributing a piece of the puzzle. Mei's amulet wasn't just an artifact. It was the key—a tool that, when activated by the combined effort of humans, Suedes, and ACs, would trigger the power to travel through Sol Gate.

James was the one doing most of the talking. "The amulet is part of a much larger system," he explained, "but it only works if all three species cooperate. It was designed this way, intentionally. It needs the resonance of each species, working together, to unlock the gate."

Jessica picked up from where James left off. "Once we've activated the amulet, the connection to Sol Gate will open up. We'll be able to travel anywhere in the universe, as long as we have the coordinates and the right alignment."

Kiran added, "It's not just a matter of putting it in the right place. We need to sync our vibrations. All of us. Humans, Suedes, and ACs. The amulet only responds when that alignment is right. If we don't have all three species involved, it won't work. And that was on purpose—the Galactic Federation wants us to show that we can set aside our differences and work together before we're allowed to travel freely throughout the universe."

Junia looked around at all the young people in the cave. Everyone was sitting forward and listening carefully They all looked excited and ready to help. Even the quiet Suede kids, who never said much, were talking now, asking questions and sharing their ideas.

It was so different from the meeting in the Community Hall. The elders said the Suedes should never, ever work with humans or the Alpha Centaurians. They were scared that if they did, everything would fall apart, and the Suede Nation would be in danger. They said humans were too violent, and the ACs weren't their problem. The elders always reminded everyone that the Suedes had to take care of the Earth crystal, and they couldn't risk that by letting other people get involved.

The elders were afraid of change—and that's why they tried to scare everyone and keep the Suedes away from the others. They didn't want to know what might happen if they let anyone in. They wanted to keep things the same. But now? Look at them—young Suedes, humans, and ACs—all working together. They weren't just trying to figure out an amulet, they were trying to unlock the whole universe!

Junia felt proud as she watched them. These kids, these *Bridgewalkers*, were making something brand new. They were making a new way to go forward, a way that didn't use old fears or superstitions. They were all working together, not fighting each other or looking down on anyone. And they all wanted to learn and not let the old problems stop them anymore.

Her cousin, Bowen, would have loved to have been here.

Bowen! But now Junia was remembering with love, not anger.

For a second, Junia thought back to the elders again. Would they ever change their minds? Probably not. They were happy being stuck where they were.

The real question was if the Suedes—Earth's caretakers—could leave the solar system. She already knew the answer. Not all of it, but enough. In ancient times, one of them had traveled on a Galactic Federation ship to meet with the Council. He had stayed there only two nights before he got sick and had to come home. That was as far as any Suede had ever gone.

She didn't think any Suede could travel farther. The Earth crystal mattered too much. They couldn't leave—at least not for long. They belonged to the Earth, and the Earth belonged them,.

But that didn't mean they shouldn't work with the humans and the ACs. There was so much they could do here, so many fun things ahead—nobody knew where working together could take them. Although she would never be a spacer, she could help change things here on the planet. And she was sure that the new path forward would be better than what they had now.

Junia looked back at the group. They were all talking, taking turns to share their ideas, and getting more excited as everything started to make sense. She smiled to herself. She had always thought that working together was the best way to go. And now, with the Bridgewalkers leading the way, she knew she had been right all along.

This was going to be *amazing!*

* * *

Both Ambassador Halbi and Ambassador Charis sat at the table in their office suite. It was nearing midnight, and the United Nations was quiet. They had both been working long hours, without much hope for the people who lived on this planet, but right now things felt... different.

Halbi spoke first. "Have you seen what the young people are doing? Humans, Suedes, and ACs are working together, Charis — doing things I thought impossible just a month ago."

Charis turned away from the window, and looked at him. "Yes. I've seen it — you can't miss it. It's exactly what we hoped: they're working together as equals and not letting their differences define them."

Halbi nodded slowly. "Exactly. It's not something I expected to see so soon."

Something in his expression seemed off—uneasy.

"This troubles you," Charis said flatly.

He nodded.

"Melly reported that the jade amulet has surfaced, which means the timing is right," Charis pointed out.

"But are we sure they're ready?" asked Halbi. "If they figure out how to activate Sol Gate, they will be free to travel the universe. They could cause irreparable damage without even realizing it. Do they realize how much is at stake? It will change everything for them—and for us."

Charis shook her head slightly—the time for arguments on whether humans were ready was long past. "I agree, it's a risk, but we don't have a say in the matter. The jade amulet has made itself known. That artifact was encoded with patterns and vibrations centuries ago. It was designed to reveal itself when the time was right—and apparently that time has finally come."

Halbi rubbed his chin thoughtfully. "Humans are unpredictable. Their species is still so young in terms of interstellar awareness. They don't yet understand the true scope of what they're tapping into."

"Please keep in mind," Charis said, letting a hint of impatience show, "this all started because the Tall Whites teamed up with the Partnership and interfered in human affairs. That's why we're in this situation. It was a mistake by a Federation member—not the fault of humanity. We can't hold them back now because of that."

Halbi held up his hands in surrender. "I know we can't. It's just that their development isn't following the usual path for sentient species. It's moving too fast. And it might already be too late to slow it down."

"It's not up to us," said Charis, sharply this time. "We've been over this, the Council has discussed this. Repeatedly."

She paused to control herself before continuing. "If there's one thing we can say for sure, it's that they are adaptable. Yes, they make mistakes, and yes, they can be reckless, but they learn. And this time, they're learning together. That's something we've never seen before."

"Exactly," said Halbi. "But they are still brash, daring, impulsive and violent. What will we see when these Earth species join efforts to come through the Gate? Despite their potential, they remain undisciplined, driven by emotions and impulses that could easily lead to destruction. When they step through Sol Gate, will they bring unity and cooperation—or will their unchecked nature tear apart the very fabric of the worlds they encounter? What will happen then?"

Charis remained silent. She didn't have an answer.

Chapter Fourteen

Mei stepped through the double doors and into the wide-open atrium. Her sneakers made a soft sound on the marble floor, polished but cracked in places. The light from the large front windows stretched across the room. An old chandelier hung from the vaulted ceiling. The air smelled faintly of pine cleaner.

Vicki, Calvin, and the Four had persuaded Mona to "just take a look" at the bank building to see if it could serve as both a new tai chi studio and a home. She wore her usual "convince me" expression, while the others moved through the space, excitedly talking as they explored.

Vicki walked just ahead, talking to the owner—Debbie had been friends with her sister Beth when she owned the flower shop.

"This place has had a few lives," Debbie said. "Bank, event space, retail... but it still has good bones. When Beth was alive, we held the block Christmas party here. We're all sorrier than we can say that she's gone. She was the spark that pulled the shopkeepers together—we're a community now."

When Mei noticed Vicki wipe a tear from her eye, she looked away. She barely knew how to manage her own emotions, let alone someone else's.

They followed Debbie as she led them through the building. The main level had the atrium, a seating area, a row of small offices, a conference room, and public bathrooms. The second level—more a half-story than a full floor—was used as Debbie's living quarters. It was a surprisingly complete living area. Three modest bedrooms, a narrow kitchen with updated appliances, and a living room with clean windows and light hardwood floors.

"It's too large for just me. I had originally renovated this level with the goal of renting it out for additional income," explained Debbie, "but I saw how convenient it was for Beth to live above her business, so I decided to do the same."

"Why do you want to sell?" asked Jessica as Debbie led them back down the stairs.

"My daughter just gave birth to twins. They live in Florida. I want to be near them."

But now Brad wandered over to the vault; Debbie had skipped it when she had shown them the first floor. "What's in here? Or has the space been converted to something else and you just kept the doors for show?"

Debbie smiled. "It's still a vault, but there's something unexpected in it. Let me show you."

She stepped up to the metal door, gripped the handle, and pulled it firmly to the left. The old mechanism engaged, and thick bolts slid back with a clunk. Using both hands, Debbie pulled at the heavy door, which slowly swung outward on its massive hinges.

"Call me paranoid, but I had the locking mechanism disabled," said Debbie. "I was afraid I might somehow lock myself in there by accident."

She stepped in, turning on a light. The room was the size of a small bedroom, with sturdy shelves lining one wall, and rows of safety deposit boxes lining the opposite. There was a door at the far end. "This is the surprise," said Debbie, opening it. "Be careful."

Cool air spilled out from the dark space beyond.

"No lights?" asked Brad.

"Sorry." Debbie flicked a switch.

A single lightbulb lit the stairway leading down into a concrete and stone-lined corridor. They all tramped down, with Mei at the back. She'd been fine with the caves, but this corridor made her feel a little claustrophobic. While it wasn't falling down, it had seen better days. Some of the concrete had broken away in places, exposing the original timber supports.

"But what's it for?" asked Brad. "It's just a hallway; it looks like it ends right here." He was standing just 20 feet from the bottom of the stairs, facing a brick wall—literally.

"Exactly," said Debbie. "When the building was originally constructed, this was a tunnel that ran down the block to a nightclub."

They all turned to stare at here.

"This is one of the oldest surviving buildings on the block," Debbie explained. "It was built in the 1920s during Prohibition. The story goes that armored cars, heavily guarded, would unload liquor here at the bank. Then the liquor was moved secretly through the tunnel to the nightclub—which was a speakeasy then—so powerful men could drink despite the law. They ran money and crates of Canadian whiskey back and forth—whiskey to the speakeasy, money to the bank." She paused. "The tunnels are sealed now, as far as I know. But the stairs still work fine if you want storage."

"Cool!" said James. He was geeking out over the history of it.

Mona ran her hand along the concrete wall. "This place has some serious structure, but some of it's a little... old."

"I know," Debbie said. "It's why I didn't left it alone when I renovated the building. It passed inspection, but only if I kept it off limits to the public."

Mei had had enough of this damp, closed-in space. She started back up the stairs, and everyone else followed. As they made their way back out, Mei felt like she could breathe again. In comparison with the tunnel, the space felt airy.

Mei glanced over at Mona, who was standing in the middle of the atrium. Her arms were folded, but her expression had changed—less tense. Calvin gave her a small nod. Something passed between them that Mei didn't need to interpret.

"I'm sorry about the tai chi studio." Debbie was talking to both Calvin and Mona.

"Thanks," Mona said quietly.

"I'm not trying to get rich here. If it helps you rebuild, I'll shave some off the price. Call it a neighborly gesture."

Vicki started to speak, but Debbie waved a hand. "You're all doing something here. I've seen it. This place could use people like you running it. This neighborhood could use people who want to make it their home. What we *don't* need is more big box stores."

Debbie reached into her bag, and pulled out a folder. "If you can meet my price, we can make it simple. I'd rather sell it to you than to have to list it."

Vicki turned to Mona and Calvin. "We could do it today," she said, earnestly. "Jessica and Brad have their portion ready. If you agree, we can start today. You'll be able to resume classes and filming this week."

Calvin and Mona looked at each other, then at Vicki. They nodded.

Vicki looked back at Debbie. "They'll take it. And they'll pay in cash."

Debbie raised an eyebrow. "All of it?"

"All of it."

She closed the folder and smiled. "You've bought yourselves a building."

No one cheered, but Mei let out a breath she hadn't known she'd been holding. The last few months had been a roller-coaster. She had lost her family and home. She had found a place to live with the Coopers, and a place to belong at the tai chi studio. The loss of the tai chi studio had been a disaster. But now? Now they had an entire building right next to the old flower shop where the Four lived and worked. It was more than she could have hoped for. Hopefully, this time it would stick.

"Let's go upstairs," Mona said. "I want to see that kitchen again."

So they did.

* * *

Jessica didn't follow the others when they went back upstairs. They were still talking about the kitchen and the size of the bedrooms. Her mind was on other things.

She was relieved Calvin and Mona agreed to take her and Brad's money. When they'd first offered, Mona had balked, not wanting to accept anything she hadn't earned herself. Jessica had worried that Mona would not only refuse but also make the situation awkward. James' parents had worked hard for their old studio, and losing it had been a blow. Jessica didn't want them to feel like charity cases.

It wasn't as though she and Brad needed the money. They were fine. Better than fine. And the vibrational shift mattered far more than any bank balance. In the end, no one knew how wealth would even be measured in a higher-dimensional reality. Whatever it was, it probably wouldn't involve dollars in an account.

If it came up again, and Mona or Calvin started feeling uncomfortable, there were options. They could place the bank building in a trust so everyone shared ownership. If Vicki agreed, they might even include the flower shop. That way Mona and Calvin wouldn't feel indebted to her and Brad—it would belong to all of them.

Her thoughts went back to the tunnel under the vault. She couldn't shake the thrill she felt when she saw the stairs and heard the history — being underground changed everything. She suspected the others hadn't made the same connection: if the tunnel structure was still intact, sealed or not, it might be possible for Junia and the Suede Nation to make an entrance from their community straight into it. That would mean the young Suedes and ACs could travel to the middle of Los Angeles instead of to a cave in the mountains. Humans, Suedes, and ACs could meet right in the bank.

That would make things simpler. No need to coordinate schedules or rides, or worry about drawing attention. More frequent meetings would mean more time to train together—and more progress. She glanced at the group as they returned down the stairs, the sound of their voices echoing in the big lobby. They had no idea yet, but this building could be much more than a replacement for the tai chi studio.

It could be the center of everything.

* * *

OMR OBSERVATION MEMO
Classified Briefing – Internal Use Only

Subject: Escalating Global Deviations – Environmental, Sociocultural & Cognitive Frequency Shifts

- **[Pacific Coast Ledger]**
  "From the Plains to the Coast: Unprecedented Migration Trends"
  Quarterly real estate data shows a 26% increase in households relocating from interior agricultural states to coastal cities and towns, despite rising sea levels. Analysts cite "non-economic drivers," with one broker stating, *"They don't seem concerned about jobs or housing costs—just where they feel they should be."*

- **[North Shore Sentinel]**
  "Historic Fishing Towns See Population Tripling"
  Municipal planners report sudden overpopulation in several small coastal towns. Infrastructure strain noted, yet no conflicts—residents describe "knowing" the newcomers belong.

- **[Campus Current]**
  "Legacy Admissions Rejected by Legacy Students"
  Admissions office confirms multiple cases where students with guaranteed legacy acceptance voluntarily withdrew

before orientation, citing "irrelevance of degree prestige in post-shift society."

- **[National Academic Review]**
  "Elite Schools Face Identity Crisis"
  Analysts note similar declines—though less severe—at comparable institutions. Several universities have commissioned "existence audits" to determine how to remain relevant if conventional socio-economic structures collapse.

- **[Federal Education Monitor]**
  "Inspectors Return Empty-Handed"
  Four separate investigative teams disbanded after failing to confirm the existence of assigned inspection sites. Internal report redacted in full.

- **[Soundwave Chronicle]**
  "432 Hz Takes Over Emerging Music Scene"
  Young musicians abandoning conventional 440 Hz tuning in favor of 432 Hz, claiming it resonates with the natural frequency of the universe. Playlists tagged #432Shift grow exponentially. Listener comments describe reduced anxiety, improved focus, and "feeling more connected to each other."

- **[IndieWire Pulse]**
  "Major Labels Lose Grip on Youth Sound"
  Executives admit inability to market 432 Hz tracks using standard algorithms; claim the music "feels uncontainable" in commercial spaces.

- **[Department of Education Internal Bulletin]**
  Multiple inspection teams dispatched to verify operational status of school systems that have ceased reporting attendance or performance metrics. Several teams unable to

physically locate campuses—finding vacant lots, unmarked woodland, or non-existent addresses in GPS databases.

- **[Metro Cultural Review]**
  "Harmony Over Hype"
  Emerging venues now advertise "432-only nights." Attendees report synchronized breathing and unplanned group singing during performances.

- **[PetLife Global]**
  "Animals Show Heightened Awareness"
  Veterinary clinics note increased pre-storm movement, grouping before owner arrivals, and apparent anticipation of seismic activity.

- **[Wildwatch Weekly]**
  "Urban Wildlife Shifts Habits"
  Raccoons, foxes, and crows documented forming mixed-species foraging groups, with coordinated dispersal when observed.

- **[Hudson River Wire]**
  "Unknown Youth Assemblies in Vacant Lots"
  Drone footage from upstate New York shows large gatherings of mixed-age youth in unused industrial areas. Overhead audio captures low-frequency humming and rhythmic clapping. No signage, leaders, or posted events.

- **[Southside Bulletin]**
  "Flash Gatherings Leave No Trace"
  City cleanup crews report spaces left cleaner than before gatherings. No graffiti, litter, or property damage.

[OMR Action Items – Restricted Circulation]

1. Monitor and map all convergence zones involving migration, missing infrastructure, and frequency-based gatherings.

2. Investigate potential subterranean or cloaked facilities connected to educational disappearance cases.

3. Assess behavioral synchronization and cultural shifts emerging from harmonic events and youth assemblies.

END OF BRIEF

Chapter Fifteen

A nne stood at the counter in the kitchen, opening a bottle of wine. The house was quiet now, save for the hum of the refrigerator and the faint murmur of conversation coming from the backyard. The boys—Josh and Adam—were both asleep, their bedtime routines having gone smoothly for once. It had been a long day, but a good one. Jerry had finished up at the office, and now they were enjoying a quiet evening together with Vicki. The night air was cool, and the grill on the back deck was cooling off as Jerry used tongs to transfer the meat to a plate.

Anne felt a sense of calm, though she knew that the conversation happening just outside the kitchen would shift everything. Vicki had called earlier to say she needed to speak with both of them about something important, and Anne had a feeling it was related to Vicki's position at the Department of State. Jerry had told her something was brewing, and since Vicki had requested to meet with them as soon as she returned to Washington two days ago, she suspected she knew what it was.

Anne carried the bottle and three wine glasses to the deck, and placed them on the table within easy reach of Jerry and Vicki. Jerry poured the wine, and Vicki took a sip. She was holding something back and it was weighing on her. Anne could sense it.

"Everything okay, Vicki?" Anne asked as she took a seat at the table.

Vicki looked at her, giving a small but tired smile. "Yeah, I'm fine. Just a lot on my mind." She hesitated for a moment before continuing. "I'm leaving the Department of State."

Anne raised an eyebrow, not surprised so much by what Vicki said, but by the bluntness of her statement. "You've decided to quit?"

Vicki nodded, taking a deep breath. "I've decided that I need to step away from my role as Deputy Assistant Secretary of OMR. It's not just a career change, Anne. It's something I've been thinking about for a while."

Anne already knew that—Jerry had told her about it.

"You're sure about this?" Jerry asked.

"Yeah," Vicki replied, her voice even. "I'm sure. It's not the job. It's the bigger picture. I've accomplished my goals—Disclosure has happened, and we've created a system to deal with it."

Anne set her glass down on the table; there was more beneath the surface of Vicki's decision. "So, what does that mean for the rest of us? For the work you've been doing with the Department of State?"

Vicki turned her eyes toward the ground for a moment, as if deciding how much to say. "It means I'm offering you the job, Jerry." Her words came out quickly, as if she wanted to get them out all at once. "If you want it, the position is yours. I can't stay in it. But I think you could do the job as well as I did."

Jerry looked at her, his expression unreadable. "You're serious? You want me to take your place?"

Anne knew Jerry wasn't surprised at the offer—Vicki had been hinting at it before she left for Los Angeles. But she could also tell he wanted Vicki to lay it all out for them.

Vicki met his gaze. "Yes. I think you'd be the best person to fill the role. You're connected with what's happening in the State Department, and you've got the right perspective. But there's something I need to tell you before you make any decisions."

Anne watched Vicki closely. She could tell this was what was bothering Vicki. "What's going on?" she asked gently. "What's got you so upset?"

Vicki looked at her hands and breathed in. "The job itself is great — higher pay, more visibility for Jerry, he'd become one of the most well-known people in government. The problem is the shift. The vibrational shift is already happening, and anyone in this job will get buried in the minutiae of bureaucracy. I don't want to be stuck in that lower vibrational reality when it happens. I don't want to remain here when everything else changes. And if Jerry takes the job... I'm worried that I might be condemning your family to stay stuck in this place, too."

Anne exchanged a glance with Jerry. Her heart tightened as she thought about the implications. Money, influence... being left behind.

"Vicki," Anne said softly, her voice calm, "I know you're worried. I can hear it in your voice. But you don't have to make that decision for us. If Jerry takes the job, that doesn't mean we're stuck. We have the choice to grow, too. And if he decides not to take it? There are other competent people who work at the Department. You won't be abandoning OMR."

Vicki nodded, though her gaze was still troubled. "I want to believe that, Anne. I really do. But it's hard. The world is shifting, and I'm not sure where any of us fit anymore."

There was a long silence, the night air cool around them. Finally, Jerry broke the silence again. "We'll make it work. We always do."

Anne agreed, offering Vicki a reassuring smile. "You don't have to carry all the burden alone, Vicki. We're here for you. Whatever happens, we'll figure it out."

Vicki seemed to relax slightly, and she nodded. "Thanks. That means more than you know."

* * *

"You don't want me to take the job, do you?" asked Jerry. Vicki had left half an hour earlier, and he and Anne were scraping plates and loading them into the dishwasher.

"Do you *want* to?" asked Anne.

"You're a lawyer—the better thinker. Why don't you walk me through it—pros, cons, options, and unknowns."

Jerry already had a good idea of what he was going to do, but he wanted to hear Anne out. His wife always had an elegant way of explaining complicated issues.

"We've done very well for ourselves professionally," she started out. "I'm an attorney who will likely be making partner in the next two or three years. You're a high-ranking government official and a key player in addressing issues of global importance. Anyone who looks at us will see that we've got it made."

She paused, but Jerry didn't say anything. Instead he poured more wine for both of them.

"And that's just professionally," she said as she took a sip from her glass. "We have two amazing sons, a wonderful place to live, a good work-life balance, and we love each other."

The two of them looked at each other and smiled. Jerry finished putting dirty silverware in the cutlery basket, and started loading glasses in the upper rack. Anne continued.

"But we've found out during this last year that reality is much different that we've assumed." She set her glass down. "It isn't just about getting the next promotion or making the right investments. The vibrational shift—whatever it really is—means the rules are changing. Not just for governments and agencies, but for everyone."

"So," said Jerry. "We could either keep our wonderful life, or risk everything for the possibility of... we don't know."

"What we *do* know is that the rules that helped us succeed won't work for our boys. What's valuable here and now in this reality probably won't be in the next."

Jerry didn't say anything. He was filling up the soap dispenser.

"I've spent the last month leading CE-5 activities here in the neighborhood."

Jerry looked up. "And what did you learn?"

"That there's more out there than we know, and that I don't want to limit myself—or limit us."

Jerry smiled as he closed the dishwasher and pushed the power button. The low rush of water filled the kitchen, followed by the soft, rhythmic hum of the cycle beginning. "I'm glad you feel the same way."

"You do?" Anne looked simultaneously uncertain and relieved.

"I do." Jerry took Anne in his arms and kissed her lightly. "If even half of what I've seen at OMR is how the new reality will work, our future will be incredible. Our *kids'* future will be incredible. It would be foolish of us to slow that down. It would be wrong of us to try and keep our boys from that."

"You *knew!*" she said accusingly. "You already knew what you wanted to do."

"Yeah, but I wanted to be sure that you knew too—knew it for yourself, not just trusting me. Because it's not going to be easy."

Anne nodded slowly, still wrapped in his arms. "Then we're agreed."

"We're agreed," Jerry said, holding her a little tighter.

The water cycled and the dishes rattled faintly, but neither of them moved for a long time.

* * *

Robert Thomas, Deputy Assistant Secretary in the Department of State's UN Liaison Office, couldn't believe his luck. Vicki Heywood and Jerry Smith had just sat across from him with coffee in hand and invited him to step into Vicki's position. For a moment he could hardly process it. This wasn't just a promotion—it was a chance to be at the center of decisions and negotiations that would shape the world for decades . The role meant tackling the hardest global issues and working directly with people and groups most leaders only heard about in briefings. It was his chance to move from the sidelines of history to the center.

Money didn't factor into his excitement—he was already a DAS, after all. The appeal was the work itself—the complexity, the constant challenge, the responsibility of helping to guide the Department during a time of unprecedented global changes. He could already imagine the projects, the problem-solving, the long hours that would feel more like intellectual puzzles than a job.

Vicki had been upfront with him about the downsides. Whoever took the role would probably stay in the lower vibrational reality while much of humanity moved forward with the shift. Robert listened carefully, then told her what she didn't yet know—what no one at the Department of State knew. His son Gerald, thirty years old, battling addiction and facing minor legal trouble, was the only family he had left. Robert would not abandon him. If staying meant he could remain present for his son, then so be it. The job wasn't less valuable because of that—if anything, it made the work more meaningful. He could serve where he was needed, both in the office and at home.

Robert's only reservation was why Jerry wasn't taking the role—he was the most experienced and the most deserving. Robert didn't want the job if Jerry had been passed over and would resent it. But Jerry only smiled and said he and his wife had agreed they wanted to take a different path.

That led to the question of staffing. Vicki assured him that most personnel in the Office of Multispecies Relations would choose to stay on, but with the workload growing so fast, he could bring about half a dozen of his own people when he transferred. That was a bonus—Vicki had already vetted his staff while tracking down the leak in OMR. The only remaining question was the deputy role. Robert had asked Jerry point-blank if he intended to stay.

"For the meantime," Jerry had answered. "And if I decide to leave, I'll be sure to have possible successors lined up for you."

This all felt too good to be true. It was rare in a career to be offered something that was both the natural next step and the kind of challenge you dreamed about. Every part of it—the scope, the urgency, the history-in-the-making—spoke to why he had joined the Foreign Service in the first place. The decision was easy. He would say yes—he was pretty sure that Vicki and Jerry already knew that.

He was so lucky. And this time, the work ahead would be as much about protecting what he loved as it was about serving the country.

Chapter Sixteen

Lewis followed Brad down the short hallway on the bank building's main floor, the faint smell of sawdust and fresh paint still in the air from recent renovations. Brad carried a black plastic crate filled with cables, routers, and a small metal box with blinking lights that Lewis recognized by memory—but not by use—as a network switch.

From upstairs came the thumping sounds of furniture being dragged across the floor, followed by voices—Mona's sharp but cheerful tone giving directions, Jessica responding with a laugh, and Mei saying something about where the dresser would fit best. A soft thud echoed through the ceiling, followed by the muffled rip of a cardboard box being opened.

"The flower shop's router is strong, but it's not going to to be able to reach through all these walls," Brad said, dropping the crate onto a desk in one of the empty offices. "We'll run a dedicated line from the shop and piggyback the signal here. You okay with pulling cable through the wall cavities?"

"Sure," Lewis said. "I haven't done it myself, but I've seen enough videos."

Brad grinned at him. "Yeah, I bet you have. But this'll be the real deal. I'll mark where we need to drill, you fish the cable through, and I'll handle the terminations."

Lewis nodded, watching him set out tools in neat rows on the desk. Brad didn't look at him the way the people at the Partnership had—the quick, sidelong check that took in his size, his military frame, and the unspoken calculation of what he could do to a person. Brad talked to him like he was just another guy.

Out in the main lobby, the sound of footsteps padded across the hardwood floor—James and Kiran, walking in slow loops, pausing here and there. Lewis heard Kiran say, "This corner could work for warmups," just as James added, "We could use the vault as a storage area for towels and stuff. It's a little creepy, but it's a useable space."

They moved into the lobby to drill the first hole, the sound loud in the high-ceilinged space. Lewis fed the bright orange cable down the wall while Brad caught it below. It was simple work, but Brad kept up a steady stream of conversation—about signal strength, firewall settings, and a "mesh node" they'd put in upstairs.

"You're really good at this," Lewis said at one point.

"It's in my blood. Or my code, depending on how you look at it. Melly's upgrade made a lot of this second nature. But honestly? Having you here makes it way faster." Brad grinned at him. "We're a good team."

The impact of the words caught Lewis off guard. No one in the Partnership had ever said something like that to him. Back then, he had been just a piece of equipment—useful until he wasn't anymore. Now Brad was talking about being a team in a way that suggested they were... maybe not friends yet, but friendly coworkers. Brad was treating him like he mattered in the process.

From upstairs came the thud of something heavier hitting the floor, followed by Jessica shouting, "We're fine! It just slipped, it's fine!" A burst of laughter followed.

After they ran the second cable into the vault—just in case they ever needed secured connections there—Brad wiped his hands on a rag and glanced toward the row of offices along the lobby wall.

"You know," Brad said, "we should turn one of those into your space. Private security office. We could put in some decent monitors, maybe a desk with a view of both doors. You could have camera feeds from the flower shop and here, side by side."

Lewis blinked at him. "For me?"

"Yeah. You're running security, right? We need better security, and to provide that, you'll need a base of operations. Somewhere you can work without people stepping over you." He walked over to the row of offices and peered into the door of the first one. "You can choose one for you."

Lewis felt an unfamiliar pull in his chest. People had assigned him duties before—missions, targets, guard rotations—but never a place. Never something that was his.

"I'd like that," he said quietly.

Brad nodded and went back to unpacking the network gear, all business again. "Good. Once we get the network up, we'll order the monitors. I have a couple of good online sources; we can look at them together, and we'll get whatever you recommend."

Out in the lobby, James called, "Hey Brad, are you guys going to need any of these offices for electronics, or can we use them for advanced sessions?"

Brad stuck his head out the office door. "We'll need one for the security office. The others are all yours."

Lewis stayed there for a moment longer, holding the coil of cable in his hands. He had the entirety of the internet in his head, but somehow, this simple offer—a room with a desk and screens—felt like the most valuable thing anyone had ever given him.

Lewis liked being part of a team. Always had. Even when he'd been with the Partnership, there was a certain comfort in knowing the plan, knowing his role in it. But Brad's comment earlier about being a good team had been different. When he was at the Partnership, "team" had meant other people giving orders and him carrying them out without question. Here, it meant him and Brad working together.

The thought bothered him. He'd promised the Four he'd protect them all—their group and anyone close to them—but maybe that wasn't enough. If they were going to do this shift thing, if they were going to go wherever the Sol Gate portal led, maybe he needed to go all out. No halfway loyalty. Not just standing guard.

He was either in. Or he was out.

As Brad plugged in the switch and began securing the cable ties, Lewis leaned against the doorframe. "Hey, Brad... once you figure out how to use that jade amulet, how are you going to get to the Sol Gate?"

Brad stopped tying the knot and looked over his shoulder. "Good question," he said, frowning. "I guess that' something we'll have to figure out. Last year, when we traveled through the portal to meet with the Galactic Federation, the Kewpies took us. But Melly told us, that was a one time thing because the Council needed to talk with us. From now on, we'll need to do it on our own. It has to be the three species—humans, Suedes, and ACs—working together without outside help."

Lewis paused. He didn't want to sound like he was making things up, or like he thought he was better than Brad. But this was something worth saying. "I... might know where one of the Partnership's spacecraft is. One of the reverse-engineered ones."

Brad straightened. "You *might*?"

"I do," Lewis said, quieter now. "It's still operational. At least, it was before the Partnership was destroyed. I've never piloted one, but I've flown in one, and I know the systems." He tapped his head, indicating his downloads. "And if it's still where they kept it, you could take it to the Sol Gate. No problem."

Brad set the cable ties down. "That's... a big deal, Lewis. Why didn't you say anything before?"

"I didn't know it mattered, and nobody asked. But if you're going to do this, you need options. This is a good one."

He took a deep breath and added more quietly, "I've all in."

Brad studied him for a moment, then gave a short nod. "Okay. We'll talk about it tonight when everyone's together. This could change a lot."

From upstairs came the sound of someone hammering something into the wall—probably Mei hanging up one of the paintings she'd carried in earlier. Kiran called from across the room, asking someone whether they could install a mirrored wall without affecting the structure. The whole building was alive with motion and voices.

Lewis felt the same pull in his chest that he'd felt when Brad suggested the security office—only stronger. He wasn't just here to guard doors anymore. He was part of the plan.

And this time, he was choosing it for himself.

* * *

The park wasn't large, but at the insistence of young people several months earlier, it had been designated as a space free from media, loud music, and surveillance drones. A small wooden sign outlined the guidelines: no recording, no posting, and no arguing. It was respected, mostly. There was a wide patch of grass surrounded by flat stones for sitting, and a few younger trees whose leaves moved slightly in the breeze.

Nearly two dozen high school students from different districts had gathered that afternoon as part of the outreach Junia had encouraged. The goal was simple: to support calm awareness and cross-species connection. At first, the public meditations were organized through the truthsplosion.net website, but they had since shifted to an independent signal thread shared among teens across the city. There were no uniforms, no banners, no formal introductions. People simply came.

On the grass, two younger boys—eighth or ninth graders—sat quietly with their eyes closed, focusing on their breathing. Next to them, a girl from North Central High School explained how to let distractions pass without reacting to them. She looked nervous and self-conscious, but she kept going.

Near the edge of the circle, three young Alpha Centaurians had arrived. One of them, a girl, wore a scarf over her elongated head to avoid drawing attention, but had pulled it off once inside the park area. The others stood with her. They didn't speak, but they joined the outer ring of seated teenagers and bowed slightly. Several human kids nodded back.

"Hey!"

The voice came from behind them. An older man with thinning hair and a paunch, stood on the sidewalk, arms crossed. Another, wearing a grey windbreaker, stood beside him. Both were glaring. The first man spoke again.

"What are you all doing? Meditating with the murderers who nearly wiped us out?"

The group didn't respond at first. One of the younger boys opened his eyes and looked at the AC nearest to him. She had stiffened, but didn't move.

The second man took a few steps closer. "You all know who they are, right? They're the reason a third of our planet's land mass became uninhabitable. You know how long it took humans to recover from what they did?"

Several of the human students stood up. They kept their voices calm.

"That was thousands of years ago," said one. "These aren't the same people."

"They knew!" the first man said. "Their people knew how risky it was and what could happen—and they didn't stop it. They didn't care about humans back then. You think they're sorry now? You think they care?"

"They've risked more than you have," said a girl. "They came above ground knowing people like you would say this. They still came."

"Because they're scoping out our territory!" The veins on the man's forehead were bulging out. They caused a disaster, hid from it underground, let humans live—and die—with the consequences, and now that the planet's recovered, they want to come back."

"No way we're going to allow that" the second man said. "You can't erase history."

"No one's trying to erase history," said said one of the boys. "We're trying to make sure what happened isn't repeated."

The group had formed a physical barrier between the hecklers and the ACs without planning it. No one had coordinated it. It had just happened. The three young Alpha Centaurians remained silent, but one of them nodded. Not as a gesture of agreement, but of acknowledgment.

The first man shook his head. "You kids think you know everything."

"We don't," said one of the girls. "But we know enough not to blame someone for what their ancestors did thousands of years before they were born."

The two men didn't say anything else. After a moment, they turned and walked away.

There was no cheering. No one shouted after them. The students returned to the circle and sat down again. One of the young ACs closed his eyes and resumed their breathing pattern, and the others followed.

The girl from North Central High School down beside one of the younger kids and touched her knees to the grass. "Let's try again," she said. "Inhale slow, and count to four."

The sound of breathing filled the space again.

Chapter Seventeen

Amanda sat at the corner table in the back of the coffee shop. Her laptop was open, a half-finished cappuccino getting cold beside it. Outside the window, people walked past in pairs or small groups, many of them younger, many of them wearing the loose, neutral-colored clothes that had become popular among those who followed the vibrational shift movement.

Amanda ignored them. She focused on her screen.

She had just sent another pitch to *Chronicle Point*, a digital news outlet based out of Boston. She had sold two stories to them in the past month—one arguing that the so-called "vibrational shift" was a psychological contagion, and another connecting certain alien disclosure advocates to fringe financial scams. Both pieces had generated decent traffic, and she had expected more assignments to follow. Instead, they had gone quiet.

She checked her inbox again. A new message had arrived.

From: Dana Espinoza <despinoza@chronicle-point.org>

To: Amanda Riley <amandarileynews@gmail.com>
Subject: Re: Story pitch: "Alien Tech, Real Estate, and Manufactured Scarcity"

Hi Amanda,

Thanks for the pitch. I read it, and I appreciate the work you've been putting into your reporting. You're a sharp writer and you've clearly been doing the research.

That said, we're going to pass on this story and future pitches along these lines.

The editorial team met last week to talk about our current focus. Since the Disclosure Conference in Geneva and the follow-up statement from the UN Working Group on Inter-Species Relations, we've seen a marked decline in interest for pieces that argue against Disclosure or that position the vibrational shift as a hoax or threat. It's not just a traffic issue—it's also a matter of editorial direction.

Our audience, and most of our partner publications, are moving toward integration-based reporting. That includes coverage of new governance protocols, legal frameworks, and cultural adaptation. The skepticism space just isn't where our readers are anymore.

I know this might be frustrating to hear, but I'd rather be direct with you now instead of letting pitches hang unanswered.

If you do decide to pivot toward stories that cover the Disclosure transition from a policy, legal, or civil liberties angle, feel free to reach out. But for now, we're not publishing anti-Disclosure content.

Best of luck,
Dana

Amanda read the email twice.

She opened a reply window, stared at the blinking cursor, then closed it again.

She clicked over to another tab where she had a half-finished draft titled *"The Shift Is Not Scientific"*. It detailed inconsistencies in statements made by former officials, and criticized the vibrational curriculum now being taught in some charter schools. She had footnotes. She had sources. She had even secured a short interview with a neurologist who had privately expressed concerns about the social effects of "vibrational alignment ideology."

It didn't matter.

She checked her other email folders. Her pitch to *WorldData Review* from four days ago was still unopened. *MediaFront* had responded yesterday, but it was an auto-reply.

She opened a folder on her desktop labeled *Pending Pieces* and looked at the list. Six drafts. Three of them finished. Two of them were expansions of previously published stories she had been proud of. None of them had found a home.

Amanda sat still for a long moment. In the background, a group of young people walked into the coffee shop, laughing. One of them wore a shirt with the symbol of the Suede Nation. Another had a temporary tattoo in the shape of a resonance grid.

She took a sip of her lukewarm cappuccino, and looked out the window. What should she do now?

Around her, the coffee shop had gotten louder. The baristas were exchanging orders with customers at the register. A couple near the window was talking about their plans for a group meditation event at the park. Someone behind her was watching a news clip on a tablet at low volume. Amanda didn't listen closely, but she caught a few words: "joint operations," "AC youth council," and "Department of State coordination."

She checked her email again, even though she didn't expect anything new.

There was a new message in her inbox. It had arrived two minutes ago.

From: [REDACTED]@protonmail.com
To: Amanda Riley <amandarileynews@gmail.com>
Subject: Rumor You'll Want to Check Out

Amanda—

Something interesting might be happening.

I've heard from two separate internal sources that Vicki Heywood may be stepping down from her role of Deputy Assistant Secretary at OMR. Nothing official yet. No press release. But the way it's moving—staff reshuffling, meeting cancellations, briefing reassignments—it fits.

The timing is weird. The Office of Multispecies Relations has more funding and visibility than ever, so why would she walk away now? Either it's something personal or someone's trying to bury something before it comes out.

Figured you'd want to know. I always respected what your uncle tried to do, and I know you've been willing to ask the questions others avoid. Maybe this is one of those moments.

If you decide to look into it, I'll keep my ears open.

—M

Amanda's eyes stayed on the screen. She read it again, then a third time. The use of her uncle's name had caught her attention, though it hadn't been written directly. Everyone in her family still called it a "disgrace," but Amanda had never fully accepted that. Her uncle had raised questions about extraterrestrial operations that weren't part of the official disclosure narrative. He had refused to back down, even under pressure. He'd lost his position, he'd been court-martialed, but he hadn't recanted. Neither had she.

She tapped her finger on the trackpad and sat back in the chair.

Vicki Heywood leaving OMR would be a major change. She was one of the few government officials with cross-agency authority since the public acknowledgment of aliens. Trusted by Congress, respected by Galactic Council representatives at the UN, and seen as a reliable source even by the most skeptical national security journalists, she could call almost anyone—anywhere—and they would answer.

Amanda opened a new browser tab and ran a few quick searches. Nothing. No news hits in the last 48 hours with Heywood's name. No updates on the OMR site. No mentions in the official press room channels.

That didn't mean it wasn't true.

She thought about the last few months. Rejected pitches. Cold leads. Editors who used to take her calls now having their interns reply. Even some of her older contacts—once eager to leak emails, fragments of transcripts, and redacted memos—had stopped returning messages.

If Vicki Heywood really was stepping down, and there was a reason no one was talking about it yet, Amanda could be the first to put it together. If there was a scandal—or even just a power vacuum—it would be a way back into the conversation. A way to prove she wasn't finished.

She opened a new draft in her notes app and typed:

Working: Rumor—Heywood out at OMR?

Below that, she started a checklist:

- Confirm Vicki Heywood schedule changes

- Request comment from OMR comms office

- Cross-reference Senate oversight briefings

- Review relevant OMR activity logs, press transcripts

- Contact [REDACTED] again for clarification

- Compare with DOD reshuffle patterns from last 30 days

Amanda stared at the list for a moment, then saved it and closed the tab. She reopened her inbox and moved Dana's rejection email into a new folder labeled *Archive - Not Aligned*. Then she opened a new message window.

To: [REDACTED]
Subject: Re: Rumor You'll Want to Check Out

Thanks. I'll look into it. Let me know if you hear more.
—Amanda

She hit send, sat back, and reached for her cappuccino. It was cold, but she drank it anyway.

She didn't know if the story would go anywhere. It might be nothing. It might be too late.

But it might also be the start of something new.

* * *

Brad sat on one of the long benches in the flower shop's common area. The room was more crowded than usual. Everyone was there: Mona and Calvin, Mei, Jessica, Kiran, James, and Lewis. Extra chairs had been pulled in from Brad's office and Jessica's studio, and a couple of floor cushions were set near the bookshelf. Brad shared his bench with James and Lewis. Jessica and Kiran sat together on the love seat, Kiran's arm around his sister's shoulder.

Cheesy, thought Brad. But he didn't say anything aloud.

The conversation had shifted to the renovations at the bank building. The updates had gone fast once the permits cleared. Fresh paint, the addition of two classrooms on the main floor, and a working HVAC system. The electricians had been there all week.

Brad didn't tell anyone he was the reason the permits cleared so quickly. What was the point of being a genius hacker if he didn't use it now and then to make life easier? He hadn't done anything illegal—just pushed their applications higher on the list.

"We'll be able to restart the tai chi classes by Monday," Calvin said, "and we'll have room to handle more students. Mona and I can lead classes in the new classrooms. Filming can take place in the atrium."

Brad nodded. He had already run the network cable through the main rooms and tested the signal strength upstairs. The router mesh was stable, and Lewis had spent the last two days organizing the security feeds. They were ready.

Jessica looked across the room. "How are you guys settling in upstairs?"

"Fine," Calvin said. "We've got the kitchen stocked. Still figuring out where to put a couple pieces of furniture, but nothing major."

"It feels like home," Mei said.

Mona smiled, then glanced toward her son. "I'm sure James was thrilled to find out that we no longer opposed him rooming with Brad here at the flower shop."

Brad turned his head slightly. James didn't react. His expression stayed neutral, but Brad could see the way his hand was tapping against his leg. It was the same rhythm he used when he was trying not to grin.

Brad leaned over and bumped his elbow into James's side. James gave him a quick side look and shrugged, but he didn't stop tapping.

"There are three bedrooms upstairs," Mona went on, "but one of them is going to Vicki."

Everyone turned toward her.

"She's made her decision—she's leaving the Department of State," Mona said. "And she's going to move into the bank building with us."

Jessica blinked. "She's really stepping down?"

Mona nodded. "She told us this morning. Vicki said it's time for her to shift her focus."

"She'll be with us full-time?" Kiran asked.

"That's what she said," Mona confirmed. "She wants to be here with all of us."

Brad leaned back against the bench. He hadn't heard the news before now, but it made sense. Vicki had looked different during her recent visit. Not tired, but ready for something else. The kind of ready that meant she had already made up her mind.

Jessica leaned forward. "So does this mean Jerry will be taking over management of OMR?"

"Actually, not. Jerry was offered the job, but he declined," Mona said. "The new head of OMR is someone from State's UN office."

Brad looked around the room. It felt different with everyone here. Tighter, but not uncomfortable. This space had been the center of their work for months. Now, with the bank building open and Vicki joining them, everything was starting to move forward again.

He flipped to a new page in the notebook on his lap. Everyone had been going back and forth about the studio reopening, about training groups and furniture deliveries. Now seemed like the right time to shift the focus.

"There's something we need to talk about," Brad said, looking around the room. "Lewis asked me a question earlier while we were working on the bank building network. He wanted to know how we were planning to get to Sol Gate once we figure out the jade amulet."

The room quieted. No one interrupted.

Brad continued. "The only time we went through it, the Kewpies took us. But Melly made it clear that was a one-time assist. From here on out, it's supposed to be us—humans, Suedes, and ACs—doing it together. No shortcuts."

Jessica nodded slowly. "We've talked about that. We know we need to coordinate. But we've also never figured out transportation."

"Well," Brad said, glancing toward Lewis, "Lewis told me something."

Everyone turned in his direction.

"He knows where one of the Partnership's reverse-engineered spacecraft is."

Silence followed.

Lewis shifted on the bench. "I think it's still there. I can't say for sure it hasn't been moved, but not very many of us knew where it was stored."

"Wait," Kiran said, leaning forward. "You're talking about a functioning ship? Not parts? Not diagrams?"

"A whole one," Lewis said. "It's not large. It was used for personnel transfer. Not cargo. It's fast. And the last time I saw it—about eight months ago—it was operational."

Jessica looked at Brad. "Is this real?"

Brad nodded. "I asked him about it. He knows the systems. He hasn't piloted one, but he's flown in one and understands how it works. He's got the knowledge—he'll be able to fly it."

Kiran exhaled through his nose. "That changes things."

"It really does," James said. "We've been acting like transport would be the main obstacle."

"We'll need to test it," Jessica said. "And check for tracking devices. The last thing we want is for surviving Partnership supporters knowing what we're doing."

"We'll do all of that," Brad confirmed. "But it's a place to start. A real option."

"Where is it?" Kiran asked.

"In a remote storage facility on the other side of Joshua Tree," Lewis replied. "In a simple underground bay—not a base. For security reasons, its location was never listed in the Partnership's network files. But I know where it is—and I know the access codes for the facility."

"This changes our timeline," Jessica said. "If we have transport, then once we decode the amulet and synchronize the three species, we're no longer waiting for outside help."

"We'll be able to reach Sol Gate on our own," Brad said.

Jessica. "We'll still need a pilot."

"We have Lewis," Brad said.

"*Not* through the portal, we don't," she reminded him. Biologic constructs couldn't raise their vibration high enough to pass through any portal.

Brad reddened. He had forgotten.

"I can teach you," volunteered Lewis, unperturbed.

James raised a hand eagerly. "I'm in. Whatever it takes."

Jessica glanced at Lewis. "You're sure no one else knows about the ship?"

Lewis shrugged. "I don't know if anyone knows about it or not. But most of the ones who *did* know about it are dead."

Everyone was quiet for a moment.

Jessica spoke up. "Like I said, this changes our timeline—and our focus. Now that we know we have transport, we need to shift our attention to the jade amulet, and figure out how we activate it."

"But we need to check out the craft first," Brad said. "We need to verify it's there and it's operational. If we move carefully, we might be able to get to the ship by next week—and put it somewhere where no one else will find it."

"We need to verify everything first," James reminded them.

"Yes," agreed Brad. "Let's get eyes on it before we make promises to anyone."

Chapter Eighteen

Vicki sat cross-legged on the concrete floor of the underground corridor, just past the stairs that lead up to the old bank vault. The air was stale, but cool against her skin. The overhead bulb flickered occasionally. No one else was around.

She closed her eyes and let her breathing settle. At first, the sounds of the building above pulled at her focus—footsteps, a door opening, the scrape of a chair—but they faded as she slowed her breath and let the tension drain from her limbs.

Jessica's question came back to her. It had been clear she had been bursting with... something, but Jess had waited until they were alone to ask.

Earlier that day, they had been sitting together in Jess's studio at the flower shop when she asked if the Suedes could create an underground entrance to the vault's tunnel.

"I know it might not be possible," she said, holding back her excitement, "but haven't they done this from caves before? Wouldn't it be easier—and safer—for the Suedes and ACs to travel straight from home to us? If Junia or her people could open a passage, we could skip all the traffic and carpool headaches. It would also lower the risk of exposure, since the bank building is private and we control who comes in."

"Besides," she continued, "we need to expand the size of our group. We need to get serious about Disclosure."

At the time, Vicki had just stared at her, blinking. It had never occurred to her. The obviousness of it now was slightly embarrassing.

She exhaled slowly and opened her eyes. Across from her, the tunnel wall was cracked near the base. Pieces of the concrete facing had broken away, revealing the packed earth behind. Someone had tried to reinforce the surrounding area years ago, probably with a quick cement patch, but moisture had made its way in anyway. But that exposed section—with it's direct connection to the planet—suggested that the Suedes might be able make one of their passageways.

The idea had merit. The tunnel wasn't as fragile as it appeared. While it wouldn't last forever, it held for now. If the Suedes or the ACs could shape an entrance to the tunnel—maybe even strengthen it while they worked—it would change everything. Fewer risks. Faster exits. More flexibility. The human youth wouldn't have to schedule around rush hours or limit attendance by how many vehicles they could find.

Vicki closed her eyes, sank into meditation, and reached into the Earth.

* * *

Junia was waiting when Vicki arrived. She could always sense when her human friend—her first ever—was moving through the planet in a higher vibrational state, and had gone to meet her in the grotto. It was the same place where they had first met.

When Junia thought about the past few months, she still felt surprised at how much had changed—and that she was the Suede who had helped make it happen. The elders hadn't wanted her to, but she had met with young humans and young ACs. Now they were all part of one group—the Bridgewalkers—working together.

As Junia watched Vicki's higher vibrational form appear in the space, she narrowed her topaz-colored eyes. "Why do you feel different?" she asked.

"Different? In what way?" asked Vicki, smiling at her.

Junia shook her head, sending her coppery-dark hair flying around her face. She was still puzzled. "You don't feel so heavy—you feel kind of floaty."

Vicki laughed. "I left my job at the State Department—I'm living right next to the Four now. And the tai chi studio's in the same place. Everything's coming together—a one-stop shop."

Now *that* sounded interesting. "I wish I could see that," she said wistfully. picturing the people moving around inside the flower shop, talking and laughing, maybe working on something she hadn't heard about yet. It was like all the fun stuff was happening without her.

"Maybe you can," said Vicki, and explained about the bank building and its underground tunnel that led to nowhere. "Can the Suedes create an entrance to it?"

In the middle of that big human city—Los Angeles? Junia knew that she couldn't do it, but maybe the adults could? She mentally signaled to Alun to let him know she was bringing someone, then grabbed Vicki's hand and pulled her through the ground until they arrived at his dwelling.

As she watched Vicki look around, Junia realized this was the first time the human had been to her uncle's home—probably the first time she had been inside any Suede's house. This was where Junia had grown up, raised by Alun after her parents were killed. She and her cousin Bowen had spent their childhood here.

Bowen! The humans had killed him.

She couldn't start thinking about that. She shook her head to make the thoughts go away.

Alun stood up from his desk. "Vicki—I didn't know you were visiting."

Vicki tried to respond, but her eyes kept looking around the room. Junia tried to see what she was looking at: stone walls with etched patterns, some holding small crystals for light. Water jars in one corner. Shelves built into the walls. Lichen mats covering the stone floor. Rounded corners instead of sharp ones. Nothing that seemed interesting. Junia turned to her uncle.

"Vicki is living with the Guides now, and she wants us to make an entryway to there." Junia didn't like to waste time if it involved something that might be fun.

Alun looked up from a low table where he was sorting pieces of carved stone. "The Guides live in the city you call Los Angeles, right?"

At Vicki's nod, he continued, "We can't do it. We can't make entryways connecting the Suede Nation to human population centers. It's complicated and dangerous. There are have water pipes, sewage lines, power cables, and metrorail tunnels. We would need to zigzag around them all. And with so many humans nearby, it's only a matter of time before someone notices."

Junia sighed. Uncle Alun was acting like the elders, being afraid of anything different.

"But the humans are going to notice us pretty soon anyway," she said. "When the vibrational shift happens, all of them will be able to see us, not just some."

Vicki nodded in agreement. "I understand the risks. But right now, the Bridgewalkers have nowhere that's easy for everyone to get to. Meeting in caves outside the city is difficult, and only a few can go at a time. Too many, and it would attract attention. Meeting in a private building in the middle of Los Angeles would solve that."

Alun shook his head. "Complications are better than mistakes."

"This isn't just about convenience," Vicki said. "The Four live in the flower shop and we just bought the building next door — together they're a hub for Disclosure. If young Suedes and ACs could come there instead of a cave, we could bring in more humans. Right now we have to limit participants. We need more Bridgewalkers. This is about the vibrational shift: the sooner our three peoples work together, the sooner the planet's vibration will rise."

Junia shifted her weight, watching Alun. "It wouldn't have to be a fancy passageway" she said. "Just enough for Suedes and ACs to use. We don't need to add the frequencies for humans."

Alun set down the piece of stone in his hand and looked at Vicki directly. His eyes stayed on her for a long moment before he spoke.

"You're right," he said finally. "As the Earth crystal's caretaker, I know better than anyone that we need to do everything possible to make sure the vibrational shift happens smoothly. I lose sight of that sometimes. The elders come to me every day with their fears—fears of change, fears of humans, fears of losing control. There's constant pressure to slow things down."

Junia watched him. She knew it wasn't only the elders that made him stop and think so much. Losing Bowen had changed him. He hadn't been the same since that day. He didn't talk about it much, but Junia could tell he was always thinking about her cousin. Sometimes it felt like he was trying to protect the whole Suede Nation so nothing bad could ever happen again.

Alun rubbed the back of his neck, then looked between Junia and Vicki. "But you're right," he repeated. "The Bridgewalkers need a place they can reach without danger or delay. If that place is already a center for Disclosure, then that's where it should be."

Junia's eyes widened. "So you'll do it?"

"I'll get a team together," Alun said. "Not just anyone—we'll need Suedes with skill in mapping human infrastructure, ones who can build without disturbing what's already there. And we'll make sure the entrance is hidden from anyone who is in a lower vibrational state. No one will be able to go through it accidentally."

Vicki's shoulders eased, and she smiled. "Thank you, Alun. This will make a real difference."

Junia could feel Vicki's excitement, and for the first time since the conversation began, she felt it herself. The Bridgewalkers would have a place in the city—right in the middle of human life.

And for the first time, she was going to see it for herself.

* * *

Brad sat at his desk in the back office of the flower shop, three monitors lit in front of him. Each screen showed a different set of maps—topographical, satellite, and road access overlays. Kiran leaned against the corner of the desk, arms folded, scanning the images. Lewis stood behind them, pointing at the satellite view on the center screen.

"There are three main approaches to the Joshua Tree facility where the spacecraft is warehoused," Lewis said. He tapped one of the routes with his finger. "Here, from the north—this is a dirt access road that branches off the highway. Surveillance cameras along here." He slid his finger to the east. "Second option: approach through the service track from the ranger station. That's monitored too—there are motion sensors, at least there were last time I was there." He moved his hand to the lower part of the map. "Third approach: across open desert from the south. No official road, but it's passable. Aerial drones patrol in a grid pattern there."

Kiran frowned. "Still? Even though the Partnership's gone?"

Lewis nodded. "Probably. Because this place wasn't just a Partnership property. It was a joint site—Partnership and military. Those systems are still running."

Brad shifted in his chair. "So we don't have a way in without being seen."

Lewis shrugged. "Not without some kind of diversion. But this facility won't have physical guards—it's just an unmanned bay. They rely on their electronics."

Kiran leaned in toward the monitor. "And once we get there? We take it, and then what? We can't exactly fly it around the city."

"There's a bigger problem," Brad said. "We need somewhere to park it—big enough to hide it, secure so no one finds it, and still easy for us to access when we need it. The parking lot behind the shop won't work."

Lewis glanced between them. "Do you have a place like that?"

"Not yet," Brad said. "Right now we're only figuring out how to get to the facility and grab the craft. But it's pointless to go in without knowing where we'll end up."

Kiran pushed off from the desk and straightened. "So what do we do?"

Brad turned his chair toward him. "To get us in, you're going to have to use the junk DNA Melly activated in you—your clairvoyance, pathfinding ability, whatever you want to call it. Look at our options, all the possible paths forward. Figure which route gives us the best chance of getting in and out without being caught. And maybe even where we can take it afterward."

Kiran didn't answer right away. He looked at the map, then back at Brad. "I'll need some time."

Brad nodded and started closing the unnecessary tabs on his screens, leaving the maps up. "You have it. Getting our hands on a spacecraft means nothing if we can't figure out how to use the jade amulet."

Lewis stepped back toward the door. "I'll keep on looking for blind spots in their coverage and possible approaches."

Kiran moved to stand directly in front of the largest monitor, his eyes fixed on the image of the desert and the facility marked at its center.

Somewhere—beyond that image—the spacecraft waited.

Chapter Nineteen

Jerry spotted Sam at a corner table in the back of the Rosslyn pub. The place was busy but not loud, and the booths were high enough to block most lines of sight. Glasses clinked at the bar, and the low murmur of conversations blended with the hum of an overhead fan. Sam already had a pint in front of him and was watching the door.

"Glad you picked here," Sam said when Jerry slid into the seat. "Crystal City would have been easier, but half my building drinks there after work. I didn't want to run into anyone I knew."

Well, that was interesting. Jerry flagged the server, ordered a beer, and leaned back. "When you asked to meet, you did tell me it was sensitive."

Sam nodded once. "It is. That's why I didn't want to put it in an email or risk having an audience. Leadership is getting used to the new reality of Disclosure—State's Office of Multispecies Relations leading the process, with the military in a supporting role. There's grumbling, but they'll adapt. This is different."

Jerry waited.

Sam kept his voice low, barely audible over the background noise. "There's something the top brass agree on—every one of them. They want to bury the Tall Whites trade agreement. You know the one from back in the '50s. Advanced alien technology in exchange for unrestricted access to human DNA samples.

Jerry's expression didn't change, but he felt a knot in his gut. That agreement had launched the Partnership: companies reverse-engineered alien tech for the government, then kept the best parts for themselves. And, in return, ordinary people were taken by aliens against their will and subjected to terrifying medical procedures. The military then ridiculed and humiliated them to make the victims look crazy and hide the truth.

The two men went silent as the server arrived with Jerry's drink, setting it down before moving to the next table. Jerry took a sip of his beer, then put the glass down. "Bury it? How?"

"Never let it into the public record," Sam said. "Not in any Disclosure report, not in hearings, not in the press. Pretend it never happened. They'll file it under a black program and call it done."

"Isn't that what's already happened?"

"It is," agreed Sam. A burst of applause rose from the bar as a highlight replayed on the television. "But now everyone is seeing all the information come out—the information about human-alien interactions throughout history. People at the Pentagon are noticing. And, sooner or later, this story will come out."

"It will," agreed Jerry. "But why are you telling me? What are you hoping I'll do with this information?"

"I'm telling you because you're the Deputy in OMR. At some point, this story—or a version of it— is going to come out, and the Department of State will be asked to verify the truth of the Tall Whites agreement. The military's position will be to deny it outright. If you push it, they'll stonewall or claim national security."

Jerry considered the implications as he watched a server bring a tray of beers to a nearby table. "So... damage control and business as usual. What about you? What do you think?"

"I think it's wrong," Sam said. "But I'm not in your chain of command. And I'm not high enough in my chain to change the directive—it comes from the highest levels in the Pentagon. I can only warn you what's being planned."

Jerry's voice was even. "So, the choice is either go along with a cover-up, or put OMR into a direct fight with the Pentagon."

"That's what it looks like," Sam said. "And the people above me are already digging the hole for this thing."

Jerry glanced around the pub. No one nearby was paying attention; the couple in the next booth was focused on their food, a trio of young men were watching the sports news. "What happens if it gets out anyway?"

"Depends on how," shrugged Sam. "If it leaks through OMR channels, you'll be accused of compromising national security. If it comes from someone else—well, I don't know."

Jerry sat forward, elbows on the table. "But you think the story will come out eventually?"

"I can't imagine it won't," said Sam. "It looks like everyone's secrets are coming out."

"What do you think is going to happen to the military when this gets out?" Jerry asked. Sam had been dodging the core question. "How do you think the public will react when they find out their government basically traded them to aliens?"

Sam grimaced. "It won't go well. Best case scenario? The entire top level of the Office of the Secretary of Defense will be forced to resign—if they're not court-martialed first. That's if we're lucky. I wouldn't be surprised if there's public violence—lots of it."

"But you're warning the State Department first."

Sam gave a crooked smile.

"I figured you'd want to warn Vicki and the kids, assuming they don't already know. But mainly, the military isn't going to change its position on this. I think someone should have the chance to walk away with at least some of their honor intact."

"But maybe..." Jerry said, slowly, "maybe it would go better if we got out in front of this."

Sam raised an eyebrow. "Leak it ourselves?"

"Not quite, but I know someone who is sniffing around for a big, juicy story."

* * *

The atrium was empty except for Mei; it was early morning, and classes weren't held on Sundays anyway. The air was faintly cool from the overnight temperature drop. Mei moved slowly through the tai chi postures, her attention on balance and breath, the smooth surface of the floor firm beneath her bare feet.

"Hi!"

Mei turned sharply, her heart in her throat. Junia stood only a few steps away, her topaz-colored cats' eyes fixed on Mei.

"Junia—" Mei stopped, trying to slow the pounding in her chest. This was... unexpected. "What are you doing here?"

Junia's gaze wandered past Mei to the vaulted ceiling, the rows of tall windows, and the reception area near the entrance. "This is my first time in a human building."

She turned in place, taking in the details of the space—slowly at first, then faster until the coppery ropes of her hair flew outward.

"Vicki told us the Suedes would make an entrance under the vault. No one said it was finished. I hadn't known they'd even started."

Did Calvin and Mona know this was going to happen?

Junia finished twirling and faced Mei. "It's finished," she announced.

The sound of a door opening carried from across the atrium. Lewis stepped out of the security office, his body in a ready position, his expression alert as his eyes swept the atrium. They stopped on Junia, then flicked to the open vault door.

Mei hadn't realized he was in there. Did he spend the night in his office?

"Who came in?" Lewis asked. His voice was flat, but Mei could sense the challenge. "I'm security. It's my job to know who's here."

Mei stepped toward him. "It's all right, Lewis. This is Junia," she said, gesturing to her. "She's the one who's working with the

Four, and she came through the new entrance the Suedes made under the vault."

Lewis studied Junia for a long moment, assessing her.

From the door to the vault, two young Suede males emerged, their coppery hair neatly bound back, their posture straight as they looked around curiously. Three young Suede females followed. A moment later, several AC youths stepped through the same point, shyer, crowding behind the Suedes. Lewis stared at them all.

Mei reached for her phone. "I need to call the Four," she said. "They're part of the Bridgewalkers. If there's going to be a meeting, humans need to be here too—this only works if all of us are in it together."

She stepped aside, pressed the call button, and waited for James to answer.

"The Bridgewalkers are in the bank building," she blurted out as soon as the call connected. "They came through the passageway under the vault which, it seems, has just been completed? Lewis is pissed that people are here without any notice; apparently it violates his security protocol. Anyhow, I explained who they are. It's Junia and her Suedes and ACs—more than before. We're going to need the high schoolers here too."

"Got it," James replied, hurriedly. "We'll be right over."

Mei ended the call and slipped the phone back into her pocket.

With the Bridgewalkers gathered together, they might finally reach the stars.

* * *

OMR OBSERVATION MEMO
Classified Briefing – Internal Use Only

Subject: Escalating Global Deviations – Environmental, Sociocultural & Cognitive Frequency Shifts

- **[Continental Housing Monitor]**

"Relocation Patterns Defy Conventional Risk Models"
Latest quarterly real estate market reports show a 19% rise in residential sales, with notable spikes in cross-regional migration. Analysts are puzzled by an even split between households relocating to high-crime metropolitan centers and those moving to historically low-crime rural areas. Economic indicators do not align with the movement—average income, employment opportunities, and cost of living appear secondary to an unspecified draw.

- [National Legislative Tracker]
"Species Harassment Bills Divide State Assemblies"
At least fourteen state legislatures have introduced bills criminalizing harassment of nonhuman species, aligning penalties with those for hate crimes. Conversely, six states are advancing "Species Autonomy Clarification" measures, which codify the right to "freely express human dominance" over nonhuman entities. Early polling shows deep regional divides, with 47% of respondents stating they would "never" live in a state where their view was in the minority.

- [Capital Ledger]
"Major Donors Suspend Political Contributions"
Political strategists across multiple parties report sudden withdrawal of financial support from long-standing donor networks. Several congressional campaigns are reportedly on hold due to insufficient funds. Anonymous sources suggest donors are redirecting resources toward "independent contingency projects" with no disclosed oversight.

- [Global Market Wire]
"Commodity Whiplash Shakes Global Markets"

Commodity exchanges experienced a sharp plunge in energy and grain futures, followed by an equally abrupt recovery within a 48-hour window. Financial analysts warn of an emerging "hyper-cyclic" trading environment tied to untraceable off-market transactions. Stock indices mirrored the turbulence, triggering multiple automatic trading halts in both domestic and foreign markets.

- **[Innovation & Commerce Bulletin]**
  "Vibrational Research Funding Surges Amid Commercialization Push"
  Private and public investment in projects studying vibrational phenomena has risen 42% in the last two fiscal quarters. Venture capital firms are partnering with academic physics departments, biotech startups, and "human potential" enterprises to explore applications ranging from energy generation to materials stabilization . Regulatory bodies have yet to issue guidelines, creating a "first-mover advantage" climate where investors accept elevated legal risks in exchange for market dominance.

- **[Civic Infrastructure Journal]**
  "Ghost Transit Routes in Metro Systems"
  Urban transport operators in three major cities confirm activation of rail lines absent from official maps. Surveillance shows passengers boarding and exiting trains on these routes, yet no ticket sales, maintenance logs, or staff assignments exist for the lines. Authorities claim these routes do not exist.

[OMR Action Items – Restricted Circulation]

- Track migratory flows into high-crime and low-crime regions to determine potential convergence triggers.

- Continue legislative monitoring of species harassment laws; assess likelihood of federal intervention.

- Investigate donor network redirections for links to off-market commodity fluctuations.

- Deploy reconnaissance teams to inland maritime sites; analyze structural purpose.

- Confirm origin and destination points of undocumented metro lines; assess potential nonhuman or interdimensional transit links.

END OF BRIEF

Chapter Twenty

K iran stood near the back of the atrium, his arms folded, taking in the group spread across the open space. The building was quiet, its Sunday morning emptiness making their voices carry a little farther than usual. The polished stone floor reflected the sound of shuffling feet and occasional murmurs.

The Four—Jessica, Brad, James, and Kiran—were there, along with Mei, the human high schoolers, Junia and her young Suedes, and the young Alpha Centaurians. Vicki stood off to the side, speaking quietly to Lewis. As their security specialist, the biologic construct was unhappy that so many people had entered the bank building without his permission—or even his knowledge.

No one had noticed the construction—or even heard it—finished just a few days after Vicki and Alun's discussion. Kiran thought this was because the Suedes had used resonant touch-singing—shaping spaces along energy flows and natural elements. Only higher-frequency beings like the Suedes and ACs could do it, and only they could use the passage it created. Lower-frequency beings, like humans, couldn't use it or even detect it. He hoped this would calm Lewis's concerns.

But now all the young people—the Bridgewalkers—were seated on the floor around Mei, who stood in the center, her hand closed over something she had been holding since they all arrived. She opened her fingers to reveal the jade amulet in her palm.

"My grandmother gave me this," she said. "She told me it had been in our family for generations, handed down secretly. It's not jewelry—she told me it was a tool. She didn't know what it was for."

Jessica stepped forward. "Melly told us it's more than just a traditional heirloom," she said. "It's an artifact—a type of cheat code or a key—that can unlock interstellar travel through the Sol Gate."

A ripple of interest ran through the group. Kiran could see one of the ACs elbowing another in the side.

"May I look at it?" Astran asked.

Mei nodded and held it out.

The young AC bent slightly, examining the surface. "The trigrams are placed in a circle around this crystal in the center," she said. "My mother is an design architect in our city. She has a tool that uses a similar configuration. If the correct energies are applied, a three-dimensional structure—hidden until then—will pop up. It's like a type of hologram."

Brad tilted his head. "What kind of structure?"

Astran straightened, handing the amulet back to Mei. "I don't know. My mother's designs are used for spatial configurations—sometimes buildings, sometimes energy frameworks. The structure that would appear here might not be physical in the usual sense."

Jessica asked, "And the energies—do you know which ones?"

Astran shook her head. "That's the problem. My mother's tool uses harmonic frequencies that are specifically tuned to the purpose of urban design. If this one is meant to facilitate travel though Sol Gate, it will probably require something different.

Vicki, who had been listening, stepped closer to the circle. "Then we need to find out exactly which which resonances to use. And we'll have to figure out a way to test it safely."

"The answer is tai chi," James said.

The others paused and looked at him.

"Think about it. We—I'm talking about the humans now—first reached higher levels of vibration by practicing tai chi. We made contact with Melly the same way. Tai chi has the eight gates. Mei's amulet has the eight trigrams. We're looking for a way to activate a way through Sol Gate—one of the Eight Gates of interstellar travel—something the ACs already know about."

"That... actually makes sense," Jessica said slowly.

Brad slapped James on the back. "You've got it!"

Kiran didn't want to put a damper on all the excitement, but there was a lot they *didn't* know. He shifted his weight and looked around the circle.

"If we're going to connect tai chi's eight gates, the trigrams, and Sol Gate, we need to be exact. We need to know *how*. The positions, the movements, the timing—none of it can just be a guesstimate."

Junia spoke from where she sat with the young Suedes. "In our home, the place of things is important—it changes the way the energy flows. So the pathways, the buildings, the gardens—they're all connected, and together they make a single pattern. But we're never used trigrams or tai chi."

Astran glanced at her. "The eight trigrams of the bagua each represent a force—heaven, earth, thunder, water, mountain, wind, fire, and lake. In my mother's work, each trigram can also be assigned a direction. Tai chi's eight gates also have directions."

Mei looked at the amulet again. "So, if we used the eight gates as movements and paired them with the trigrams' meanings, we might produce the right resonance for the amulet?"

Kai, one of the young humans, leaned forward. "But the trigrams aren't just directions, right? Each one has a specific pattern."

James nodded. "Yes. And I'm betting those patterns can be expressed through movement, sound, or form. If we align all three, we could generate the kind of multi-layered resonance Astran's mother uses in her work."

Caffo, one of the Suedes, spoke next. "Our touch-singing can hold a harmonic frequency while we move—that's how we created the passageway here. If the humans perform the eight gates at the same time, the frequencies might overlap in a way that fits the amulet's design."

Brad frowned. "And the ACs?"

Nevik answered. "We can match the harmonic intervals and reinforce the structure of the pattern. Our resonance carries more stability in higher ranges. That could help keep the configuration active long enough to trigger the effect."

Jessica tapped her finger against her knee. "That means humans provide movement, Suedes provide harmonic shaping, and ACs provide stabilization. Three groups working together to produce a pattern."

Vicki turned to Mei. "Is there any marking or sequence on the amulet that shows where to start?"

Mei shook her head. "Not that I can see. The trigrams are evenly spaced around the crystal. We'd have to figure out the starting point by experimenting."

Kiran glanced at James. "We also don't know if this requires all eight gates in sequence or just one specific one. And if it does need all eight, we need to know the order."

"That's true," James admitted. "But the way we learned the energies or forces—the eight gates—in tai chi class is a sequence. *Peng, lu, ji, an, kao, cai, lie*, and *zhou*. We can start with that."

Astran added, "If the amulet responds at any point, we'll know we're on the right track."

"We'll have to set up controlled tests," said Jessica. "One group at a time, then combined. We need to document the results so we don't lose track of what worked and what didn't."

Kiran watched as the group nodded in agreement. They were eager, but he knew this was going to take time.

Time that they might not have.

* * *

Amanda Riley was already in the Arlington coffee shop when Jerry and Sam arrived. She sat in a corner booth with her back to the wall, sipping a cappuccino. The empty plate covered in pastry crumbs suggested she'd been there for a while. Jerry wondered why she had come so early—did she suspect some sort of trap? Was she that distrustful? He didn't know. He and Sam slid into the booth across from her.

Jerry leaned forward, resting his forearms on the table. The hiss of the espresso machine intruded, followed by the sound of steaming milk. A spoon clinked against a ceramic cup at the counter.

"Thanks for agreeing to meet us," Jerry said. "I understand you're looking for a story."

Amanda tossed back her long hair and set her cappuccino cup down on its saucer. "Always. And right now, the one I'm hearing about is Vicki leaving OMR. Why? Was there some kind of scandal? Was she fired, or will something embarrassing going to be made public?"

Jerry shook his head. "There's a bigger story than Vicki. Much bigger. If you're brave enough to break it. But maybe you're not the right person for it."

Amanda's expression tightened. "Why not?"

"Because your past stories have shown you have an agenda," Jerry said. "You've argued against Disclosure, and you've done it on orders from certain people in the military."

Amanda leaned back in the booth, crossing her arms. "I'm on the side of the truth," she said. "That's what sells. If you've got something big, I'll print it."

A server passed by, setting down a muffin and a drink at the next table. The smell of fresh coffee drifted across the booth. Sam shifted in his seat.

"This is the kind of story your uncle, Colonel Riley, would fight against," Sam said. "He's been court-martialed, but if he weren't, he'd be the first to try to bury it. Are you up for that?"

Jerry was glad Sam had agreed to wear his uniform. It served as a subtle reminder to Amanda that the military was more than just her uncle.

Amanda's voice was level. "Doing my uncle's bidding never got me anywhere. If the story's solid, I'll run it."

Sam gave a short nod. "Good. Because even though it might look like what we're about to give you is anti-military, it's not. A lot of people in the military want this information made public."

The espresso machine hissed again. Jerry caught the faint sound of someone laughing near the front door.

"The people who don't want it out," Sam said, "are the ones who are guilty. The ones who benefitted from keeping it quiet."

Amanda picked up her cup, and took a sip before setting it back down. "Then let's hear it."

Jerry glanced at Sam. They had her attention.

Sam reached into his messenger bag and pulled out a thick manila envelope. The papers inside shifted as he placed it on the table between them.

He slid it toward Amanda. "This is what you need to see. Read it later, somewhere private. But I'll tell you what's in it."

Amanda's fingers rested on the envelope, but she didn't open it.

"It's proof," Sam said, "of a government agreement with a group known as the Tall Whites. In exchange for advanced alien technology, they were given unrestricted access to human DNA."

Amanda's brow furrowed slightly, but she stayed quiet.

"The Tall Whites kidnapped people with the government's permission," Sam continued. "They subjected them to medical procedures. Afterward, the military discredited them—called them unstable, called them liars. In many cases, they made sure to destroy their reputations so no one would believe them."

The espresso machine hissed again, punctuating his words. Jerry watched Amanda's posture shift slightly forward.

"This wasn't the entire military," Sam said. "And it wasn't the whole government. In the first years, the agreement was shared among high-level officials across the government. But then it changed. Knowledge of the deal was restricted to a small faction inside the military. Other senior government leaders—even those at the highest levels—were no longer briefed on it."

Amanda's eyes stayed on the envelope. "You're saying the rest of the government didn't know?"

"That's right," Sam said. "And most of the military didn't either. Plenty of them would have shut it down if they'd known. But the ones who did know—those are the ones who benefitted. They quietly maintained the arrangement for years. It didn't end until the Galactic Federation stepped in and the Partnership was shut down."

A coffee grinder whirred behind the counter, then stopped. Amanda's hand closed over the envelope and pulled it toward her.

Jerry studied her expression. He could see she was calculating—measuring the risk against the story.

Sam leaned in slightly. "You asked for something big. This is it. But once you print it, you can't take it back. You'll be famous, whether you like it or not."

Amanda nodded once. "Then I'd better make sure I get it right."

"You'll need to," Jerry said, "because we'll know if you try to write something false or slant the information to justify what happened."

And they would. Brad had volunteered to handle that. He had even admitted to Jerry that he hoped Amanda would mess up, given how she had smeared Jessica in the past. He would enjoy taking her down. He would like getting revenge.

Amanda started to speak—likely a comment about freedom of the press—but Jerry kept going before she could say anything.

"We could have done that with any of your other stories, too—we have the means. We just didn't bother because we didn't think they were important—and they weren't. But this story *is* important, and if you agree to do it, we'll hold you responsible."

Jerry could tell his remark about her earlier stories not being important stung Amanda's pride. Her mouth snapped shut, and she leaned back, eyes flashing. She picked up Sam's manilla envelope and stood up.

"I'm a professional," she said, tossing her long hair back again.

Then she walked out of the coffee shop without looking back.

CHAPTER
TWENTY-ONE

L ewis moved carefully along the line of storage containers. This time he hadn't gone straight to the abandoned industrial lot. Instead, he parked a mile away and approached with caution. Now he stopped at a corner and listened.

Malcolm had been asking to meet for weeks. The last time they met here, Lewis had walked away before anything happened. This time, he wanted to be sure there were no surprises.

From his position, Lewis could see the lot through a gap in a fence. Malcolm had told him that there were only six of them—half a dozen biologic constructs—that survived the destruction of the Partnership. He spotted three of the remaining super-soldiers standing in plain view near the center. He recognized Malcolm by his broad build and close-cropped hair. The other two stood slightly behind him, watching the area.

Lewis stayed still for several minutes, scanning the surroundings. A faint movement on the far side of the lot caught his eye. He circled around, using the cover of the storage containers, and found a fourth super-soldier crouched behind a stack of pallets. The man was watching the meeting area, holding a weapon low at his side.

Lewis kept moving and spotted the fifth one in the narrow space between two warehouses. This one was closer to the main group but still out of sight from the lot. He was also armed.

Lewis pulled out his communicator and typed a short message to Malcolm:

All five of you need to be in the open together before I come over.

He waited in position where he could see the reaction. Malcolm checked his own device, and his expression changed immediately. His jaw tightened, and he looked toward the hiding spots where the other two were stationed. He raised a hand in a sharp signal, and the two hidden men stepped out reluctantly.

Although all five were visible, Lewis stayed where he was, watching them. Malcolm scanned the lot, then looked toward where Lewis was hidden. Malcolm was just as good a tracker as Lewis—he could figure out where someone would need to be to spot both his hidden men. His voice carried across the space.

"So, you've been scouting," Malcolm said. "You found them."

Lewis didn't answer. He could see from Malcolm's expression that the plan had been to corner him. Malcolm's shoulders stiffened, and he gestured to the others to hold their position.

"You're making this harder than it needs to be," Malcolm called out. "We wanted you with us."

Lewis stayed silent. He could guess what "with us" would mean. He typed another message: *What do you want that would need guns to get me to come with you?*

There was frustration on Malcolm's face. "We just didn't want waste time," he called out. "We know how long it takes you to understand things. It's for your good—and ours. All six of us together. We're starting our own outfit, just us. And since we're the last super-soldiers, we'll be in demand—we'll get rich. But we need another man."

Lewis felt the heat rise in his chest. He didn't like it when people talked about him like that—slow, not understanding things.

The Four didn't talk to him that way. The Bridgewalkers didn't either. They treated him like he was part of the team.

Malcolm's voice carried clearly across the lot. "Think about it—half a dozen biologic constructs, all flying around in a spaceship. We'd be unstoppable."

The words caught Lewis off guard. A quick tightening spread in his stomach. Did they know? Did any of these men know where the ship was? The one he had told the Four about? If they did, they'd go after it. If they got to it first, there'd be no stopping them.

Malcolm went on, his tone shifting between coaxing and commanding. "We've been scattered too long. We should be together. You're wasting your time with those kids and those aliens. They don't understand what we are."

Lewis stayed still, watching the five of them. The way they stood—spaced just enough to cover each other's angles—wasn't casual. The two that had been hiding still kept their hands close to their weapons.

"You know I'm right," Malcolm called out. "We're the last. Nobody else can do what we can do. And with the right jobs, the right contracts, we could own this field. Security, retrieval, enforcement—whatever pays best."

Lewis shifted back into the cover of the shipping containers, moving as quietly as he could. He needed to tell the Four. If Malcolm's group suspected anything about the ship, they couldn't leave it where it was.

He took one last look around the corner. Malcolm was still talking, raising his voice as if Lewis were still in earshot. "You'll see I'm right! You can't hide from what you are. This is your chance!"

Lewis moved farther away, keeping his steps silent. By the time Malcolm realized he was gone, Lewis would already be over the fence.

Behind him, Malcolm's voice was still carrying through the lot, sharp and insistent.

* * *

Amanda sat cross-legged on the floor of her apartment. The coffee table was covered with stacks of documents, and more were spread out in uneven piles on the rug around her. The room smelled faintly of paper and printer ink from where she had run copies of some of the files earlier in the day.

She picked up the manila envelope Sam Burger had slid across the table in the coffee shop and checked the contents again. Every page had some combination of military letterhead, signatures, or diagrams. There were typed reports, memos, and what looked like minutes from closed-door meetings. The words "Tall Whites" appeared in multiple places, always tied to phrases like "technology transfer" and "human genetic material."

It was the kind of material that could end careers, maybe even send people to prison—if it was true.

Jerry Smith's name and title gave the claim credibility. She had known who he was before the meeting. Deputy Director of OMR was a position that carried authority. He had been visible enough in the public sphere that she didn't need to check his identity. Captain Samuel Burger was different. She had not heard of him before, but his uniform and insignia were authentic. She had verified them online the moment she returned home. His service record matched the details he had given her.

She thought about their warning—how they would know if she tried to twist the story into something else. She didn't like how certain Jerry's tone had been. The comment had been brief, almost casual, but it stayed in her mind. How would they find out? The most likely explanation was alien technology. OMR had access to things no one else did. If they had surveillance or tracking devices far beyond anything in commercial use, she would never see it coming. The safest choice was not to test them.

Her gaze moved over the piles again. This was explosive content. If she published it, she would have the biggest story of the year—maybe the decade. She imagined producers calling her for appearances on national talk shows. Editors would compete for her next piece. She would be in demand everywhere.

A faint unease tugged at her thoughts. The public's reaction could be unpredictable. There might be a backlash blaming the military. Would it be violent? Would she—as the one who blew the whistle—be blamed for provoking it? But she pushed that aside. This was her opportunity. She could handle whatever came after. The important part was to get the story out—and make sure her name was on it.

She reached for a pen and a fresh notebook, flipping to the first page. If she was going to write it, she needed to map out the opening line now.

* * *

Jessica stood near the front windows of the bank building—the new tai chi studio—watching the last of the students walk down the sidewalk. Outside, streetlights lit patches of the pavement, and a passing car's headlights swept across the glass before disappearing down the block. Inside, the atrium was dim, lit only by a couple of overhead fixtures near the reception counter. Somewhere upstairs, a door closed with a muted thud.

The rest of the group was gathered around Lewis, who stood outside the door to his security office, feet planted and body straight, as if delivering an official report.

"I met with the others," he said. "The remaining super-soldiers. There are only six of us left, and they wanted me to join them."

Jessica crossed over to stand by Kiran, then looked over at Lewis. While his tone was matter-of-fact, she noticed the way Vicki's shoulders tightened.

"They're starting their own business," Lewis went on. "Security, enforcement, that kind of thing."

Brad frowned. "And what did you say?"

Lewis almost smiled. "Nothing. I just left. It didn't deserve an answer. I want to stay here."

Jessica felt some of the tension in the room drop. Vicki exhaled quietly.

Then Lewis smiled—the first time Jessica had ever seen him smile. "I left, but they didn't know it. They were still talking when I was gone."

Brad covered a grin and clapped Lewis on the back. But then the super-soldier's expression turned serious

"There's something else. Malcolm mentioned a spaceship. He said a team of super-soldiers flying around in a spaceship would be unstoppable."

The room went silent again. Even the sound of traffic outside seemed to fade for a moment.

Jessica's thoughts jumped immediately to the craft Lewis had told them about before. "Are they talking about the same spaceship you told us about? Do they know where it is?" she asked.

"I don't know," Lewis said. "If it is and they do, we need to get to it first. I want to go tonight. It's just about four hours away, and traffic will be light at night.

Vicki started worrying out loud. "But if we get it, what then? We don't have anywhere to put a spaceship."

Jessica thought for a moment. "What about our property—the one that belongs to Brad and I? We haven't sold it off yet, and it's a full two acres with just trees and the burned-out remains of the house. That's it. The property is fenced, and the gates are locked. There's still even police tape up."

"It's not perfect, but it would be hidden enough for now," agreed Brad.

Kiran nodded. "We'd have to make sure no one is watching the place."

Jessica reached over and took Kiran's hand. She could feel the energy shifting again as the idea took hold.

Calvin spoke. "If we're doing this, we need to prepare. Vehicles, fuel, whatever we need to move it."

"We're going to go get a spaceship!" crowed James. He and Brad high-fived, the sound sharp in the quiet space.

Mona was the voice of reason. "But what do we do if the other super-soldiers are already there?"

Lewis's voice was confident. "I can handle them if they're there."

Jessica wasn't sure if that was true. She knew Lewis *wanted* it to be—and that he saw it as his duty to make it true. But what could they—a few humans and one biologic construct—really do against five of the most powerful fighters on the planet?

The risk wasn't just about the confrontation. The spacecraft was their only possible way to reach Sol Gate. Without it, space travel was nothing more than a dream. With it, they had the means to act—a chance to open the way to interstellar travel for all of humanity. A way to step up as a full member of the Galactic Federation. But if the other super-soldiers got to the ship first, they would use it for power and control—just like before. And there would be nothing the Four or the Bridgewalkers could do to stop them.

Jessica could see Lewis understood this. His eyes stayed on the others in the circle, his expression calm. He didn't talk about his feelings, but he had chosen to stay with them when he could have joined his former unit members. For Lewis, going after the spaceship wasn't a risk—it was a duty. If he had to stand between them and the super-soldiers to keep the ship in their hands, he would.

Vicki gave a short nod. "All right. We go tonight. No delays."

Jessica squeezed Kiran's hand once before letting go. The decision was made.

Chapter Twenty-Two

C alvin kept his eyes on the road, the headlights catching the reflective paint of highway signs as they headed east through the city. The nighttime Los Angeles traffic might be light, but it still demanded his attention.

Vicki sat in the passenger seat, phone in hand, scanning the map and glancing up to check the exits. In the row behind them, Jessica and Kiran sat side by side, looking out the window. Lewis was in the far back, his muscular frame filling most of the space. James and Brad were the extras—one riding with Lewis, the other with Jessica and Kiran.

The farther they drove from downtown, the darker the road became. Beyond the congestion and suburbs, the orange glow faded, and the desert air turned cool. With each mile, they drew closer to Joshua Tree—and to the secret storage bay just beyond it, where Lewis claimed a reverse-engineered spaceship was hidden. The thought of it waiting underground, functional and ready, kept the car quiet for long stretches.

Calvin was glad they decided to take his vehicle—a Chevy Traverse—because it meant he was the designated driver and he got to come along to retrieve the spaceship. Everyone had wanted to go and his SUV held the most people. As it was, Mona and Mei had to stay behind.

Mona hadn't wanted James anywhere near the underground bay. She had argued for over an hour, pointing out the risks and the fact that the facility was guarded. It wasn't just the military they might face—the surviving biologic constructs could be there too. There were five left, and none of them on their side.

She had looked at Calvin like he was out of his mind for agreeing to drive. But she also knew how little control either of them had once James made up his mind. In the end, it was better for one of them to go than for both to stay behind.

Calvin understood her. He was protective of their son too. But things were different now. James wasn't just a high school kid anymore. He was rooming with Brad—just like he'd wanted—while talking to aliens and moving in the same circles as Vicki and other high-profile people. If things kept heading in this direction, Calvin couldn't see their son filling out college applications—or even finishing high school. That life didn't fit anymore. Maybe if James got his GED, Mona would feel calmer. At least it would put the high school question to rest.

College was harder. Maybe James should teach instead of study? UCLA's history department was nationally respected, and Calvin was sure they'd welcome James teaching a class on human-ET history. Although only a teenager, James would be the most qualified person on Earth—courtesy of the memory crystal—to do it. He thought that might satisfy Mona, at least for a while. Long enough for the next phase to become clear.

Road signs started showing exits for the park, but Calvin drove past them, keeping his speed steady. He worried about what lay ahead. Lewis had warned there would be military surveillance—and guards once they spotted them. These weren't people you could bluff past.

That thought brought him back to his brother, Larry—another biologic construct, but one who had chosen differently. Larry had fought the Partnership from the inside and had given his life to make sure the kids got out.

Larry had struggled with being a super-soldier. He struggled with doubts about what he was and whether he was still worthy of being considered human. Calvin had argued that he was, but he wasn't sure Larry had believed him. Tonight, driving toward whatever waited for them in that underground bay, Calvin hoped that Larry—wherever he was—could see him. And that he would approve.

* * *

Jessica checked the time on her phone as their vehicle turned down an unmarked service track—the kind that would be used by park rangers. Just after three in the morning. The air outside was cool, but inside it felt warm and close. She could see the shape of the building ahead in the headlights.

It was exactly where Lewis had said it would be. As they slowed to approach, she stared at it. The building looked like nothing more than a plain cement box. No paint. No markings. No windows. Just a single utility pole beside it, its light flickering.

"That's it?" she asked, keeping her voice low. Kiran squeezed her hand.

Lewis glanced up from the back seat. "This is just the entrance. The rest is underground. Size of two football fields—it goes three levels deep."

She nodded once but kept her eyes on it, hoping Kiran had been right. He had used his pathfinding ability to help them plan the theft of the spaceship, working through possible approaches and weighing the odds for each. His conclusion was that the best route was to approach the facility from the south along the ranger access road.

Roads like this were often used by young people looking for privacy—to drink from a bottle they weren't supposed to have or to make out without being interrupted. A vehicle going down this road would be noticed, but not investigated right away. Kiran had estimated they would have a couple of hours before anyone came to check.

Driving out was another matter—going back the way they came was not an option. Kiran believed the dirt road heading north was the best way out, but said Vicki would need to do something to make it possible. He hadn't said what and Vicki didn't ask. She only gave a sharp nod when Kiran brought it up.

The timing for leaving in the craft had been set. Sunrise. When the sun was low on the horizon, any flash from the hull could be mistaken for an airplane or a trick of the eyes. Lewis had flown in these crafts many times, and had been confident about that part. Kiran hadn't been quite so confident, but he agreed sunrise was their best chance.

Calvin slowed the car and took them around the side of the building. The tires crunched over the dirt and gravel. The walls looked the same from every angle—flat, featureless cement. No windows. No signage. A single metal door that appeared to be rusting.

Calvin parked behind the building—out of sight from the service road. The engine noise faded, leaving only the faint ticking of cooling metal.

As they all got out of the car, Jessica looked at the others. Lewis was already scanning the area. Vicki's expression was unreadable. Calvin and the boys stood looking at the building, waiting for direction. The night was bright with stars.

She took a slow breath. "Will this work?"

No one answered right away.

* * *

"Of course this will work," Brad said after a brief pause. He regretted taking those extra moments—he should have answered confidently right away. The short delay made it clear to the others that he wasn't completely sure.

Lewis called everyone's attention toward the corners of the building. "Cameras," he said. "If anyone is looking, they'll see us now, but they won't come for a while."

Brad looked closer and saw the small black domes fixed high near the roofline.

Lewis walked over to the door. He reached up, running his fingers along the top of the doorjamb until he stopped at one point. Brad saw his hand press something, then slide a narrow piece of wood to the side. Behind it was a panel with several buttons. Lewis pressed them in a sequence—four quick presses, a pause, then three more.

A mechanical click came from inside the door. Lewis pulled the handle and opened it.

Brad stepped in behind him. The room was plain, with a desk and two metal chairs sitting against one wall. There was no other furniture. The walls were bare, painted gray.

Staring at the empty space behind the desk, he said, "No one's here. That's sloppy. A guardhouse at the entrance to something this important and not a single person in it?" He shook his head once. "Either they've gotten careless, or they're expecting no one would make it this far."

James came up from behind and elbowed him in the side, ""Guess we shouldn't complain if they're making it easy for us."

Lewis crossed to the far wall and put his hand against it. He pressed along the surface until something gave way. A section of the wall swung inward to reveal a stairwell leading down.

The air inside was cooler than outside. Lewis started down the stairs, and everyone followed. At the bottom was a wide corridor with smooth concrete walls. Lights in the ceiling triggered on as they passed and went dark again once they moved beyond.

Lewis kept moving. After about thirty feet, they came to another metal door. It had no handle, only a panel with a slot. He took a card from his pocket, slid it through, and the door unlocked with a short buzz.

Beyond it was another corridor, narrower than the last, with several closed doors. On the walls, signs were mounted in both English and another language none of them recognized. Some had symbols above the text—circles intersected by triangles, diagrams that looked like engineering schematics. One read: Quantum Field Containment – Authorized Personnel Only. Another: Temporal Synchronization Lab – Keep Door Sealed.

Brad slowed as they passed a third sign: Propulsion Core Access – Radiation Clearance Required. He glanced at James, who was already studying the markings beside the English text, tracing them with his eyes as if committing them to memory.

They came to a corner and turned right down another hallway which was wider, with a smooth floor and reinforced doors on either side. Small transparent panels beside the doors glowed faintly, displaying lists of numeric codes. They kept walking until they reached another security checkpoint—a second metal door with no visible lock. Lewis placed his palm flat against the wall beside it. There was a pause, then the door slid open.

The chamber beyond was enormous—a true warehouse. The ceiling arched high overhead, and the walls were lined with maintenance platforms at different levels. In the center sat the craft.

It was classically saucer-shaped, with a smooth silver surface that reflected the overhead lights. The outer edge tapered thin, and the underside was recessed, showing dark openings that might have been vents or ports. The hull's curve was unbroken except for a single narrow band that circled it near the top.

"Look at the seams and rivets," said Brad. "Shows it's reverse-engineered rather than extraterrestrial."

It was also easy to focus on—not fuzzy looking—which was how the ET spaceship manned by the Kewpies had looked. But Brad didn't want to get bogged down in details.

"And no sense of living chi," agreed Vicki.

The scale of the craft filled the space. Even without knowing its systems, Brad could see it was intact. He looked from the landing struts to the smooth dome, trying to imagine it lifting from the ground.

"How does it fly out of here?" asked Kiran. Everyone looked to the arched ceiling, but it was solid.

Lewis gestured toward the wall opposite the craft. "The far wall isn't solid. It's a door. Once we power up the spaceship, it automatically slides open."

Then he reached the control console and tapped a sequence into the flat, dark panel. Lights came on across its surface, forming rows of status indicators and readouts. He glanced at the group.

"Maintenance mode," he said. "It's offline now, but the systems are stable. No fault indicators."

Brad stepped closer, still keeping his eyes on the ship. "How do we get inside?"

Lewis pressed another sequence. A faint hum came from the far side of the craft, and a section of the hull shifted, revealing a narrow ramp that extended to the floor. "Boarding ramp's manual override is locked from this panel. I'll keep it extended until we're all inside."

Vicki moved toward the ramp, scanning the edges of the chamber. "How long to power it up for flight?"

"Full readiness?" Lewis checked the display. "Forty minutes for core ignition, another ten for flight systems. If everything runs clean."

"So we're ready?" asked Vicki.

Lewis nodded.

"Then I guess it's time for Calvin and I to go stand guard."

"What?" asked Jessica. "Aren't you guys coming with?"

"Someone needs to drive the car back," said Calvin, smiling.

"And Kiran knows that someone needs to slow down the guards who will be coming for us. That person is me," Vicki said, her face now serious.

What? Brad looked at Kiran, who was nodding. Then he remembered Kiran saying that Vicki would have to "do something" for the plan to work. And he remembered exactly what Vicki had done to bring down the Partnership.

He swallowed. "You'll let us know if something comes up?

At this, Vicki smiled. "Believe me, you'll know—you'll feel it. She joined Lewis at the console. "Sunrise window still holds?"

"Yes," Lewis said. "But we'll be ready before then."

"Be ready," said Vicki. "Calvin and I will do what we can."

Chapter Twenty-Three

V icki studied the road. Calvin had parked the car on the service road, facing north and ready to go.

"See anything?" Calvin asked, tapping the wheel. Mona hadn't asked how they would handle both the car and the spaceship. She probably hadn't considered the possibility that he and James might need to split up. He wondered how she'd react when she found out. It was't really something he looked forward to.

Vicki shook her head. "No. Based on what Kiran saw, we've got about half an hour. They'll be coming up the service road from the south, same way we did. As soon as we spot headlights, I'll do my thing, and then we'll head north. There's a dirt road a little farther up that should eventually take us back to the highway."

"So what's going to happen? What are we supposed to do?"

"I'll slow them down," Vicki said, "using Earth energies. When Melly activated my junk DNA, she strengthen my connection to the natural forces of the planet. I did it at the Partnership's compound; I can do it here."

Calvin froze, remembering the Partnership's destruction. *Vicki* had caused all that? He hadn't known. But he also realized he'd never asked what had really happened.

Tonight, he would find out.

* * *

James followed Lewis up the ramp and into the spaceship, with the other three close behind. For the second time, they'd be flying in a spaceship! He hoped Lewis would be willing to teach him how to pilot it himself.

Though brightly lit, the interior was dusty—the craft hadn't been used in months, maybe a year. The space was circular, with smooth walls curving up. Along the front wall, two large viewports rose to the ceiling, giving a wide view ahead. Below them, the main control consoles sat in a semicircle, each with screens, levers, and rows of glowing indicators. To the left, a recessed area held storage compartments with sliding doors. Some were marked with symbols; others were blank.

Around the outer walls, evenly spaced seats were built in. Each one was contoured and fitted with restraints to hold passengers securely during flight. Between some of the seats, small access panels and storage compartments were set into the wall. The center of the room remained open, leaving enough space for people to move freely between the seating area and the control station.

James kept part of his attention on Lewis, who crossed the deck and looked through the forward viewport to inspect the far wall on the other side of the underground facility. A section there had shifted open, revealing the exit ramp they would use. Satisfied, Lewis moved back to the consoles, pressing sequences of buttons, watching readouts, and scanning monitors. A low hum began to build as he powered up systems.

James sat in the co-pilot's chair, his eyes still fixed on Lewis. The man moved carefully, scanning each console and panel as though checking items off an invisible list. His hands hovered over the controls, pausing now and then as he reviewed the sequence in his head.

It was clear that even though Lewis had never flown the ship before, the instructions were already inside him—detailed and complete.

Behind them, the others spread through the cabin, running their hands over smooth surfaces, pointing at displays, and whispering in awe. James stayed silent, watching as Lewis went over the ship again and again until every control was locked in his memory.

"When are we leaving?" James finally asked.

"As close to sunrise as possible," Lewis said without looking up. "Easier to blend in when sunlight is streaming into peoples' eyes."

James's phone buzzed. He answered, and after a short exchange, his expression tightened. "That was my dad. We've got incoming—some of them are super-soldiers."

Before anyone could react, the deck jolted violently beneath them. A deep rumble filled the chamber, and everyone grabbed for the nearest solid surface. Storage doors rattled, and one of the overhead panels flickered.

"Earthquake," Brad said through clenched teeth, bracing himself.

"It's Vicki," Kiran said with a nod, pulling something from his pocket.

"Time to go," Lewis ordered. He moved quickly across the controls, switching on the flight systems. The hum grew louder, and the ship's displays shifted to new readouts.

"I need a line of sight to the door—the one we came through when we entered," Kiran said urgently. "Can you open a viewport in that direction?"

Lewis worked the controls, and a panel slid aside, bringing the door into view.

About eight minutes later, the sound of pounding came from the main door leading into the bay. The door shuddered. With a sharp crack, it gave way, and armed figures in combat gear forced their way in—super-soldiers, weapons raised, advancing quickly toward them.

* * *

This was the part he was unsure of—the part of his vision that was cloudy. Kiran's pathfinding ability never gave him the equivalent of a neon blinking sign saying *Do This* or *Go This Way*. Instead it gave him options, possibilities, and probable results. Success was not guaranteed. Which is why he took the metallic cylinder out of his pocket. Something to increase the odds of success.

Shoes scraped on the deck behind him as someone shifted position. A low mutter from Brad carried over the hum of the craft's systems. "Crap."

The device felt cool in his hand. The photonitron transmitter—3D holographic projection tech he had helped create for the Partnership—produced images that looked solid and even showed up on radar. He had prepared by loading several holo reels ahead of time.

A sharp click echoed from the front consul as Lewis toggled a switch. "Just a few more seconds," Lewis called out without looking back.

He crouched against the wall by the back viewport and switched the device on. The projection unit emitted a faint hum, and the air in front of him shifted as the first image sequence loaded.

"Make it count," Jessica said quietly, putting her hand on his arm. He hadn't realized she was standing so near.

He selected the one he and Brad had created while still working at the Partnership: a life-size hologram of the top executives. He aimed it out through the viewport to a spot about 40 feet in front of the spacecraft. The men appeared exactly as he remembered—standing in a loose group, talking among themselves.

One of the figures turned toward the direction of the approaching super-soldiers and raised his hand in a casual wave.

From his vantage point, Kiran saw the reaction. The super-soldiers slowed. They stopped a short distance away, their attention locked on the projection. None of them moved closer immediately.

Kiran knew the truth. Every one of the people in that projection was dead. They had died when the Partnership compound was destroyed. But the rendering was flawless. The clothing moved naturally, the lighting matched the environment, and the body language was consistent with real people having a private conversation. The added radar signature would show them as living individuals on any scanner.

"They're buying it," Brad murmured.

Recognizing the men in the hologram as the Partnership's top executives—and their bosses—the super-soldiers stayed in place. A couple of them shifted position as if unsure whether to attack or put down their weapons.

Kiran watched the seconds pass. The projection had bought them time—90 seconds so far. He kept his hand on the transmitter, ready to switch the reel or shut it down the instant they needed to move.

A shout broke the stillness. One soldier was yelling at the others, his voice carrying over the distance. Kiran couldn't make out the words, but the tone was sharp, commanding. The soldier raised his weapon and fired at the hologram. The shots passed through with no effect.

"They're not going to wait much longer," Jessica said.

Weapons fire erupted from multiple directions, aimed at both the hologram and the spacecraft.

"Time to go!" called out Kiran.

Lewis was already guiding the craft smoothly up the launch corridor, the landing struts clearing the bay floor as the opening above widened. The hull brushed the edges of light spilling in from the outside as they rose, leaving the facility and the super-soldiers behind.

"Tell me you brought the other holo reels," Brad said, his voice tight.

Kiran allowed himself a brief smile but kept his focus on the transmitter. As soon as they cleared the upper perimeter, he switched reels. The image shimmered and reformed—now there were two identical copies of the ship flanking them. Both appeared solid and carried the same radar signature as the real craft.

"They'll never know which one to go for," James said.

He adjusted the spread, sending the projections out to either side so they matched the real ship's position, but with slightly different movements. From the ground, or on scanners, the three would appear to be three distinct physical spacecraft.

The morning light was faint but growing brighter. The sun's rim was just lifting above the horizon, its angle making the silver hulls flash briefly as they moved. Below, the damage Vicki had caused was visible in sharp detail. The service road was torn apart—sections collapsed into deep gullies, others buckled into steep ridges. Cracks branched across the ground in all directions, and loose debris covered the space between them.

"Look at that," Brad said, leaning to see past Kiran and Jessica. James joined them.

"I'm glad Vicki is on *our* side," said James, awe in his voice.

On the far side of the destruction, military trucks and personnel were clustered in a loose line. Some soldiers were crouched at the edge of the broken ground, pointing toward the facility. Others were standing back, talking into radios. While the super-soldiers had managed to cross and get to the facility, the rank-and-file military had not; the gaps were too wide for vehicles, and the buckled sections too unstable for foot traffic.

Lewis banked the ship while Kiran kept the projections in tight formation, sometimes dropping behind, sometimes moving ahead. Not knowing the transmitter's range, he kept them close. From the ground, they would look like three flying saucers traveling together.

Kiran laughed to himself. It's not as if one would be any more believable than three. But radar—both civilian and military—wouldn't be able to differentiate between the holo flying saucers and the real craft.

The terrain changed as they turned north toward Los Angeles. Ahead, a thin ribbon of dirt road cut through the desert. Calvin's car was visible on it, heading away from the facility.

Lewis brought the craft down just enough to hover over the vehicle. The car stayed on course, dust trailing behind it as it moved toward the horizon.

"Looks like they made it," Jessica said.

After a moment, Lewis pulled the ship back up to altitude. The projections followed as they accelerated toward the city.

* * *

Three UFOs Seen Over Los Angeles at Sunrise
By Marlene Ortega | Los Angeles Sentinel | Staff Writer

Los Angeles residents waking early this morning reported seeing not one, but three disc-shaped craft flying in tight formation over the city. The objects appeared just after sunrise, moving silently across the sky before disappearing to the northwest.

Witnesses described the craft as "smooth, silver, and perfectly round," each reflecting the early light. "They weren't like planes," said Westwood resident Andy Carlson. "No wings, no noise, and they kept perfect distance from each other the whole time."

While local and federal agencies have yet to release an official statement, the sightings have already sparked debate online. Some speculate that the craft are part of ongoing government tests. Others believe they could signal a new stage in contact between humans and extraterrestrials.

California's open coastline, cultural diversity, and history of technological innovation have led some residents to hope the state might serve as a natural base for any future alien presence. "If they're looking for somewhere to settle, why not here?" said Mar Vista shop owner Leila Tran. "We've always welcomed people from everywhere. Now maybe it's time to welcome beings from... well, anywhere."

No unusual activity was reported at local airports, and the FAA declined to comment.

Chapter
Twenty-Four

It took ten minutes to get to Los Angeles. The Four kept talking about how fast it was. They thought it was amazing. But this was nothing—Lewis kept the ship going slow on purpose. When they learned to fly it themselves, they would see what it could really do.

Brad and Jess pointed the way, telling him where the property was. They didn't tell him when to turn or when to go lower. They didn't know what the spacecraft could do, but he did—he was the one in charge. It made him feel good that they trusted him.

The city stretched out below them—rows of streets, lines of traffic, clusters of taller buildings, and the Pacific further off in the west. Lewis ignored the conversation inside the craft while they flew. He focused on the landmarks Brad pointed out, checking the map in his head.

Lewis flew steadily until he saw the spot ahead. He slowed to a full stop, hovering in the air. The young people stopped talking. He looked out through the front viewport, scanning the sky for planes from the Santa Monica airport. A small one passed in the distance, heading toward the runway.

Once he was sure it was all clear, he pushed the controls straight down.

The ship dropped quickly but smoothly, heading straight for the ground. He heard the others react—James gave a short laugh, Jessica said "whoa," and Brad muttered something under his breath. No one complained. When they set down, the craft didn't even shake.

Lewis looked out at the grounds. He remembered it from before—wide green lawn, tall hedges, trees along the edge, and lots and lots of flowers. The big house was gone now, only the blackened frame standing in the middle. The grass and trees were still nice, but they had grown a little wild.

Lewis saw both Jessica and Brad stop talking. They just looked at the burned house. He guessed it meant something to them. It had been their home before the Partnership destroyed it. He understood that, but to him, a building was just a thing. What mattered was having your people with you.

In the military, his people were his unit. In the Partnership, they were the other super-soldiers. Now it was the Four. That was who he had.

He thought about what would happen when they went through Sol Gate. He couldn't go with them. He would have to stay. He didn't know what he would do then.

He had brought the ship down onto the back lawn, hidden from the street by trees and hedges. The grass flattened under the landing struts.

"That was a nice landing," Brad said.

Lewis only nodded and started shutting the systems down.

* * *

James couldn't stop smiling. He had flown in a spaceship again! The first time had been in the Kewpie's ship, which had felt borrowed and out of reach. This one felt close. This one felt possible. He could imagine his hands on the controls for real, not just watching over a shoulder. He could imagine learning.

They had set down on Brad and Jessica's property now. Systems were cycling down in progressive steps, lights lowering on the console in front of Lewis. The cabin was filled with silence. James pulled out his phone and typed fast.

> Made it to LA. Landed at B&J's place. Everyone okay. – J

He sent it to his dad, cc'ing Vicki.

He hovered over his mom's name and then locked the phone. They hadn't gone into detail when making the plan to steal the spaceship, and he was pretty sure she thought he and his dad would be staying together the entire time. If James texted now, it would start a storm. Better to let his dad decide what to say—and when.

He checked the time. Calvin and Vicki would get here in about three hours if traffic held. That gave them room to breathe. Lewis opened the hatch, and Brad, Jessica, and Kiran went down the ramp. Warm air drifted in, bringing the smell of ash and burning that seemed to mark the place, even though the fire had happened several months before. James watched from the top of the ramp.

Jessica had her arms wrapped around herself. She was quiet. Kiran put an arm around her shoulder and left it there. Brad scanned the grounds and the black skeleton of the house without saying anything. None of them had been back since the night it burned. James stepped back into the ship. Brad and Jess needed this moment. He needed a different one.

Lewis was still at the console, making checks. He moved slowly, without rushing. James stood beside him, trying to take in each step.

"I want to learn," James said.

Lewis looked up. "Good."

"Not just theory. I want to fly it."

"You will," Lewis said. "All of you will. I can't go through Sol Gate. I can't raise my vibration—you know this. The other biologics constructs can't either. You will all need to be pilots."

James nodded. He had known the outline of that, but hearing it said out loud made it real. "So can we train now?"

"We can," Lewis said, nodding. He tapped the display. "Here's what I did when I landed. I kept the speed slow on purpose. Still faster than a jet, but much slower than this ship can fly. You'll see how fast later."

James grinned. "Everyone thought it was already lightning-fast."

Lewis gave the smallest smile. "I wonder how they'll like real speed."

James leaned over the panel. "Show me the basics you used from approach to hover."

Lewis slid his hand along the left control strip. "This is the vector hold—it keeps the ship pointed where you want it," Lewis said, tapping the control. "You use this so it doesn't start sliding sideways."

"You're talking about drift?" James asked.

"Yeah. Sideways drift. You don't want that. These here are the field shapers. They keep the upward push even so the ship stays level. If the push is stronger on one side, you'll start leaning, and it feels wrong real fast. You don't want that."

James nodded, watching where Lewis's fingers moved. "And for stopping?"

"For stopping in the air, you use this." Lewis pointed to a dial. "That's called the predictive arrest. You set how far you want before the stop, and the ship smooths the last bit for you automatically. If you try to do it all by hand, you'll wobble. Let the system finish it—it's better than you."

"Makes sense," James said.

"Coming down straight, like we just did, you add more on the field shapers," Lewis continued. "That's what drops you fast without turning. The ship's built for it, so don't fight it. Just keep it stable, and it'll hold level all the way down."

James grinned. "I want to try it."

"You will," Lewis said. "All of you will."

James repeated the sequence under his breath. Vector hold, field shapers, and predictive arrest. He could memorize steps. He had done it with tai chi forms. This felt like the same kind of work.

"You flew other places," James said. "In space, and on Europa. Can you tell me about it?"

Lewis sat back and looked past James toward the open ramp. For a moment he said nothing. "Europa was cold," he said, and then he corrected himself. "The numbers said cold. You don't feel it when you're inside the facility. The mining station had three docks. Sometimes we brought ore up from the pits, processed it, and shipped it out in blocks. But mostly there was ore delivery from asteroids. The ships came in on a tight schedule. There wasn't a control tower because we needed to stay hidden. Pilots guided their ships in using beacons and sensors, and tried not to make mistakes—if they did, they might crash into another spacecraft."

"How did they do that?" James asked.

"Pilots had to come in close, and keep their ship on course. Line up on the two beacons and keep them the same distance on the screen. Sometimes ice plumes would shoot up from the surface. You watched the sensors so you would get a warning before it happened. If it did, you waited outside the lane until it dropped. If you didn't, the ice would hit the hull and everyone got mad."

James pictured the console alerts and the approach lines. "And deep space?"

"We had to fly between markers," Lewis said. "We locked on to the corridor and kept the ship steady. No windows. No stars we could use."

"You miss it?" James asked, curious.

Lewis's jaw worked once. He nodded. "Yes."

James hadn't expected such a direct answer. Lewis rarely shared his feelings, usually focusing only on tasks. Hearing him say yes meant a lot. James realized the challenge with Lewis wasn't just the Four trusting a former Partnership biologic construct—it was also about Lewis trusting them. He had to believe they wouldn't leave him behind now that they had what they needed: the ship, the path to Sol Gate, and a future he couldn't share.

"We're not leaving you out here," James said. "When we go, it won't be because we stopped needing you."

"I know," Lewis said."

James shifted back to the panel. "Okay. Show me the startup from cold. I want to see the order."

Lewis walked him through it. Environmental checks first. Hull integrity. Power routing. Field shapers in passive. Navigation core in standby. Communications muted by default unless they needed to spoof. He flagged the emergency drop sequence and made James repeat it twice.

"You say it," Lewis said.

James went through it. "Emergency drop. Kill lift here, vector hold off, a matter of seconds for freefall. Field shapers to soft catch at five percent. Predictive arrest back on. Land on struts."

"Good," Lewis said. "Don't panic in that sequence. It feels wrong, but it's normal."

From outside came faint voices. Jessica said something low, and Brad answered. Kiran's voice carried a little louder, but also unintelligible.

James glanced back at the hatch. "They'll be okay out there?"

"They need it," Lewis said. "They lost this place."

James nodded. "It looks smaller without the house."

"We're not staying long," Lewis said. "We hide the ship, we rest, we plan. When Calvin and Vicki get here, we'll decide the next move."

James checked his phone again. His dad had replied.

> Saw you. Good. Stay put. We're fine. I'll text Mom. We'll be there in 2 1/2 hours.

"Can I try a hover?" James asked. "Just a little. Without leaving the ground."

"No lift," Lewis said. "But you can practice the controls. Put your hands on, but don't engage the power. Get comfortable with it."

James slid into the pilot chair. The surface adjusted to his shape. He placed his hands where Lewis told him. He traced the path from vector hold to field shapers to predictive arrest. He watched how small a motion the controls needed. He repeated the emergency drop sequence again with the power safe.

"You're learning," Lewis said.

"I want hours," James said. "Real ones."

"You'll get them," Lewis said. "We'll rotate. You, Jessica, Brad, Kiran. You all need it."

"Mei too?" James asked. It felt bad there hadn't been room for her to come along.

"She can do it," Lewis said. "All of you can."

They fell quiet for a moment. The craft clicked as one of the systems cooled. A small status light blinked.

"Tell me one more thing about Europa," James said. "Something I need to know if I ever go there."

"You won't," Lewis said. "You'll go farther. But if you did, the station's empty now. No people, no cargo, no ships coming in. They always shut it down when Jupiter and Earth get too far apart. Costs too much to operate then, even for the Partnership. But it still works. Power's on everywhere. You could go in, flip a few systems on, and be working again in minutes."

"Okay," James said. He filed it away with everything else.

Footsteps sounded on the ramp. Brad came back up first, then Jessica and Kiran. Jessica's eyes were red, but she looked calm. Kiran kept a hand on her shoulder until they were inside.

"How's our ship?" Brad asked.

"Quiet," Lewis said. "Hidden. She'll be fine."

"James getting his first lesson?" Brad asked, pointing at the console.

"Ground school, only," James said. "Flying will come later."

"Good—I look forward to it," said Brad.

"We've got a couple of hours before Calvin and Vicki arrive," said Kiran, checking his watch. "I'd like to walk around the edge of the property to make sure the gates are still locked, and the police tape is still there."

"I'll join you," Jessica said.

Brad looked at James and Lewis. "While they're doing that, can I watch you run a simulation?"

Lewis nodded. "Have a seat."

James waited for Brad to sit down before placing his hands on the controls. He didn't press anything, just rested his fingers on the buttons as he went through the steps: vector hold, field shapers, predictive arrest, and emergency drop sequence. He repeated the sequences over and over until it felt natural, saying each step out loud for Brad's benefit. By the end, Brad was reciting the words along with him.

James kept his focus on the panel and listened to Lewis talk through the checklists one more time. He would happily spend the next few hours here. He would train for more than that if they let him. He was ready to learn.

He was ready to fly.

Chapter
Twenty-Five

Mei sat across from her grandmother. There was no sound in the room. Her grandmother's hands rested on her lap, holding the jade amulet. The green surface was smooth, aside from the bagua etchings, the small crystal in its center catching the light. Mei looked at the amulet and then at her grandmother's face, but her grandmother kept her gaze down on the amulet.

The amulet slowly began to glow. First a faint brightness in the crystal's center, then a steady light that grew stronger. Mei's eyes stayed on it. The crystal's light shifted, a narrow beam projecting upward about a foot.

Above the amulet, shapes appeared—geometric and sharp. The first shape turned slowly, its lines clear. It dissolved into a second, then another, each one appearing in a set order. Mei counted eight before the sequence looped back to the first shape and started again.

Her grandmother kept watching until the shapes had cycled several times. Then she looked up at Mei. Her expression was calm, and a broad smile formed. She lifted the amulet, holding it out for Mei to take.

Mei reached for it. The shapes above the amulet were still forming and dissolving, one after another. She felt the weight of the amulet in her hand, cool against her palm.

The room was silent. Neither of them had spoken.

* * *

Mei opened her eyes in her new bedroom in the bank building. The light coming in through the blinds was faint; the room was still dim. She was lying on her side, her book next to her on the bed. She remembered planning to stay awake until the Four came back with the spaceship. She had wanted to hear their first impressions and know they were safe.

She shifted on the bed, pushing herself up on one elbow. There hadn't been enough space in Calvin's car for her to go. She had been disappointed at the time, but she just swallowed it. She knew she was lucky to have been included in as much as she had been. Most people would never see or experience even a fraction of what she had in the last few months.

The dream came back to her in full. It had been unusually clear—every detail sharp. Her grandmother's hands, the way the light had emanated from the crystal, the exact order of the shapes—it all sat in her mind as if she had just opened her eyes from watching it happen in the waking world.

She swung her legs over the side of the bed, and her hand went to the nightstand. The jade amulet was where she always left it, resting in a shallow dish. She picked it up and turned it over in her hands. The crystal at the center was small, smaller than the nail of her pinkie finger, but the edges caught the dim light from the window.

She tilted it, studying the surface. The green of the jade was deep, like the moss in a forest. She touched the crystal with her thumb. It felt as it always did—cool, smooth, and still. No light, no shapes, no movement.

She remembered her grandmother's smile—it had come with a look full of warmth and understanding. A look full of hope that Mei was ready to take the amulet.

Mei held it a moment longer, then placed it back in the dish. She sat on the edge of the bed, looking at the book she had left open. She had been halfway through a page when she must have drifted off. The clock on the nightstand told her it was still early; the Four would not be back for a while.

She thought about going to the kitchen for tea but stayed where she was. Her fingers went to the amulet again, tracing its outline in the dish.

In the dream, her grandmother had not explained the shapes. Mei had not asked. But they had appeared in a specific order, each one following the last in quick succession. She tried to picture them again in her mind, recalling the angles and the way each shape transitioned to the next. Eight shapes, then the loop back to the first.

She wondered if the sequence meant something, if it was a pattern she should know. This dream wasn't like the random ones she usually forgot by morning. This one stayed with her.

Mei took the amulet in her hand again; it felt the same as always. But now, in her mind, she could still see the beam of light and the floating shapes. She wondered if she should tell Vicki when she arrived, or wait and see if the dream returned another night.

Mei lay back on the bed. She stared at the ceiling and listened to the quiet, thinking of her grandmother's hands and the way she had held the amulet out to her.

* * *

It was late afternoon. Although it had only been a few hours since Lewis and the Four had returned from successfully stealing the Partnership's reverse-engineered spaceship, they—and Mei—had already gone back to Brad and Jessica's place. For flight lessons!

Vicki had planned to go with them. She wanted to learn to fly a spaceship too! But instead, she stayed.

Earlier that day Jerry had called to say he and Sam had given Amanda Riley the documents about the military's trade agreement with the Tall Whites. They'd been planning it for weeks. The military had been locking down files and restricting access. The information needed to be made public before evidence was destroyed. For years people had said aliens had kidnapped them and subjected them to medical procedures; they were mocked and had their lives ruined. These documents backed up their claims — proof they weren't crazy.

It was also proof they had been betrayed by their own government.

On the call, Jerry said, "We handed the whole set to Amanda. Source documents, internal memos, meeting summaries, the draft MOUs, the final signatures. She has it all."

"I'll tell Brad the project is live and to keep an eye on it. He'll let us know if there are any changes to the files. If she tries to twist the story, we'll release the originals with a timestamp."

They also reviewed the risks. Jerry calmly listed them: public protests, attacks on government targets, anti-ET demonstrations, and even possible government collapse in places where trust was already thin. Vicki had added disinformation campaigns and smear operations. They agreed the risks were worth it—these people deserved the truth about what their government had done to them.

That was why she didn't go to learn how to fly the spaceship.

Instead, she made calls. She reached a civil rights group that had asked for guidance months ago. She told them a major Disclosure story was coming and to prepare de-escalation teams and legal observers. She called a community organizer who had handled tense rallies in the past and asked for a quick plan for nonviolent demonstrations. She left a message with a doctor who had been treating abduction trauma. She asked for a short statement affirming that consent and dignity are nonnegotiable in any medical context, human or nonhuman.

By early evening she had a folder ready with five short statements: one for release with Amanda's story, one for their backup release, one for public safety officials, one for community leaders, and one for international contacts who would ask what the United States was doing. She was no longer at the Department of State, but her responsibility hadn't ended. She still had people who would take her call. She sent notice to three of them: *You will see a story soon. Do not deny. Acknowledge and say you are reviewing. Do not attack witnesses. Do not attack the press.*

She closed the laptop and sat for a minute.

She had wanted badly to learn how to fly the spaceship. Vicki remembered being on the Kelpies' saucer—the endless black of space, broken only by sharp points of light. Inside the craft, the the systems quietly hummed, the walls close and solid. The ship moved smoothly, whether passing a planet or crossing open space, and the only sense of speed came from watching the stars shift through the viewports.

Right now, Vicki wanted to be on the spaceship with the others, not reading briefings or drafting statements.

But wanting it didn't change her role here. The Four could learn to fly without her. Lewis could teach them everything they needed to know. Mei could take her turn at the controls. They would be fine.

On Earth, things were different. No one else had her combination of connections, experience, and understanding of how these crises had played out. If she left, she would be leaving Mona, Calvin, Lewis, the Suedes, and the ACs to fend for themselves. She couldn't pretend the work was done just because she had stepped away from her title.

The disappointment sat with her, but so did the knowledge that she was where she was needed most. She would see the ship another day. She would be ready for the shift when the time came.

For now, her job was here.

* * *

Amanda Riley walked into the lobby of the network's headquarters with her head high and her bag swinging at her side. The building's glass doors slid open as if they knew she was coming. She told the receptionist her name and that she had an appointment with the producer. The receptionist's polite nod felt like confirmation that she was in the right place, that the next step in her career was about to begin.

This was the story that would put her back on the map. After months of dead ends and polite rejections—ever since her uncle, Colonel Riley, had been court-martialed—she was going to be relevant again. More than relevant. Famous. Her pieces on the dangers of Disclosure had stopped being picked up after his trial, editors claiming her credibility had been compromised. She knew the truth—they were cowards who didn't want to be associated with someone speaking hard truths.

And now she had something bigger than anything she had written before. Jerry Smith of State's Office of Multispecies Relations and Captain Samuel Burger from the Pentagon's OSD had handed her proof—actual proof—of a secret agreement between the U.S. military and the Tall Whites. The trade was straightforward: advanced alien technology in exchange for unlimited DNA sampling of the human population.

She had felt a small twinge when she realized she would be attacking the same military she once championed. But it was fleeting. Principles were fine, but opportunities like this did not wait around. It wasn't about loyalty to a position; it was about telling the biggest story. And this story would be *hers*.

She had sent the proposal to one of the largest media outlets in the country. She had been careful—professional headline, concise summary, a bullet-point list of the supporting documents she held. She had expected it to be a week before she heard back. Instead, the next morning, she had been invited to come in and meet with the producer directly.

The elevator ride up to the meeting room felt like the ascent to a higher tier of journalism. She imagined the moment when her name would be attached to a breaking news segment that would dominate the headlines for weeks. She pictured interviews and guest appearances—maybe even a book deal.

When the elevator doors opened, a young assistant was waiting to escort her to the meeting room. The assistant smiled but didn't say much as they walked down the hall. The producer was already there, sitting at the head of a long table. He gestured for her to sit.

Amanda set her bag down and pulled out her notebook. She was ready to discuss timelines, document handling, and how they would release the story.

The producer leaned back in his chair, hands folded. "Ms. Riley," he said, "I appreciate you coming in on short notice."

"Of course," she said, keeping her tone professional but warm. "I'm excited to work with you on this. I think you'll agree it's—"

He held up a hand. "Before we go further, I want to be very clear about something. We will not be publishing this story."

The words came with an abruptness that caught her off guard. "I don't think you've seen the material yet," she said. "These aren't rumors or anonymous tips. I have the full documentation—"

"It doesn't matter what you have," he said. "This is the kind of thing that will not see daylight through our network. You need to drop it. If you know what's good for you, you'll let it go."

Amanda stared at him, searching his expression for some sign that he was bluffing or testing her. "Are you saying you're refusing to even review the evidence?"

"That's exactly what I'm saying," he replied. "We're not interested in this story, and neither is anyone else who values their job or their company's stability."

"I don't think you understand," she said, keeping her tone measured. "This is the biggest national security and human rights story of our time. People will demand answers once it's out there. And if I don't do it, someone else will."

"You're free to shop it elsewhere," the producer said, his voice flat, "but we've already consulted with our lawyers. It's too dangerous. My advice is to consider your career and your personal safety before you try to publish this."

The words hung in the air, matter-of-fact and final. Her excitement drained, replaced by something colder. She forced a tight smile, thanked him for his time, and left the office, her mind already working through her next move.

If they thought she would just walk away, they didn't know her at all.

CHAPTER
TWENTY-SIX

M ei sat strapped into the rear seat, her hands gripping the armrests tightly. The craft was in flight, but when she closed her eyes she couldn't tell—its movement was so smooth it felt nearly motionless. They were above the Earth now, past the heavy air, past the faint blue that clung close to the curve of the planet. She forced herself to breathe steadily. She was in a spaceship—an actual flying saucer!

She hadn't been with Lewis and the Four when they stole the ship. There hadn't been room in Calvin's car for everyone. When it came down to deciding who would go and who would stay, it made sense for her to remain behind with Mona. But sitting here now, she could admit to herself that she had been afraid that this was how it would always be—that she would be the one who was left behind. The Four would take the risks, make the discoveries, live the experiences, while she watched from the sidelines. That fear had troubled her more than anything.

But now she was here. She hadn't been left behind. She was in a flying saucer, and it was flying above Earth.

She looked around at the others. Per Lewis's instructions, they all remained seated. James had already spent a few hours earlier in the morning learning the displays, so he was at the console, holding an animated discussion with Lewis. Beside him, Brad looked ready to burst, his excitement overflowing into questions he couldn't stop asking. Jessica and Kiran sat together, talking in soft voices that Mei couldn't hear.

Vicki wasn't with them. Mei still didn't understand why not. At first, they had assumed Vicki was just running late, but she had said no, she had other work to do. She had told them it was important, though there had been regret in her eyes as she said it. Mei had seen that look, and it bothered her. Hadn't Vicki left the Department of State so that she could work alongside them, free of rules, free from the bureaucracy? If she had given all that up, why had she chosen to stay behind now?

Mei pushed the thought away and focused on Lewis. He was at the console, fully in control. His hands moved over the unfamiliar surfaces as though he belonged there. His voice was calm as he explained.

"Cruise speed is different here than what you'd expect from atmospheric flight," he said. "Once you're clear of drag, you don't push harder to stay fast. You touch the field and let it hold. Push again only if you need a change. Otherwise you're wasting energy."

James leaned forward. "So how do you slow down?"

"You balance. Drop power to the forward field shapers. Let the pressure ease. It takes a feel—you don't slam it. You ease it down, then trim."

Brad frowned. "Trim?"

Lewis tapped a set of glowing symbols on the panel. "Here. Adjustments. Keeps the orientation stable. Stops unwanted movement. If you let it go too long, you start sliding sideways. You don't want that, not in traffic."

"Traffic?" James repeated, surprised.

Lewis nodded once. "Not here. But out where the lanes are marked—closer to Europa—yes. You fly the corridor that's already been established. The asteroids have been cleared away, so it's safe. In open space, though, you're on your own. You need to watch for debris. You can only rely on yourself.

"Markers don't care if you're tired. They don't care if you're off by half a degree. You stay on point. If you miss, you'll drift into someone else's path or into asteroids. That doesn't happen if you're trained."

Brad was practically bouncing in his chair. "We'll get trained, right?"

Lewis looked back at him, his face unreadable for a moment.

"Yes. Right here, right now. *This* is your training. You all need to learn. I can't take you through Sol Gate—you know that. Which means every one of you has to be a pilot. It's not optional."

Mei let those words sink in. All of them, including her. She hadn't thought of herself in that role. She had assumed she would stay in support, maybe help organize things. But fly?

The thought was both terrifying and thrilling.

* * *

Brad could hardly keep himself still. He wanted to lean forward and take the console in his hands. They were in space. Not watching from a telescope, not looking at blurry camera feeds or simulations—actually in space. Every second of it seemed impossible and yet here it was, laid out in front of him on the displays.

He thought back to the early morning. The theft. It felt like days ago, but it had only been hours. The secret bay had been enormous—an underground bunker. They had gotten the ship free, powered it, and then lifted into the air. That part had been amazing, but what impressed Brad the most was what happened next.

As they cleared the facility, Vicki's "distraction" unfolded below them. At first, he hadn't believed what he was seeing. Earth energies. She had spoken about them before, but seeing the destruction firsthand—fissures in the earth, vehicles overturned, armed men scattered as if control had been ripped from them—was sobering. He had always thought his own DNA upgrade was impressive. His ability to read code, to sense the structure of networks and systems, to find the weaknesses and flow in circuitry—that had seemed like the coolest thing in the world. But compared to what Vicki had unleashed, his skill suddenly felt small. He couldn't imagine harnessing that kind of raw force. The memory humbled him.

The present drew him back. Lewis's voice carried across the cabin. "You can get up now. Fifteen minutes before we reach the Europa facility."

Brad's restraints were off in a flash. He stood, stretching his legs, then moved closer to the forward viewport. Jessica and Kiran stayed seated, talking quietly, while Mei looked around with wide eyes, still gripping her armrest with one hand as if she wasn't entirely convinced it was safe to stand. James followed Brad up, his curiosity just as strong.

Lewis pointed to the viewport. "You'll see Mars out there."

Brad followed the gesture. The red planet was distant, a sharp circle against the black, but larger and clearer than any view from Earth. It wasn't just a dot. It was a body, real and reachable.

"It looks so close," Brad said.

"Closer than you're used to," Lewis replied. "From Earth, the atmosphere hides detail. Out here, nothing blurs it. You'll learn to judge distance properly. It's important when you start navigating for yourself."

Brad nodded quickly, committing the information to memory.

Lewis tapped another display, bringing up a data readout. Lines moved across in repeating patterns, some bright, some faint. "Solar winds. Magnetic fields. You need to know them. A burst can interfere with controls, knock out systems, and even turn a stable orbit unstable. You can't ignore them."

Brad leaned closer. "So these graphs—this tells us what's coming?"

"Correct," Lewis said. "You read the spikes. You check the angle of field strength. It won't stop you from moving, but it can change how the ship responds. Always adjust for it."

They moved onward. Soon, the asteroid belt began to register. Blips on the scanner. Lewis slowed the ship just enough to demonstrate, pointing out the clusters and strays. "This is where you practice awareness. Small objects can destroy you if you ignore them. See the shadows on the display? That's the trajectory. You plot your path through the gaps. Always assume there's more out there than the system is showing you."

He ran a hand across another control, and the ship tilted slightly. On the screen, a rock the size of a house slid past, missing them by what felt like a narrow margin.

Brad exhaled, adrenaline sharp in his chest. "That was close."

"It wasn't," Lewis said flatly. "It looked close, but the margin was correct. You'll learn to trust the displays, not your nerves. Your nerves will lie to you."

Brad absorbed the lesson, fixing it in his mind. He couldn't wait for the moment when he would be the one at the controls, proving to himself he could do it.

They pressed deeper into the belt, passing the massive moons of Jupiter. Ganymede appeared first, its surface striated and scarred. Then Callisto, dark and ancient, with craters upon craters. Brad had seen them in books and in photographs, but none of those compared to the sight of them outside the viewport, occupying space not as pictures but as worlds.

Finally, they approached Europa. The icy moon gleamed pale, its cracked surface like a frozen map stretching into the distance. Lewis angled the ship lower, scanning across the surface before bringing them toward a jagged divide.

"There," he said.

At first, Brad thought it was a canyon, but then he realized it was ice split open, a rift that went deep below. Lewis guided the ship carefully, lowering them through the narrow opening. The walls of ice rose around them, reflecting light from the ship's glow. The descent was controlled, then the walls widened and the structure below became visible.

It was the Partnership's mining facility. Built into the ice, its metal surfaces gleamed faintly under the lights. It looked dormant, waiting for them.

Lewis settled the ship down within the open bay. Systems clicked as they powered into rest mode.

Brad stood at the viewport, heart racing. They had made it. Not just through the sky, not just to orbit, but all the way across space to Europa. He couldn't stop smiling. They would train here. They would learn. And he would be a pilot.

* * *

Jessica kept her eyes on Lewis as he worked the controls, the sound of switches clicking sharp in the quiet cabin. The ship eased downward, bringing itself in line with the structure below. Metal struts, docking clamps, and the faint glow of a guidance beacon came into view through the forward viewport.

Lewis's voice spoke up. "The airlock shows no activity in over ten months. System logs confirm it." He adjusted a dial and glanced at another display. "That matches my information. This facility was mothballed when Jupiter's orbit shifted too far from Earth for profitable runs. Asteroid mining was put on hold until the next favorable alignment. Operations would normally have resumed last month."

Jessica frowned, leaning forward in her seat. "You're saying no one has been here the entire time?"

"That's what the logs show." Lewis moved his hand to another panel, flipping a row of switches. A low hum reverberated through the cabin as power channels began feeding into the external connection. "I'm reactivating the power flow and life support now."

Jessica exchanged a glance with Kiran, then asked, "But how do we really know? What about the super-soldiers? They need less air, less food, less heat. They could survive where others couldn't. If the Partnership left even one behind, we might never detect it."

The cabin went silent for a moment. Everyone looked at Lewis.

He looked Jessica in the eye. "Procedures are always followed," he said. "Mothballing a facility means leaving it empty. Biologic constructs aren't left idle at outposts — they're too expensive and valuable. If the Partnership were still active, it would be deploying super-soldiers on Earth to fulfill contracts, not leaving them sitting here."

Kiran nodded slowly. "That makes sense. Still, maybe we should do something to make sure no one else will be able to use this place in the future. Just in case." He gestured toward Brad, who was already standing near the secondary console, scanning the unfamiliar displays hungrily. "Brad could dig into the schematics, reset access controls, and rewire passwords. If we lock down the system—key it to just us—then we'd be the only ones who could get in."

Brad grinned at the suggestion. "I can do that. If I get inside the central processing system, I can reroute command authority and put up new gatekeepers. Even if someone tries, they'd need months to break through."

Jessica let out a breath she hadn't realized she was holding. "That would make me feel better."

Lewis gave a short nod. "Fine. Once we're docked and the airlock cycles, we'll secure the facility. But keep in mind—speed matters. We're not here to play with systems all day. Yes, Brad can do a reset once we're in. But after that, we train."

The airlock clamps closed around the ship. A vibration passed through the hull as seals engaged. Lewis monitored the readings, his hands still moving over the switches. "Pressure equalizing. Oxygen stable. Temperature rising. Facility systems are responsive."

The inner doors opened, revealing a corridor that stretched into the base.

Jessica led the way behind Lewis, with the others falling in step. The air felt faintly stale but breathable, warmed by the facility's environmental systems slowly restoring balance.

The first corridor was industrial—thick walls, exposed conduit, and reinforced flooring. The Partnership had built for durability, not aesthetics. Frost clung to some of the surfaces, melting slowly as heat flowed back through the vents. Their footsteps echoed lightly in the emptiness.

Jessica scanned each doorway they passed. Some led to storage alcoves stacked with dormant equipment. Others opened into wide work bays, lined with robotic arms, heavy drills, and processing units. The machines were silent, locked in standby mode, their indicator lights dark until power could be fully restored.

Brad stepped into one of the bays, his eyes already mapping the network junctions in the walls. "It looks like the controls are hardwired into the host system. I'll find the operations core and lock it down."

"Later," Lewis reminded him. "Tour first to confirm the layout. Then you can secure it."

They moved deeper. Jessica's awareness sharpened as they passed through each section. Living quarters lined one wing—small rooms with bunks bolted to the walls, desks folded down from hinges, lockers stacked in rows. Everything carried the look of a methodical shutdown. Beds stripped. Personal effects removed. It matched what Lewis had said: procedure.

In another wing, they found the mess hall. Long tables were anchored to the floor, chairs still arranged in neat rows. The kitchen area was clean, surfaces wiped, machines disconnected but intact. There were no signs of recent use.

Kiran ran his hand along one of the tables. "Feels like they walked out and closed the door."

Jessica nodded. "Good. That's what we want."

Finally, they reached the control center. The doors slid open a little sluggishly, as though the mechanism hadn't been engaged in months. Inside, rows of consoles faced a massive wall screen. Lewis stepped directly to the primary station, activating power nodes. Lights flickered across the displays, bringing the room alive as they slowly pulsed.

Brad stood beside him almost immediately, scanning the schematics that scrolled into view. His expression was already focused, his mind moving ahead.

Jessica crossed her arms, standing in the center of the room. She let herself take in the space. It was secure. Empty. Just as Lewis had said. But still, she couldn't shake her wariness. "I know I'm probably paranoid, but let's lock it down anyway," she said firmly. "There's no reason to take chances."

Brad smiled faintly, not looking up from the screen. "Already on it."

Chapter Twenty-Seven

C aptain Samuel Burger adjusted the knot of his tie before stepping into the conference room. Today's meeting wasn't a routine briefing for a Pentagon official—it was at the Department of State. His friend, Jerry Smith from OMR, was already inside, standing beside the window, hands folded as he looked over a stack of documents.

At the head of the table sat Robert Thomas, the newly appointed Deputy Assistant Secretary for OMR. His jacket was sharp, his posture formal. He was still settling into the role, but so far he had proved to be a good fit.

"Gentlemen," Robert said as Sam entered. "You asked for this meeting. What do you have for me?"

Sam took his seat beside Jerry. "Of course. This one can't wait."

Jerry slid a folder across the table. "Amanda Riley. She's about to publish."

Robert raised an eyebrow. "On what exactly?"

"The military's secret trade agreement with the Tall Whites," Sam said plainly. He watched Robert's reaction carefully.

For a moment, Robert didn't move. Then he drew in a breath, opened the folder, and scanned the first page. "This is serious."

Sam leaned forward, resting his elbows on the table. "It's not a rumor, it's not conjecture. She's got hard evidence—enough to make it stick."

Robert looked up sharply. "How did she get the evidence?"

Sam kept his expression neutral. This was the moment he and Jerry had anticipated. They had agreed days ago: they wouldn't reveal their own role in leaking the documents unless it became absolutely necessary. That way, Robert could maintain plausible deniability. Sam let the silence draw just long enough before answering.

"She has it," Sam said. "That's what matters."

Robert studied him, then shifted his gaze to Jerry. Jerry gave a slight nod, as if confirming the same boundary.

Finally Robert exhaled. "Fine. Then we move on to what this means. If she runs with this—and it sounds like she is—fallout is guaranteed. Should we try to contain it? Keep the information hidden?"

Sam almost smiled at the question, though there was nothing amusing in it. He glanced at Jerry, who was already pulling another folder from his bag.

"I've prepared talking points," Jerry said calmly, laying them on the table. "When the crap hits the fan—and it will—we'll be ready. Framing is critical. This isn't about chaos. It's about accountability."

Robert tapped the folder but didn't open it. "Accountability is fine in theory. But Disclosure has already stretched the public. Do we really want to risk panic by throwing fuel on the fire?"

Sam spoke then, his tone measured but firm. "We can't bury it, Robert. That's exactly the kind of thinking that got us into this mess in the first place. People were taken. Abducted. Had their DNA sampled. For decades they were dismissed as deranged, liars, or worse. They deserve to know they weren't imagining it. That their government not only knew, but actively cooperated."

Jerry added, "And if we don't let it out now, someone else will. The longer the delay, the worse the betrayal looks when it finally surfaces. We're on better footing if we show we're willing to face the truth."

Robert folded his hands on the table. "And the military? You're both well aware how this will be received. The idea that we made trades with non-humans in secret... The idea that we traded our own citizens for technology—it'll spark outrage."

Sam nodded. "It *should* spark outrage. Government isn't above the law. And the military isn't exempt from accountability. If we want to lead through this new era of Disclosure, we have to be honest about the past. Otherwise, everything collapses under the weight of the lies."

The room settled into silence for a moment. Sam watched Robert carefully. The man was weighing not just the argument but the political implications.

Finally Robert said, "You both sound like you've rehearsed this."

Jerry shrugged lightly. "We've had this conversation before. We knew the day would come when the hidden agreements would come out. Better to be ready."

Sam leaned back slightly. "Look, Robert. This isn't about protecting institutions at the expense of people. The victims come first. If we ignore that, we're no better than the Partnership was."

Robert tapped his fingers on the table. "You're asking me to endorse a strategy that will almost certainly damage trust in the government."

Sam met his gaze directly. "No. We're asking you to endorse a strategy that will rebuild trust, because it doesn't shy away from the truth. People can forgive mistakes. They don't forgive cover-ups."

Jerry slid the talking points folder closer. "This is the path forward. It'll be rough. But it's the only path that stands a chance of holding together when the story breaks."

Robert stared at the folder, then finally opened it. His eyes moved over the neatly typed pages, his face unreadable.

Sam waited, composed, keeping his thoughts focused. They had done their part. They had brought Robert into the loop, but not so deeply that he'd be implicated. If he played it right, he could stand as the face of reason when the backlash hit.

After several long minutes, Robert closed the folder. "All right. We'll proceed with this line. But understand—I don't want to be blindsided. If there's more out there, I need to know before it lands in the press."

Sam inclined his head. "Understood."

Jerry gave a small smile. "Then we're agreed."

The meeting ended without ceremony. But as Sam left the room, he felt a certain sense of relief. The line had been drawn, and the truth was coming out.

* * *

Lewis sat at one of the long tables in the mess hall, tearing open the brown plastic pouch of the MRE. The air inside the facility smelled faintly stale, even with the ventilation system running again. The heaters hummed in the walls, and the fluorescent panels overhead flickered once before settling into a steady glow. The food looked the same as it always did—dense, colorless, and unappealing. Around him, the young people made faces as they poked at the contents of their trays.

Brad set down his fork with exaggerated frustration. "This tastes like cardboard dipped in salt."

Jessica smirked. "At least it's consistent."

Kiran gave a small laugh. "Consistent isn't the word I'd use."

Mei bit into her ration bar and wrinkled her nose. "Does it always taste this bad?"

""Yes," Lewis said simply, chewing through his own portion. He wasn't about to pretend otherwise. He had eaten more of these over the years than he cared to count. Complaining about them had never made them taste any better. The packets were designed to last on a shelf for years, to survive extremes of temperature and rough handling. Taste had never been a priority. Most of the entrées were bland, the textures off, and the seasoning far too heavy on salt to make up for everything else. The side items were no better—powdered drink mixes that never dissolved completely, crackers that broke into dry crumbs the moment you touched them, and dessert bars that clung to your teeth long after you'd finished chewing.

James leaned forward, squinting at the packet of rehydrated stew on his tray. The chunks of meat looked swollen, floating in a sauce that had separated into layers. "I can't believe people actually survived on this for months at a time."

They did," Lewis replied. "And they worked while doing it. Long shifts. Heavy labor. This was all they had, and it kept them alive. You'll be fine for a few days."

Brad tapped his spoon against his tray and groaned. "I'd trade my entire stash of ration bars if anyone's got something edible hidden in their pack. Even half a candy bar."

Jessica laughed. "You don't have anything worth trading. Who'd want a ration bar in exchange for real food?"

"Speak for yourself," Brad said, pointing at her tray. "I'd happily take your powdered mashed potatoes. At least you can pretend they're food."

"They taste like chalk," Jessica shot back.

"That's still a step up from cardboard," Brad said, lifting his fork dramatically.

Mei gave a shy grin. "When I was little, I used to think space food was going to be special. Like astronaut ice cream. I thought it would be colorful, maybe even fun." She looked down at the blocky ration bar in her hand. "This isn't what I pictured."

Kiran raised his eyebrows. "You thought it would be colorful?"

"Yes," Mei said firmly. "On TV, everything in space looked advanced. I thought the food would be too. Not... this."

Brad chuckled. "See? Even Mei agrees with me."

Lewis set down his fork and shook his head slightly. "Every generation thinks space will be different than it is. The truth is simple: you eat what you're given. You work. You move forward. There's no time to worry about whether you enjoy the taste."

"Easy for you to say," James muttered. He pushed a limp chunk of vegetable to the side of his tray. "You've had practice. We're new at this."

Lewis gave him an even look. "Then consider it training. Start small. If you can handle eating these for a few days without losing focus, you can handle worse."

Jessica tilted her head at him. "So you're saying choking down flavorless rations is a survival skill?"

"Yes," Lewis answered readily. "It's about discipline. Discipline keeps you alive."

Brad sighed and took another bite. "I still think discipline would taste better with some hot sauce."

That broke the tension, and laughter circled the table. Even Lewis allowed himself a small smile before finishing the last of his portion in silence.

Lewis let the conversation fade while he thought about the past two days. He hadn't known how long training would take, but they picked it up quickly—faster than he expected. The ship's controls weren't as complicated as most assumed. Built from alien tech, they responded almost directly to intention, intuitive in a way no car on Earth could match. Still, maneuvering through obstacles wasn't instinctive. Judging distance, predicting movement, shifting fields to avoid impact—those skills took practice. And they had practiced until they could handle it.

When he turned his attention back to the table, the group was still talking, their voices animated.

"Admit it," Brad said, pointing his fork at Mei, "you're the best pilot out of all of us so far."

Mei's eyes widened. "No, I'm not. James is better."

"Not true," James said at once. "You're smoother with the turns. Lewis saw it."

Mei looked up uncertain, glancing toward Lewis as if for confirmation.

He gave a single nod. "You're steady," he said. "You don't overcorrect. That's important."

Her whole face brightened at the words. She looked down quickly, but not before he noticed the way she was beaming.

"See?" Brad said triumphantly. "Kick-Ass Quartet is no more..."

"We were never the Kick-Ass Quartet," interrupted Jessica with a glare.

"...Now we're the Kick-Ass *Quintet*," finished Brad, winking at Mei.

Jessica raised an eyebrow. "That doesn't roll off the tongue."

Kiran smirked. "But it's accurate. Seriously."

The table broke into light laughter. Mei ducked her head again, but the pleased expression never left her face. Lewis noted it quietly. She had wanted to belong, and now she did.

After a few minutes, the talk shifted. Mei set down her fork and looked thoughtful. "I had a dream before we left. It was so clear, I can still see it now."

"What kind of dream?" Jessica asked, her tone sharpening. They had had experience with vivid dreams.

Mei paused before speaking. "My grandmother was holding the amulet—the one she gave me. A light came out of the little crystal in the middle and projected shapes. They floated in the air, one after another. They were patterns—three-dimensional, like geometry but alive. The patterns repeated over and over again. I can't explain it better than that."

The others grew quiet. Brad leaned forward, suddenly serious. "Did your grandmother say anything to you?"

Mei shook her head. "She just looked at me and smiled."

"That doesn't sound like just a dream," said Jess.

Kiran nodded. "Vivid dreams oftentimes mean something. They're not random."

James crossed his arms, thinking. "Especially with everything else going on. We should pay attention."

Jessica studied Mei carefully. "Did the patterns mean anything to you? Did you recognize them?"

Mei shook her head slowly. "Not really. But they felt important. Like they were meant to be remembered."

Lewis stayed silent, listening. He had heard of such things, but he didn't interrupt. Dreams had carried messages before. If this one did, they would figure it out in time.

Brad exhaled, leaning back. "First you turn out to be a natural pilot, and now you're having message dreams. You're full of surprises."

Mei looked startled by the attention, but she didn't shrink from it. "I just... thought you should know," she said.

"You were right to tell us," Jessica said firmly. "If it means something, we'll figure it out together."

Around the table, the others nodded in agreement.

Lewis took another bite of his ration and watched the group settle into the new rhythm. For two days, they had been students, straining to absorb everything he told them. Now, they were more than that. They were becoming a team, each of them pulling the others closer, each of them finding their place.

Chapter
Twenty-Eight

Mona leaned against the wall of the atrium, watching the five young people come in the front door. Two days was not long in the grand scheme of things, but something had shifted. They walked together with an ease she hadn't seen before. They were bumping shoulders, tossing words back and forth, laughing at inside jokes. Even Lewis, following behind, moved as if he were part of the group.

She wanted to let them enjoy it for a while longer, but the call from Mei's cousin Tian was still in her mind, and she couldn't put it off. She had known Mei would need to hear it from someone who cared about her, not just an unfriendly voice over the phone.

Mona stepped forward and raised a hand. "Mei," she said, keeping her tone quiet but firm enough to be heard.

Mei looked over, her smile faltering only slightly, then jogged a few steps to close the distance. "What's up?"

Mona didn't answer right away. She tilted her head toward a quieter corner of the atrium. Mei followed without question. When they were out of immediate earshot, Mona took a slow breath.

"I got a call earlier," Mona said. "From your cousin Tian."

The name brought a small crease to Mei's brow. "What did *he* want?"

Mona drew a breath, then delivered it as directly as she could. "Your grandmother passed away."

Mei didn't flinch or cry out. Instead, her face went still, as if a mask had slipped down in place. She lowered herself onto a nearby chair, controlled and quiet.

Mona kept her gaze even. "He said the family wouldn't welcome you at the ceremony. That you should stay away from the funeral parlor."

Mei's shoulders dropped a fraction, but nothing else changed. Her hands rested neatly on her knees. Her voice, when it came, was even and distant. "Of course he said that."

Mona felt the old irritation rise in her chest. Tian had been a student at their tai chi classes for several years. Self-absorbed, sharp-tongued, always ready with a criticism for someone else. Mei had been his favorite target. Mona had disliked him from the beginning, and this cruel phone call only deepened it—he had only called to make Mei suffer more.

"You don't deserve that," Mona said.

Mei didn't answer. She stared past Mona at nothing in particular, expression unreadable. Mona recognized it for what it was—years of practice hiding every reaction, every vulnerable part, behind that blankness.

The sound of footsteps drew closer. Mona turned to see Jessica leading the others over, concern written across all their faces. They must have noticed the shift in Mei's expression, the way her energy had dropped away from their easy camaraderie.

"What's wrong?" Jessica asked.

Brad looked from Mona to Mei, worry plain. "Something happened?"

James crouched down in front of Mei, searching her face. "Hey. You okay?"

Mona glanced at Mei, silently asking whether she wanted her to say it. Mei gave the slightest nod.

Mona spoke evenly. "Her grandmother has passed away. Tian called to tell her."

"Tian?" said James with contempt.

Mona knew that James disliked Tian as much as she did.

"He called to tell Mei that her grandmother died *and* that she wasn't welcome at any of the ceremonies," clarified Mona.

"So, rubbing it in." Brad's voice was full of disgust.

The group fell quiet. The joking atmosphere evaporated. Jessica's hand lifted and hovered near Mei's shoulder before she finally placed it gently there. "I'm so sorry."

Mona spoke up. "I know you are estranged from your family—with good reason—but I also know you loved your grandmother. And I know that your grandmother both cared for and respected you—you were the person she gave the the family heirloom to."

Mona was talking about the jade amulet

"I don't hold with people telling me who I can and can't love and honor," continued Mona, a tight control on her anger. "So I called around and found the funeral parlor where your grandmother's ceremony will be held. Until then, there's a wake in a viewing room."

Mei finally lifted her eyes and looked at Mona.

"The Rose Hills Mortuary in Alhambra," said Mona.

"I'm not ready to face my entire family—I can't go to the ceremony—but I would like to pay my respects beforehand."

Lewis, who had been a step behind the rest, finally spoke. And it was a statement, not a question. "We will go with you."

Mei looked up at him for a second, her blank expression cracking just enough for Mona to see the strain behind it. Then she straightened her back, returning to her composed mask.

Mona watched them close ranks around Mei without needing to discuss it. Their short training on Europa had knit them together in ways Mona hadn't expected. Now, even in silence, their unity showed. They didn't ask more questions. They just stayed near, forming a quiet shield around their friend.

Mona folded her arms and exhaled, her frustration with Tian simmering under the surface. Whatever poison he thought he was spreading, it wouldn't reach here. Mei wasn't alone.

Not anymore.

* * *

Mei sat. Breathing in. Breathing out. Her hands resting on her knees, and her back straight. The news of her grandmother's death had hit her hard, though she gave no outward sign. She had practiced this concealment for years. To show grief in front of people who would use it against her had never been safe. But the stillness did not make the pain any less sharp.

She loved her grandmother. The elderly woman had been stern, but Mei had felt seen by her in ways the rest of her family did not. Now that was gone. The loss was more than the end of a life. It was the end of a dream Mei had carried quietly—the dream that one day the others in her family might soften and look at her with approval instead of criticism. Her grandmother had been the one person who might have opened that door for her, who might have brought the rest of them around. With her gone, the door was closed for good.

While she hadn't been on the call with her cousin Tian, she knew what the words—relayed by Mona—really meant. In telling her not to come, he was saying to never think she would ever belong. He had always been that way, even as a boy. Now, nearly an adult, his disdain had only sharpened. It burned to hear it spoken so bluntly, even though she had long known it was true.

She lowered her gaze, letting her breath settle. Her thoughts slipped back to the last two days on Europa. The contrast was stark. There, she had not been unwanted. There, she had not been measured against impossible standards. She had sat at the controls of a spaceship and, after only a short explanation, felt the rhythm of the systems under her hands. When Lewis had told her to take them into orbit, she had done so with a steady hand. Brad had clapped her on the shoulder afterward. Kiran had said, with a grin, that she flew cleaner than he did. James and Jessica had cheered, their voices rising in support. Even Lewis had given her one of his quiet nods that meant more than most words.

They had called her part of them now. Not the outsider who sometimes tagged along, but officially inside the circle. The *Five*. She belonged.

That memory steadied her now. She let herself feel the grief for her grandmother, but she refused to let Tian's voice define her. She would find her own way to say goodbye—to honor the woman who had mattered to her. Family obligations still weighed on her, but they no longer had the power to hold her back.

Her family was *here*. Jessica, Brad, James, Kiran, and Lewis. They were the ones who celebrated her successes instead of cutting them down. They were the ones who made space for her without condition.

She straightened her back once more, her eyes clear. Whatever Tian thought, whatever the others said or withheld, she knew where she belonged now.

* * *

Amanda pressed her back against the cold brick wall and tried to slow her breathing. Her chest rose and fell rapidly, her own pulse pounding in her ears. Only minutes ago, she had been walking down the street, lost in thoughts about the latest round of rejections, when the sharp crack split the air.

She knew that sound. It wasn't a car backfiring. It wasn't a door slamming, a balloon popping, or a jackhammer on a construction site. Her father had taken her shooting every summer when she was a teenager, and her brothers owned firearms. She recognized it immediately.

It was a bullet being fired.

She hadn't seen the shooter. She hadn't even seen where the shot had landed. But she had heard the sharp impact against metal just a few feet in front of her. She had ducked around the corner and flattened herself against the rough wall, her eyes scanning the shadows.

For weeks she had told herself the warnings were exaggerated. Editors at national outlets had given her polite declines. The story wasn't their mission. It didn't fit their focus. They didn't have the resources to handle something of that scale. Then came the one editor who leaned closer, lowering his voice, saying it was too dangerous. She had scoffed when she left his office. Too dangerous to print the truth? Too dangerous to do the work of journalism? She had been convinced he was making excuses. Just like the others.

Yesterday she had nearly been clipped by a speeding car while crossing the street. The driver had come out of nowhere, tires screeching as the vehicle cut so close its side mirror brushed her jacket. At the time, she told herself it was just an impatient commuter.

But now—with the sound of the gunshot still ringing in her ears—the memory felt different. What if it hadn't been an accident? What if someone had already been trying to silence her?

Amanda lifted her head, eyes darting from one end of the alley to the other. Nothing moved. No more gunshots. A woman passed by the corner, glanced in, then kept walking.

Amanda forced herself to stay still. If someone was watching, any sudden movement could give her away.

The story she was trying to publish was real. That had never been in doubt. She had documents and first-hand testimony, and the pieces all fit together into something bigger than anything she had ever worked on. In her mind, it was the story of the century.

She had expected editors to fight over it. Instead, she was met with silence, closed doors—and finally, an uneasy warning. She hadn't let that stop her. Not until now.

Her thoughts spun through the few options she had. If someone was willing to shoot at her in broad daylight, what did that mean for the security of her apartment? Her phone? Her email accounts?

She thought of all the hours she had spent at her desk—typing notes, saving files in folders on her laptop.

If they wanted to, whoever was behind this could already know everything about her. Every place she had been. Every contact she had made.

She couldn't go to the police. What would she say? That she had a story she couldn't publish, and now someone was trying to kill her? Without proof, without evidence beyond the sound of a gunshot and a close call with a car, she doubted they would take her seriously. Worse, what if some of them were already compromised?

Amanda shifted her weight, the brick wall rough against her back. She needed to decide quickly. Staying exposed on the street was a mistake. But where could she go that no one would find her? A hotel would require her name and credit card. Friends' houses would be obvious. A relative's place was out of the question.

She thought of the city's outskirts—motels that took cash, places where no one asked questions. She could disappear there, at least for a short while, long enough to decide her next move. She would have to change her routine. No phone. No social media. No predictable patterns.

Amanda inhaled slowly, forcing her hands to still. She pulled away from the wall and scanned the alley once more. Nothing. Her heart was still pounding, but her legs obeyed when she told them to move. She kept close to the buildings, ready to dive again if she had to.

Dangerous, the editor had said. She had dismissed it then. But now she knew he had been right.

How far did the danger would reach? Did she have anyplace left to hide?

Chapter
Twenty-Nine

T he van moved through the quiet streets of Alhambra. The dashboard clock showed it was nearly midnight. Mei sat still, hands folded in her lap, watching the dark rows of storefronts slide past.

She had chosen this late hour because there would be fewer visitors. Even so, her grandmother's body would not be left unattended—the mortuary staff would remain, and family members would keep vigil until the cremation. Mei knew some of them would still be there when she arrived.

She had thought about waiting until the next day, but there would be fewer relatives in the middle of the night, and she wanted to avoid confrontation. All she wanted was a moment to bow, burn her offering, and say her goodbye.

The van turned into the driveway of Rose Hills Memorial Park. The mortuary was lit, but the wide parking lot was mostly empty. Lewis found a space near the main entrance.

Jessica, Brad, James, and Kiran stepped out with her, their footsteps echoing softly against the pavement in the still night. They had all insisted on coming. Mei had told them it wasn't necessary, but they hadn't budged. She had let it go.

Now, surrounded by them, she felt a quiet gratitude.

Inside, the air was cool and smelled faintly of incense. At the reception desk, an attendant looked up and offered a short nod. Mei gave her grandmother's name. The attendant gestured down a long hallway. "Lotus Room," she said simply.

They walked in silence, the polished floors reflecting the overhead lights. The Lotus Room door was slightly open. Mei pushed it wider and entered.

The room was spacious but subdued. Rows of chairs lined either side of a central aisle. At the far end stood the casket, raised on a platform and draped in white cloth. A table nearby held incense sticks, candles, and a metal urn for burning offerings. A few vases of flowers stood against the walls.

But Mei immediately saw she was not alone. Half a dozen family members sat scattered among the chairs at the front—an uncle she barely knew, two aunts, and several cousins. And Tian.

They looked up as she entered. Some faces showed surprise, but most narrowed with disapproval. No one spoke.

Mei gave no sign of recognition. She walked forward slowly, her friends following a respectful distance behind her.

At the casket, she bowed three times. She drew the folded paper amulet from her pocket. She had made it earlier, cutting and shaping the paper to mirror the jade amulet her grandmother had gifted her. Holding it now, she felt its lightness against her palm. She touched a match to the edge, watching the flame take, and placed it into the urn. The paper darkened, curled, and turned to ash. The faint smoke rose into the air.

She stood still, eyes lowered, letting the offering burn down. Behind her, she heard the quiet shifting of chairs. The other mourners watched, their silence heavy with judgment.

Then the sound of footsteps came from the side. Mei turned her head. She had expected to see Tian approaching; instead, it was her mother. She wore a dark dress and carried herself with the same rigid posture Mei had grown up seeing. Her expression was cold.

"So you came after all," her mother said, her voice low but sharp. "And at midnight, like a thief slipping in. Burning scraps of paper, as if that means anything. Do you think this makes up for all your failures? Do you think this honors her?"

The words landed with the familiar sting. For years Mei had absorbed them, swallowing each insult, showing no outward resistance. But something inside her had shifted.

She faced her mother, but her words were for everyone else in the room—her voice was calm, clear... and dismissive. "I don't recognize this woman standing in front of me."

The room went still. Family members looked up, startled. Her mother's eyes widened, shock breaking through the hard mask on her face. She had never heard Mei answer back like this. She had expected silence, the same quiet acceptance that had always followed her criticism.

But Mei hadn't shouted or cried. She hadn't lowered her head in shame. Instead, she had made one thing unmistakably clear: she no longer saw this woman as her mother, and she no longer accepted her place in the family as defined by their disapproval.

Her mother opened her mouth as if to reply, but no words came. She stood frozen, her expression shifting between disbelief and offense.

Mei did not give her the chance to recover. She turned away. The rest of the Five had risen from their seats and came over protectively. Lewis stepped forward last, silent but solid.

Together, they formed a quiet line behind Mei as she walked down the aisle. She didn't look back at her mother, or at the cousins whispering among themselves. The only sound was the measured steps of her group leaving the room.

* * *

The air in the common area of the old flower shop carried the faint aroma of brewed tea and coffee mixed with the sweetness of

cocoa. James had his hands wrapped around a mug of hot chocolate. Jessica and Brad had mugs of coffee. Kiran and Mei were both
drinking tea.

James's eyes went to Mei. She had changed so much in the past
couple of months that it was hard to remember what she had been
like before. Back then, she had been a little loud, a little awkward,
and always tense, as if waiting for someone to blame her for something. And that was only in tai chi class. He knew that at home she
had been the family scapegoat, a role she had accepted because it was
what her family expected of her.

Now she sat with her back straight, her face calm, and radiating
a confident energy. She was the youngest person here—only a few
months younger than James himself—but she had shown more
courage than most people ever would. It took real guts to leave her
family, and just hours earlier at her grandmother's vigil, to stand
before them and declare her independence.

James caught himself staring and pulled his attention back to
the conversation. Mei was speaking, and the others were listening
carefully.

"In my dream," she said, "my grandmother was holding the
amulet. She didn't say anything. At first she only stared at it, and
then a thin beam of light shot up from the little crystal in the center.
After that, shapes began to form—eight of them—one after another, turning so I could see each one clearly. The sequence repeated
three times. Then my grandmother looked up at me, smiled, and
handed me the amulet."

James cleared his throat and everyone looked over at him.

"I'd like to point out," he said, "that Mei's grandmother was in
the hospital when Mei had that dream. In his call, Tian scolded Mei
for not visiting during the week when she was in the hospital in a
coma. Of course he didn't bother to let her know until the day after
she passed away."

"So Mei's grandmother was in a coma—a different level of consciousness—and that's when she reached out with a message for her," Kiran agreed.

The others nodded.

Jessica leaned forward, tilting her head slightly. "What shapes did you see?"

Mei lifted a hand, ticking them off one by one. "The first was some sort of geometric shape I didn't recognize. The second was a cube. The two after that I didn't recognize either. The fifth shape was a pyramid. The sixth was another mystery shape. The seventh looked like lightning bolts—zigzag lines breaking outward. The last one looked like a donut, but it moved, like it was spinning or flowing."

The others looked at her in surprise.

"I had the feeling I was supposed to remember them—both the shapes, and the order they came in," explained Mei. "Like I said, I don't have any idea what four of the shapes were, but I'd remember them if I saw them again."

Jessica stood up, grabbed a marker, and began writing on the whiteboard that stood against the wall. She wrote quickly:

1. Unknown

2. Cube

3. Unknown

4. Unknown

5. Pyramid

6. Unknown

7. Lightning Bolts

8. Spinning Donut

She turned back to the group. "All right. Does this mean anything?"

Kiran spoke up. "The spinning donut—that sounds like a torus."

Brad nodded immediately. "Definitely. A torus has a donut-shaped surface. The energy flowing through it makes it dynamic. That makes sense."

"Okay, torus then," Jessica said, erasing *Spinning Donut* and replacing it with *Torus*. "So what about the rest?"

Brad opened his laptop and shifted so the screen was visible to the group. "Let's run through some of the classical geometric shapes. Maybe one will click."

The glow of the screen lit his face as he pulled up a list of Platonic solids. "First, tetrahedron. At first glance you'd think it's a pyramid, but it has four triangular faces—the three sides and the base. A true pyramid has four triangular faces and a square base.."

Mei leaned forward. "Yes. That was one of them—the fourth one."

Brad clicked to the next. "Cube—already got that. Next, octahedron. Eight triangular faces."

"That one too," Mei said quickly. "Number six."

Brad smiled, clicking further. "Dodecahedron. Twelve pentagonal faces."

Mei pointed at the screen. "That was the first one."

Brad brought up the last of the main five. "Icosahedron. Twenty triangular faces."

Mei sat back slightly, her eyes narrowing in thought. Then she nodded. "Yes. That was number three."

Jessica turned back to the board and began writing again, her marker squeaking against the surface, substituting dodecahedron, icosahedron, tetrahedron, and octahedron for shapes 1, 3, 4, and 6.

She capped the marker and looked at Mei. "So that's all eight. Are you sure?"

Mei nodded. "Yes. In the dream, it was like I had to learn them. Even though I didn't know what some of them were, I memorized what they looked like."

James took a slow sip of his hot chocolate. He was impressed—not just by Mei's memory, but by the clarity with which she explained it.

Kiran leaned back in his chair, tapping the edge of his teacup. "That's interesting. The Platonic solids plus a pyramid, a torus, and lightning bolts. That makes eight exactly. And we're trying to figure out the Eight Gates. Normal people would say it's a coincidence, but I think we can all agree that our lives aren't normal anymore."

James started laughing and snorted some hot chocolate.

Brad's eyes were on the laptop screen, his fingers busy as he typed. "The Platonic solids are often tied to elements. Tetrahedron is fire, cube is earth, octahedron is wind or wood, icosahedron is water, dodecahedron is ether or heaven. The torus is about flow, cycles, maybe energy fields. Pyramid... that could be stability or focus. Lightning bolts... well, that's force. Disruption."

Jessica wrote those associations next to the list on the board. She underlined the words as if to fix them in place. "So, can we agree Mei's dream wasn't random? Her grandmother wanted her to remember the shapes for a reason."

Mei's expression didn't change, but her fingers tightened around her teacup. "I think so too. But it's also connected to the amulet."

Kiran leaned forward, resting his elbows on his knees. "Do you think the amulet itself is the key? Or is it about the shapes?"

Mei looked at him. "Both. The amulet holds them, but the shapes are the lesson. I don't know why yet. But I know I need to keep them in mind."

James looked at everyone. They were forgetting something.

"Don't forget tai chi," he said. The others looked at him blankly.

"It all started with tai chi," he reminded them patiently. "Meeting Melly in meditation, getting our junk DNA upgraded, and everything else. We're trying to figure out the Eight Gates of interstellar travel, but we shouldn't forget that tai chi also has eight gates."

"You're right," said Jessica, slowly. "But where would they fit in this list?"

"The trigrams," James said. "The trigrams on Mei's amulet and the trigrams of tai chi. Each one is tied to a direction—north, south, east, west, and the points in between. The numbers and shapes you've written down"—he nodded at the whiteboard—"are also associated with directions. If each shape represents a Gate—an interstellar portal—and they're in sequence..." He glanced at Mei, who gave a quick nod. "Then Gate #1—the dodecahedron—connected with heaven, would also link to the trigram for heaven and the direction south. In tai chi, the movement tied to this is *Lü*, or *Roll-Back*. Its energy is about redirecting and neutralizing."

"Ok, this is getting complicated," muttered Brad.

It was. And it took them another hour to come up with an outline of what they were finding out.

THE EIGHT GATES

1. Gate One: Dodecahedron, Heaven, South, *Peng* (Ward Off)

2. Gate Two: Cube, Earth, North, *Lü* (Roll-Back)

3. Gate Three: Icosahedron, Water, West, *Ji* (Press)

4. Gate Four: Tetrahedron, Fire, East, *An* (Press Down)

5. Gate Five: Pyramid, Mountain, Northwest, *Kao* (Shoulder Strike)

6. Gate Six: Octahedron, Wind/Wood, Southwest, *Cai* (Pluck)

7. Gate Seven: Zigzag pattern, Thunder, Northeast, *Lie* (Split)

8. Gate Eight: Torus, Lake/Marsh, Southeast, *Zhou* (Elbow Strike)

The group fell quiet for a moment, each of them considering the list on the board. None of them understanding what it meant.

"Maybe it's a cheat code," suggested Brad. "But I don't think we can do this by ourselves."

James nodded.

"We need to talk to the Bridgewalkers."

Chapter Thirty

Representative Brandori stood at the far end of the chamber, hands folded behind his back, while Varan faced him from the other side of the rectangular table that anchored the room. The crystal walls glowed faintly with the rhythmic pulse of the city's energy network, but neither of them looked at the surroundings. Their focus was inward as they spoke mind-to-mind—the default method of communication between adult Alpha Centaurians. It was a sign of respect.

"It is not wise to permit your young ones to mingle so freely with the Suedes and the humans. You know the history. You know what was nearly lost because of recklessness," said Varan.

Brandori bit back a sharp reply. He had wondered why this Alpha Centaurian—a member of the Galactic Council—wanted to meet with him. He had imagined the Council might finally be ready to welcome the Earth ACs back into intergalactic life—to restore their voices after a millennium of hiding.

Instead, he found that Varan was here not as a Council member, but as a politician concerned only with reputation. It had been thousands of years since the ACs on Earth had been able to communicate with their home planet, and now this man was *lecturing* him.

Brandori drew in a breath, smoothing out the energy of his mind speech. "*The danger is not forgotten. We live with it every day. Yet you speak as though I have never given the warnings myself. I have told the young ones. They have been cautioned.*"

Representative Brandori wasn't about to tell this self-important spacer that the issue of young ACs meeting with the Suedes and humans had driven a wedge between the adults and the teenagers in their community. He would not be spoken to as if he were a child.

"*And yet they are not cautious,*" replied Varan. "*They join in group activities, they speak freely, they exchange ideas about accessing interstellar portals. It should not be allowed. The humans do not understand the risks. The Suedes are too eager. The shame will fall on all Alpha Centaurians, as it did before.*"

Brandori bristled at the words. Varan showed no concern for the struggles of their youth or for the fragile balance the Earth ACs worked to maintain between caution and growth. All he cared about was how their actions might look to the rest of the galaxy. Varan wasn't a kinsman offering support—he was a politician protecting appearances, blind to the cost of survival his people on Earth had paid for thousands of years.

"*You speak as though we are reckless children,*" Brandori answered. "*We are not. You, who live among the stars, know Earth's history only through records. We know it because we live it every day. For thousands of years, we've endured the consequences without any help. For thousands of years, you kept your distance. And now you come to us acting as if you have the right to decide how we should live? You do not.*"

Varan's thought was sharp. "*The Earth disaster is why you should be more careful now. This could affect all Alpha Centaurians. If you dismiss my counsel, you will likely repeat the same foolish mistakes your ancestors made.*"

Brandori didn't say anything. He couldn't without saying something he might regret.

Varan continued, *"I am offering guidance. Guidance that I acquired through long service in the Galactic Council. I pass it on to you because you have been cut off for so long, and you no longer understand your place among Alpha Centaurians. You no longer remember your duty."*

He dares! Brandori's anger flared, then settled into a cold burn. The time for being polite had passed. Now when he spoke, he did so out loud, no longer using the mind-to-mind speech of adults.

"It is time for us to agree that we have changed. You call us Alpha Centaurians, but that name no longer fits us. We are not the same as those who live among the stars. We are not your people. We are Earth's people. We are Earthlings now."

Varan barked out a harsh laugh, responding in kind. "Earthlings? You would throw away your own kind to claim allegiance to those who live in pettiness and ignorance? You live up to your ancestors' reputation."

Brandori's voice did not rise; if anything, it grew softer. Varan had just made the decision easy for him.

"You offer no solutions, only scorn. You have no right to stand here and speak as if we are beneath you."

For the first time, Varan's composure cracked. His face tightened, his mouth drawn hard, and his words were spoken with contempt.

"Then you are lost. You cut yourselves off not only from us but from your own name. I will not waste more words on those who choose to shame themselves."

He turned sharply, the movement abrupt and dismissive, his cloak brushing against the chamber floor as he strode toward the exit. The crystalline walls picked up the sound of his steps, each one echoing. He did not look back.

Brandori remained where he stood. This had been unexpected. The other ACs in the city would be angry with him—not for what he said, since Brandori would make sure they knew exactly what

Varan thought of them—but for making the decision without their input.

Still, the time for regrets had passed. What mattered now was the path forward.

Vicki had once mentioned that the ACs should consider leading seminars on architecture and building methods. Maybe the Bridgewalkers could help him arrange that.

* * *

Amanda left the condo before sunrise with two duffel bags and a backpack. Her hands were steady—she couldn't afford to lose control. The night before had taken care of that.

The police had stood in her living room for almost an hour, checking the window and the footprints below it, asking for a description she couldn't give. They only came because her next-door neighbor had called. He'd seen the figure at her window, phoned it in, and shouted until the intruder fled.

Creepy Lyle always watched her condo. He always found a reason to talk to her. He called her "sweetheart," winked, and had already asked her out three times.

He also may have just kept a break-in from becoming something worse.

By morning, her condo looked as if a storm had passed through. Every drawer was open, shoes were scattered across the floor, and last summer's suitcase sat half-packed as she tossed items in and pulled them out again.

She forced herself to think about blending in, not standing out. She chose simple clothes—two pairs of jeans, one pair of black slacks, three button-downs, two sweaters, underclothes, sneakers, flats, and a windbreaker. She rolled everything tight, filling the gaps with chargers, a notebook, and a box of pens. She emptied her medicine cabinet into a zip-lock bag. She pulled her passport and social security card from her desk drawer.

Then she closed the door behind her—and didn't look back.

At the bank, Amanda stood in line behind retirees and a contractor in a paint-stained hoodie. When the teller asked if she wanted a cashier's check, she said cash. When asked how much, she slid a piece of paper with the amount written on it across the counter.

The teller's eyes widened, and she called over the manager. He asked Amanda if she felt safe. She said yes, even though it wasn't true—it was just what she had to say to end the conversation.

After signing the forms, Amanda left with one envelope tucked inside another. She stopped at a pharmacy, bought a cheap tote, slipped the cash inside, and stuffed it all into her backpack.

By late morning, she was across the city at her cousin's house. She parked a block away, walked the rest, and knocked. Elise answered in socks and a bathrobe, her hair tied back.

Amanda smiled—people usually gave in when she did—and asked if she could borrow her Civic for a few days. She explained that she was working on an important story and needed a plain car she could use on a stakeout. Elise's eyes lit up. When Amanda asked her to keep it quiet, she agreed—on the condition that Amanda promise to tell her everything once it was over.

They traded keys in the kitchen—Elsie's Civic for Amanda's sporty Miata. The Civic was a hand-me-down from Elise's parents and had a scratch on the rear door and a coffee stain on the front passenger seat. It would be perfect for staying under the radar.

As she drove out of the city, she thought about where to go. When Jerry and Sam had given her the evidence for the Tall Whites trade agreement, they'd warned her there would be backlash. She had their numbers, and both men were smart—they could probably help her figure something out. But they also lived nearby. If someone was watching her, they were probably watching them too. She crossed both names off her mental list and kept her eyes on the road.

The truth was, she couldn't trust *any* of her usual contacts anymore. Someone had warned off the news agencies—the last two she'd reached out to shut her down before she could even explain the story. She racked her brain. Had one of the friends she'd shared her excitement with alerted the authorities because she had classified material? Or was it someone in one of the newsrooms? It didn't matter now—she needed to find someone no one would expect her to contact. Someone everyone knew was her enemy.

The first hour didn't feel real. The highway signs were the same ones she had driven past for years. The sidewalks held the same runners and dog walkers. She repeatedly checked her rearview mirror. A black SUV followed for three exits and then turned off. A white sedan passed and cut in front of her, then vanished. She kept to the speed limit and moved with the traffic.

By midday, she pulled into a gas station just off the interstate. She filled the tank and bought an old-fashioned paper map from a rack near the door. The cashier rang her up without ever looking at her face.

Outside, she sat in the car and mapped a route west—mostly interstate, then smaller highways. She had decided: her destination was the Pacific coast. Someone now lived there whom no one would expect her to turn to.

By late afternoon, she reached a small town with three motels, two fast-food places, and a grocery store. She chose the motel with a vacancy sign and a front desk behind glass. She paid in cash, declined the loyalty card and Wi-Fi password. The clerk slid a key card across the counter and pointed to a map of the property with her room circled.

The room smelled of cleaning chemicals. The bedspread was patterned with squares. She wedged the chair under the door handle and propped the luggage rack against the sliding window. She charged her phone for ten minutes, then turned it off.

She lay on top of the bedspread, fully dressed, and set the alarm on a small travel clock. Sleep came in short bursts. Twice she woke and listened. The parking lot was still except for a delivery truck passing through and a couple arguing beside a pickup.

At dawn she was back on the road. She kept her stops brief. Coffee. Gas. A sandwich. She sent a single text to Elise from a prepaid phone she had picked up at a big box store before crossing the state line: *Car runs fine. Be back soon.* She switched the phone off and removed the battery, storing it in the glove box.

The miles added up. The Civic ran smoothly. State lines slowly came and went. The country opened and folded again into cities. The weather stayed mild. She kept the radio off. She didn't want company or noise—she wanted distance.

On the morning of the fourth day she placed a call to someone who was surprised to hear from her. The line rang four times before a voice answered.

"Hello, who's calling?"

"It's Amanda Riley—don't hang up," she said. "Please, don't hang up."

There was silence on the other end.

Amanda continued. I'm on the road, heading west, just a few hours out of LA. I can't explain everything now, but I need a place to stay. A place to hide. Just for a few days, nothing more. I won't be a problem—I promise."

Another pause, the voice was incredulous. "You're serious?"

"I am. I wouldn't ask if it wasn't necessary." There was desperation in her voice—she hated that.

Silence stretched, then the voice returned, softer. "All right. I'll give you an address where we can meet. I'll find a way to make it work."

Amanda closed her eyes for a moment. "Thank you, Vicki. I owe you."

Chapter Thirty-One

The old bank building was quiet except for the low murmur of conversation as the Bridgewalkers gathered in the atrium. Folding tables and chairs had been set out, but were pushed aside so everyone could sit together on the floor. Humans, Alpha Centaurians, and Suedes mixed into a single group rather than clustering by species. That was deliberate.

Jessica had spoken quietly with Junia before the meeting, and together they made sure the young people didn't sit only with their own kind. The message was clear: they were meant to be one team, not three separate groups pretending to cooperate.

Jessica had assumed the jade amulet would be the first—and maybe only—topic of the meeting, but before she could speak, one of the ACs cleared her throat.

"We need to tell you what Representative Brandori announced yesterday—it affects all of us here," said Astran, glancing nervously at Nevik and Calix. "The Alpha Centaurians here on Earth have officially declared our independence from our Alpha Centauri home planet—and from the rest of our species. Brandori has proclaimed we are Earthlings now. Not Alpha Centaurians."

The words echoed in the atrium, and all the young people sat up straighter. Jessica frowned. "What does that mean exactly?"

"It means our people will no longer take orders from the Alpha Centaurians who stayed in the stars—the spacer ACs," said Nevik, the word *spacer* clearly meant as an insult. "We will make our own decisions as Earth citizens. We will act in the best interests of Earth ACs—and in the best interests of this planet, not Alpha Centaurians as a whole."

Kiran nodded slowly. "So you're not just visitors anymore. You're invested."

"Yes," Astran said. "And because of that, we're freer to work with all of you. Before, we were ordered to hold back. Now, we're being told to help."

Calix piped up. "Representative Brandori and the Alpha Centaurian from the Federation had a fight."

Jessica covered her mouth to keep from laughing as Astran glared at Calix. Luckily for him, they were seated on opposite ends of the circle. Nevik hurriedly picked up the story.

"But it also means we won't have access to the benefits of Galactic Federation membership. Before we declared ourselves Earthlings, we had the right to request transport to other star systems. Now, we are planet-bound, the same as everyone else here. Unless we find a way to travel through Sol Gate, we are all trapped together."

"Well, we have a spaceship," said James. "We also have the jade amulet and a possible cheat code."

A sudden outpouring of surprised chatter followed as the Five explained what they had done—stealing the spaceship from the Partnership's underground bay, learning to fly it, the geometric forms projected from the amulet in Mei's dream, and how those shapes matched the trigrams and the eight gates of tai chi.

In response to questions, Jessica opened a notebook and flipped through pages filled with diagrams. "We've matched trigrams to tai chi gates. For example, the trigram for Thunder connects with the tai chi force of *lie*, which is opposing forces moving in different directions . The trigram for Mountain connects with *kao*, the shoulder or whole body force. There are overlaps, but not perfect ones. The amulet seems to bridge the gaps."

Tara, one of the high school students, raised her hand. "So you're saying it might be a translator of sorts? Between systems?"

Brad shook his head. "Not a translator. More like a stabilizer. If we can align movements, the trigram patterns, and the geometry at the same time, the amulet should resonate. We've tried it, but haven't had any success."

"Well, Melly *did* say the amulet could only be activated through a joint effort of all three Earth species—human, Suede, and AC," James said. "If only humans tried to use it, it was bound to fail."

Nevik's expression grew intent. "So the amulet is keyed to group alignment, not individual use?"

James nodded. "It requires cooperation, at least at first. It's actually a test to see if Earth's peoples can work together. If so, we prove we're worthy of interstellar travel. Melly told us that once we successfully pass through Sol Gate as a group, we'll have the freedom afterward to travel independently if that's what we want."

Astran looked around at the group. "Then it's time to test together. No more holding back. We'll share everything our elders taught us. They told us to keep it secret, but we're Earthlings now, and that changes everything. This is our responsibility too."

The young people shifted and traded glances across the circle. Even though it had gotten late, nobody looked eager to break off the meeting.

Jessica closed her notebook and set it on the floor. "Then the next step is simple," she said. "We test what we can, with everyone involved. No theories left untried."

Heads nodded around the atrium. The amulet, the spaceship, the gates—none of it would sort itself out. If they were going to make progress, it would be by putting in the work side by side.

* * *

Junia sat cross-legged on the atrium floor, the cold marble pressing through her clothing. Around her, the Bridgewalkers huddled in small clusters, speaking in low voices, passing the jade amulet from hand to hand. The light above was dim, but she could see the green surface catch every movement, alive with faint patterns that none of them had yet learned to control.

She felt proud of them. Proud of what they were doing together. Suedes, Humans, and Alpha Centaurians, all together in one circle. They hadn't listened when their elders told them what to do. Every one of them had disobeyed warnings. Every one of them had broken rules. They wanted change, and they had decided to make it happen.

She felt especially proud of the young Suedes. Even though they couldn't be a long time away from the Earth, they were here helping the humans and the ACs learn how to do something the Suedes could not—travel to the stars. That was the test—the amulet required all three species. Without the Suedes, there could be no passage through Sol Gate.

Junia's gaze drifted to the doors. She wondered where Vicki was. Her human friend had said she quit her important job to spend more time with the Bridgewalkers. If that was true, why wasn't she here now? Junia had expected her to be standing among them, helping and guiding.

Junia kept her thoughts to herself. The others were focused, leaning over the amulet, trading notes and diagrams, experimenting with careful gestures. She stayed quiet, proud and watchful. The Bridgewalkers were strong, stronger than she had hoped, stronger than anyone had expected. She couldn't wait to tell Alun all about it.

This was going to be *fun!*

* * *

Amanda entered the coffee shop, shoulders tight, eyes darting around the room. She spotted Vicki already seated at a corner table, back to the wall, with a half-finished cup of coffee in front of her. Amanda took a breath before walking over. She hated being in this position—asking Vicki for help after everything she had written about her. Every headline, every column criticizing Vicki and the Disclosure movement seemed to echo in her head. The humiliation of having to sit down and ask for help was almost more than she could stand.

But there was no one else. She would be safe with her enemy.

Vicki looked up, her expression calm, voice even. "You came."

Amanda slid into the chair opposite her. "I didn't have much choice."

"You always have a choice," Vicki replied, watching her carefully. "So why now?"

Amanda gripped her cup of coffee too tightly. "Because someone has been trying to kill me."

Vicki's expression sharpened. "Tell me."

Amanda recounted the incidents of the past week—nearly being hit by a car, the gunshot, and the attempted break-in at her condo.

"I know why it happened," she said. "I'm trying to publish the story about the Tall Whites trade deal. I have the documents—names, memos, the official procedures for discrediting human victims, even the signed trade agreement itself."

Vicki sat back. "And you think I should help you because...?"

Amanda's face flushed.

"Because I don't trust the police. Because I no longer trust my friends or media contacts—someone must have talked. Because I don't know who's watching me. And because this is all tied to the Partnership, and you—your people—you were the ones who took them down. I know you'd want this story to come out."

Vicki studied her for a long moment. Amanda fought the urge to fidget. She needed to look credible, not desperate.

"You've written enough about me to ruin my reputation ten times over," Vicki said at last. "Why should I believe you aren't just trying to get closer, to sniff around for another exposé?"

"Because I wouldn't humiliate myself like this for a scoop," Amanda shot back. "You think I like sitting here, begging for help from someone I criticized in print—from someone I don't even like? I'm here because I don't want to die."

After several seconds, Vicki nodded slightly and—to Amanda's surprise—smiled.

"Fine. But understand this—you need to follow instructions."

Amanda exhaled shakily. "What do you want me to do?"

Vicki pulled out her phone and tapped in a number. Amanda heard her say, "Mona? It's me. We've got a situation—Amanda Riley. She's here and needs a safe place to stay."

Amanda couldn't hear Mona's words on the other end, but the tone was unmistakably furious. Vicki listened for a while, expression neutral, before continuing.

"Yes, I've checked her. She's telling the truth, and she has a story we'd like to see publicized. So what do we need to do to make sure that happens? Lewis handles security—what would he recommend? Can you put him on the phone?"

Amanda's body felt heavy. Days of stress and driving pressed down on her all at once. She drifted in and out of focus, dimly aware of Vicki's voice.

"All right," Vicki said into the phone. "We can put a cot in one of the offices off the atrium and let her stay there. Surveillance? Audio only—tell Brad to install it, but no video. That's a step too far. He wants to know whether she has a car?"

Vicki glanced at Amanda and raised an eyebrow. Amanda nodded wearily.

"Yes, she does." Vicki listened for a moment, then "A chop shop? Seriously? Fine. Can you have someone pick it up from here?"

Amanda pressed her lips together. The Civic wasn't even hers—it was her cousin's. Guilt pricked at her, but she tried to reason it away. Her cousin still had the Miata, and that was the better car anyway. Anyone would prefer to keep that one. She repeated the thought until she believed it.

"Two hours will be fine," Vicki said into the phone. "Bring Brad when you pick us up—he'll want to take a look at her electronics before anything goes near the Five."

When Vicki ended the call, Amanda tried to sound calmer than she felt. "You're made arrangements?"

"Yes."

"You're dismantling my life."

"We're keeping you alive. If someone's tracking you, any detail could put you at risk."

"Safe but caged," Amanda muttered.

"Temporarily," Vicki said. "Until we're sure no one can use you to get to us. Until after you publish your story, and no one can bury the truth by killing you."

"Who are Lewis and Brad?"

"Lewis is security. He'll escort you whenever you leave the building. Brad's technical. He'll install audio surveillance in your room. That way, if you try anything that could hurt us, we'll know."

Amanda looked down at her coffee. Cold now. She hadn't touched it.

"So I become your prisoner?"

"You become someone who lives long enough to finish her story," Vicki corrected. "Unless you'd rather take your chances outside."

The words stung because they were true. Amanda was desperate enough to accept. She gave a short nod. "I'll do it."

Vicki's posture eased slightly. "Good. Then we wait here until they confirm everything's ready."

Time stretched. They sat in the coffee shop, conversations and the clatter of dishes filling the background. Vicki checked her phone now and then, scanning the room whenever the door opened. Amanda picked at a muffin without tasting it, trying not to imagine eyes watching her, men with guns waiting outside. The humiliation pressed down, but beneath it ran a current of stubborn resolve. If she survived this, she would get her story out. No one was going to silence her.

Two hours later, Vicki's phone buzzed. She read the message, then looked at Amanda.

"They're ready. We'll leave by the back door. Someone will meet us outside."

Amanda gathered her bag. It felt lighter than it had that morning, as if part of her life had already been erased. She followed Vicki through the narrow hallway, out into the alley, and toward whatever came next out of this uncomfortable alliance.

Chapter
Thirty-Two

Lewis waited at the curb outside the back entrance of the coffee shop, engine running. Brad sat in the passenger seat, his jaw tight, hands still. He had been silent the entire drive. Lewis knew why. Amanda Riley had smeared Jessica in the media, writing pieces that were personal and deliberately cruel. Brad hadn't forgotten. Brad was working hard not to take revenge.

Vicki stepped out first, scanning the sidewalk, with Amanda close behind. Lewis got out and held the back door open. Both women climbed in. He noticed Amanda's features—pretty, but tense and washed out.

Without offering a greeting, Brad turned in his seat.

"Phone," he demanded.

Amanda hesitated, then handed it over.

Brad powered it on and ran a quick check, his eyes moving over the list of background programs. He went through the outgoing connections one by one, watching the indicators without saying anything. When he was satisfied, he shut it down and set it on his knee.

"It's a burner," Amanda said. "I bought it when I left Washington."

Lewis gave her points for that. He liked people who were careful enough to protect themselves. People who weren't careful got hurt.

Brad didn't say anything. He opened a utility on his own device, connected the burner, and wiped it clean. Then he snapped off the back, pulled out the SIM, and broke it into pieces with a quick twist. Both the wiped phone and the SIM fragments went into a bag.

Brad held out his hand again.

"Computer."

Amanda handed it over.

Brad gave the laptop a quick inspection, powering it on only long enough to see it worked. Then he wiped it and booted it up from his own drive. The screen of Amanda's laptop came up with a bare operating system.

He cleared out any running programs, checked recent activity, and shut down anything unnecessary. Finally, he reviewed the browsing history without logging into any accounts. He took his time.

After ten minutes, Brad gave a short nod without looking at anyone.

"No active trackers. No obvious implants."

Amanda's shoulders eased slightly.

"So it's fine?"

Brad closed the lid.

"Clean enough for a civilian—not for us. If they planted anything in the firmware, we wouldn't catch it in time. If they've already got your accounts, this laptop is a beacon. If you bring it with you, you bring them to you."

Amanda stared at him.

"That's my work. Everything I've written."

"You have the physical documents," Brad said, looking at Vicki, who gave a short nod. "You can rebuild the draft. The hardware is the risk."

Amanda's voice thinned.

"So you're just going to trash both?"

"Exactly," Brad said. "Clean doesn't cut it. Safehouse rules—no outside electronics."

Amanda nodded once and didn't argue further. Lewis gave her credit for holding back. She had already taken several hits in a short time, and she was still holding herself together.

Vicki checked the time.

"We need to deal with your car. Get what you want from it and leave the rest. Leave the keys in the ignition. Someone will pick it up soon."

Amanda's mouth opened, then closed.

"It's my cousin's," she said. "She loaned it to me."

She had already overheard Vicki's earlier phone call and knew the Civic was headed for a chop shop. Still, she couldn't stop herself from making one last protest.

"We can't do anything about that," Vicki replied. "You can make it up to her later. Right now the vehicle is a liability."

Amanda hadn't expected such a military-style setup, but she followed instructions. She climbed out, went to the Civic, pulled out a tote with her clothes, makeup, and documents, and left the keys in the ignition as Vicki had told her. When she stepped back, her posture slumped. No longer was she Amanda Riley, rising media personality.

She had nothing left.

By the time they arrived at the bank building, Mona had the ground-floor office ready. A cot sat along the inner wall, piled with blankets and a pillow. A table, a lamp, a folding chair, shelves, and a bottle of water completed the room.

"This is temporary," Vicki said. "You do not step outside without Lewis. If you need something, ask. Brad has installed audio surveillance in the room. While you told me the truth tonight, that doesn't mean we trust you not to switch sides again. You have no phone or laptop, but you do have your documents. You can work with paper for now. You won't have any outside contact unless one of us clears it, and I don't think we will—you're in too much danger."

Amanda nodded. "All right."

Lewis looked at Amanda's face. The earlier tension had given way to a flat, tired look. Her eyes were red at the edges. Her hands were still, but held close to her body. She answered questions with single words and short sentences. No attitude, no sarcasm.

Vicki laid out the routine.

"We'll bring you your meals. If you need to shower, tell Lewis. If you need clothes, give Mona your sizes and we'll sort it out. If you remember anything about the Tall Whites story that could affect your safety—names, dates, who knew what—you tell us. Once you rewrite your article, let us know. Brad can get it out to more readers than you could on your own."

Amanda sat down on the chair, and everyone filed out of the room. Lewis was the last one to leave.

"You'll have a longer briefing later," Lewis said. "For now, rest. If you need anything, knock on the door or call my name."

"Thank you," she said, almost under her breath.

Lewis closed the door to the room. When the others were gone, Lewis went back to the security office—right next to the room where Amanda was staying. He adjusted the earpiece connected to Brad's feed. The line was quiet except for the small sounds of movement inside the room. He took a deep breath and let his shoulders settle.

His thoughts went back to the pickup. Brad's silence in the car. The way Amanda had paused before handing over the phone. How Brad had taken it without a single polite word. The scan, the wipe, the broken SIM in the bag. The methodical check of the laptop. The verdict: no active trackers, no obvious implants—and still not safe enough. The blunt reminder about safehouse rules.

And Amanda's face when she understood she would be losing both devices. The quick nod, the decision not to fight. A choice to comply—at least for now—in order to survive..

Lewis was surprised to realize he respected Amanda—at least parts of her. He still disliked her past media coverage, but he respected anyone who adjusted to reality without wasting time.

He thought about Jessica, who had done nothing to deserve being smeared. Brad had carried that anger with him into the car and into the room. He had kept it contained, but Lewis had seen it. He would keep an eye on that too. Internal friction led to mistakes, and he would not allow mistakes near a protected person—even one he did not like.

He also thought about the risk. If someone had already tried to kill Amanda, then someone had the resources and motive to keep trying. The chop shop would remove her vehicle from any surveillance nets. The burner was gone, and so was the laptop. The flower shop and the bank building were still under the radar. For now, it should be enough.

Lewis checked the doors and the stairwell again. He walked the perimeter, then returned to his office.

He didn't try to predict what Amanda would do tomorrow or guess at her next choices. He focused on the next hour, then the one after that. He kept his eyes on the camera feed showing the alley and service door. The receiver was on, volume low. The street outside stayed quiet. He noted the time.

It seemed like Vicki couldn't sleep, because she came back down to check. Lewis gave a concise report.

"She's resting. Feed is clear. There's no movement outside the buildings."

"Good," Vicki said. "Thank you."

"Brad?" Lewis asked.

"In the flower shop," Vicki said. "He'll cool off."

She went back upstairs to her bedroom.

The building settled into silence once more. Lewis kept watch. He let Brad's earlier anger fade from his mind. That was what he was supposed to do. Nothing else mattered.

It felt good to have a job.

* * *

James lay awake in the dark, staring through the ceiling glass of the greenhouse room that served as a bedroom for him and Brad. The rest of the flower shop was quiet, but he had never been good at falling asleep quickly. His thoughts kept circling back to the day's events—the ACs announcing their allegiance to Earth, working with the Bridgewalkers, and making real progress on the jade amulet. They had already decided on each group's role: the humans would do the tai chi movements, the Suedes would handle harmonic shaping, just like they did when tunneling through the planet, and the ACs would balance the two energies and provide stabilization. They had practiced a little and felt something, but they weren't quite there yet.

But soon.

The door swung open and slammed against the wall. Brad stomped in, letting it shut behind him. His steps were hard against the floorboards, and he didn't bother to keep his voice down.

"I can't believe we're doing this," Brad said. "Letting Amanda stay here, after everything she's written about Jessica? All the hit pieces on her? What the hell is Vicki thinking?"

James thought for a minute, then it clicked.

"You mean Amanda *Riley*?" he asked incredulously.

"Yes, Amanda Riley," Brad snapped. He dragged out the chair by the desk and dropped into it. "She's trashed Jessica in the press. She's trashed all of us. Disclosure, the extraterrestrials, everything we're trying to build—she's made a career out of smearing it. And now she gets a safe bed and protection like she's one of us?"

James sat up, pulling his blanket aside. "Why is Vicki doing it?"

Brad let out a sharp laugh without humor. "Because Amanda's working on some story. Supposedly it's a big deal. Something about a Tall Whites trade agreement? And that's why someone's after her. Supposedly someone's trying to kill her." He shook his head. "I don't care. I don't care if every Partnership remnant out there wants her dead. She's a bitch, James. She doesn't deserve us risking everything for her."

James froze, his chest tightening. Those words—*Tall Whites trade agreement*. From the memory crystal, he knew what that meant—he knew details none of the others had seen. He forced his face to stay neutral, though inside he went cold.

"The Tall Whites trade agreement," he repeated, voice low.

"Yeah." Brad's tone was flat. "Some conspiracy crap, probably—everything Amanda Riley writes is crap. Vicki thinks it matters. She thinks it's worth putting all of us at risk for."

"If she really has documents about that," James said slowly, "then I'd agree with Vicki that it's in our interest to keep her safe."

Brad shot him a disbelieving look. "Are you serious? After everything she's done to us?"

"I never told you about it," James said, "but I found it on the memory crystal. It's an agreement between government officials and the Tall Whites—advanced alien tech in exchange for access to human DNA. This is a story that could bring down politicians, maybe the whole government. When I first found it a couple months ago and told Vicki, she said to ignore it for a while, that it wasn't time yet. I guess it's time now. And better Amanda than us—'shoot the messenger' is a real possibility here."

Brad glared at him, his hands tightening on the edge of the chair. "You want to trust her? After she smeared Jessica? After she called us liars and frauds?"

"I *don't* trust her," James said firmly. "But that's not the point. The point is, she's already in danger. Someone wants her dead because of what she knows. If she dies, the story dies with her. But if she lives long enough to release it, the truth is out. We need that."

Brad shook his head, restless. "You're saying we should just swallow our pride and babysit her? Like none of it matters?"

"I'm saying we can use this," James said. "We don't have to like her or forgive her. But if protecting her gets the story out, it's worth it. There could be riots, investigations, everything. Better if Amanda takes the spotlight. She becomes the face of the government's betrayal, not us. That keeps us out of the line of fire."

Brad leaned back in the chair, arms crossed tightly over his chest. His face was hard, but he didn't argue right away. The silence stretched.

James pushed a little more. "You think Jessica wants to see Amanda get hurt? After everything Jessica's been through, do you think she wants us to ignore someone being targeted because of Disclosure?"

That hit home. Brad looked away, jaw still clenched, but the anger in his posture shifted. "Jessica's too nice for her own damn good," he muttered. "She'd forgive anyone. Even Amanda."

James didn't answer. He lay back against the pillow.

Finally, Brad exhaled sharply and stood. He paced once across the small room, then stopped with his hands on his hips. "Fine. We keep her alive. But I don't have to like it. And I won't pretend I'm doing it for her."

James gave a small nod. "Do it for the truth, then."

Brad didn't reply. He pulled off his shoes, tossed them aside, and dropped onto his bed with his back to the room. Within minutes, his breathing slowed, though James doubted he was fully asleep.

James stayed awake longer, staring into the dark. Brad hadn't thought it all the way through. Keeping Amanda safe wasn't just about keeping her alive. It was about keeping her away from people who would be willing to make her rich for burying the story.

Yes, this was better for everyone.

Chapter Thirty-Three

J essica kept quiet count of the days since Amanda moved into the bank building. Four days.

On the first day Amanda kept to herself. Lewis brought meals to the ground-floor office that now doubled as her bedroom and escorted her whenever she needed the bathroom or shower. She didn't ask about schedules or rules. She followed every instruction without argument. Everything seemed calm, but Jessica kept her distance. Amanda herself seemed... broken.

On the second day, Mona set a place for Amanda on the table upstairs for lunch, and mentioned that Mei would be teaching breathing to the high schoolers in the late afternoon. The class was held in the atrium when the lobby was quiet. That afternoon, Jessica saw her sitting at the edge of the group, shoulders tight, knees drawn up. Mei led the count: breath in, breath out, hold. Nothing complicated. After ten minutes, Amanda's shoulders dropped a little. When the class ended, she returned to her office bedroom, escorted by Lewis.

By the third day, Amanda had begun to appear in the second-floor living area in the mornings. She carried a legal pad and pens. She wrote while sitting at the far end of the couch, knees together, papers balanced on a clipboard. When a page filled up, she tore it off the pad and set it under the clip. She organized her notes with paper clips and adhesive tabs Mona found for her in a supply drawer.

Her work came in bursts, broken only when she poured another cup of coffee or asked Mona for more paper. She never asked for a laptop. She never mentioned her phone. Her documents stayed close, stacked neatly in a manila folder at her side.

Jessica noticed the change. On the first day, Amanda had used silence as a shield. By the third day, the silence had become work. She sometimes lifted her head to listen when the voices of students echoed up from the atrium. She nodded if someone greeted her. She rinsed her cup at the sink and set it to dry. She even asked Mona if she could help with anything—and meant it.

The shift wasn't major, but it showed in small acts.

Jessica's feelings were mixed. She remembered Amanda's articles. They hadn't just been critical, they'd been cruel. They twisted facts and made her seem emotionally and mentally stunted. She had spent days angry, then finally just tired. Instead of arguing about what she couldn't change, she chose to focus on her work.

Now the author of those articles sat at the same table and slept in a small office under their protection. The two facts existed side by side, and Jessica couldn't ignore either of them.

On the fourth day, Jessica went upstairs looking for Mei—she wanted to check the amulet. In the living area, Amanda was at the far end of the couch with the legal pad and the manila folder. She was writing quickly, eyes moving as she formed each line. A cup of coffee sat steaming on the low table beside her.

Amanda looked up. "Jessica," she said. "You got a minute?"

Jessica stopped, wary. "Sure."

Amanda pressed the cap onto her pen a little harder than necessary, then dropped it onto the pad. "I owe you an apology."

Jessica folded her arms, waiting.

"I wrote crap about you," Amanda said flatly. "Stuff that was exaggerated, twisted, and sometimes flat-out false. I made you out to be someone who was weak-willed and slow because it made for better copy. I wanted the clicks, and you were an easy target. That's on me."

Jessica felt her chest tighten. The words weren't soft, but they were clear. She could say it didn't matter, but it had. It had mattered a lot. She drew a breath.

"Thank you for saying it. It hurt me, and it made everything harder. But I'm still here, and we're still doing the work." She gave the smallest smile. "And now you're here too—under our protection. Not what we expected."

Amanda gave a short nod. "Yeah, I didn't expect it either."

"None of us did," Jessica agreed. "But there are bigger things at stake here than our egos."

Amanda smiled without humor. "I'm starting to get that. I'm writing this by hand, and for the first time I'm thinking about what the words will actually *do*—not what they'll earn me." She tapped the folder with two fingers. "I'm not chasing likes or name recognition. Not this time."

Jessica nodded, "It's easier to live with yourself when you focus on something bigger."

Amanda gave a half laugh. "Maybe. All I know is I've already been sleeping better. The breathing stuff that Mei teaches actually works."

Jessica studied her face. "You're starting to loosen up."

"I guess." Amanda leaned back. "I spent years hunting the next big headline. But then last week, someone was hunting me—I thought every corner had someone waiting to put a bullet in me. When I stopped waiting and started breathing, I actually got work done—for the first time in months."

Jessica nodded. "It takes a while for most people."

"I was wrong about this place," Amanda said. "About all of you. I thought I was better than everyone, and I wasn't. I thought I couldn't be touched, and I was."

Jessica caught the edge in her tone, a mix of resentment and honesty. "You're not the first person who's had to figure that out," she said.

"I know," Amanda said. "I've spent years in back rooms,—too much coffee, too little sleep, staring at screens until midnight. This—" she gestured vaguely at the room "—isn't that. It's different."

"It is," Jessica said. "And it's not complicated. That's what helps."

Amanda picked up the pen again and set it down. "I really hope so. It's the only thing keeping me from losing my sanity."

* * *

Anne sat on the sofa, a folded blanket across her knees. The house was quiet except for the hum of the dishwasher; dinner was over, and both boys were finally asleep in their room down the hall. Jerry had come home a little later than usual, kissed her cheek, and slipped a small note into her hand before taking off his shoes.

She had read it quickly at the kitchen counter: *We are probably being bugged.* Her fingers tightened around the paper before she slid it into the pocket of her cardigan. She hadn't asked questions. She wouldn't—not here.

Jerry settled into his chair with a glass of water. He didn't look tense, but Anne knew him well enough to notice the control in his movements. His eyes swept the room once, then returned back to her.

They spoke of small things. How Josh had spilled juice at lunch. How the neighbor's dog had barked all afternoon. Anne mentioned a coupon that had come in the mail. Jerry nodded, offered a few words here and there, keeping the conversation light. Nothing important. Nothing that would stand out if replayed.

Anne wondered who had warned him. Which contact had told him their house might not be secure. She wanted to ask if the message had come from his office or from someone closer, but she held the questions back. If anyone was listening... She tucked her feet under the blanket and leaned back, careful to mirror his calm.

Then Jerry said, "You know, I found myself daydreaming about Hot Springs today. I'm glad we decided to fit in a short vacation before you go back to the law firm full time—it'll be good to get away for a bit."

Anne's fingers went still against the blanket. *Hot Springs?* There was no vacation planned. She was due back at the firm in three weeks, and they hadn't booked anything. They hadn't even mentioned leaving town. Her stomach tightened, but she kept her face neutral.

Jerry took a sip of water. "The boys will love the pools there. We should remember to bring Josh's goggles. He hates getting water in his eyes."

Anne forced her lips into a faint smile. "Yes. He'd enjoy that."

"And the trails," he continued. "Easy ones, short enough for Josh; Adam will be fine in his baby carrier. We should pack good shoes for everyone. And layers. It can be cool in the evenings."

Anne felt her hands grow cold under the blanket. She understood. He was telling her they needed to get ready. The trip was not a vacation. It was a signal. Jerry had been keeping a go-bag with their important papers in the front hall closet, but now he was telling her to get clothes ready for all four of them. They needed to be prepared to leave sometime within the next couple of weeks.

She nodded slowly. "I'll make sure everything's set aside. They'll be excited."

Jerry gave her a small look, just long enough for her to catch it, then shifted his attention to the glass in his hand. "Good. Maybe we should bring the board games too. We'll need something for the evenings."

"I'll add them to the list," Anne said faintly.

In the kitchen, the dishwasher clicked off, leaving the room even quieter. Anne kept her breathing even. Tomorrow she would start discreetly pulling items together, making it look like she was reorganizing drawers or rotating seasonal clothes.

Jerry leaned back, stretching as if the day had finally caught up with him. "It'll be good for all of us," he said in a level tone. "Hot Springs will be a change of pace."

Anne nodded once more, folding the blanket tighter around her legs. She gave no sign of the thoughts running through her head, only the calm agreement of a wife listening to her husband talk about a vacation that did not exist.

* * *

FOR IMMEDIATE RELEASE

Alpha Centaurians Launch Global Conference Series on Architectural Design and Crystal-Based Construction

For the first time, the Alpha Centaurians are opening their expertise in design and construction to the public through a series of international conferences. The subject is architecture and sustainable building, with a focus on how crystal materials can be shaped and adapted for use in inexpensive and eco-friendly construction.

The conference is scheduled to be offered six times over the next two months. Each event will take place in a different location across the globe, allowing broad access to attend in person. According to organizers, the aim is to demonstrate practical techniques that could be applied immediately in human building projects.

Interest has been intense. The first three conferences, all announced last week, have already sold out. Tickets were snapped up by architects, engineers, policy makers, and environmental groups who see crystal-based materials as a possible breakthrough in sustainable construction. For those unable to attend in person, each event will be livestreamed and archived with free video replays.

Practical Applications

The Alpha Centaurians have described their methods as accessible and scalable. Crystal shaping techniques, they say, do not require the kind of heavy industrial infrastructure associated with steel and concrete. Instead, crystals can be grown, cut, and assembled using a fraction of the energy. The resulting material is durable, resistant to weather, and maintains thermal balance without extensive insulation.

Human engineers who have seen demonstrations confirm the potential. Some note that crystal construction could drastically lower the carbon footprint of the building sector, one of the largest sources of global emissions. Others point to the possibility of reducing costs in affordable housing projects, where durable but inexpensive materials are in short supply.

Representative Brandori's Remarks

At the announcement event, Representative Brandori of the Alpha Centaurian delegation emphasized the importance of shared responsibility. "Earth is the future of the Alpha Centaurians here on this planet ," Brandori said. "We need to make sure we do our part to ensure everyone thrives."

Brandori's statement has been widely interpreted as a sign that the Alpha Centaurians see their presence on Earth as permanent and intertwined with human progress. By offering technology and methods openly, they appear to be signaling a willingness to invest in long-term collaboration rather than selective partnerships.

Media Speculation and Industry Response

Media outlets around the world have raised questions about what this development might mean for the future of architecture and construction. Industry commentators suggest that the introduction of crystal-based methods could disrupt conventional supply chains for concrete, steel, and glass. Construction firms may face pressure to adapt quickly if the new techniques prove cost-effective at scale.

Universities and research institutes are also expected to respond. Departments of architecture and civil engineering may integrate Alpha Centaurian methods into curricula as soon as reliable data and training materials are available. Some observers predict a wave of pilot projects in cities that have signed early cooperation agreements with Alpha Centaurian representatives.

Not everyone is convinced the transition will be smooth. Skeptics argue that building codes, safety standards, and regulatory frameworks are not yet ready to handle the introduction of entirely new materials. Insurance providers and developers may be cautious about committing to crystal construction until comprehensive testing is completed under human oversight.

Public Access and Next Steps

The decision to make livestreams and free video replays available has been described as a move to ensure transparency. Anyone with an interest in sustainable building will be able to observe the methods, even if they cannot secure a seat at the physical events.

The next three conferences are expected to take place in Asia, Africa, and South America. Specific venues are being kept under wraps until security arrangements are finalized, but organizers state that each location was chosen to highlight local needs for affordable, resilient construction.

For many, the Alpha Centaurian conference series represents more than just a technical demonstration. It is being seen as an opening step toward reshaping how humans and Alpha Centaurians build together, balancing environmental needs with social priorities. Whether crystal materials will become mainstream remains to be seen, but the discussion has already begun across design studios, government offices, and construction sites worldwide.

CHAPTER THIRTY-FOUR

Vicki stood near the edge of the atrium as the sounds in the room settled. The Bridgewalkers were gathered in a wide circle around the amulet, which rested on a folded cloth in the center. Human students were spaced evenly, with the young Suedes sitting in a ring behind them and the Alpha Centaurians forming the outermost layer.

They had been at it for an hour, testing different combinations of movement and tone. The humans concentrated on tai chi, working through the Thirteen Postures and the eight gates. The Suedes took that energy and tried to harmonize and shape it into geometric forms. The Alpha Centaurians focused on stabilizing both, keeping the human and Suede energies in balance.

Vicki heard someone call out, *"Reset!"* after the latest failed attempt. She admired that the young people weren't discouraged. They simply adjusted and tried again. But she could tell *something* was happening, because she could sense the energy building—it was becoming almost physical. But the final step still remained out of reach.

Vicki watched Mei, who stood a little apart, eyes fixed on the amulet as if turning something over in her mind. As the others began moving again, Mei stepped into the circle.

"Let me check the bagua etchings; there might be a sequence in the lines we've missed."

Her fingers closed around the jade. The moment her skin touched the amulet, a narrow beam of soft light projected from it.

Everyone froze, and the beam of light disappeared.

"Again," Kiran said. "Mei—stay where you are holding the amulet. Humans, Suedes and ACs—you all know your parts."

As the humans moved through the Thirteen Postures, the Suedes harmonized their energy, and the Alpha Centaurians worked to balance the flow. A beam of light appeared once again above the amulet. This time, the Bridgewalkers kept moving. They held their focus, and while they waited, three-dimensional geometric shapes began to form above the amulet. One after another, the shapes appeared, slowly rotating in sequence.

Vicki was awestruck—the Bridgewalkers had cracked the code! Mei waited until all the geometric shapes had cycled three times, before she put the amulet down and the projection collapsed.

"So that's it," Kiran said. "There's a hereditary factor. Someone of Mei's family line has to be in physical contact with it."

"Did you see that?" James asked, his voice quick with excitement. "Each geometric form appeared when a different tai chi energy was being used. Every shape matched one of tai chi's eight gates!"

"We ACs say the Eight Gates are different interstellar portals," Nevik said. "Since the tai chi gates activated the amulet, we need to figure out which one represents Sol Gate. Do we have to perform all of them to use Sol Gate, or only the specific one?"

"Good question," muttered Astran.

"Only one way to find out," said Brad helpfully.

Everyone looked at him, and he continued.

"We have a spaceship. There are several of us here who can fly it. We'll need to go to Sol Gate and try."

"Who gets to go?" asked Calix in a small voice. There was longing in the young AC's voice.

The room fell silent. Everyone wanted to go. And just as clearly, they wouldn't all fit.

"Mei needs to go. Obviously," said Kiran. "The rest should be representative of our three groups."

In the end, it was agreed that all the pilots would take part in the first trip. Junia explained that only three Suedes were needed to manage the harmonizing, but warned they could not remain away from Earth for more than a day or two. That limit made it necessary to keep the initial journey through Sol Gate short. The Alpha Centaurians could also carry out their part with just three of them.

As the young people began chattering excitedly, Vicki felt a tug in her chest. She wanted to follow where this was going—she wanted to be with them on the spaceship. She wanted to show that interstellar travel didn't belong only to a government lab or a hidden group.

But she also knew where she was needed most. Her place was on Earth, helping humanity through the vibrational shift. People were both frightened and hopeful. Policies were changing, communities were adjusting, and conflict and cooperation were rising together. Amanda was preparing to publish a story that would shake the public's trust in their leaders. Vicki had a role here.

The team in front of her had their own irreplaceable gifts. When they opened a path through Sol Gate, she wouldn't be on the first trip. That was okay. There would be other trips, and the planet needed her help to keep things balanced.

Vicki felt proud of the Bridgewalkers. Proud of the Five, who had endured so much. Proud of the Suedes, who had looked past the violence aimed at them and still chosen to stand here. Proud of the Alpha Centaurians, who had tied their future to Earth's. They had all earned this moment.

She felt anticipation for what was ahead. Vicki wouldn't go this time, but there would be other journeys. For now, the world needed her here.

* * *

Brad leaned back in his chair, the glow from three monitors reflecting across his desk. Today had been good. Better than good. The amulet had responded. Mei's touch had unlocked the sequence, and with everyone working in tandem, they had caused the artifact to produce the geometric shapes. Tomorrow they'd be practicing on the spaceship. For once, everything was going right.

On his right-hand screen, a secure site displayed three incoming messages from the past hour. Brad smiled—Graham, one of the scientific advisors at the State Department's Office of Multispecies Relations, was nothing if not relentless. The subject line on the latest email read: Quantum *Threader Release.*

Brad typed: *The schematics are solid. Everyone understands stitches. This will be less disruptive than either free energy or the medical regeneration chamber. It's all good.*

Kyle answered a minute later: *You're certain?*

Brad replied: *It'll make headlines, but that's the point. We've already drafted talking points.*

Brad leaned forward, elbows on the desk. The quantum threader would be a success. A device that could stitch jeans, close cuts, or repair damaged infrastructure at the push of a button was exactly the kind of practical technology that could sway public opinion. No abstract theories, no talk of "vibrational shifts." Yes, it could realign atomic structure using sacred geometry protocols. But most people would just see it as a tool they could hold in their hands and use.

He was drafting a quick outline for the rollout plan when the knock came. Before he could answer, the door opened. Lewis stepped in, solid as always, and behind him Amanda carried a stack of papers held tight to her chest.

Brad exhaled, already feeling his shoulders tense. "What?"

Amanda gave him a narrow look. "Nice welcome." She crossed the room and set the papers on the edge of his desk. "This is my best draft. I think it's ready to go, but it needs a second pair of eyes. Vicki said you're the one who could get it to the public, who would know how the story would resonate."

Lewis stayed near the door, silent.

Brad glanced at the stack without reaching for it. "You're supposed to stay in the bank building."

"I needed a copier," Amanda said. "And I needed someone to read this who knows what they're looking at. That's you."

Brad turned back to his screen. "I'm busy."

"We're all busy," she shot back. "You think I came over here to waste time?"

Lewis shifted slightly, the faintest suggestion that Brad should give her a chance. Brad muttered under his breath and finally pulled the papers closer. He flipped to the first page.

The title line read: *The Trade We Weren't Supposed to See.*

His first instinct was to dismiss it, the same way he had dismissed her before. She had worked to tear down Jessica's image in print, painting her as weak and unstable. Brad had no reason to give her the satisfaction of attention.

But his eyes caught on a detail in the first paragraph: specific serial numbers, models of Tall Whites trade equipment, and the dates they had been moved through hidden channels.

He turned another page. There were interviews, anonymous but detailed. Descriptions of storage facilities, equipment crates, and the language of the contracts. She had pulled in data he hadn't seen compiled anywhere else. His irritation dulled as he skimmed faster.

When he reached the third page, his hand stilled. He leaned closer, the words pulling him in. The account described ordinary people taken against their will by the Tall Whites, subjected to invasive medical procedures, and then—once released—faced with humiliation and hostility from their own government. An official set of psyops—psychological operations—had been used on these victims: defamation, ridicule, and harassment. Jobs were lost. Marriages collapsed. Entire lives were dismantled.

All at the behest of their own government.

Amanda wasn't just speculating; she had evidence that confirmed every detail. If this story reached the public intact, it would reshape how people saw Disclosure and expose the hidden machinery of power behind it.

Brad looked up at her, frowning. "Where did you get all this?"

Amanda crossed her arms. "I can't reveal my sources."

"Someone wants you dead over this," Brad said flatly.

"Yeah," Amanda answered. Her voice had an edge to it. "I figured that out."

Brad went back to the stack. He skimmed another section and shook his head. "This isn't just a story—it''ll blow the lid off the government."

Amanda leaned against the desk. "Yeah, you think?."

He didn't answer right away. The transformation in his own head annoyed him—the shift from brushing her off to calculating how this would ripple once it broke. The thought that Amanda was being helpful. He set the last page down and rubbed the bridge of his nose.

"You know they'll call this treason," he said.

"They call everything treason when it's inconvenient," Amanda said.

For the first time that evening, Brad felt the tug of respect creep in.

Amanda tapped the edge of the stack. "So, are you going to help me with this? Or just glare at me until I walk out?"

Brad pushed the papers back toward her. "You've got something strong here. But if you drop it raw, they'll bury you under lawsuits before it even hits the wire."

"I've survived worse," Amanda said.

"No," Lewis said from the door, his first word in minutes. "You haven't."

Both Brad and Amanda shot him startled glances, then returned to their conversation.

"We should lead with what the trade agreement is, then how it affected average people. How they were traumatized—first by the Tall Whites, then by their own government. The tech details can come later—the public already knows something about that because of what the Partnership did."

Brad's fingers drummed on the desk. He hated that he cared enough about Amanda's story think about it.

"We need to do more than drop the story on hundreds of websites," said Amanda. "We need to build a campaign. Threads, video snippets, coordinated shares. People don't read blocks of text anymore. They watch, they scroll, they click. Give them entry points and they'll chase the details."

Brad raised an eyebrow. "You think I don't know how social media works?"

"I'm afraid you might ignore it because of who I am and what I did to your sister," Amanda admitted. "But that can't matter now. What matters is this story."

Brad stared at her. The abrasive edge in her tone was clear, but so was the logic. She wasn't wrong.

"What would you suggest?" he asked, voice still curt.

Amanda blinked, surprised that he'd asked. "Short videos. Two minutes max. Package them for different platforms. Push the text story alongside, but let the videos carry it. Lead with the clips and the headlines people can't ignore, then give them the documents to back it up. If you want reach, you have to hook them in first."

Brad considered her words. It wasn't how he preferred to operate, but it was the kind of delivery that could flood channels fast.

"Fine," he said at last. "Draft me an outline."

Amanda gave a small, half-smile. "Didn't think you'd say yes."

"Don't read too much into it," Brad said. "You and I are not friends."

"Noted," she replied.

Lewis exhaled softly, the closest thing to relief Brad had heard from him all day.

Amanda gathered her papers back up, the faintest shift in posture suggesting she knew she had scored a small victory. Brad let her have it. Grudge or not, they had work to do.

Chapter
Thirty-Five

The meeting room was larger than the one the AC Council usually used, but this time the public had been invited. Everyone wanted to witness what promised to be a pivotal gathering—citizens from all three Alpha Centaurian cities had come. At one end of the room stood a long table where the council representatives were already seated. Rows of chairs faced them, filled with onlookers. When Brandori entered, faces turned toward him—council members and citizens alike—watching with expectation.

He took his seat at the head of the table and began the briefing.

"The conference series on alternative building materials and construction methods has concluded," he said. "Attendance was nearly double what we projected. Delegations from over forty human nations took part, and engineers and architects joined every workshop. Demonstrations of crystal-based composites, rapid-form housing, and non-destructive load-bearing methods were all well received. The closing sessions produced public commitments from twelve governments to fund pilot projects. We can say with confidence: this effort has built real goodwill between humans and our people."

Several heads nodded. Representative Lacino leaned forward, his notes spread before him.

"I'd like to add some detail," he said. "Human engineers are eager to continue these exchanges, especially in adapting their existing equipment. Take coal mining, for example—the infrastructure is huge but built on destructive methods. Several companies have approached us about repurposing drills and conveyors to extract crystal in controlled, sustainable ways. They've also suggested turning abandoned mine shafts into stabilization chambers for crystal growth. So far, though, most of the interest has come from companies based in Quiet Zones."

Someone raised their hand, "Why in the Quiet Zones?"

"Location is a factor," Lacino answered. "The energy patterns within Quiet Zones align with our methods, which makes conversion of existing infrastructure more feasible. But there is also the matter of trust. The firms within them view cooperation as a way to ensure stability and build harmony. By contrast, those based outside the Quiet Zones fear that cooperation will erode their profits. They see change as a threat to their established models, rather than as an opportunity for sustainable growth.

Brandori noticed the approving looks around the table. Quiet Zones were often the only places where humans and ACs could work together without constant resistance. Building on those connections made sense.

But the moment of agreement broke when an audience member spoke. The elder, Seren, was known for her attachment to tradition and her unwillingness to embrace change. Her voice carried across the room, calm but edged with reproach.

"You speak of cooperation and adaptation as if the dangers have vanished," she said. "Have you forgotten what brought us here? You speak of aligning with humans, but you never explain why Representative Brandori declared us separate from our kind among the stars. That was not a decision made with counsel. The elders were not consulted. It was made by one voice alone."

A murmur spread across the room.

Neecon, seated two rows behind Seren, spoke next. His voice was slower but just as firm. "Seren is right. What gave you the authority to decide this? Separating from the rest of our people is no small matter. It shapes how humans and the Galactic Council see us."

A low murmur spread through the audience—some nodding, others shifting uneasily. Brandori straightened. He had expected this question since the day he made the declaration.

"You ask what gave me the right," he said. "I will answer. Necessity gave me that right. You know what Varan told us when we asked to resume contact with our people. He dismissed us. He called us remnants. He said the survivors on Earth were not true Alpha Centaurians, that we were worth less than the our relatives in space. He called our past shameful and told us to accept whatever scraps they gave us. That was not recognition. That was contempt."

Seren's eyes narrowed. "So you thought declaring separation would fix contempt?"

"I thought declaring our separation would keep us from being defined as worthless." Brandori said. His voice rose slightly. "We are not scraps. We are not shadows of those who orbit around other systems. We live here, we build here, and we risk our lives here. The humans who attended our conferences didn't come because Varan allowed it. They came because of our knowledge and skill. They came because of what we gave them openly, not what was filtered through disdain. We are Earth ACs. We are our own people."

The chamber was quiet for a long moment. Lacino looked between the speakers, his hands resting on his notes. A younger councilor shifted uneasily.

Neecon broke the silence. "You take a great burden on yourself, Brandori. Declaring a people is not a small matter. You may be right that Varan held us in contempt. You may be right that we must act on our own. But you should have brought it here, to the council, before you spoke for all of us."

Brandori inclined his head. "I accept that. I should have called for a vote. I should have sought counsel. I did not. I judged that delay would cost us the moment. Varan was already moving. Silence would have meant consent. So I chose to act. If you wish, you may call for censure. But I will not withdraw the words. We are our own people. I stand by that."

Seren leaned back, arms crossed. "You admit you acted in haste—I fear the cost may prove to be too high. You have set us on a path we cannot step away from. Humans will now expect us to speak as a separate people. And the Galactic Council may choose to ignore us altogether."

"They ignored us already," Brandori answered. "They accepted Varan as our representative, and he had publicly stated that we were inferior. At least now we speak in our own name."

Lacino raised a hand. "The dispute is real. But I remind the council of today's facts. Humans are eager to work with us. They see us as partners. They speak of Earth ACs with respect. That is new. Whatever path we are on, we should note this outcome."

Several nodded. Even Neecon gave a small sign of agreement.

Brandori pressed home the point. "Varan—the AC representative on the Galactic Council—called us lesser. I say we are not. We have survived what others did not. We endured isolation, destruction, and suspicion. Yet we stand here holding conferences that draw thousands. We inspire humans to rethink their own building methods. We propose sustainable practices they had never imagined. These are not the actions of a lesser people. These are the actions of a people who know their worth, and who know the value of what they create."

The silence that followed was contemplative. Seren did not argue further, though her expression remained hard. Neecon gave no approval but also no renewed challenge.

Brandori looked around the table. "If you demand a vote, we will hold one. If you wish to censure me, I will not resist. But I will not apologize for claiming dignity for our people. Not while Varan treats us as less. Not while humans show us more respect than our own kin in the stars."

Lacino cleared his throat. "Then let us record both matters: the success of the conferences, and the disagreement over Brandori's declaration. Both will shape our next steps. We should not forget either."

Brandori nodded. That was fair.

The meeting shifted back to practical matters: project proposals, delegation assignments, and budget allocations. But the words spoken—his and theirs—hung in the chamber. Brandori knew this was only the beginning of the debate.

* * *

The Tall Whites Trade Agreement: A Dark Chapter in U.S. History

By Amanda Riley, Investigative Correspondent

Introduction

For decades, whispers of alien contact have been relegated to the margins of serious debate, dismissed as conspiracy or entertainment. But newly corroborated documents, eyewitness testimony, and insider accounts have revealed a shocking truth: a secret agreement was signed between senior members of the United States military and an extraterrestrial race known as the Tall Whites.

This arrangement—known within classified circles as the Tall Whites Trade Agreement—gave the U.S. military access to advanced alien technology. In exchange, the Tall Whites were granted unlimited access to human DNA. The consequences of this deal have reverberated for generations, hidden under layers of secrecy, psychological manipulation, and deliberate misinformation.

The story that follows is not speculation. It is the record of a systematic betrayal of the American people by officials sworn to protect them.

What the Agreement Entailed

The Tall Whites Trade Agreement, negotiated in the mid-20th century and renewed multiple times under classified directives, was premised on a simple but devastating bargain: technology in exchange for human genetic material.

The Tall Whites promised breakthroughs far beyond the frontier of human science—propulsion systems, communications networks, biomedical advancements. In return, they required access to human DNA, ostensibly for their own genetic research. The agreement contained no limits on how this access would be obtained.

This carte blanche authorization opened the door to decades of human abductions carried out with the full knowledge of the military. American citizens were taken without consent, subjected to invasive medical procedures, and returned without explanation. The agreement treated the American population not as citizens, but as a genetic resource.

The Human Cost

The most disturbing consequence of the Tall Whites agreement was its impact on abducted citizens. While most were returned physically intact, the psychological trauma was profound. Survivors describe waking in unfamiliar environments, surrounded by beings who performed clinical procedures without explanation. Needles, incisions, tissue samples—all conducted while the subjects were paralyzed or restrained.

What compounded the trauma was the reaction of our own government. Far from receiving help or acknowledgment, abductees were subjected to a coordinated campaign of psychological operations designed to discredit them. Military information specialists planted stories labeling them as delusional, unstable, or attention-seeking. The victims of abduction became victims once again, this time of their own country's propaganda.

The collateral damage was immense. Marriages collapsed under the strain of disbelief. Careers ended when individuals were ridiculed for speaking out. Families fractured as relatives argued over whether to trust their loved ones' accounts. Some abductees, unable to reconcile their experiences with the gaslighting they endured, took their own lives.

These were not isolated tragedies. They were the predictable consequences of a policy that prioritized secrecy and technological gain over human dignity and safety.

Technology and the Rise of the Partnership

The advanced technologies obtained through the Tall Whites Trade Agreement did not remain solely in military hands. Instead, they were channeled into private aerospace and technology firms under the guise of "black projects."

These firms formed what came to be known as the Partnership, a conglomerate of corporate and military interests working hand in hand to develop the alien technology for commercial and strategic purposes. Officially, the Partnership did not exist. In practice, it wielded enormous influence, shaping both defense policy and private industry in ways that bypassed public oversight.

Among the Partnership's projects, one stood out as both groundbreaking and deeply sinister: the creation of biologically constructed bodies. The aim was to produce human-like forms that would never fall ill, would possess enhanced strength and intelligence, and could house human consciousness.

But embedded within this technology was a fatal flaw—or, more accurately, a design feature. These bodies came with an override mechanism. The Partnership could deactivate them at will. Individuals who underwent the procedure would live in a state of constant powerlessness, knowing that their very existence could be "shut off" by the push of a button.

This was not the promise of human advancement. It was the blueprint for a new form of slavery.

Why the Truth Was Buried

Even as the truth about the Tall Whites Trade Agreement has begun to surface, elements within the military continue to fight to keep it hidden. The reasons are twofold.

First, there is guilt. Those who authorized and perpetuated the agreement understand that history will not absolve them. They presided over decades of human rights abuses against their own citizens, traded away freedom for power, and undermined the very Constitution they swore to defend. Exposure would mean disgrace, accountability, and potentially criminal charges.

Second, there is power. The technologies obtained from the Tall Whites remain a source of strategic advantage. Control of those technologies equates to control over industries, economies, and governments. To relinquish secrecy is to relinquish that power. A small but determined faction of officers and officials remains committed to maintaining their grip, no matter the cost to truth or justice.

The Path Forward

The revelations surrounding the Tall Whites Trade Agreement are not merely about past abuses. They point toward a fundamental choice facing humanity today.

We stand at the threshold of what many scientists and spiritual leaders describe as a vibrational shift—a transformation of human consciousness that exceeds the capacity of current science to predict. This shift promises profound changes in how humans understand themselves, their place in the universe, and their potential.

But there is a catch. This transformation can only occur if we remain fully human—unaltered, and free of technology designed to enslave us. The biologically constructed bodies envisioned by the Partnership would sever us from this potential, locking humanity into dependence just when independence is most essential.

The Tall Whites Trade Agreement was a bargain struck in fear and ambition. It is not the path forward. The path forward lies in embracing humanity itself—in our resilience, our creativity, our willingness to confront even the darkest truths and choose a different course.

Conclusion

The Tall Whites Trade Agreement will be remembered as one of the most shameful episodes in American history: a pact that handed citizens over to alien experimentation, destroyed lives through deliberate disinformation, and built a shadow empire of technological control.

Yet exposing this history also opens the possibility of redemption. By acknowledging the truth, we can ensure that no agreement of this kind is ever made again. By rejecting the lure of enslavement through technology, we can claim the future that is rightfully ours.

Only by being fully human—by trusting in the depth of our own potential—can we navigate the challenges of the vibrational shift and build a society worthy of the name.

CHAPTER THIRTY-SIX

The security office was calm, quiet, and filled with the hum of equipment and blinking lights. Lewis kept it organized. Two monitors displayed exterior cameras, two showed interior feeds, another logged entries, and one large screen handled reports and message traffic. He liked knowing how every cable connected, and which switch controlled what. It made problems manageable.

This morning, the problem wasn't connected to any cable. It sat in his chair, scrolling quickly through feeds.

Amanda had asked to check the reaction to her story. Vicki allowed it with one rule: either Lewis or Brad had to supervise. Brad was on three calls, so Lewis stayed. He didn't mind. Amanda had proven herself by writing an unbiased article that accurately presented the evidence, even though she hadn't always done that in the past.

Now she sat at his desk. He stood behind her shoulder, close enough to monitor the screen but far enough not to crowd her.

On one monitor, the cameras cycled through every access point: front, alley, roof, delivery door, and two hidden angles watching the street. Nothing stirred. On Amanda's screen, the headline glowed.

THE TALL WHITES TRADE AGREEMENT: TECH- NOLOGY FOR HUMAN DNA

Amanda had written it. Brad had published it, attaching documents and sending the package to websites and news outlets across the world. Within hours, every news site, feed, and platform carried it. Podcasts rushed out emergency episodes. Roundtables debated it on live TV. Comment sections filled with arguments. Streams ran nonstop. Messages refreshed so fast counters froze.

Amanda opened a live analytics page and exhaled. "It's still climbing."

Lewis nodded. He didn't need statistics to confirm it. People always chased the truth.

She scrolled. Some responses were thoughtful. People said they had always suspected something was wrong in how abductees were treated. Academics linked old studies on sleep paralysis and trauma, now asking if those had been highlighted to hide other explanations. Veterans hinted that they had seen things on deployment that matched parts of the story, though they could not speak in detail. Families posted photographs of loved ones lost to suicide with short captions: *We believe you now.*

But those weren't the loudest voices.

The loudest accused Amanda of lying, seeking fame, or betraying her country. Some called her a disgrace. Others demanded she be arrested for threatening national security. A few claimed she was an agent for foreign powers.

Lewis leaned in closer. Many of the accounts used identical wording, posted within seconds of each other. Same grammar mistakes. Same cropped images. Coordinated. He marked the patterns in his head to tell Brad about later.

Amanda opened a thread under a republished version of her article. The top comment read: *She should be in prison for endangering the country.* The next: *People like this don't care if soldiers die.* Another: *No such thing as Tall Whites. She just wants attention.* Replies accused her of inventing sources, of not being a real journalist. A video host had crumpled a printed copy of her article and thrown it in the trash. The clip had hundreds of thousands of views in hours.

Amanda's hand trembled on the mouse. She put it down, pressing her palms together. "I knew it would be bad," she said quietly, "but I thought there would be more people who cared about the evidence."

Lewis kept his tone level. "There are many who care, but they don't post as much. The loud ones post more."

"That's not really helping," she said, but gave a short, strained laugh.

Lewis scanned the camera feeds again. All clear. When he looked back, Amanda had switched to her mentions. Her name had been trending for eighteen hours. Another tab showed a flood of emails pouring into the public address Brad had created.

Subject lines rolled past: *Please talk to me. This happened to my wife in 1999. You are a liar. Cease and desist. I can prove what you wrote. You will pay.*

Amanda clicked one, read a few lines, then closed it and rubbed her nose.

"I'm used to attention," she said. "Even negative attention. That comes with the job. But this feels different.Before, when I wrote sensational stories, people argued about the issue, not about me. Now they're going after me. I wasn't ready for that. I trained to grab headlines, not to be the target."

"You trained to ask hard questions," Lewis said.

She stared at the screen again. On a news panel clip, two retired officers said that even if her story was partly true, it never should have been published. They called secrecy necessary. One implied that abductees misunderstood their experiences. A comment under the clip called Amanda a traitor.

Amanda muttered, "Do they want me dead? Do they want someone to try again?"

Lewis kept his voice plain. "The ones posting aren't the problem. They're only venting. The danger comes from the quiet ones. The ones who don't post, who don't announce themselves. They're the dangerous ones."

Amanda turned, startled. "I never thought of it like that. I've just been counting clicks and likes." Her voice dropped. "I feel like crawling into a corner and staying out of sight."

He remembered that feeling from his own past—moving through crowds after missions, unsure who might be a threat. He put his hand on the back of her chair.

"You're safe here," he said. "We check every access point and rotate procedures. We expect attempts, so we aren't surprised by them."

She nodded. "Thank you."

She opened another outlet. They had posted a timeline with disclaimers. A rival site published doubts about her sources. Lewis could see that Brad had responded in a thread with declassified memos proving the agreement existed and had been renewed. His rebuttal had only half the shares of the attack.

"The anger is so much louder," she said.

"Doing the right thing often makes people mad," he answered. "It shows them *they* aren't doing the right thing."

Amanda turned. "You think I did the right thing?"

"Yes," Lewis said. "And I'm glad you're finally being brave."

"Brave?" she echoed. "I just broke the story because it was big—it was an exclusive. Because no one else would print my other ones."

"Yes, but you wrote it even knowing people were trying to hurt you," he said. "You decided the truth was more important than safety. That's brave."

Amanda looked at him for a long second. Her expression showed confusion first, then a sort of stillness. "I hadn't thought about it that way."

"It's good," he said. "I admire that."

Her cheeks colored, and she looked back at the screen.

She opened a spreadsheet Brad had set up to track reactions. One column listed the names, another the links, a third rated tone—supportive, neutral, skeptical, hostile—and a fourth logged connections to the old Partnership network. She began filling it out, marking patterns. Hostile media outlets clustered around corporate families with defense contracts. She added a note to cross-check with budget lines in the leaked memos.

"This will be useful," she said.

"It will," Lewis agreed. "Patterns show plans."

She began sorting threats. "Should I flag the worst ones for Brad?"

"Yes. Sort them into a folder. He'll follow up. But don't read threats too closely. There's no point."

"Too late," she said with a tight smile, but she followed his advice with the next batch, clicking through quickly.

A new testimonial thread appeared, detailed and anonymous, echoing abductee accounts Amanda had seen in interviews. Another post came from a doctor describing patients with unexplained scars and conditions that didn't fit known medicine. She invited colleagues to share data. Amanda bookmarked both.

"This is the other side," she said. "People stepping forward."

"They needed someone to go first," he replied.

She shook her head. "I didn't go first."

"You went first with the evidence that almost got you killed," he countered.

The reaction kept building. Some of the worst comments slowed as moderators intervened. Fact-checks appeared. A few outlets issued corrections after repeating false claims about Amanda. Supportive messages increased.

A quiet stretch followed. The equipment hummed. The feeds stayed clear. Amanda's breathing evened out. She opened a new document and began drafting a follow-up. The outline included four sections: the Partnership's corporate structure, oversight failures, the psy-ops campaign against abductees, and a final section titled *What Being Fully Human Requires*.

She considered changing the last title, then left it alone.

Lewis watched her work. Before, he had only seen Amanda as someone acting in her own self-interest. Now he saw a woman who had been frightened to the edge of panic, but who chose to sit in the chair and face what came.

He thought she was pretty. More than that, he thought she was learning—and that mattered more than the type of person she used to be. He and Amanda had a lot in common. He was glad she was with them.

He moved to where he could watch both her and the cameras. He felt focused, alert. He logged a note for Vicki: *Amanda adapting to pressure., but recommend continued supervision.*

Amanda kept typing. Lewis kept watch. Ready for the next alert, the next knock, the next turn in the story. Ready to protect the team—and the woman now learning to stand her ground.

* * *

OMR OBSERVATION MEMO
(Classified Briefing – Internal Use Only)

Subject: Escalating Global Deviations – Environmental, Sociocultural & Cognitive Frequency Shifts

- **[Defense Watch]** *"Recruitment Numbers Plunge"*
  Department of Defense reports enlistments have fallen 38% in the two weeks since the Tall Whites Trade Agreement story was published. Multiple state recruitment offices have temporarily closed due to threats and vandalism. Parents cited widespread distrust in leadership.

- **[Financial Journal]** *"Factory Production Goes Local"*
  Economists note a sharp reorganization of manufacturing supply chains. Local and regional sourcing has increased 24% over the last quarter. Analysts describe a shift toward "simple and resilient" goods, produced close to point of

sale. Unconfirmed reports suggest that 'Quiet Zones' are harmonizing activities with each other to "minimize risk."

- **[Capitol City News]** *"Protests at Pentagon Turn Violent"*
  Demonstration escalated when crowds pushed through barricades. Dozens arrested, multiple injuries. Protesters chanted *"We are not experiments."* Police deployed tear gas by mid-afternoon.
  [Social Media: @activistDC] *"They fired gas on families with kids. Nobody trusts them anymore."*

- **[Denver Post]** *"Quantum Threaders Spark New Small Businesses"*
  Threader-based enterprises surge nationwide, from clothing repair to small appliance repair. Informal "threader cafés"—half clinic, half social hub—are opening across several states. Local officials say attempts to regulate the new industry have been rebuffed.

- **[National Education Review]** *"High School and University Enrollment Declines"*
  Enrollment down 25% nationwide. Families cite distrust of institutions and new alternatives. Universities report unprecedented drops in applications; students prefer apprenticeships, energy training, and tai chi instruction. Regional colleges explore possibility of converting to meditation campuses.

- **[Better Business Bureau – Press Release]** *"Psychic Accreditation Streamlined"*
  The BBB confirms a formalized accreditation track for psychics. Quote: *"The number and quality of talented individuals has increased so much that recognition is overdue."*

[Social Media: @clairvoyantvoices] *"About time psychics get recognized as professionals."*

- **[Armed Forces Monitor]** *"Officer and Enlisted Resignations Spike"*
Pentagon insiders report voluntary resignations up 41% in the past two weeks, affecting both junior enlisted and mid-career officers. Exit interviews cite "loss of trust" and "moral conflict" following the Tall Whites revelations. Several units face critical staffing shortages; deployment rotations already extended in response.

- **[Global Culture Review]** *"Alpha Centaurian Conference on Architecture a Success"*
The AC-sponsored architecture series exceeded attendance records. Forty-two national delegations committed to testing design principles focused on harmony, durability, and energetic alignment in urban projects. In associated news, firms specializing in concrete, rebar, lumber, brick and plastics have experienced a business downturn.

Assessment

Public trust in traditional institutions—military, government, and education—is collapsing. Violent protests at symbolic sites (Pentagon) indicate rising instability. Simultaneously, alternative sectors—local production, small businesses powered by alien tech, accredited psychics, and Alpha Centaurian cultural initiatives—are expanding rapidly. Observed trend: decline of legacy systems, emergence of parallel structures.

END OF BRIEF

Chapter
Thirty-Seven

T he small house sat a couple of miles inside the quiet zone. From the window, Anne could see hills stretching into the distance. There were no sounds of traffic, even though a mid-sized town was only a short drive away. Both boys were napping—Josh in the bedroom, Adam in her arms. She sat with Jerry on the small sofa, while Vicki took the armchair across from them.

Vicki's car had arrived half an hour earlier. She greeted them warmly, but Anne still noticed the faint weariness in her eyes—the kind that came from too many choices and too many consequences pressing in at once. Anne recognized it right away; she and Jerry had worn that same look often in recent months.

Jerry got right to it. "Sam told me straight out," he said. "Our house was being bugged. Anne and I were placed on a surveillance list by the same people trying to bury the Tall Whites trade agreement. That was enough for me. Truth is, it scared me."

Anne's stomach tightened as Jerry spoke. She remembered the moment he had handed her the note after coming home from work, and then, two days later, when they had talked about it while taking the boys to the park. She recalled the quiet anger in his voice, sitting alongside the fear he tried to hide. She shared both his anger and his fear—and the recognition that there was little they could do to change the situation.

And things had only gotten worse after Amanda Riley's story about the trade agreement with the Tall Whites was published. Angry protests erupted outside the Pentagon and other government buildings, many turning violent. When several demonstrators were killed, it made their decision easier.

Jerry continued. "I spent the last two weeks at OMR doing nothing but training a replacement. I told them I was going on vacation to Hot Springs, Virginia. Instead, we just kept on driving."

Anne remembered the drive clearly. Jerry already had a go-bag with their documents and cash, and she had packed clothes, family photos, snacks, and toys. They loaded the car quickly, pretending it was just a family trip. Jerry cracked jokes to keep everyone cheerful. Anne sang songs and played games with Josh in the back seat, smiling as she told stories. But inside, a knot of fear stayed with her. Each mile between them and Washington felt like one step farther from danger, yet also a step closer into an unknown.

They had taken back roads, avoided big hotels, and eaten sandwiches from the cooler, constantly checking the news to ensure they didn't drive into a violent demonstration. At night, after the boys fell asleep, she and Jerry whispered about where to go next, how far to keep driving, and what they would do if anyone followed. By the time they reached the quiet zone, the exhaustion had given way to relief. For the first time in weeks, Anne felt she could breathe without fear.

Now Vicki's gaze turned toward her. "Why here?" Vicki asked. "Of all places, why this?"

Anne straightened. She had been waiting for this question.

"When you told us you were leaving OMR," Anne said slowly, "you said you could be more useful elsewhere. Jerry and I kept thinking about that. We realized we felt the same way. We don't want to run anymore. But we don't want to prolong the life of a system that's dying. We want to build something."

Vicki tilted her head. "What kind of something?"

Anne drew in a breath. "The vibrational shift is changing everything. People are confused—some are scared, some are trying to profit. Here, we're in a quiet zone, they're already going through the shift. But people still need help. I can organize CE-5 events, and bring people together to try direct contact. People need that. Jerry can work with the local government. He knows how the financial systems work. He can help them prepare for being cut off from places that aren't shifting, and make sure the transition doesn't hurt people unnecessarily."

Jerry nodded beside her. "I don't want to be part of a bureaucracy anymore. I want to help people understand what's coming in practical terms—budgets, food, infrastructure. Regions like this need to learn to be flexible and find ways to cooperate with others so everyone can thrive if their usual resources disappear. They need to be ready for whatever comes."

Anne looked down as she cradled Adam in her arms. "And we want a future for the boys. Not just survival. A real future—one where they grow up knowing that when everything broke apart, their parents did more than just hide. We need to help shape what comes next."

The room was quiet after she finished. Vicki studied both of them carefully. Anne could see the calculation in her eyes—always weighing risks, always deciding how much to share. Finally, Vicki smiled.

"I understand," she said. "When I left OMR, I wasn't sure where I belonged. But I see now it isn't about where I belong, it's about where I can make the most difference. If that's what you're choosing too, then we're actually doing the same thing."

Jerry leaned back in his chair. "I wonder what the boys will think of all this when they grow older."

"They'll understand," Anne said softly. She looked at Vicki again. "We're not trying to be heroes. We just want to stand where we can help. If enough people do that, maybe the shift won't tear everything apart."

For the first time since leaving Washington, Anne felt she was speaking words meant not only for survival but for living. The decision to leave had been born of fear. The choice to stay here, to work here, felt intentional. It felt like a beginning.

Vicki reached for her glass, took a drink, and set it back on the table. "Then maybe this is the right place for you," she smiled.

* * *

The ship rested on its struts, hidden in the trees on the Martinssons' property. Inside the cabin, the air was still, filled with the quiet hum of dormant systems. Mei stood a few steps back, watching.

Everyone who was tagged to make the first trip through Sol Gate was here. Nevik, Calix, and Astran from the Alpha Centaurians, along with Junia, Caffo, and Ilar from the Suedes, moved eagerly around the consoles. Their voices rose as they pointed out displays and traced lines of symbols across the panels.

Jessica, Brad, Kiran, and James were already at one console, explaining what they had learned: the navigation display, the engineering monitors, and the command interface.

Lewis remained near the hatch, alert but at ease, his eyes shifting between the group and the entryway.

Mei held the jade amulet in her hand. It was no longer just a family heirloom; it was the key to aligning the energies of Earth's three species—the piece of the puzzle that would let them travel through Sol Gate. But humanity's future—at least the chance of it—also rested on her.

She wrapped her fingers around the stone. How could she have ever imagined this? Other kids her age worried about classes, homework, and who was dating whom. But here she was, inside a stolen alien spaceship, preparing to help guide it through a portal at the center of the sun. She was lucky. Despite the risks, she knew it.

The humans, ACs and Suedes moved with excitement . Nevik traced the lines of the pilot console, asking rapid questions about interfaces. Jess and Kiran were showing Calix storage compartments. James was explaining to Caffo how the power system distributed load across redundant circuits, while Ilar and Junia climbed up to examine a stowed emergency cradle. Their energy filled the ship.

Mei smiled faintly but stayed where she was. Watching the others made her wonder how her own family would react if they saw her now. Tian would accuse her of showing off. Her mother would shake her head, certain she was wasting her life. None of them had ever believed she could do anything important. It all came to a breaking point at her grandmother's viewing, when her mother tried once more to drag her down, and Mei declared her a stranger. She didn't regret it.

Family was supposed to build you up. Hers had only ever cut her down. That was over.

She let her thoughts settle on the Five—Jessica, Brad, Kiran, James, and herself. They were the real family now. They lived together, trained together, risked their lives together. They had believed in her when no one else would, even when she doubted herself. With them, she was not just tolerated. She was necessary.

Lewis moved closer, glancing at the activity inside the ship. "They're treating it like a toy store," he said, his voice low but not disapproving.

Mei nodded. "They've never had this much access before."

"Neither has anyone else," he replied.

It was true. Until now, the ship and everything inside it had been knowledge the Partnership had deliberately withheld from the rest of humanity. Now it belonged to them, theirs to learn from and to use.

Mei listened in as Brad and Kiran had a conversation near the main console.

"When the Kewpies took us through Sol Gate," said Brad, "they used a navigation crystal that they mounted on a pedestal. How are we going to do this?"

Kiran replied, his voice low but firm. "The amulet *is* the crystal now. But without the pedestal, we need a living anchor. The resonance has to come from her." His eyes flicked to Mei. "She'll take the part of the pedestal. The system will treat her as the base, and the amulet will align through her."

Mei's hand tightened around the amulet. The idea that she herself would take the place of a machine left her both excited and unsettled. She had always known the amulet was important, but not that it would make her the center of the ship's passage. Her grandmother had once admitted she didn't know its purpose. What would she say now, seeing her granddaughter about to serve as the heart of a spaceship?

Astran emerged from what looked like a hole in the wall, brushing dust from her hands. She had opened up a panel and been crawling through it. "The connections look good. If the system checks are clean, it's good to fly."

Mei shifted on her feet. The excitement of the others was real, but for her, the responsibility made her feel a little sick. If she faltered, the alignment would fail. The ship would never cross safely. She told herself again: she was lucky. Few ever had a chance like this.

Lewis caught her expression. "You're quiet."

"Thinking," she answered.

"About what?"

"That my grandmother gave me this amulet. That everything depends on it now."

He studied her for a moment. "It depends on all of you. But yes—without you, and without the amulet, the ship will never pass through Sol Gate."

She nodded as the truth sank in. Whatever her family had thought of her, whatever names they might have thrown at her, here she mattered. Here, she was indispensable—part of something larger than herself.

Junia called from the other side of the cabin, "We should review seating and assignments. Everyone needs to know their roles before we approach the portal."

The group began to gather near the ramp. Mei tucked the amulet back in her pocket and walked over. She could hear the hum of the ship's systems, the soft sounds of the ACs comparing notes with the Suedes and the humans. Lewis stayed at her side as they joined the circle.

She looked around at the faces—Bridgewalkers from three species, a super-soldier, and herself, a girl who had once been dismissed as insignificant. This was her family now. The mission belonged to all of them.

Chapter
Thirty-Eight

Malcolm watched the bank building from a bus shelter across the street. The morning foot traffic had settled into its rhythm—couriers, office workers, and shopkeepers. A food truck idled at the corner. He'd been observing the flow for three days.

Jamal leaned on the shelter's glass wall with a to-go cup of coffee in hand, eyes quietly scanning the block. Pete circled on a scooter with a delivery box strapped behind him. He had done a dozen short loops already to normalize the sight of his helmet and jacket. Their setup was simple and boring by design.

Malcolm liked things simple. His years with the Partnership had taught him that teams only survived when they prepared carefully and avoided shortcuts. Rushed plans usually got people killed. Lewis had survived mostly through luck and stubbornness. Malcolm didn't like luck.

Malcolm disliked the bank building too. There were too many sightlines to the outside, and the street was too busy. But this was where the kids were, and Lewis had followed them, turning into a guard dog for a group of young humans who thought they could handle projects that had brought governments to their knees.

The plan had started out simple: take Lewis when he went out alone. A van would pull up, side door open, grab him, and be gone in under a minute. Two days in a safe house and Lewis would be back with them—they'd talk sense into him and he'd see the logic; he'd realize how good it felt to be back among his own kind. No noise, no unnecessary damage. Quick and clean.

Malcolm's reasoning was practical. Five super-soldiers didn't divide evenly. With six they could work in pairs, split into teams with balanced capabilities, or rotate positions. Six gave them three pairs for moving through streets, or two fire teams for stairwells and tight spaces. Six allowed one person to rest while the others worked, and it gave better coverage during convoy runs. In cities, six covered blind spots where danger could appear anytime. Urban work was picking up again after the Tall Whites story—protests, convoy escorts, riot control, VIP extractions. People wanted to move assets and people, and they were willing to pay well. A sixth man raised the daily price and opened contracts. Six not only meant survival, it meant profit.

All of that had seemed straightforward until last night, when Jamal had brought him new information. His cousin—one of the teenagers caught up in the current craze about the so-called vibrational shift—had mentioned that the next stage of humanity's evolution would involve flying a spaceship through the sun. From that, it wasn't hard to figure out who had taken the ship. The only surviving Partnership people with the skills to fly it were the super-soldiers.

And the only surviving super-soldier not already on their team was Lewis.

They'd all been there that night the Partnership's remaining spaceship had been stolen—right from under their noses. All five of them had been there as it flew away. Things would have been different had that crazy earthquake not slowed them down. At the time they hadn't known who had taken it. He had seen the craft rise and vanish, and had felt a roar of frustration in his chest. He had kept it in check in front of the team, but it had stayed with him. That ship had been their backup plan for after the Partnership—a ticket to independent work, a way to move without worrying about borders or checkpoints. Watching it disappear had been like watching a safe door close while the combination was erased.

So now Lewis and the kids had the ship. They had hidden it somewhere—either in the city or in the nearby hills. That made the plan of grabbing Lewis alone less useful. If they took only him, the kids would still have the ship, and that meant competition. Every job the ship made possible was a job the team would lose. If they took both, they would control the craft and the operator. Lewis wasn't smart, but he was trained, strong, and deadly in his own right. With both the spacecraft and Lewis on their side, no one would be able to match them. Malcolm could work with that.

"Movement," Pete said. "Door."

Lewis stepped out of the bank building. Loose jacket, baseball cap, bag slung low. He scanned the street casually, then crossed to the far side and walked north. Alone.

"Hold," Malcolm ordered. They shadowed him. Jamal paralleled on the opposite sidewalk. Pete drifted behind on the scooter. Malcolm blended into the crowd.

Lewis's stride was even, unvaried. He wasn't running counter-surveillance—just moving through his routine. After several blocks, he knocked on the window of a taco truck. After exchanging a few words with the person inside, he passed over a few bills and received a bag of food in exchange. Then he retraced his steps back to the bank building.

They regrouped in the parking lot of a store opposite. Pete set the scooter on its kickstand and took off his helmet.

"We should amend the plan," he said. Jamal only drained the last of his coffee, then threw the empty cup in a nearby trash bin.

"We already have," Malcolm said. "We're not taking him today. We follow him until he leads us to the ship. Then we take both."

"We're taking a risk," Pete said. "Maybe they just want to keep it hidden—this could take a long time and in the meanwhile we'll be losing jobs."

"The ship changes everything," Malcolm said. "If we just take Lewis, it helps with a few jobs. If we take both Lewis and the spacecraft, it sets us up for the next decade. No more paying for transport. No more dealing with customs. We move where we want, when we want, and we gain leverage in every negotiation."

"And what about the kids?" Jamal asked. "From what my cousin said, they're going be on the ship when it goes through the portal."

"If they're there, we try to leave them out of it," Malcolm said. "They're not the target. If they resist, we push back. Avoid casualties if we can—but we're not losing the ship again."

That night, Malcolm rented a cargo van with fake plates, secured a warehouse near the river, and paid a hangar operator in cash. With preparations in place, they worked in shifts. Pete circled the block, Jamal watched the the front entrance, and Malcolm managed logistics.

At dusk they met in the van. They handed out radios, mapped routes, and set fallback positions. "Be ready for this to take days," Malcolm said. "We don't move unless we have to. If he stays inside, we watch the access points. If he comes out, we follow him. With the kids involved, our best chance is if Lewis comes out with them."

Malcolm stopped talking, and the three men settled in to watch. They wouldn't move on him that night. They would let Lewis lead them to the hidden ship. When they took the ship, they would take him too. Six men, one craft, a fresh start.

And this time, Malcolm promised himself, they wouldn't lose it.

* * *

Mei materialized in the pocket-out-of-time reality for the first time. She stayed close to the energetic forms of the others—Jessica, Brad, Kiran, and James—as the vast space took shape. But "shape" wasn't the right word, because no matter how hard she tried, Mei couldn't see anything beyond the shimmering shapes of the Five. She lifted her arm—it was sparkling too.

Then, a short distance away, another being appeared—taller than any human she had ever seen, with an angular frame, short forelegs and a burgundy cape. The eyes in its triangular-shaped head were huge, iridescent, and constantly shifting.

She froze for a moment, forgetting to breathe. The creature dipped its head in acknowledgment as the other four humans stepped forward and one after another steepled their hands over its forelegs in greeting. This was Melly, the mantis being who represented the Galactic Council. Mei had heard the others describe her, but nothing had prepared her for this. Her knees felt weak, and she struggled to stay upright. Gratitude, awe, and disbelief all hit her at once.

"Mei," said Melly. "You have arrived." Her words were measured, with an overlay of bells and gongs. "It is time you learned what your presence has made possible."

Mei pressed her hands together, bowed her head briefly. "I'm honored. Thank you for allowing me to come here."

Melly tilted her head. "We have not given you a gift—you have provided the key. The passage of the spacecraft through Sol Gate requires more than technology. It requires harmonics, resonance, and balance. Those will be provided by Earth's three species working together. But that would still not be enough without the integrating force that comes from your bloodline. Without it, the craft would not be able to cross."

Mei's mouth went dry. She nodded slowly, trying to find the words. "My... bloodline? My family? What does that mean?"

The whorls of color in Melly's eyes shifted. "Blood and DNA carry frequencies. Centuries ago, because of your family's superior character and qualities, your bloodline was chosen to guard the ability to unlock what had been sealed. The amulet anchored that role. The Galactic Council feared your family's character had weakened too much to fulfill its duty. But your presence proves otherwise. Without you, this path would have stayed closed."

Overwhelmed, Mei lowered her eyes. Her pulse raced. For years her family had told her she was a failure. Now Melly, a member of the Galactic Council itself, was telling her she had made the difference. She swallowed, her voice small but steady. "I didn't know. I thought it was just luck."

"It was not luck," Melly said. "It was character. You stand here because of who you are."

Jessica stepped forward, giving Mei a quick glance, then faced Melly with practical questions. "What will happen when the ship goes through Sol Gate? Where will we come out? We don't have a navigation crystal like the Kewpies did."

The feeling of small bells. "The first passage is fixed. All who cross a Gate for the first time arrive at the same place—the spaceport where the Galactic Council meets. It is the same location you visited when the Kewpies carried you. That is where we will meet you again, and where the Federation will greet you."

James frowned thoughtfully. "So, automatic docking at the Council? That means no chance of coming out anywhere else?"

"Correct," Melly said. "The first time is bound. Afterward, your vessel will require a navigation crystal—the Council will provide one. With it, you may set coordinates to other destinations across the Federation."

Brad looked at Mei. "And the amulet?"

"Every sun is a portal that allows travel within a galaxy, but interstellar travel is possible only through one of the Gates," said Melly. "Each time you access a new Gate, the amulet is required. It establishes the first resonance needed for passage. Afterward, with a navigation crystal in place, you may move freely along the routes associated with that specific Gate."

Mei gripped the amulet in her pocket more tightly. Now that she understood its role, it felt heavier. Her grandmother had guarded it for years without knowing why. Its true purpose was... astonishing, unbelievable, mind-boggling.

James raised another question. "You've upgraded the junk DNA of all the Five except for Mei. Will you be doing the same for her now?"

For a moment, Melly was silent. Then she turned her eyes fully on Mei. "No."

The single word hit Mei like a slap. She blinked and forced her face into a neutral expression, but the disappointment rose before she could stop it. Her friends had been chosen for something extraordinary. She had assumed this meeting meant the same for her.

Melly's tone softened—muted gongs. "Do not mistake this answer for rejection. The vibrational shift is already moving through you. Your abilities will appear on their own—as they will for the rest of humanity in time. You will not be left behind."

Mei let out a slow breath. She had managed to hide her disappointment behind an impassive face, but Melly's words eased some of the sting. "So... it will happen naturally? For me, and for everyone?"

"Yes," Melly confirmed. "The shift touches all of Earth. Those who are prepared—like you—will move faster, but no one will be excluded. The process is underway, and it cannot be stopped."

Kiran spoke next, his voice careful. "That means humanity will catch up? Not just us?"

Melly's eyes turned toward him. "As your planet goes through the vibrational shift, everyone on it will change as well. Some will resist. Some will adapt. But the path is already set."

Melly unfolded her forelegs slightly, her voice carrying finality. "Your task now is to prepare for the crossing. You have the vessel. You have the key. The Council awaits. When you arrive, you will not stand alone. Human, Suede, and Alpha Centaurian together will be received. The Federation looks forward to your emergence."

Mei's throat tightened. She managed a whisper: "Thank you." Gratitude rose sharp inside her, not just for herself but for the chance to be part of this moment. For the first time, she felt not like an outsider, but an integral piece of the pattern.

The space around them began to dissolve at the edges. The lines of Melly's tall form blurred, and the iridescent eyes shimmered once more before fading.

Mei blinked as the pocket-out-of-time released them. She stood once again in the common area of the flower shop, her hand gripping the amulet firmly. The others turned to her, faces bright with excitement, but she barely saw them. Her mind replayed Melly's words again and again.

She was the key. Her bloodline would open Sol Gate. And when all the Earth's peoples crossed through, the Federation would be waiting.

Chapter Thirty-Nine

They left before sunrise to avoid both traffic and the neighbors. The residential area where the Martinsson property was located was heavily landscaped with trees and foliage; most houses were hidden from the road. The mansion that Brad and Jessica had lived in had also been hidden, but that was before the Partnership had burned it down. There was still yellow police tape at the front entrance, but they went in via the service entrance at the back of the property.

This was a celebratory day—the Bridgewalkers were going to take the spaceship through Sol Gate—so they took two vehicles so that everyone could be there when the craft took off. Calvin was at the wheel of his SUV with Mona, James, Jessica and Kiran. Vicki drove her car with Brad, Mei, Lewis and Amanda.

Brad had argued with Vicki about Amanda the night before. "I know she did that Tall Whites story," he said, "but that doesn't make up for how she deliberately went out of her way to humiliate and mock Jessica. I think it's a mistake to let her near the spaceship."

"She's coming anyway," Vicki said. "If she stays behind, there's no one to watch her. Lewis will be with us. He won't let her near anything she shouldn't touch."

Now, in the car, Amanda stayed quiet. She had learned to be careful around Brad.

When they reached the property, the Suedes and the Alpha Centaurians were already waiting by the spaceship, their bags at their sides. They stood as the humans arrived. A general feeling of excitement and nervousness filled the air.

Lewis immediately took charge. "I'll do a systems check as we power up the ship. They should be ready to fly in about thirty minutes." As he opened up the hatch, the young people swarmed forward with him. With a quick glance at Vicki and the Coopers, Amanda slowly followed.

Vicki joined Calvin and Mona by their SUV, watching the young people go up the ramp.

"I keep flashing on James's first day of kindergarten," Mona said. "He had a backpack that was too big for him. He wanted to carry a notebook because he thought that made him official." She smiled without any tears. "Now he's flying off in a spaceship."

Calvin's mouth twitched. "He's not just flying *in* a spaceship—he'll be piloting it himself, at least part of the way."

Mona nodded. "I know. I also know that today changes everything. We hoped for a college campus in California or maybe a school out-of-state. We thought there would be tuition and roommates and that he would call on weekends. We thought there would be a major, a degree, and then a job. We pictured him coming home for holidays. We thought we knew the the path his life would take."

Calvin kept his gaze on the spaceship. "It won't be that," he said.

"No," Mona answered. "He'll be flying around the universe in a spaceship. He'll be visiting places I can't begin to imagine, and making choices I don't understand. And that's fine. I kept trying to fit him into the plan I had in my head. I was wrong." She made a face. "That plan isn't right for him. He belongs where he's needed and where he can grow. That's not life at college. That's this."

Calvin turned to her, surprised. Vicki saw it—he had expected Mona to object, not accept. Something in his face relaxed.

From the interior of the ship came the sound of boxes sliding, and low conversation. James's voice rose and fell as he counted system checks. The Suedes laughed at something Mei said. Lewis was giving final instructions on setting a flight path for Sol Gate. Everything was falling into place.

Suddenly Vicki stiffened. Something was different. She closed her eyes and reached out with her senses.

She could hear Lewis calling out to the young people. "Pressure green. Coolant stable. Power core warmup at eighty percent. Three more minutes until launch readiness." Kiran repeated back the numbers.

Vicki focused. What was she sensing? Oh, that was it—chi. Several people were approaching. But their chi was... unmoving. The people approaching were biologic constructs!

"Go, go, go!" shouted Vicki, her voice desperate. "Super-soldiers are almost here! Get out—I'll hold them for now, but you need to leave!"

* * *

Amanda jerked at the sound of Vicki's scream. The word *super-soldiers* rang in her ears and for a heartbeat she froze.. Then she turned instinctively toward the open hatch, ready to run down the ramp and see for herself. Before she could take two steps, a hand like a vise clamped around her arm.

Lewis loomed beside her, his voice clipped and absolute. "Sit. Now."

"I—"

"No time. It's not safe outside." He shoved her lightly but firmly toward one of the padded seats along the cabin wall. His tone left no room for argument.

Amanda stumbled back, caught herself, and sank into the seat. Her pulse pounded in her throat. The others were already dropping whatever they held and rushing for their stations. The chatter cut off. Feet slammed on the deck as everyone lunged for their seats.

Mei slid into the pilot's chair, James into the co-pilot's. Their hands flew across the controls with an ease that revealed practice. The young people all strapped themselves in. Lewis stayed near the hatch until the last moment when it closed with a pressurized hiss, sealing them inside. A sequence of locking sounds followed.

Amanda clutched the harness straps across her chest. Her palms were slick with sweat. She had covered headline-grabbing stories before, oftentimes when violence threatened, but this felt different. There was no buffer between her and the threat. This time she was in the middle of it.

The ship hummed louder as the power core surged. Mei called out, her voice controlled but strained, "Systems warming. Sixty seconds to launch readiness."

James repeated, "Sixty seconds." His eyes never left the board.

Amanda forced herself to look up at the forward viewport. The trees framed the lawn and the burnt-out ruins of the mansion. At first she saw nothing. Then a flash of movement.

A white van sped into view, skidding to a halt about a hundred yards away. The side doors slammed open, and five men jumped out.

"That's the rest of them," Lewis said flatly. "The remaining super-soldiers."

Amanda's breath caught. The men moved with an unnatural grace. No wasted motion, no delays. Their heads turned—almost in unison—and tracked the ship.

"They're running," Jessica said, her voice tight.

Amanda blinked. The five figures had started forward, closing the distance at an impossible speed. Their strides ate the ground. It looked wrong, like a video played at double speed.

"Thirty seconds," Mei said, eyes fixed on the controls. Her voice didn't shake.

Amanda's heart hammered. She knew Lewis had said it wasn't safe outside, but every instinct screamed at her to move, to *do* something. She gripped the armrests until her knuckles hurt.

Through the viewport, Vicki stepped into view. She stood halfway between the van and the spacecraft. Her arms were at her sides. Amanda saw her lips move though she could not hear the words through the sealed hull.

The super-soldiers closed in. Forty yards. Thirty.

Then Vicki dropped suddenly to the ground, legs folding under her as if she had chosen to sit in the grass. She smacked her hands on the earth.

"What's she doing?" Amanda whispered.

Before anyone could answer, the ground in front of the charging men shifted. A dark line cracked open beneath their feet. The earth sagged, then tore wider. The five men scrambled, but the collapse was faster than their reflexes. A sinkhole yawned open, swallowing them whole.

The sound was muted through the hull, but Amanda felt the vibration through her seat. Dust and clods of earth billowed upward. The men vanished from view.

"Fifteen seconds," Mei called.

"Power core stable," James added. His voice was calm, clipped, as if he had shut off any panic.

Amanda stared at the viewport. The hole was still there, raw and jagged. Vicki sat a few yards away from the edge, unmoving. Calvin and Mona were farther back, standing together near their vehicle, their faces pale.

"Ten seconds," Mei said.

Amanda pressed her lips together, fighting the urge to shout. She wanted to know what had happened to the soldiers. Had they been buried alive? Or were they climbing out even now, ready to attack again? But the ship vibrated slightly beneath her as the engines began to hum.

Jessica gripped the straps across her chest and muttered, "Come on, come on…"

The ship shuddered as systems came online. Mei's hands moved across the board in fast sequences. "Five seconds."

Amanda's stomach tightened. She glanced back at Lewis. His eyes were locked on the viewport, his jaw tight. He gave no sign of relief.

Then the engines roared fully to life. The deck vibrated harder. Mei's voice was firm. "Ready for lift."

James: "Launch sequence green."

The restraints bit into Amanda's shoulders as the ship rose, impossibly smooth, but with increasing force. Sunlight flooded the viewport, obscuring the scene outside. She caught one last glimpse through the light: Calvin's arm around Mona's shoulders, both of them staring upward, eyes fixed on the rising spaceship. Vicki was still seated on the ground, her head lowered. Then Amanda's view was lost in the cloud.

The ship climbed higher. Thin wisps of low clouds. A deepening blue sky above, paler toward the horizon. The horizon curving slightly. The cabin tilted as Mei angled the vessel toward its departure vector.

Inside, no one spoke. The only sounds were the regular updates from Mei and James, the occasional confirmation from one of the Alpha Centaurians, and the continuous hum of the core.

Amanda sat rigid in her seat. Her throat was dry. She forced herself to breathe slowly. She wasn't supposed to be here. While she didn't know the entire plan, she had overhead enough to realize the Bridgewalkers' destination was Sol Gate—and she wasn't the type of person who could survive the trip.

The pressure eased as they broke into the blackness of space, the background scattered with sharp pinpoints of stars. Below, the Earth was curving visibly now, oceans and continents stretching wide beneath them.

Brad's voice broke the silence. "That was a close call, but now we have a problem. We have two people on board who won't be able to survive going through the portal. Maybe we can return and let them off somewhere?"

Amanda immediately bristled. This wasn't her fault. She opened her mouth to say something biting, but Lewis spoke first.

"No," Lewis said immediately. "It's too risky. But it's a short trip to Europa. You know how to fly there, to dock at the mining facility, and to navigate through the asteroids. The station has been powered on and we are the only ones who have access because you changed the access code."

"*And* because we're the only ones with a spaceship right now," muttered James, his eyes not leaving the controls.

Lewis continued, "Amanda and I can stay there until you return. Your first trip will be short because the Suedes will need to come back to Earth."

He looked at Junia, and she nodded.

Amanda let out a long breath she hadn't realized she was holding. Her hands were still shaking. She looked around at the faces of the youth, the Suedes, the ACs. All of them were focused. No one was looking at her. She was just cargo now, an observer strapped in the corner.

Did she want to go to Europa with Lewis? She wasn't sure. But she was very sure she didn't want to die. Maybe she could make this into another story. She could write an entire series—*Intrepid Reporter Travels Through Space.*

Her eyes went back to the viewport. Earth was receding, growing smaller. Somewhere down there, Vicki sat by a sinkhole with enemies trapped inside. Were the super-soldiers dead, or would they claw their way to the surface to attack again? She didn't know.

Amanda tightened her grip on the harness straps. She had known Vicki was only bringing her along because there was no one left to guard her at the bank building. She had been hoping it would give her a story. Now she realized she was in it whether she wanted to be or not. There would be no distance, no protective wall of detachment, no safety.

This was her life now.

Chapter Forty

L ewis listened until the docking clamps settled and the last vibrations ran through the corridor. The lights shifted to solid
green, confirming the ship had disengaged from the mining facility
and had left Europa. He remained in the narrow airlock until he
was sure of the readings. Only then did he move forward, Amanda
following closely with her bag pressed to her side.

The hatch cycled open. Cold air flowed from the station. It
smelled of metal, cleaning solution, and old coolant lines. Lewis
remembered that smell; he had worked rotations here before. The
Partnership had wanted the biologic constructs to know every corner of their facilities. He stepped in first, scanning with a soldier's
discipline. Amanda entered behind him, glancing around quickly,
her expression alert but not panicked.

The airlock sealed, leaving them alone in the station.

The Bridgewalkers would return for them in forty-eight hours.
That was the agreement. They needed to travel through Sol Gate,
meet with the Galactic Council, then return the Suedes to Earth
before they grew sick from being away from Earth's field too long.
He briefly wondered what it would be like to travel through the
universe, but that was impossible for biologic constructs—unable to
reach higher levels of vibration, he would have died going through

Sol Gate. Him and Amanda both, although she might be able to do it in the future if she trained for it.

Lewis thought of the flight between Earth and Europa. He had watched Mei and James guide the ship through the asteroid belt before docking. Their work had been calm and exact, with no wasted corrections. He was confident they'd have no trouble with the Sol Gate transit. Then he stopped thinking about them. His task was here, to manage the wait and protect Amanda.

Amanda shifted the strap of her bag higher on her shoulder. "So it's just us?" she asked.

"Yes," Lewis said. "We're alone here. We'll be ready when they return in two days."

She gave a short nod. He wondered what she was thinking. She had been dragged into things she couldn't control, but she stayed calm. He respected that. He also noticed how her eyes moved along the corridors, observing details carefully. She was smart. He thought she was adjusting better than most civilians would have.

"You are the first person here who isn't a Partnership employee or one of the Five," he said. "Would you like a tour?"

Amanda raised her eyebrows. "The first?"

"Yes," he said.

Her mouth curved in a small smile. "Then yes. Show me everything."

Lewis turned toward the central corridor. He had walked these halls many times in the past. Training had drilled the layouts into him, but the schematics were already downloaded into his brain.

They passed through the entry hub, a circular space with four branching corridors. The walls were lined with doors that led to work bays, storage alcoves, and offices. The cameras in the corners were active, but Brad had fixed them before so that the feed could be accessed only by the Five. They weren't a concern.

"This is the main hub," he explained. "From here you can reach different wings—living quarters, kitchen and mess hall, the medical wing, the mining control section, and the observation gallery. Red lights mark restricted corridors, sealed since the Partnership left."

Amanda nodded and kept pace with him.

He led her first to the observation gallery. The heavy doors opened onto a row of thick viewports. Beyond them stretched Europa's ice plain, scored with long ridges and fractures. Overhead loomed Jupiter, its bands stark and its storms in constant motion. The view was silent, the only sound the faint hum of the facility's systems.

Amanda pressed her hands lightly against the glass. "I never thought I'd see this with my own eyes. More than that—I never dreamed such a thing was possible."

"Few people have," Lewis said. "The Partnership built this facility but kept it secret. It wanted everything for itself."

When Amanda finally stepped back, Lewis guided her down another corridor. In the kitchen wing everything was still stocked, though lightly coated in dust. He opened the storage cabinets to check supplies. Rows of freeze-dried packets lined the shelves. Water tanks read as full on the monitors.

"We have more than enough for two days—for two years if we needed," he said.

He already knew this—he had been here with the Five just a couple of weeks ago—but he thought it might make Amanda more comfortable he went through the motions of checking.

In the medical wing, Lewis opened the cabinets. Sterile packs were sealed. Analgesics and wound care supplies were in date. Two blood expanders remained. The Partnership stimulants were still stored in the back, but he closed that cabinet without comment. Instead, he showed her the gym: basic machines bolted to the floor, tether bands, and a squat rack.

Amanda lingered in a doorway. "You know this place well," she said.

"I worked a rotation here," Lewis replied. "The Partnership moved us often, but I remember everything."

"Does it feel strange, being back?"

"No," he said. "It feels the same. My work has changed, that is all."

She seemed to accept that answer.

They moved on to the mining control wing. Consoles glowed on standby. Lewis inserted his badge and accessed the logs. The last entries showed automated runs to the surface, processing ice into water and metals into storage. A probe had been lowered into a borehole, then retrieved without error. No record of human activity for the past eight months.

Amanda stood behind him, reading over his shoulder. "So it's abandoned."

"Operational, but unmanned," Lewis corrected. "The Partnership pulled the crews out when Jupiter's orbit swung away from Earth. Now it's in reach again, but there's no one left."

Lewis could see that Amanda understood what he wasn't saying—that the Partnership had been destroyed and key personnel were dead—but instead of asking questions about that, she changed the subject.

"Are those sealed corridors dangerous?"

"They might be," he said, "if you pushed buttons and pulled levers without knowing what they did. I will keep them locked. We do not need to go there."

She gave a short nod. "That's fine by me."

"You're handling this well," he told her.

She looked at him. "I don't have much choice, do I?"

"Some people fail under pressure," he said. "You don't."

She shot him an expression he didn't understand. "Thanks."

They returned to the wing that housed the living quarters. Dormitories held bunks, lockers and wash stations. A nearby lounge held sofas and an entertainment system.

"We can use these bunks," he said. "It will be quiet."

Amanda unstrapped her boots and slid them under a lower bunk. "It'll do. I've stayed in worse places."

He nodded once. He would sleep lightly, even though there was no threat. That was how he had been trained.

Amanda leaned back on the bunk and looked at him. "You said I'm the first outsider here. That feels... big."

Lewis met her eyes but didn't say anything.

She gave a short laugh. "I spent so long searching for the next big thing, and when I stopped looking, it dropped into my lap."

The lights shifted to evening mode, dimming slightly. The ventilation cycle changed tone. Lewis listened, mapping the sounds. Everything was running as expected.

"I'll make patrol rounds before rest," he said. "Check the fire doors and vents."

Amanda nodded. "I'll be fine here. And... thank you. For trusting me. For showing me the station."

He only nodded.

When he stepped back into the corridor, he felt grounded. He hoped she liked him. She was smart, careful, and strong in a way most people weren't. For now, he would guard her. He would see that the next two days passed without incident.

* * *

The ship moved smoothly and silently, leaving Europa behind. James sat in the co-pilot's chair, eyes fixed on the navigation displays and the broad viewport beyond. At his side, Mei worked the controls with careful focus, her voice calm as she called out headings and corrections.

Europa shrank quickly, its fractured ice plains fading into the dark as Jupiter loomed behind it, massive and banded. As the ship angled outward, the giant world became a backdrop, its glow diminished by the growing distance.

Ahead stretched the inner solar system. Through the viewport, James could see the asteroid belt sliding past on either side. Rocks of every size turned slowly in their orbits. Some reflected faint light, others remained in shadow. Mei threaded a path through them, each correction small but sure. The Suedes and ACs sat quietly behind them, watching, their attention fixed not only on the view but also on the energy patterns that surrounded the ship.

Beyond the belt lay Mars, a faint red disk against the dark. The instruments picked out its thin crescent, sunlight catching along its edge. Farther still, the blue-white glow of Earth and its Moon showed as a pinpoint, familiar and distant. James thought of his parents, standing, watching as the spaceship had taken flight just a few hours earlier, and then focused again on the task ahead.

The Sun dominated the center of the viewport now, a sphere of white and gold. Even filtered through the ship's shielding, its surface moved with constant activity. Streams of plasma arched from its corona. Darker spots pocked its surface, shifting and stretching with the churn beneath. The crew watched as the light grew stronger, filling more of their view.

Mei checked her board, then looked at James. "It's time," she said.

James nodded. The Five had had many conversations about what they would need to do. He unbuckled, slid from the co-pilot's chair, and took the pilot's seat, his hands moving about the controls. He was ready for this.

Mei stepped to the center of the cabin. She took the jade amulet from her pocket and held it up. Its surface caught the light. She closed her eyes briefly, centering herself, then lifted it with both hands.

The others moved into position. Jessica, Kiran, and Brad stepped to form a triangle around Mei. Their movements slowed and steadied as they began the tai chi forms they had trained together for months. Their breathing synchronized, each of them grounding and extending their arms with deliberate care.

The three Suedes—Junia, Caffo, and Ilar—stood behind them, their voices rising in low tones. The sound resonated, each of them weaving in harmony with the others. The vibration filled the cabin, firm and constant.

The Alpha Centaurians—Astran, Nevik, and Calix—took their places near the rear bulkhead. Their eyes closed, their hands lifted slightly, palms outward. Their bodies swayed with faint, measured shifts as they balanced the energy the others generated, smoothing it, guiding it so it flowed evenly throughout the space.

The cabin became quiet apart from the hum of the ship and the voices of the Suedes. James guided the controls, feeling the ship respond as if it too were aligning.

Then it began.

The first geometric shape appeared, faint and translucent, hanging in the air above the amulet. It was simple, clear in outline. It glowed briefly, then faded. Another appeared after it, different in structure, then another. One by one, eight shapes formed, each distinct, each lasting only a moment before the next replaced it.

James kept his attention divided between the controls and the vision before him. He saw the way the shapes built on one another, each one marking a stage of alignment.

Kiran's voice cut softly through the resonance. "Because we are from Earth and going through Sol Gate, the corresponding shape is the cube. The associated tai chi movement is Lü—Roll Back."

Jessica and Brad exchanged a look and shifted smoothly into Lü, their arms circling outward, drawing and redirecting. Kiran matched them. They moved as one, their flow constant.

The Suedes kept their tones level. The ACs' balancing presence grew stronger, their movements subtle but sure. The amulet in Mei's hands pulsed faintly, the green stone glowing with inner light.

James adjusted their trajectory as the Sun swelled before them. In this higher vibrational level, glare no longer blinded; instead, structure emerged. The corona revealed fine lines, arcs, and lattices of geometry woven into its brilliance. They pulsed in a rhythm that matched the resonance inside the cabin.

The Sun no longer looked like a uniform blaze. Depth unfolded in its layers. Gold, silver, violet, and unfamiliar hues shimmered across its surface. Patterns rotated slowly, locking into alignment as though responding to the Bridgewalkers' state.

At its center, James saw the Gate itself. The geometry converged, forming a stable opening. It was not a hole but a region where the patterns bent inward, aligned and clear. Beyond it, stars flickered into view, impossibly visible through the solar glare. Space folded in ways no ordinary instrument could have recorded.

James breathed evenly, his hands on the controls. The ship obeyed, smoothly drawn toward the convergence.

Behind him, the humans continued Lü, their movements perfectly measured, their breathing steady. The Suedes' tones held strong and unbroken. The ACs' balancing presence steadied the cabin, the flow of energy even and smooth. Mei stood in the center, the jade amulet lifted high, her face calm and focused.

The convergence brightened, the framework of geometry locking into place. The Sun's light bent around it, creating a clear path forward.

James set their heading and confirmed the trajectory. His voice was calm, the same tone he had used in every rehearsal. "All stations secure. Entering Sol Gate."

The ship moved forward. The Sun filled the viewport. The patterns widened, opening into a corridor of light and structure. The jade amulet glowed brighter in Mei's hands.

Then they crossed the threshold.

Chapter
Forty-One

Junia sat forward in her chair, fighting to keep herself from bouncing in her seat. The chamber of the Galactic Council was large, and species she had never dreamed of before were sitting there listening to them. They had made it! They had crossed through Sol Gate, and now they were sitting with the Council as equals.

Jessica stood a few feet ahead, facing the semi-circle of Council members. Her voice carried evenly, calm and measured. Junia listened to the words without focusing on the details. She trusted Jessica to speak well, to represent them honestly. Jessica was careful with language, and Junia admired that. She knew Jessica would not agree to anything that put the Bridgewalkers or Earth at a disadvantage.

That left Junia free to look at everyone else.

Kiran sat straight, his face calm. Brad was looking more relaxed than he probably was—he was good at that. James was serious, his gaze fixed on Jessica. They had already been here once before, and it showed. They weren't fidgeting. They weren't wide-eyed. They were holding themselves like they belonged. Junia admired it, though she didn't feel the need to copy them. She liked the way the excitement rushed through her.

The three Alpha Centaurians—Astran, Nevik, and Calix—sat a little straighter than usual. Their bodies were still, their eyes bright. Junia could tell they were proud. She knew why. The space ACs had been insulting, mocking them for being "Earth-bound," for having failed, for being weak. But now the Earth ACs had crossed Sol Gate without the help of their spacer cousins. Junia grinned just thinking about it. The ACs deserved this moment.

Her smile faded a little when she looked at Caffo and Ilar. Both of them were slouching in their seats, their attention drifting. Junia understood. She felt the pull herself, the odd sense of being stretched too far from home. The Suedes couldn't stay away from Earth long. Two days at most, or sickness would set in. The thought buzzed in her mind. She hoped Jessica would remember to push for an ending before that happened. For now, though, she wanted her fellow Suedes to hang on. This was too important to let discomfort distract them.

She took in all of them, the Bridgewalkers together: human, Suede, and AC. They looked young, but they commanded attention. All the elders on Earth had argued for caution again and again. They had wanted to keep the boundaries in place, to hold fast to the order they knew. Junia had listened to them long enough to understand they would never change on their own.

That was why the Bridgewalkers existed.

Her mind went back to all the arguments they had faced. The Suede elders had warned them about taking risks. The AC elders had pressed for more unity with the space-born factions before making any moves. Human leaders had gone in circles with endless meetings and delays. None of them had wanted to move fast. None of them had believed the young could carry out this responsibility. None of them believed the young should be *allowed* to have this responsibility.

Junia wanted to laugh out loud, not because anything was funny, but because the feeling inside her was too big to stay quiet. She was only fifteen, but she had insisted they do this. She had wanted a path that was not just about repeating the old patterns. She had declared they need not wait for permission. Now she could see it in front of her. Jessica's calm voice, the humans composed, the ACs proud, and the Suedes holding on through the strain. They were here.

A Council member leaned forward, asking Jessica a pointed question about Earth's readiness for more contact. Junia listened as Jessica answered carefully, acknowledging the difficulties but making it clear that Earth's youth wanted cooperation. The Council members murmured among themselves, and Junia caught the way a few of them nodded. She wanted to nudge Caffo and Ilar, to make them see it. The Council was listening.

Caffo sighed beside her, and Ilar's eyes drooped half-shut. Junia touched Caffo's arm gently, letting him know she understood. He gave her a faint smile, but she could see the strain in it. They needed to get back to Earth soon. She tucked the thought away. They would manage until then.

Junia lifted her chin and looked at all of them again. This was the beginning of the life they had wanted. Not the life the elders had wanted to hold onto. This was the beginning of something new. The Bridgewalkers were showing that the young from Earth could step forward and do what the elders could not.

She did not need to speak it aloud. She only needed to hold it inside: the certainty that they had made the right choice. Whatever the Council decided, the Bridgewalkers had already changed what was possible.

Junia sat straighter, letting herself feel the energy of being here, together. This was the life they had wanted.

This was going to be fun!

* * *

Mei sat stiffly in her chair, her hands clasped tightly in her lap. Her heart beat too quickly, and she tried to keep her breathing slow. The chamber was filled with beings she had never thought she would see in person. She had known about aliens for almost a year now, but knowing was not the same as sitting in a room with them while one of her friends spoke on behalf of Earth.

Jessica's voice was composed. Mei admired her for that. She spoke confidently as she explained who they were, how they had traveled, and why they had come. Mei tried to focus on her, but her eyes kept straying.

Melly sat a few seats away, legs folded neatly, the color of her eyes swirling as she listened. To Mei, Melly looked calm, maybe even at ease. Mei realized with a sudden jolt that she no longer thought of Melly as strange. An eight-foot-tall mantis being had become ordinary to her. Mei laughed quietly to herself. The idea that Melly was normal now showed her how far she had come.

Her gaze drifted to the line of Council members seated in front of them. She recognized one of them immediately. His hair was dark, his eyes intense. He looked human in almost every way, except for his light blue skin. A Pleiadian. She remembered the news footage from Earth, showing the Pleiadian ambassadors who had come after Disclosure. Those envoys had often felt distant in interviews. This Council member watched more carefully.

Next to him sat a pale figure with light-colored hair covering an elongated skull. Mei knew without being told: an Alpha Centaurian. The stillness of his shoulders suggested he held tension low in his frame.

She glanced quickly at Astran, Nevik, and Calix—the three Earth ACs who had come through Sol Gate with them. They were sitting straight-backed, proud, their eyes bright with confidence. They had been mocked and dismissed by the space ACs, but they had proven themselves now. Mei could feel the pride radiating from them.

She looked back at the Alpha Centaurian on the Council. He had his head angled down. His eyes stayed on the surface of the table. He did not acknowledge the Earth ACs. He avoided looking at anyone. Mei's jaw tightened. Was he ashamed? He should be. The Earth ACs had been treated unfairly, insulted, and excluded. Now, they had achieved something remarkable, something that gave them equal standing. The Council AC could not hide from that fact, no matter how much he pretended not to see them.

Mei forced herself to turn back to Jessica who was describing the crossing in plain words. She was telling the Council how the Bridgewalkers—humans, Suedes, and Earth ACs—had traveled through Sol Gate using the jade amulet. Mei could see the Council members shifting, murmuring softly among themselves. The explanation had captured their attention.

Jessica continued. "The amulet carried resonance from all three of our species. The humans moved with tai chi, the Suedes harmonized, and the ACs balanced the flow. The Sol Gate responded to all of us together. That is how we were able to access it."

The murmuring grew louder. Several Council members leaned toward each other. One of them, a tall being with pale gray skin and no hair, lifted a hand. "You claim this crossing was achieved without guidance from the established interstellar fleets?"

"Yes. We prepared ourselves and worked together," Jessica responded firmly. "We didn't wait for approval or instruction. The young from our three species chose to act together."

The Pleiadian leaned forward slightly. "And the jade amulet. Where did this artifact come from?"

Jessica's gaze did not flicker. "It came from Earth. It has been hidden—kept safe—by Mei's family for generations."

The Council members exchanged looks.

The presiding member nodded once to Jessica, then looked towards the Bridgewalkers as if seeking someone out. Other Councilors followed his gaze. One by one, their eyes moved to Mei. She flushed. The heat rose higher. She kept her gaze straight ahead. She did not blink more than normal. She kept her features still. She had practiced this type of control in her family home for years. Her parents had expected silence and composure. She had learned how to give them that while thinking her own thoughts.

A Council member leaned forward and addressed her. Part snake, part dragon, with a scaled head and a neck that moved in a smooth, sinuous motion. Two small horns rose from his brow. His eyes had vertical pupils that narrowed under the lights. His fingers were long and ended in blunt keratin tips. His clothing was simple and formal, with a high collar that framed a narrow jaw and an elongated snout. His voice was low but carried across the chamber without strain.

"Mei," he said. "Thank you for staying true to the responsibility assigned to your family. One of my ancestors was part of the circle that selected your line. We believed your family could keep the secret for generations and hold the power ready for a time of need. We believed your line would pass the amulet to a person of character who could use it properly to access Sol Gate. My ancestor wrote that the your line showed both restraint and resolve. Lately we feared we had made a mistake. But today I have the evidence—I am satisfied that the choice was sound."

Mei turned his words over in her head. She had spent years being measured by her family and found wanting. She had spent years measuring herself, and had found faults and gaps. Now she understood that at least one Council member had been measuring too. He had looked for signs that the old decision been the right one. He had wondered if his ancestor had chosen well. His statement told her he had carried his own doubt. He had reached his conclusion here, in this room, with her present.

Mei bowed her head low. She kept it down long enough to show respect without seeming theatrical. When she raised it and was once again facing the Council, she smiled.

"Thank you," she said. "I am learning every day to be worthy of what was entrusted to me. I did not carry it alone. My friends stood with me, and we made the crossing together."

The Council member with scaled skin inclined his head. "That is recorded," he said. "Cooperation made the crossing possible. Duty was honored. We will consider next steps with that in mind."

Jessica took a half step forward and resumed speaking.

Questions continued. Jessica answered. Kiran added a short clarification on tai chi forms and their alignment with the bagua and the geometric shapes. Brad gave a concise note on safety protocols inside the ship. James explained how the pilot switched with the co-pilot to allow Mei to hold the amulet at the correct phase. Junia spoke of how the Bridgewalkers were created. Astran explained how the Earth ACs had carried out their part without help from the spacer ACs—the AC council member hunched over even more when she said that.

The presiding member called a short recess. The Council rows broke into quiet clusters. Some members left the room through side doors. Others spoke with aides.

It wasn't long before the Councilors returned to their seats. The voice of the presiding member carried across the room. "The Earthlings have presented their achievement. We recognize that they have crossed Sol Gate by their own skill and cooperation. We will deliberate further on the implications. For now, we acknowledge their standing among us, and we award them observer status in the Galactic Federation."

The room echoed with a low hum of approval. Mei's hands unclenched. She realized her shoulders ached from holding them so tightly.

The next phase would bring conditions, timelines, and procedures. Mei felt ready to hear them. She felt ready to travel further among the stars. She looked around at her friends, and could tell they were ready too.

The Bridgewalkers—and all of Earth—had been acknowledged.

Epilogue

Ambassador Charis sat at the long table near the window, her hands resting on the polished surface. The pale blue of her skin caught the reflection of the Geneva sky. Ambassador Halbi stood opposite her, a slate tucked under his arm.

"They made it through Sol Gate," he said. "I still can't decide whether to be impressed or alarmed."

Charis gave a thin smile. "Both are reasonable. But what we feel is irrelevant. The Council has made its decision—the three species of Earth stood before them and were acknowledged. Earth is now a provisional member of the Federation."

Halbi started pacing, then realized what he was doing and stopped.

"That's the part that unsettles me," he admitted. "They've been violent toward each other for as long as they have existed. Their history is one cycle of wars, collapses, and brief truces. And now we are expected to treat them as peers among civilizations that have lived with stability for centuries."

"Not all members of the Federation lived in stability when admitted," Charis said dryly. "Do you remember the debates around Davenar? Their clan wars had not even ended when the Council voted. Many feared they would export their feuds into interstellar space."

"You can't compare the two," protested Halbi. "The Davenar did not have arsenals capable of planetary extinction. The humans do."

"We need to keep in mind that Federation members and the Council forces themselves unleashed violence and death on this planet thousands of years ago. And as recently as this last century, another Federation member was responsible for their leap in technical know-how. The Federation has much to answer for."

"You sound convinced," said Halbi, "but uneasy at the same time."

"I sound practical," sighed Charis. "I'm not ignoring the risks, Halbi. I've read the same histories you have. I know about their exterminations, their slave systems, their ideologies that drove millions to death. Those accounts are real. But so are the accounts where they abolished such practices. They are contradictory, yes, but not fixed.

"Contradictory is one word. Unstable is another."

Charis nodded. "I agree, but the Council judged that engagement would restrain their instability more than isolation. If left outside the Federation, they would still be attempting spaceflight. They would still transit portals and spread throughout the universe. Only then, they would do it without guidance, without limits."

"Engagement is surrender disguised as pragmatism. You're betting the stability of the Federation on the hope that humans will restrain themselves."

"It's recognition of reality. Earth is not a backwater colony. It is a populous, inventive, restless planet. It's currently going through a vibrational shift. Containing it is impossible. Engaging it is the only workable path—this gives the Federation oversight."

Halbi shook his head. "You speak as though Federation oversight can tame them. I don't believe it can. Their capacity for violence is coupled with a capacity for justification. They convince themselves they act for justice while committing atrocities. That combination cannot be managed by rules alone."

"You know the rules aren't symbolic—they're binding. If Earth acts out of line, suspension will follow, as it has for others. Membership depends on conduct, and the Council has revoked privileges before—including access to the Gates."

"Suspension is not the same as prevention," grumbled Halbi.

"True," said Charis. "But that's the burden of history. We cannot live only in fear of what might be. If that standard had been applied to every new world, the Federation would have remained a council of a dozen cautious species. Instead, it became a network of hundreds."

Halbi's mouth tightened, but he said nothing. For a long moment, they let the quiet of the office settle between them. Then he spoke.

"I admit I am weary of being the voice of caution. Yet I cannot ignore their history—it speaks for itself."

"You shouldn't," said Charis. "Your caution balances my pragmatism. But remember—it's not our job to reopen the Council's decision."

"So Earth is in, whether we like it or not."

"For better," agreed Charis, "or worse."

Δʙᴏᴜᴛ ᴛʜᴇ Δᴜᴛʜᴏʀ

Nancy Nelson retired after 25 years as a diplomat with the U.S. Department of State, then spent a few more years launching her kids, and traveling the world. Now she lives in California and explores the possibilities of humanity's future paths.

Sol Gate is the third of the Disclosure Files Series, and is Nancy's attempt to weave a story of people facing the need to choose who they wish to be in a future with many options.